In Falling Snow

MARY-ROSE MacCOLL

Allison & Busby Limited
12 Fitzroy Mews
London W1T 6DW
www.allisonandbusby.com

First published in Great Britain by Allison & Busby in 2013.
First published by Allen & Unwin, Sydney, Australia.

A CIP catalogue record for this book is available from
the British Library.

First Edition

ISBN 978-0-7490-1333-2

Typeset in 10.5/16 pt Sabon by
Allison & Busby Ltd.

The paper used for this Allison & Busby publication
has been produced from trees that have been legally sourced
from well-managed and credibly certified forests.

Printed and bound by
CPI Group (UK) Ltd, Croydon, CR0 4YY

MARY-ROSE MACCOLL grew up in Brisbane, Australia, with her parents, both journalists, and three brothers. MacColl worked as a journalist, nursing assistant, photocopier operator and corporate writer while studying towards degrees in journalism and creative writing. She is the author of four novels and a non-fiction book, as well as short stories, feature journalism and essays.

In memory of Elizabeth J. Cooley
1927–2011

'It was a lesson about ordinary people and the lesson was that they were not ordinary.'

Australian Prime Minister Paul Keating,
Remembrance Day 1993

Paris 1917

Afterwards, she would find herself unable to describe the old man with whom they shared the elevator, other than a lascivious smile, as if he knew. She would forget the hotel lobby, the desk clerk, the room, even the view out the window which she knew must be the Luxembourg Gardens. I want . . . he said, but she stopped him with a kiss and pulled him into the room. She worked her hand through the front of his coat, shirt and undershirt to the warm smooth skin of his stomach. She felt the kick all the way up her arm.

Still locked in the kiss, he undid the buttons of her blouse, pulled up the camisole and ran his arms around her waist. This time the feeling started deep in her chest, spreading heat from there. They squirmed out of their clothes and stood there in boots, pants puddled around their ankles. He started walking forward towards the bed, she backwards, baby steps, still joined in the kiss. She tripped and he caught her in his strong arms before she fell. Together they collapsed onto the floor, laughing as they pulled off their boots. Naked now, they embraced again. He lay on his side and drew a line with his fingers from her toes up one leg over her hips belly breast and face and down the other side. He moaned when she touched him. They made love there on the floor.

Later she got up and surveyed the room, their clothes leading from the door, his boots, the last thing to come off, at the bottom of the bed. She would remember none of those details but would never forget the long lateral muscles of his back, where angel wings would start. And the shame. She would never forget the shame.

He looked up at her and smiled and she saw momentarily in his face the face of her brother. What? he said.

Nothing, she said. You're beautiful.

Iris

The envelope was at the bottom of the small pile of mail, as if it planned the surprise. I'd already been to the shop for the newspaper and the girl, the new one, had counted my change incorrectly and I'd said so and she'd said aren't you the sharp one, which she'd never have said to a twenty-year-old. I felt like saying and aren't you the stupid one but didn't. On the way home, I'd stopped under the tree outside Suzanne's place, even though I knew they weren't likely to be home; the younger children's piano lessons are on Wednesdays and they'd have left already. I was about to keep going when I noticed, on the ground under the tree, a tiny possum, lying on its side as if sleeping. I don't know how I'd missed it on the way up. I had to take my time bending down. I looked back at Suzanne's house; definitely no one home.

The possum was breathing but its breaths were fast and shallow, as if it might not be long for this world. I dropped my satchel and walking stick, sat down on the ground beside the possum and picked it up gently. I could find no obvious injuries, but ants were making their way over the underside of the poor little creature's face and neck, no doubt anticipating their attack once the elements had done their work. I brushed off as many as I could and took my cardigan from my satchel and wrapped the possum up. It didn't resist me, had no fight at all.

I'd seen a possum like this with its mother and twin on the wires in the early evenings lately, making the journey from Suzanne's house to the mango tree in my front yard. Ringtails not brushtails, creatures you might have as a pet if their smell wasn't so powerful. 'You should be with your mother,' I said, 'not sleeping on the footpath.' I held the possum against my chest. It nuzzled straight down into the cardigan, perhaps feeling a measure of safety with this new giant that had come into its life, or perhaps just too exhausted to care. The sun was already high in the sky, and although there was a freshening north-easterly breeze I felt it was going to be a warm day. We sat for a while, the possum and I, both of us too weak to do much else.

I was just contemplating how I might manage to stand up when I saw the young man from the grocery store on his way to work. 'Hallo!' he called out as he charged down the hill towards me. 'Are you all right, Mrs Hogan?'

'Well, clearly not, Patrick,' I said. 'I've gone and sat down and now I need to stand up. I have a possum.'

'So you do,' he said, moving closer to give me his arm. 'That's the one was there last night.'

'You saw it last night?'

'Yeah,' he said, 'on my way home from work.'

'Why didn't you pick it up?'

'It's just a possum, Mrs Hogan.' I gave him my free hand

and he fairly pulled me up – I really don't think I had much to do with it – and then held the possum for me while I put my satchel over my shoulder. 'Stinks,' he said.

I took the possum back and sent him on his way. 'I'm glad I'm not a possum or you might have left me here. Anyway, thank you, Patrick,' I said and then noticed his name badge said Mark. So nice of him not to correct me. I smiled and patted his shoulder.

'Seeya, Mrs H. Have a good one.'

Most mornings I see Geoffrey, the postman, who always has something interesting to say about the world – yesterday it was people in Sydney whose gaiety was a problem for the police in a way I couldn't understand; I'm not even sure what they were happy about because I missed the beginning of the story and then felt I was too far behind to ask – but today he must have come early. He sometimes does if his satchel is very full. The children next door on the uphill side were standing to attention at the gate in their uniforms, their mother at the top of the stairs yelling at them; nothing unusual in that household, frankly. I smiled as I passed the children and said, out of their mother's hearing, 'Is that a dragon I can hear?' They didn't respond but the older one, a boy of about ten, smiled back and craned his neck to look at what I carried. 'I'll show you later,' I said, feeling I needed to get inside and put down my load. I collected the mail and from the bottom of the stairs called to the children's mother, 'Lovely day.' She pretended not to hear. They're new to the neighbourhood.

I put the mail down to open the door and took the possum, still in my cardigan, and set it down in the umbrella box. It was breathing more easily, I thought, although it was totally incurious about its new surroundings. Exhaustion, I decided, and exposure. Somehow it had been separated from its mother. I picked up the mail and left it on the hall table while I went to warm some milk and sugar and put on the coffee. I found an eye dropper in the bathroom and washed it out. I took the saucepan of sweet milk to the front hall and filled the dropper. At first the possum showed no interest but I persisted, pushing the dropper towards its tiny mouth until it took a first little lick and then guzzled. 'Hungry too,' I said. I filled a hot-water bottle and put it in the box, unwrapping the possum from my cardigan and wrapping it in an old piece of flannel. My cardigan smelt musty.

I made my coffee and went to get the mail from the hallway table. It was the usual nonsense – a bill from the electric company, a rather lovely booklet from the SPCA, a David Jones catalogue – and the envelope.

I knew where it was from, the blood-red logo in the corner, the *R* with its long tail, but even though I knew, it took a moment to recall the word, as if I had it tucked away in the very darkest corner of my mind and it took time to find the light switch. Miss Ivens came first, her name, and then her face, smiling, saying, as she so often did, 'After all, Iris, we're women. We do things.' And then Royaumont, I thought finally, dear Royaumont, as I sat down on the floor in the hall, fell down really and found myself seated. I haven't heard for years, not a single word, not from any of them.

The envelope had taken a circuitous route and several months to find me, posted in June from France, addressed to Miss Iris Crane, my maiden name, going first to the house at Risdon by the look of things – I don't know how they knew where to find me – and from there to Fortitude Valley where Al and I had lived; Mr Stinson must have forwarded it from the Valley here to Paddington. I didn't open it straight away. I'd felt a little flutter and decided it was best not to upset the apple cart. I got up from the floor slowly, using the hallway table for support.

I have a heart that worked well for more years than I care to disclose before it decided, rather suddenly, that it could work well no more. I told the heart doctor Grace took me to that at seventy beats a minute, more or less, mine had beat more than three billion times. Nothing wrong with your brain, he said, in that voice reserved for women over a certain age. Or my ears, I wanted to yell back but didn't, and at any rate, my ears are not what they used to be. When he dropped his voice to address Grace, who sat beside me, she nodded but I hardly heard a word. I've noticed that old things are popular now, furniture and houses and clothes. But not people. Old people are anything but popular, as if it's a disease we've got that others might catch rather than one they already have.

It can't just be my heart. There must be other body parts of mine biding their time, my liver, my kidneys, those organs that work on and on through the night, cleaning my blood and body, my brain that won't stop, that doesn't rest even when I plead with it. My brain and its thoughts, its monkey business, as Grace called it in her brief Buddhist period. She'd become friendly with a philosophy student when she was at the university. Dying is easy, she told me when she was all of twenty-one. You just breathe out and then you don't breathe in again. I suppose I could have found her quiet confidence impertinent but it was almost sweet that someone so far from death could pretend to understand the view from here. It's not a pretty view, but it's not as bad as you might imagine.

I have turns – that's what I call them, because it sounds

innocuous, although Grace calls them coronary-somethings, I must ask her. I'm afraid I'm beyond the age at which I might be able to remember new expressions. I live with the words I already know, except the few I manage to pick up from schoolboys on the bus. I love to surprise Grace with my new knowledge. 'I went to the city yesterday,' I might say. 'It was cool.' She finds it so unlikely I would know how to place 'cool' in the vernacular, she asks what happened, did I forget my cardigan, those gorgeous green eyes that came straight from her grandfather and into her head, that can still make me take the occasional sharp breath in when I see them flash up at me from a book or task that requires concentration, those lovely eyes that have haunted me through all her thirty-nine years and will haunt, I suppose, a little longer, until I am reunited with Grace's grandfather and I no longer need haunting.

When Al died I thought my life too would end, in every sense but breathing in and out. We were not particularly physical – whenever he'd see couples strolling across the Story Bridge with arms intertwined he'd say they must have back trouble to need to support one another – but we were so used to each other, that was the thing. He was the one constant in my life. It was his breakfast that got me out of bed in the morning, his shirts needing ironing that kept me going, his dinner that made me eat. I worried about the days, how they'd pass. In the event, it was his smell I missed most. I didn't miss the ironing and breakfast at all but I kept his unwashed pyjamas by me in the bed where I spent most of my time. It was months before I gave them up to the washing.

Lately, I've got to wondering whether when you get to Heaven you'll be the age you die or some other age, a favourite perhaps. If I'm the age I die, I'll be old and most of those I

16

lost will be young. If I'm given a choice, indeed if Heaven's where I'm going, I'll pick five so I can remember my mother, or twenty so my life is yet to be decided. And then I'll do it all differently. Ah, regrets. Where do they take us? Not here, not to happiness.

After breakfast – two wheat biscuits and a cup of black tea instead of the coffee I'd made – I felt a little better. I sat down on the front porch and looked at the envelope again. It's from the Fondation Royaumont that runs the abbey these days. Inside is a folded card, the edge glinting in the sun. I open it up. It's an invitation. They've asked me back. They've asked us all back because come December they're laying a plaque to commemorate our service, to recognise us, *les Dames Écossaises de Royaumont*, the Scottish Women of Royaumont. It's sixty years since the war ended, if you can believe it, and they know if they wait for a hundred none of us will be left.

Whenever I contemplate my coming death, which I can still do without anxiety – it remains theoretical even now I suppose – I know there is one task left undone. I have found myself wondering what became of Violet, whether she's living, whether she's happy. And the older I get, the more I wonder, late in my night when it's her morning. Water under the bridge, I told her once, it's all just water under the bridge. Well, it seems Violet's not only alive but able to speak, to speak on behalf of the women of Royaumont, to speak, can you believe, about what women can do. It says so on the invitation. I finger the smooth white card, the logo embossed, the tail of the *R* so long it trails off the page. I turn the card over, half expecting the tail to continue on the back. I put the invitation back in the envelope.

At twenty-one years of age and alighting from the train in Paris, I felt as certain as I do now of my coming death that my life was truly beginning. The other life I'd lived, at Risdon with Daddy and Tom and at the Mater in Brisbane, even Al, was like a rather pleasant interval, a practice for the real life that was now mine. I remember it was a grey day and the light refracted through the grimy roof windows of the station and gave everything a singular shining beauty. I thought I would never again see people so illuminated by the stark purpose of their lives.

I sit on the steps in the sun, teacup in hand, and contemplate the likelihood of death or travel.

At first it was the summers I remembered, long warm days under the palest blue skies, the cornflowers and iris and forget-me-nots lining the road through the Lys forest, the buzz of insects going about their work, Violet telling me lies. He loves you, he loves you not, she'd recite, skipping along the road until all the petals were gone. She'd finish with 'he loves you' no matter what the flower told her. I'd seen her cheat like that. Violet showed me an iris and told me what it was. Beautiful like you, she said. She couldn't believe I'd never seen one. They're common as weeds, she said. No offence. None taken.

But now in my mind's eye, it's winter, that first winter we arrived, Miss Ivens and me alighting from the train in Viarmes, the darkness descending, no one to meet us. And there's Miss Ivens herself, charging ahead to walk, not a thought for our luggage, abandoned on the station platform when we'd failed to rouse the porter. 'Where's M Bousier?' Miss Ivens said, as if I might know. I shrugged but she'd already moved off down the hill at a cracking pace – even with my long stride I could barely match her – turning back to me every now and then, those large straight teeth somehow adding to my trepidation, all the better to eat you with going through my head. What was I doing? I'd boarded a train with a perfect stranger. I'd listened to her story for an hour from Paris and now I was following her to a place called Royaumont. 'Better to walk at any rate,' Miss Ivens said. 'Nothing like seeing it on foot,' turning back to smile, 'the world, I mean,' and then she was off again.

'You should know that you and I and the rest are at the beginning of something momentous,' she'd said on the train, a curl of her dark hair slipped from its moorings and dangling between her eyes. 'It's going to be grand,' she insisted, reading something in my face that suggested I disagreed. I'd been assigned to the British Casualty Clearing Station in Soissons, close to Amiens where we thought Tom had gone. A Sergeant Fleming would be there to meet my train unless Matron had sent word, and no one sent word of anything in these strange days, not as far as I could tell. I'd signed up in London with the Red Cross and already I'd had orders changed, waiting those three days in Paris, I assumed because of a change in the fighting. And then I'd happened upon Miss Ivens and everything changed again.

I was just what she needed, Miss Ivens said. She smiled so quickly I almost missed it. Her French wasn't the best, she said, book-learnt, she could write but no one understood her spoken word, and no one else at Royaumont had time. 'You'll be my shadow,' she said, 'my voice. Just what I need. I can't believe our good fortune. There's a little work to be done at the abbey, of course,' dismissing it like a fly with a flick of her wrist. 'The building's not quite ready. It's rather old,' making shapes with her hands, collapsing them into her lap. 'I need someone who understands the language and can liaise with the tradesmen, someone with common sense. I believe that's you.' If I was silent, she never noticed, just kept on talking, more to herself really, setting out on her fingers the work she wanted to do that night, the supplies they'd need to order before Christmas, the long list of people to meet the next day. I listened.

And then Viarmes itself, at the base of the hill, a main street, a few shops, already shut up tight although it was barely 4 p.m., a little stone square defined by the church and town hall, the smell of incense – benediction or death – and we soon saw which. There was a funeral procession ahead of us. A boy had died, we learnt from some stragglers. His leg went under a plough and no one knew to staunch bleeding. Miss Ivens was furious at that. Knowledge was something the whole world had a right to and how could they, how could they, not be told?

We turned off the main road, watched the funeral at its slow march behind a black motor vehicle – M Bousier, our taxi driver, was also the undertaker – heading across a cold field towards the little cemetery in the nearby town of Asnières-sur-Oise. We took a narrow road out of town, more a path really, which was flanked on either side by pine trees. 'Blanche de Castille rode her horses through here,' Miss Ivens said. Perhaps I looked perplexed. 'Her son built the abbey, Royaumont. Louis IX, the saint.' She sniffed the air. 'They were all white – the horses I mean. But Blanche was marvellous. Such an example to women. I'd love to have known her, just for an hour.'

We passed a grand house that at first I took for the abbey Miss Ivens had told me about. 'No no,' Miss Ivens said, 'that's the palace, built by the last abbot. Absolute indulgence. M Gouin lives there now. Delightful fellow but completely impractical,' as if I should know who M Gouin was or why we might wish he were practical.

It began to snow. Miss Ivens took no notice, walked on ahead, asked me, without turning back, what I knew about drains. Drains were a problem. I must talk to Mrs Berry. Berry knew something but not enough; we needed a plumber. I should go into Asnières tomorrow and arrange it. I should take Berry although she didn't speak the language. 'Berry is a brick, though, she's good for me. Don't know what I'd do without her.' And then forging ahead, failing at first to notice that I'd stopped, turning, seeing me, laughing, for I was looking straight up, my mouth wide open. 'Snow,' she said matter-of-factly. I must have looked blankly at her. 'You've never seen snow?'

'No,' I said. 'Frost in the winter, but nothing like this.'

'Wonderful stuff. We'll make angels tomorrow if there's time.'

By the time we turned into the abbey grounds, the day was almost gone. The pines of the long drive were newly dusted with the snow which also dotted our coats and Miss Ivens's hair. She looked wild, a little mad even. She charged ahead once more, the gravel along the drive crunching with an alarming efficiency under her boots. Snow makes the world quieter and louder at the same time, she said quite loudly. Imagine never having seen snow, she said more softly, so softly I had to strain to hear, for I'd stopped again and was standing still. I was standing still, for when you round that last bend and begin along that long drive, you see Royaumont Abbey for the first time, and you never forget it. You must stand

21

still, or you'll miss the chance. Even at the end of that cold amazing day, even with the wonder of my first snow at hand, the abbey took my breath away. And the feeling in my heart? That feeling surprised me, for it was joy, joy and fear in about equal measure. I now know the name of that feeling to be awe.

Until three months before, I'd only ever travelled between Stanthorpe and Brisbane, less than two hundred miles, the towns at each end with their proud little post offices and hotels as their architectural achievements, the space between them mostly bush. Royaumont Abbey was some other order of place, a feat of engineering or evidence of God, depending on how you saw the world. To one side were the remains of the chapel, recollecting a structure that once nudged the spires of Paris's Notre Dame in size but was now just one tall tower looking as if it might topple over. Next to the church tower were the monks' buildings, menacing in the winter twilight. I could just make out the window recesses along the front wall. No light shone within.

I know I was exhausted. My life at home had been simple, divided between Risdon and the Mater nursing quarters, with the occasional train trip to St Joseph's to see one of Tom's teachers about something he'd done or hadn't done. I knew from one day to the next what lay in front of me and mostly it was much like what lay behind me. And now this, where every day was full of the strange. And through it all – the ship journey from Australia, the days in London, the Channel crossing, the days in Paris – in the back of my mind was that other thought that could creep up on me when I least expected, as it did now, the thought of my brother Tom, telling me of his plan to run away, me agreeing, letting him go when Daddy said I should have told him, should have done whatever I could to stop him.

Tom now, just fifteen years old, somewhere out there in this cold, fighting the wicked Germans.

As we drew closer, I made out two large wooden doors. Darkness would soon be with us but no light shone inside the abbey. I looked to Miss Ivens, her hair flecked with snow, her arms out to the sides, hands not touching anything, those enormous boots. It was so cold now my breath caught in my throat. The doors looked as if they hadn't been opened for years. Miss Ivens knocked, waited, said, more to herself than to me, 'Where the devil are they?' I still heard no sound nor saw a light within. A notion lodged in my brain that there was no one here but us. It took hold quickly, the cold feeding my imagination. Miss Ivens was mad. She'd led me here to the pixie twilight on a merry chase, and her talk of drains and equipments and hospitals was nothing but a product of her madness. Oh Iris, you fool, now look what you've done, acted impulsively, followed your most wrong-headed instincts, followed this mad Englishwoman, and here you are in the middle of a dark forest with no way back.

I was not given to hysterics, but the cold, exhaustion, the newness of it all, Miss Ivens herself so much larger than life, like a character from Dickens, made me less than logical. My excited mind worked quickly. What would we do? We had no lamp to walk by, and the road was rough in parts. There had been a light in the window of the last house, the Gouin residence; Miss Ivens had pointed it out. He might be impractical, he might be Mr Ivens for all I knew, but if we could make it back we might be able to beg a room. There was sure to be a train to Paris in the morning. I could be in Soissons by nightfall. I could be back at what I was supposed to be doing.

Daddy need never know. And Miss Ivens could . . . Miss Ivens rapped on the door a second time. Just as I was about to suggest that we go quickly to try to reach somewhere before dark, the door swung open with a whine.

My thoughts were interrupted by the telephone and at first it sounded exactly like the porter's horn at Royaumont. That's what confused me. How we came to dread that sound. Of course, the porter's horn – what was her name, a big girl from Newcastle with fair hair – was nothing like a telephone but it took me a moment to come back to my senses and realise where I was, in my house in Paddington not at Royaumont waiting for wounded.

I got up slowly, felt a little dizzy in the bright sun. I stood there until it passed, using the railing to keep from falling. The phone was still ringing. I bent down and picked up my teacup and saucer and went inside. I walked carefully.

They say that our greatest sense for memory is the sense of smell and Royaumont was full of smells, the perfume we sprinkled on our beds to try to rid ourselves of the awful reek of decay that always accompanied new patients, the clean smell of snow, almost like petrol and, later, the spring flowers, the fresh cut grass of summer. But it was the sound of that horn I couldn't get out of my mind now. I can just imagine what Miss Ivens would say to me. 'Oh for goodness' sake, Iris, who cares a fig for a silly horn?' But I know she'd have remembered it too after we left. That horn ruled our lives. You'd hear it in your sleep, over and over.

The phone stopped before I reached the kitchen. Then it started again. I walked over, steadied myself on the bench. 'Hello?' I felt like my voice was coming from somewhere else.

'Iris, is that you? Are you all right?'

'Grace. Yes, I'm fine. I was just out the front in the sun and I dozed off.' My lips wouldn't work properly and I could still hear that porter's horn, in the distance now, as if I were one of the patients approaching in the ambulance along the drive. I wonder did it reassure them that someone knew they were coming, that someone would help them now, ease their suffering.

'I just rang to say I'll drop in on my way to work,' Grace said.

'You don't need to do that. I'm fine really.'

'I've got time. David's taking the girls to school and he said he'll take Henry to day care. I'll just pop in.'

Grace had started 'popping in' a lot over recent months, ever since the appointment with the heart doctor. But I didn't want to see her today. The invitation had unsettled me. Violet Heron. Violet Heron, after all these years. 'The flower bird girls', she called us, Iris Crane and Violet Heron, the flower bird girls. What young fools we were.

The door swung all the way open and there was a woman, dressed like Miss Ivens, in a long grey skirt, black boots and a coat, brandishing a candle lantern. 'Oh Frances, thank God it's you. We had no idea what had happened.' The woman was considerably smaller than Miss Ivens and me. She held the lamp high to guide Miss Ivens in. Around her everything was blackness.

'I missed the morning train,' Miss Ivens said. 'And there shouldn't have been another. They ran two today because there was none yesterday.' Miss Ivens started making her way inside, and the woman moved to close the door. 'Wait, wait,'

Miss Ivens said. 'Come in, Iris, quick, before Cicely shuts you out.'

'Who's this?' Cicely made way for me to walk past her and then quickly closed the door, although there seemed little point; inside was colder than out. I could just make out her face in the candlelight.

'Cicely Hamilton, may I present Miss Iris Crane, recently of Stanthorpe, Australia, come to rescue us from my ineptitude.'

'Charmed, I'm sure,' Cicely said, in a way that suggested she wasn't at all. 'And what will Miss Crane be doing?' I felt like a speck she'd found while dusting.

'She's a nurse,' Miss Ivens said enthusiastically, ignoring Cicely's tone. 'And she speaks French like a native.' It was the first time I saw the skill Miss Ivens had for ignoring a person's faults. Initially, I thought she was lacking perception but it wasn't that. It was that she always dug deeper to find the better feelings inside people and encourage those. Their petty feelings she simply ignored. I later saw that even the worst of them often rose to her expectations.

'Good for her,' Cicely said. 'Do we need more nurses?'

'Nice to meet you,' I said, for something to say. I felt the entire distance between Australia and England, between Cicely Hamilton and me, could be heard in our voices. I hadn't felt it at all with Miss Ivens, whose Warwickshire accent was warmer and more musical. Cicely Hamilton's voice was deep and melodious, floating above us to the cold ceilings. Next to Cicely's, my voice was harsh, like the summer sun – you couldn't escape from under it. With every syllable, she alienated me further. I wanted to remain silent, not hit the walls with my loud flat notes.

'Come through to the kitchen now,' Cicely said warmly to

Miss Ivens. 'Quoyle's done up a barley soup. No idea how. And we've bread and cheese. Oh, and a knife. Just the one, but a knife all the same. I think Quoyle got it in the village today. She's charmed the locals, you know, without a word of French.' She continued to ignore me and led the way through the abbey, holding her lamp above her head. At one stage I looked up to try to find the ceiling but the columns disappeared into darkness and then I tripped on the uneven stone floor and decided to keep my eyes on where we were going. I could smell the damp that had made its way up through the floor or down through the ceilings. There was the smell of animal droppings too. Something – rats, I assumed – scurried off as we approached.

After what seemed an age of turns and corridors, we came to a large square room with an enormous wood stove at its centre and oil lamps in makeshift holders along the walls. A dozen or so women were gathered on benches around one of two long tables. Each woman had a plate or bowl of sorts in front of her, none seeming to match any other. Most were empty. Some looked as if they'd been licked clean. In the middle of the table was a large tureen with the dregs of a thick soup beside a wooden board with torn pieces of bread and slabs of yellow butter. As I looked around the group, I was struck by how bright their eyes were.

'Look who I found at the door,' Cicely said. 'Here is Miss Ivens, home from Paris but without our beds.'

'That's not true,' Miss Ivens said, smiling. 'I found some mattresses that will do nicely, but we'll need to send up to the station for them. We've had to walk.' Miss Ivens told them about the funeral and M Bousier's being the undertaker. 'Terrible business,' she said. 'You think farmers would have some inkling that we can't live without blood but apparently not. It's asparagus they grow around these parts, isn't it, which likely doesn't bleed, and perhaps they don't keep animals. I have no idea where the local doctor was and didn't feel I should ask.' Cicely continued to watch Miss Ivens which meant I could study Cicely. Small and slightly built, full of nervous energy, she had a long handsome face, a Greek profile, and dark eyes that flitted about taking in everything except me. She couldn't have worked harder at ignoring me if she tried.

'Now what was I talking about?' Miss Ivens said. 'Ah yes, mattresses. Before you all go dreaming of feathers, they're far from that. And we'll be sharing for now. Cicely, perhaps one of the drivers could go?'

'I'll see who I can find,' Cicely said.

Although the kitchen was not warm, it was a furnace compared with the corridor we'd come from. Miss Ivens and I peeled off coats and gloves and scarves, dripping our melted snow onto the stone floor. We hung our things over the chairs that lined the wall.

'Quoyle,' Miss Ivens said to the woman standing over the stove. 'What's this you've made? Barley soup I hear.'

'Yes miss and there's plenty more. Sit down now and eat.'

I was introduced. I don't remember now everyone I met but it must have been most of them. There was Quoyle, just mentioned, who'd worked as Miss Ivens's secretary for fifteen years in Liverpool, she said. She was happy to be the cook for now. 'But I'll turn my hand to anything,' she said. 'I'd have learnt to be a nurse if it meant I could come here.' Quoyle was not a young woman, perhaps fifty, with spectacles, a substantial bosom, wide waist and hips. She looked as if she might prefer to be kind but with a temper that might at times let her down, like some of the matrons I'd worked for.

Seated at the table was Dr Agnes Savill, who seemed not much older than me, tiny with curly hair, dark eyes and high rosy cheeks. Agnes was going to be responsible for the hospital's radiological equipment, Miss Ivens said. 'Responsible's going just a tad far,' Dr Savill said to Miss Ivens, and screwed up her nose and smiled at me. I loved her immediately.

And then there was Mrs Berry, whom Miss Ivens had mentioned on the train. She'd studied with Miss Ivens, although she looked older, long greying hair parted in the middle in two plaits to the side, big brown eyes, beatific smile. She looked like someone you could trust.

I remember the orderlies too, sitting in a group at the other end of the table, Vera Collum from Liverpool who grinned and bade me welcome, and Marjorie Starr, a Canadian, who started singing a song about bears she thought I might know but didn't, the others whose names have gone now. They were like excited schoolgirls at a play, giggling and hooting and talking among themselves. They'd come to do whatever was needed, Collum told me. She was a journalist and photographer before the war. 'But here I'm happy to be a mere orderly,' she said.

Dr Savill and Mrs Berry made room for Miss Ivens and me at one end of the table. I realised I hadn't eaten since early morning when I'd set out from the pension for the station. I was hungry and the soup, fairly plain in all probability, tasted heavenly. The bread, my first taste of a fresh baguette, was a marvel.

Miss Ivens talked as she ate. She seemed to have boundless energy. 'Ruth, tell Iris about the drains. Iris knows about drains.'

At Risdon we had a bore whose water tasted of the earth

and showed its red-soil pedigree. I had no experience of drains and hadn't given any indication that I did.

'I think the cesspits need to be emptied,' Mrs Berry said, leaning forward to meet my eyes. She had a deep quiet voice. 'Either that or the grease trap's not working. We've a plumber coming in the morning.'

'Good, well have Iris with you when you meet him. She can tell him what to do. It's not the trap. It's a blockage in the pipe. I'm sure of it.' Mrs Berry smiled at Miss Ivens and then at me.

'And then perhaps you and Iris should go into town, find out who we should see about letting the locals know we're here. I'll warrant they'll be glad to have a hospital nearby. Make sure you tell them we're Scottish doctors.' I must have looked puzzled. 'The Auld Alliance. Scotland and France against the English. The French have long memories. I'm perfectly willing to be Scottish if it makes them happy.'

Dr Savill turned to me, those dark curls framing her pretty face. She asked how long I'd been in France. 'Three days,' I said. 'I'm actually going to Soissons but Miss Ivens asked if I might come here on the way.'

'She's going to be my assistant, Agnes,' Miss Ivens said. 'The new hospital administrator. She speaks French like she grew up here.'

'Isn't that my job?' Cicely said. She was standing over at the door and I was surprised she could even hear what we were saying.

'Cicely,' Miss Ivens said and smiled, 'you're our bookkeeper. You can't be running round after me all day as well.' Cicely turned and walked out of the room without saying anything more.

'Poor you,' Dr Savill said to me. 'Can you work twenty-three hours a day and keep four million things going at once?'

'Stop it, you'll terrify the poor girl and we can't have that,' Miss Ivens said. 'Tell me what's happened about the X-ray machines?' She reached across and tore a piece of bread from the loaf and spread it thickly with butter she'd put on her plate.

'Cicely wired Edinburgh again today,' Dr Savill said. 'No one will freight for us. As soon as they know who we are, they tell us there's no room.'

'Well, let's just tell them we're someone else,' Miss Ivens said. 'Is it the Scottish or the Women they object to? I assume Hospitals are all right.' She bit into the bread.

'Either? Both? Elsie's got a bit of a reputation, you know. She wouldn't come out against the hunger strikes.'

'Elsie Inglis runs our organisation,' Miss Ivens said to me after she'd swallowed the bread. 'The Scottish Women's Hospitals. You'll meet her soon.' And then, to Dr Savill, 'Let me see what I can do tomorrow. My father's company uses a Greek shipping group. They might be able to carry the heavier equipment. We're not fools, just women. If I get a chance . . .'

'Did you want me, Frances?' A new face had appeared at the door. It was another woman, tiny and slight, younger even than Dr Savill by the look of her. She smiled over to me, pursed lips, raised eyebrows, like a little pixie.

'Ah, Violet my love. Mattresses,' Miss Ivens said. 'We left them at the station. Can you go up in the car?'

'For a mattress, I'll drive to Paris,' she said. Her voice was surprisingly deep for such a little thing. She looked at me. She had green eyes like a cat, with blonde hair that fell to her shoulders in soft curls. 'You must be Iris.' She read the surprise on my face. 'Word travels fast in a house full of women. Cicely Hamilton's got your name in her book. Want to come back into town?'

I didn't. I was exhausted. 'Of course. I'll get my coat.'

I used my bread to mop up the rest of my soup – when in Rome – then got up, pulled on my coat and followed the woman out into the cold abbey.

'I'm Violet Heron,' she said just outside the kitchen door.

'Iris Crane,' I said, taking the warm dry hand she offered.

'Flower bird,' she said. I must have looked puzzled. 'Our names – we're both flower birds.'

I laughed. 'Yes, I suppose we are.'

'Well, come on Miss Flower Bird. Let's flit.'

We walked back through the abbey, taking a different route from the one I'd taken with Miss Ivens. Violet carried a lantern. 'What did you mean, Cicely Hamilton has my name in her book?' I said.

'She keeps a book on troublemakers,' Violet said. 'She thinks you're a troublemaker. But don't worry. My name's the first entry. Yours won't be the last. Eventually we'll all be in there and then she'll be alone, won't she?'

'Why?'

'Who knows? Cicely's an *actress*.' Violet said this with considerable emphasis, as if it would explain everything. 'She thinks she's in charge. Frances and the rest go along with her because she's a good bookkeeper. But she doesn't like anyone getting between her and Frances. If Frances likes you, and she does, apparently, you're doomed.'

'I think I went to school with girls like Cicely. You can never please them. You're better off ignoring them.'

'You got that right, my dear.' Violet's voice had started to echo. We'd moved into a large space.

'I can smell horses,' I said.

'We're in the refectory. The Uhlan used it as a stable, dear hearts.'

'The Uhlan? I thought Miss Ivens said they were Cistercians.'

'You're out by five centuries and a mile of vocations. The Uhlan are the German cavalry. The Cistercians are the monks who built the abbey.'

'The Germans were here?'

'My word. Two months ago, Royaumont was between them and Paris, more or less. The mayor of Asnières fled and left the poor old curé Father Rousselle to meet the Germans at the crossroads into town. Even the government of Paris evacuated. Apparently, what stopped the Germans was the taxi cabs. Some French general commandeered all the Paris taxi cabs to take more soldiers to the front. The Germans retreated. I'd retreat too if I were up against a Paris taxi cab. They're even more daring than the ones in London.'

The smell of horses, which had always seemed to me sweet and honest, was suddenly associated with the thing I most dreaded, the Germans who'd started the war. I dared not breathe lest I took some of their evil into my lungs. I thought of Tom again suddenly. I had a picture of him in my mind as clear as day, younger than he really was, a boy of twelve out there on his own in the cold snow, and I felt a pull at my heart.

Violet said she'd been in Paris in the summer but now it was like a different city. 'Miss Ivens says they've only just got over the last war with Germany. Life's just dismal. You can't even get absinthe these days.'

'Absinthe?'

'Marvellous stuff, better than champagne,' Violet said. 'But it's been banned because it makes you feel so good. We're not supposed to feel good.'

We emerged into the cloister and I was relieved to breathe the clean air. It was colder than within the abbey now and the stars were out, the snow a white so bright it was nearer blue. I wrapped the two lengths of my scarf around my neck.

Violet turned to me and smiled. 'Who taught you to wind a scarf?' She pulled at the scarf gently and repositioned it, making a long side and wrapping it twice. 'There,' she said. 'Snug as a bug.' It was something Daddy would say as he tucked Tom and me into bed at night, and I felt a twinge of homesickness.

We were walking down one side of the cloister. Violet pulled a pack of cigarettes from her coat pocket and offered me one. I took it. She pulled one out for herself and stopped and struck a match and held it. I put my face forward and sucked on the cigarette as I'd seen others do. I leant back and breathed it in and coughed violently and pulled my face away. Violet extinguished the match. 'Do you smoke?' she asked.

'No,' I said, through my cough, holding the foul thing away from me.

'Oh for goodness' sake, you don't have to,' she said, taking the cigarette from me and putting her own back into the pack as she nursed mine between her lips. 'Aren't you a trick?' She led me out of the cloister, around the back of the abbey. 'These are our garages,' Violet said. 'Mine's this one.'

'You can drive a truck?' It was an enormous contraption, two seats in front and a canvas-covered tray behind. I'd driven a car just the once, the Carsons', over their top paddock which was big enough so I wouldn't hit anything, or at least that's what Tom had said. The steering wheel rattled under my hands. The engine was louder than anything I'd ever heard. It was nothing like a fast horse, which was the way Tom had described it. I screamed at him to tell me where the brake was, slammed it on as soon as he did, stalled the car and never asked for a drive again. Tom was the opposite, of course, loved anything with a machine in it, drove the car whenever he could, much to Daddy's consternation. They would have fought about cars, Daddy and Tom, if they'd ever got to it. But they had plenty of other things to get through first.

'This isn't a truck,' Violet said. 'It's an ambulance, or it will be.' She pulled herself up into the cabin, holding her cigarette between her lips again to free up her hands.

'I might be a trick,' I said, 'but you're amazing. Did you study with Miss Ivens?'

'Study? Oh God, no. I'm not a doctor. Whatever gave you that idea?'

'I don't know. You called Miss Ivens Frances.'

'Frances is her name, darling. No, I'm a driver. I'm going to drive this ambulance.'

'So, did you know Miss Ivens from before?'

'No. They advertised for drivers so I thought I'd come along. You had to bring your own car.'

'So how old are you?' She seemed so young to have so much experience.

'Twenty-four. You?'

'Twenty-one. You own a car?' I said.

'It was a friend's but yes, it's mine now. I don't think he'll want it back when he sees what they've done to it.'

'Are all the drivers women?' I asked.

'We've brought two men because the Croix-Rouge said women can't drive in a war zone. Frances says we'll see about that and they'll just need to get used to us. But as for the rest of us, we're women, yes, last time I checked.'

'How on earth are they going to make that abbey into a hospital? It's a wreck.'

'You're not supposed to say that. We all have to pretend the abbey "just needs a little work".' It was a perfect imitation of Miss Ivens, complete with the little shake of the head. I laughed.

'So, tell me about Australia.' Violet had her right arm over the back of my seat as she reversed. She smelt like flowers and spoke like my English teacher had implored us to speak. I wondered how you could muster up the energy for such perfect diction all the time, but I suppose it was what she was used to. 'My brother had a book about Australia and I've always wanted to go there.'

'What do you want to know?'

'Is it true the men are giants?'

'Well, I've nothing to compare them with except the few little Frenchmen I met at the railway station. But based on Miss Ivens, I'd say women from Warwickshire are giants.'

'Amazons. She is truly wonderful, isn't she?' Violet said.

'Is she a bit mad?'

'Oh yes, completely, but don't you find mad people interesting? They go out in the deep where something's happening. The rest of us just bathe in the shallows. I'd like to be mad. Wouldn't you?'

'Not at all,' I said. 'No, thank you.'

'Well, I don't think you're too much at risk, at any rate,' Violet said. 'Nor me, more's the pity.'

'So, what made you decide to come here?' I said. Violet was so charming and sophisticated. I couldn't imagine her working for a hospital.

'What else would I do? Sit at home? We're at war. I don't know. Why did you come?'

'It's complicated,' I said. 'My young brother ran away and signed up. Our father told him he wasn't to go but he went

36

anyway. He's very headstrong. So I'm to find him and bring him home.'

'Is your father a pacifist? How exotic.'

'I don't know. What's a pacifist?'

'You know, peace at any cost. Lay down your weapons. I wouldn't tell anyone else if I were you. We're all pretty patriotic at the moment. God save and all that.'

'I wouldn't say my father's a pacifist,' I said. 'Actually, he has a pretty bad temper if it comes to it and doesn't mind taking anyone on. But he doesn't believe we should go to war.' Daddy's older brother had been killed in the Boer War and it broke their mother's heart. He said Australia wasn't Britain and shouldn't be in a British war.

I peered into the snow ahead of us. 'It's very dark.'

'Night tends to do that. Cicely said you were supposed to be in Soissons with the hospital there. Frances has told her to "fix it will you dear". I think Cicely's planning to ship you off as soon as she can.'

I smiled. 'I think you're right about that. The Red Cross gave me a choice – a hospital ship in the Aegean, nursing typhoid cases, or France, where there were vacancies in Soissons. When we last heard from Tom he mentioned Amiens, so I asked to go to Soissons. To be honest, I don't quite know what possessed me to follow Miss Ivens,' I said.

'I do. She's put one of her spells on you,' Violet said. 'Frances could convince rain to fall upwards.'

'She probably could.' I laughed. 'And I'm very glad to have come to meet you all. It sounds marvellous, what you're planning to do. But I really must go tomorrow. I'm supposed to be looking for Tom, not having fun.'

'Surely you can do both,' Violet said. 'We're just as near

37

Amiens as Soissons is, and we're a good deal nearer Paris, more to the point. It's criminal to be too far from Paris when one is living in France, my dear. Perhaps you could just stay with us until you find him. That wouldn't hurt.' She looked over at me, screwing up her nose and giving me a little pixie smile.

'Perhaps I could,' I said. 'I mean, it's not as if I'll be able to locate him just like that anyway.'

'Exactly. I imagine it might be quite difficult to find one young man in all this war. Even if he started in Amiens, he would have moved south with the troops by now.' I was nodding agreement. I hadn't given much thought to how I'd actually locate Tom, and Violet was right. It might take quite a bit of time. 'Hurrah,' she said, although I hadn't said anything. 'Someone I can have a laugh with. I have to warn you, Iris, the others take everything very seriously. And don't get me wrong. I like being at Royaumont and I'm frightfully serious, but goodness me a little fun now and then never goes astray.' I didn't reply.

'So why does your father want you to take your brother home?' Violet said after a pause.

'He's only fifteen,' I said. I felt a pull of emotion. 'We're very close, Tom and I.' Suddenly I thought I might cry. I narrowed my eyes to stop the tears.

'Oh, that is young,' Violet said, failing to notice my upset. 'And so you've come all that way, all by yourself?'

'Yes,' I said, recovering my composure. 'Actually, the ship journey was fun. But then we were held up in Folkestone because of the Channel storms, then Boulogne, then Paris. I've been to the train station for three days running but there were no trains to Soissons. The line's been blown up.'

Violet laughed. 'There is a war on, dear.'

'So I hear. I didn't mind at all. I loved the station, just watching all the people.'

Gare du Nord had been exactly as I'd imagined it, the rafters thickly lined with pigeons, moving about aimlessly, mirroring the people milling about below. The uniforms were there, the khaki of the British, the blue and red of the French who looked so gallant wrapped in their greatcoats with their caps low. Ordinary French people were scattered among the soldiers, their baskets and bags and need to travel in front of them like signs against enchantment. Porters were moving about slowly as if there had never been a war. They looked at their watches, at their shiny shoes, and cast sly glances at the soldiers.

On the second day, having confirmed the train was cancelled again, I'd left the station and wandered the city. 'We weren't supposed to be on the streets unaccompanied but how could I stay inside?' I said. 'It was Paris,' I added, trying to sound sophisticated like Violet. And it *was* Paris, the Paris that Claire had made so real for me. From the way Daddy had talked, I'd expected the city to be in ruins because of the war but it was nothing like that at all. You'd hardly have known there was a war on, other than that the streets seemed quieter than they did in the pictures I'd seen. I went to all the places I'd read about. I started to feel as if I could be someone else, not plain Iris Crane from Risdon but someone who might be present at important places and important moments, someone more like Violet seemed to me to be, perfectly relaxed in the world. This new Iris ate lunch in a café in Montmartre called Chartiers – baked ham with cabbage that tasted heavenly, like nothing she'd ever eaten at home – and drank red wine that came in a little glass bottle and tasted like the fruit it had once been. In the afternoon, she stood below the Arc de Triomphe. From there, she could look straight ahead to the Place de la Concorde, right to the Tuileries and beyond those to the palace and Eiffel Tower. She walked along a street on her way back to the pension kicking a little rounded black pebble that skipped along in front of her merrily. The street was empty but for an old man in a cap with an old dog and a boy playing marbles. She kicked the stone and felt she had found perfection itself.

Later I wondered if that girl, that Iris, was still there on the street in the Latin Quarter kicking the stone, and I could go back and find her, and change the rest of the story. But of course, you can't do that. If I was to be that new Iris, I would have to give up the old Iris. There would be no going back. There never is.

At dinnertime, I ate a ham-and-cheese toasted sandwich that came with more wine in a little glass jug. I felt giddy when I returned to my pension where my roommate – still waiting for her orders to be finalised – was playing solitaire as she had been when I'd left. How could you be in Paris, I thought, and play solitaire? I didn't say as much. I'd already given up on the notion that Mary Jefford and I would be friends. I was relieved she wasn't coming with me to Soissons. Mary had experience with typhoid. She'd opted to go to the Aegean to serve on the hospital ship.

I told Violet about Mary. 'In the four days we spent together, counting one night on the held-up train from Dieppe, she gave me lessons in the job of nursing soldiers. Her most memorable tip, and it had many memorable tips to compete with, was what to do when a soldier gets an erection while you're sponging him. You simply carry around a glass of iced water and a teaspoon and give his pecker a tap. That's what she called it. "Problem solved," she said.'

Violet laughed. 'No, she didn't say that.'

I nodded. She did.

On the third day, I'd been fully ready to go to Soissons. Matron had sent word that the train would surely come today and I'd be on my way. I said goodbye to Mary again and set off.

I remember seeing another nurse in a wool coat like mine hurrying along the platform with a confidence I admired. She was older than me, perhaps middle forties. I thought to wave but she didn't look my way. Nearer me was a young French couple, leaning towards one another, focusing on a bundle the woman held in her arms, an infant. They looked so forlorn, I was wondering whether I should ask them if they needed help when the man looked up past the woman and child and met my gaze. His eyes were dark and wet. He looked from my face to my shoulder, saw the red cross emblazoned on my coat, the red cross of hope. 'Please, please, will you help us?' he asked in French. 'Our little one is sick.'

I could hear the tension in his voice, like Daddy if he ever had to ask for help. I went over immediately, with no idea what I might be able to do. 'I'll do what I can,' I said. I led the mother, whose gaze was fixed on the child, over to a bench. When she did look up at me finally I saw dark smudges under her eyes and tear lines down her face. I put a hand on her shoulder and smiled with what I hoped was reassurance. She kept both arms firmly around the child. Her husband remained a little distance away.

I was trying to remember what I'd learnt about newborns, for the child looked very new. A boy, his mother told me, her voice croaky. He'd been sick with a fever for three days and they'd come to Paris but there were no doctors available because of the war so they were going back home. The night before, the boy had gone completely rigid – they'd thought he was dead – and then he'd slept. He'd been asleep all night now. The woman's voice shook with emotion. I kept my own voice as even as I could, remembering how Al would do this when faced with strong emotion and how it calmed patients. 'Is he on the breast?' I asked matter-of-factly. He was. 'Was the fever very high?' She nodded, yes. The boy had had a seizure, I surmised, brought on by the fever, no bad thing but not really relevant to the underlying condition, which was . . . 'I'll need to have a look at him,' I said. She brought the child down to cradle him in her arms. I felt his forehead. 'The fever's broken,' I said. 'That's good.' Gently, I peeled back the shawl and a blanket. I checked glands, no swelling; pupils, normal as far as I could tell; belly, no distension.

'He has a rash,' his mother said.

'Show me,' I said. There were serious illnesses that started with fevers and moved to pox. The mother cradled the child in her left arm and lifted the nightdress with her right hand. I pulled up a little vest. The skin was red with raised white papules, all around the child's torso. It wasn't chickenpox, which came out everywhere, nor shingles in a newborn. Nor measles; the spots were too small. And then I knew it. It was false measles. A high fever resolves into a rash like this that spreads. Roseola was the name. It used to be confused with measles, thus the common name of false measles.

'I'm pretty sure it's harmless,' I said. 'The fever has worn him out. Exhausted, needs fluid.' I was talking more to myself now. The little boy's lips were as dry as his mother's. 'And so do you. You must look after yourself to keep your milk. Have

42

you expressed?' I didn't know the word and made a pumping action with my hand on my own breast. The girl smiled for the first time and she was beautiful suddenly. She had, she said. 'Good. He'll wake soon, I hope, and be ravenous. Feed him as often as he likes. The rash should move out from his middle before fading in a day or so. If it does anything differently, you should find a doctor.' The girl looked worried again. 'I'm a nurse,' I said, 'not a doctor.'

The other nurse I'd noticed when I'd arrived at the station earlier was talking to the little porter. I wondered if I should ask her advice. I caught snatches of the conversation. The porter was rocking from the balls of his feet to his heels as she spoke. I'm sorry madam, he said in French then, there are no sleeping cars on account of the war. You will have to sit up like everyone else. The journey is not long. Oh, for God's sake man, she replied, can't you speak English? She made a pillow of her hands and put her head there in a mock sleep. She even snored gently. The porter told her again that there were no berths because the journey was too short. She wouldn't need sleep. Her cheeks were flushed with exasperation. She looked straight at me then and called over. 'Can you help me?' she said. 'He doesn't seem to understand.'

'Mattresses,' I said in French to the porter. 'She has mattresses she wants you to put on the train.'

'*Oui*,' said the little porter. 'Of course. Why didn't she say so?'

The porter went off to get help with the mattresses, and the woman came over. I stood. We were about the same height, a rare enough experience for me. I had been the tallest in my class all through school.

'You're a marvel,' the woman said. 'If I don't get their beds on the train, my girls will have another rough night of it. Frances Ivens.' She held out her gloved hand, which I took.

43

'Iris Crane.'

'You're not English.'

'Australian.'

'Where on earth did you learn to speak French?' Before I could answer she was looking beyond me to the mother and child.

'Have you nursed babies? This child is sick,' I said. 'I didn't look after children very much in my training.'

'You're a nurse to boot,' she said. 'Why don't you come with me?'

'What?' I said. 'Where?' But Miss Ivens had moved on to the child and his mother. She smiled and I felt a great sense of relief. 'My bag's over there, dear one,' she said, placing a hand on the young woman's shoulder. 'I'll be back,' and she strode off, returning directly with a little leather case. When she opened it up, I saw the stethoscope and instruments, and that was when I realised she was a doctor, not a nurse.

'I really didn't expect to see a woman doctor,' I said to Violet now.

'You're lucky Frances didn't bite your head off. I shouldn't think she'd like being mistaken for a nurse. She's even particular about women doctors being employed as nurses. That's what they do at some of the hospitals, employ women doctors but only to nurse. Frances says we'll never do that at Royaumont.'

Miss Ivens sat down beside the mother and confidently took the sleeping boy into her own arms and examined him while I recounted the symptoms.

'And what did you conclude?' she said, looking at me so intensely I felt nervous and unsure.

I told her what I'd told the couple. 'The rash,' I said.

'Well done. It's roseola. Reassure this poor woman her child will live.' Miss Ivens smiled at the mother. 'She must

44

make sure he takes in fluid while he has the diarrhoea. She should give him sugar water. Where are they from?'

I asked the woman. 'Senlis,' she said.

'That's near enough,' Miss Ivens said. She took out a pen and scrap of paper and wrote down an address. 'Tell them that's a hospital where they'll always find a doctor who can help them.' I told the woman who thanked us both, tears streaming down her face. 'Tell her she must bring him when he's well so we can see if he needs extra care. The seizure has probably done no harm, but . . . we don't need to worry about that just yet.'

I interpreted as confidently as I could. 'You need to bring your baby to the hospital when he's better,' I said. 'No urgency.'

'Where did you say you were going?' Miss Ivens asked me when the couple left us.

'Soissons,' I said. 'My train has just arrived.' I was disappointed, to be honest, to see the Soissons train running. I'd hoped for another day in Paris.

'That's no good,' Miss Ivens said. 'I need an interpreter. Come to Royaumont.'

'Where's Royaumont?'

'That way,' Miss Ivens said, pointing north. 'Not far. And much more exciting. Where are your things? Here's the porter with the mattresses and the train will be off soon. Hurry now or we'll miss it and I don't know when there's another.'

'But I have orders.'

'I'll take care of those.'

'And so, here I am,' I said to Violet. We'd arrived at the station in Viarmes. Violet pulled around and brought the car to a sudden stop next to the platform. Our bags and chattels were just as we'd left them, the straw mattresses piled against

45

the back wall, our luggage supporting them on one side, my own portmanteau, everything I owned in the world, standing bravely against its first French snow. The station remained deserted. We worked together quickly in the cold to pack the truck. Violet left the headlamps burning so we could see what we were doing.

When we'd finished loading the truck, we climbed back in and set off for Royaumont. 'I've still seen no sign of this war they keep talking about,' I said. 'And for all I know, Matron is writing to my father right now to say I've gone missing in Paris.'

'I doubt they'll even notice,' Violet said. 'And if they do, Frances will speak to someone who knows someone and the orders will disappear. She has a way. I know what you mean about the war, though. Royaumont's so strange. You don't imagine the war could ever touch us there.'

Violet told me she'd grown up in Cornwall where her family had lived for generations. 'We're the Cornwall Herons,' she said, with a hint of mockery in her voice. 'My father's father, Duxton Digby Heron, had an extensive collection of stamps, inherited by my father, Digby Duxton – the names are not a joke, by the way. My father sold the stamps to pursue his own hobbies of gambling and drink. Gets me where I live, he used to say. It certainly did. He died of liver failure at forty-four, no mean feat.

'My mother, from a less wealthy and less unhappy Scottish family, tolerated my father until his untimely death, and inherited the estate. No love lost, that's for sure, although the cousins are not happy about the estate falling to the Scots, and my mother does tend to rather rub their noses in it by inviting her family to stay. There's no money left, of course, so the place is slowly falling apart.'

'How old were you when your father died?'

'Sixteen,' Violet said. 'Away at school. I went home to make sure there was no mistake, that Digby wasn't lurking in some corner of the house. He was always a bit of a lurker. My mother thought me ghoulish when I insisted on viewing the body.' Violet had lost a brother too, she said, to pneumonia, when she was eight.

Violet told me her family's story as if it was all a big joke, and it was funny, the way she put it, and I even found myself laughing, but later I couldn't help thinking how unhappy she must have been growing up in a house like that. When I told her about my own family, it seemed much happier, despite the fact my mother had died when I was only six.

'My father remarried, a woman from a farm near us,' I told Violet. 'Claire's French. Thus my competence in the language,' I said in French.

'Ah, the wicked stepmother,' Violet said, in the same tone she'd told me about her own life, 'with an added French twist.'

'I'm afraid not,' I said. 'More like I was the wicked stepdaughter.'

The year I turned nine, my mother's sister Veronica visited us from Scotland. Until then, Daddy had been happy enough the way the three of us – me and Daddy and Tom – had muddled on together, but Veronica had put an idea into Daddy's head I should be among women and girls. So he packed me off to All Hallows' in Brisbane to board. I felt completely at sea among those girls with their girls' games and perfect hems on their tunics. When I went home for the Easter holidays in that first year, I said I hated school and didn't want to go back but Daddy made me. Two weeks later he came to town and brought Claire.

We met in the parlour of the convent, a neat room with heavy drapes and the smell of wood polish. Claire was a small, slight woman with straight brown hair surrounding a heart-shaped face. Much later I learnt she'd married into a family on the Italian side of the French–Italian border and she and her husband had come to Australia to run an orchard. He'd been killed when he fell from a ladder five years earlier. After his death, everyone had expected Claire would go home. But instead she stayed on and engaged a manager to run the orchard. She and Daddy met when Daddy took our bull over to service her cows.

I liked Claire instinctively, although I had no idea why they were there until they were taking their leave and Daddy put a hand to the small of her back to usher her out. 'Do you hate it here very much?' she said to me in strongly accented English. 'Would you rather be back home?' I nodded yes, unable to speak for fear of crying. The next week they married and the week after that, I was brought home.

'I should have been grateful she got me a reprieve from boarding school,' I said to Violet. 'And she worked so hard to win our love, Tom's and especially mine, even after the twins were born. But for a long time, I just felt angry. I hated her.'

Claire never tried to be a mother to Tom and me but she was kind and interested and we came to love her almost in spite of ourselves. I was worse than Tom, loyal to a mother I thought I could remember that he could never have known – she'd died of toxaemia just after he was born. To her credit Claire ignored my seething anger. She played to my finer feelings and eventually dragged them out of me. When I think back now, having lived my life, I know she was one of the most truly good people I ever knew, willing to raise someone else's children and even to love them. I came to love her too. By the time I went back to boarding school, the twins, André and René, were born. It was so different for me to be a half-sister rather than the child-mother I'd had to be to Tom. Claire welcomed whatever help I offered but never made me do more than that. She taught me French and made me love the Paris she conjured for me. She also taught me how to sew and cook, which I never would have learnt otherwise. I'd been blessed really and knew it.

As Violet drove, I watched the snow fall lazily to earth in the beams of light in front of us. Something niggled at the edge of my consciousness, vague, indefinable, as though I was doing a jigsaw puzzle and I'd just put a piece in the wrong place. It hadn't worried me at all, what Violet had said about remaining at Royaumont instead of going to Soissons. In fact, it made me feel valued. Of course, it should have worried me. I was young, so young, I think now, not yet an adult, not truly, but with an adult responsibility that had been mine since I was six, that of caring for my brother. And it wasn't as if I was deciding to abandon Tom. I wasn't deciding anything really. Violet was right. Royaumont was as good as anywhere to stay while I searched for Tom, and there was something about Miss Ivens that made a person want to muck in and help her. All those things were true. But as I look back, it was that point, the point I met Violet, so worldly and yet so welcoming, so convincing about how much fun it would all be, that was the point at which I went horribly horribly wrong.

Grace

It was 2.36 a.m. on the bedside clock. She picked up on the second ring. 'Grace, come now.' It was the night midwife, Alice Jablonsky. Grace was about to respond when she heard the click, the phone disconnecting. 'Grace, come now.' Grace knew what that meant. Don't ask questions, don't have coffee, just get in the car. She pulled the sweats on the floor over her pyjamas, slipped on socks, sneakers, grabbed a toothbrush out of the bathroom, smeared it with paste, stuck it in her mouth and chewed. David woke as she fumbled for her watch. 'On call,' she said through the toothbrush. 'Go back to sleep.'

On the way out she went into the kids' rooms. Mia wasn't there; a moment's panic until she remembered her eldest daughter was sleeping across the road at her friend Julie's. She went on to Phil who was talking nonsense in her sleep, light still on, Tolkien on the floor beside her, snoring quietly, a single tail thump when he saw Grace. Then Henry, on his back, arms splayed, covers off. Grace went in, replaced the covers, took in his little-boy smell and turned and headed out, dumped the toothbrush in the kitchen sink and grabbed a sip of water from the tap to rinse.

By 2.41 a.m. she was in the Citroën, David's car; he'd parked her Honda in – she didn't much like the symbolism but didn't have time to address it now. She drove over the Paddington hill and down through the flood plain of Milton as the moon came up over the city of Brisbane. She came in the back gate and pulled into her space outside the maternity unit. She heard a storm bird somewhere down near the river but the night was clear as glass. She went straight to the labour ward and found an enrolled nurse who looked about fifteen at the desk.

'Why am I here?' Grace said. Her voice was gravelly. She wanted coffee.

'I'm sorry?' The girl looked flatly at Grace.

'I'm Dr Hogan. Alice called me. Get her for me, would you?' A question that wasn't a question.

'Sorry, Doctor, of course.' She left the desk.

Alice Jablonsky came down the corridor with that calm, brisk gait of the best midwives and steered Grace back towards the operating theatres. They talked as they walked. 'So which one is it?' Grace asked.

'Margaret Cameri.'

'Which one was she?' There had been three on the ward when Grace left at 10 p.m.; two who should have been sent home, one a young girl from the hostel in early labour, the other with slightly elevated blood pressure but no need for hospital yet. The third was a multi in established labour, no complications, close to transition. Grace hadn't even waited. Nothing expected from outlying districts, a good registrar, a good, experienced midwife in Alice. Grace had looked forward to a night of unbroken sleep.

'Room four, third baby, straightforward, eight centimetres when she came in. Margaret Cameri.'

The transition one. 'And?'

'Labour stalled for a bit and then sped up again on its own. She pushed the baby out and he's fine. She had a bleed, maybe four hundred mils. Something not right so I called Andrew. We started some Pitocin thinking PPH but then the fundus was wrong, too low, we couldn't figure out why, and then her uterus came out. It just came out. She's lost a lot of blood.' There was a hint of fear in Alice's voice.

Take a breath, Grace thought to herself. 'Where's Andrew now?'

'He's in theatre with her. We think we've controlled the bleeding and we've ordered more blood.'

'All good.' They'd got her to theatre and stopped the bleeding. It gave Margaret Cameri her best chance. 'I'll need another consultant. Try Lindsay or Frank if they're in town. And an anaesthetist. You been through one of these before?'

'No. Anaesthetist already there. I'll find another ob.'

'We'll be fine. Alice?'

'Yes?'

'You've done very well.'

By the time her pager went off again, Grace was walking through the double doors into the theatre. Nine minutes, twenty-four seconds, a record. 'I'll be there in a sec,' she said to Andrew through the intercom.

Grace confirmed Andrew Martin's diagnosis. 'You seen one of these before?' she said quietly to him.

'Nup.'

'You know what we're going to do?'

'Yep.'

'Good.' She was glad it was Andrew Martin, easy to work with, liked by docs and midwives, didn't mind taking orders from Grace, something male registrars often had trouble with. 'Stay where you are for now.' Andrew was using a towel to compress the bleeding. Another EN was holding Margaret Cameri's hand at the head end of the bed. She looked about fifteen too, Margaret Cameri not much older and wide-eyed with fear. Grace hoped she'd had plenty for pain.

The anaesthetist was the new guy, no sense of humour, no one could remember his name, but he was good enough tonight. Frank was still on his way, from somewhere south of the city, his wife phoned to say. He should have passed so they could try someone else. Frank was one of the older consultants who wouldn't necessarily take a call-in from the likes of Grace seriously. She was never sure if it was her youth or her sex and she didn't much care. They'd have to start. At any rate, they'd only need Frank if a hysterectomy became necessary and Grace hoped it could be avoided.

Grace was helped into gloves and went to the head of the bed. She smiled her hello-I'll-be-the-doctor-looking-after-you-today smile. 'Mrs Cameri, I'm Grace Hogan. I saw you earlier tonight. You've pushed out your baby and he's fine.' She looked across at Andrew who nodded. 'But the placenta hasn't come away and when you pushed it out it's pulled your womb out,' as if this was only to be expected, happened every other day. 'Once you're asleep, we're going to do our best to put it back manually but if that doesn't work, we'll have to operate to do it. We may have to remove your womb if we can't put it back. Do you understand what I'm saying?' What Grace didn't tell Margaret Cameri was that they might not be able to stop the bleeding, they might make a mistake, they might hesitate too long moving to the hysterectomy, such a young woman, you didn't want to do it if you didn't need to, she might haemorrhage, she might die, leaving her new son and two other children motherless. These were things Grace made herself stop thinking about.

Grace's mother had died during childbirth with Grace, of a PPH, a post-partum haemorrhage, where the uterus fails to contract following birth, leaving the placental bed bleeding freely into the uterine cavity. Like an inverted uterus, it's one of the few true emergencies of childbirth. Mostly now a PPH could be avoided or averted but when Grace was born, there were none of the drugs that could make a uterus contract. They did the best they could to stop the bleeding. In her mother's case, it hadn't been enough.

Over drinks one night when they were still medical students, Grace's friend Janis Kennedy had suggested that if Grace wanted to be an obstetrician she would need to face her emotions about her mother's death. Janis was into facing her emotions at that stage. She was specialising in psychiatry, fascinated by what the mind could do. 'Otherwise, you'll be no use to patients.'

'Oh please,' Grace had said. 'I have no feelings. I might have been there but I was hardly conscious of it.' Grace hadn't had children then, hadn't understood anything about birth and mothering. She ate the glacé cherry that came with her advocaat and dry and stared flatly at her friend.

'You probably blame yourself at some level,' Janis said. Janis was thin as a rail with neat brown hair and eyes that appeared to see deeply into a person. Tools of the trade, she'd told Grace when Grace had said as much.

'I do not,' Grace said. 'And just because you're my friend doesn't mean you can practise on me.'

'What did your father do after your mother died?' Janis said.

'I have no idea,' Grace replied curtly. 'He wasn't around. I've never met him.'

'You've never *met* him?'

'No,' Grace said. 'Iris, my grandmother, knows who he is, or thinks she does. He didn't want anything to do with me.'

'So you don't want anything to do with him?' Janis said.

'That's about it,' Grace said. 'It's possible he's a doctor. He was studying medicine with my mother.'

'Wow,' Janis said. 'You're a psychiatrist's dream in terms of issues. You might meet your father.'

'Unlikely,' Grace said. 'There are a lot of doctors in the world. And I have no intention of seeking him out. Ever.'

Grace looked at her patient now, mustering her confidence. Margaret Cameri had enough doubts for both of them. She nodded vigorously that she understood what Grace had said, but she just looked terrified. 'Where's the baby?' she whispered.

Just then Alice walked in. Thank God, Grace wanted to say. Alice was much better with patients than Grace, who always set out the risks too precisely. 'He's fine,' Alice said. 'A great big boy who surprised us all. Now he's out there with Dad in the other room and they're getting acquainted nicely. They'll be there when you wake up and you can give him a feed.'

'The others?' Margaret said.

Grace was about to say what others when Alice said, '. . . are on their way into the hospital with your mum, remember? And they're okay too. Everyone's fine.'

Within minutes Margaret was asleep and the anaesthetist was doing the crossword. We don't do that here, Grace wanted to say but didn't. Tomorrow she'd talk to his boss.

Grace wasn't in the mood for teaching but she showed

Andrew Martin what to do because that's what you did. You showed the next generation, passed on the skills you could only learn by doing. This would probably be the only inverted uterus Andrew would see during training. He'd have read about it but the real thing was rare. This was the second Grace had managed in ten years, the third she'd seen.

Grace had loved anatomy, had found the cold science of the dead oddly peaceful. In medical school, she'd taken extra tutorials and everyone thought she'd be a surgeon. But few women were accepted into surgery in the sixties and Grace wasn't offered a place. She remembered the interview panel's feedback. A red-faced gastroenterologist told her they couldn't give out positions that didn't pay off. 'Before you know it, you'll be married and having kids and we'll have wasted our time with you.' She'd opted for obstetrics, happy medicine as someone had called it, but this was the part she did well, the cutting and manipulating. As obstetricians, she and David were opposites, he the warm fuzzy doctor, she the skilled surgeon. And yet, he probably operated more than Grace. Gender, he'd told her, can't quite get away from it.

With Margaret Cameri fully under, Grace guided Andrew as he grasped the fundus, the top of the uterus, between his thumb and fingers and began to push it back gently. 'The Johnson method,' Andrew said. She could see sweat beading on his forehead. It was hard work and he'd surely be nervous. Grace herself was nervous.

'You're doing well,' she said. 'Fingers towards the posterior fornix.' He worked to force the uterus back up the birth canal and through the pelvis, stopping every few minutes to check with Grace. 'And now,' she said, 'slowly make a fist and continue to push towards the umbilicus.'

Andrew was nodding, starting to relax a little. 'I can feel it. It's about like putting your hand in someone else's boxing glove.'

'Not an analogy I'd use with a new mother but yes you have the idea.'

When they'd finished and the bleeding had stopped, Grace told Alice to make sure she watched Margaret Cameri carefully. She paged Frank to thank him and let him know he could turn around and go back to wherever he was coming from and told Andrew not to hesitate to call if there were problems. 'You did well, recognising this. Go tell the husband his wife is fine.' Grace always made sure the trainees got some of the good jobs as well as the hard ones. It hadn't been her experience as a registrar and she vowed she'd never do that to someone else.

She was on her way out when Alice came running across the car park after her. 'What's wrong?' Grace said, thinking Margaret Cameri might have started bleeding again.

'No, it's another patient – private. I need someone to authorise peth.'

'Who's her doc?'

'Clive Markwell.' Markwell was a senior consultant at the hospital, a 'dong and tong' man, as David referred to them, happiest when he could knock patients unconscious and pull their babies out with forceps.

'Why can't you ring Dr Markwell?'

'I did. He said no pain relief.'

'Why?'

Alice looked at her carefully. 'I can only assume.'

'Assume what?'

'The girl's sixteen and unmarried. Baby's going up for adoption.'

'And unmarried,' Grace repeated. Alice nodded. 'This is 1978. Tell me he's not punishing her.' Alice was silent. 'Okay, let's go back in.' Grace dropped her car keys into her bag and tossed the bag to Alice.

The girl was the one who'd come down in early labour from the hostel and was on the ward when Grace had left earlier in the evening. The Sisters of Charity who ran the hospital also ran several homes for unwedded mothers including the largest one, St Mark's, which was on the hospital campus, high on the hill above the hospital itself. When Grace had been a medical student, they were admitting a couple of girls in labour every week from St Mark's. Grace had never been inside but from the outside it looked like a haunted house, dark stone walls and shuttered windows. She always felt a little sorry for the girls from up there.

When they came back onto the ward, Grace could hear the girl's screams from the desk. 'What's she had?'

'Nothing,' Alice said.

'Not even nitrous?'

Alice shook her head. 'He said not.'

'Nothing?' Grace said. She looked along the hallway. She was reluctant to go in and examine the girl but could see Alice was in a dilemma. 'She's having a tough time. How old did you say she is?'

'Sixteen. Baby's persistent OP. She's getting pretty crazy, Grace.' Occiput posterior, where the baby's back remained facing towards the mother's back. It made for a painful labour and sometimes a difficult delivery. And Alice had an uncanny knack of knowing when a woman had reached the edge of coping.

'Jesus,' Grace said. 'How could he do that?' Grace took her bag back from Alice and left it at the desk and walked down to the delivery room with Alice behind her. 'Name?' Grace said quietly. Alice told her.

Jan Michaels was lying on her side, gripping the top rail

of the bed. She was a big girl carrying a big baby. When she looked up, Grace thought of Tolkien as a puppy, completely helpless and dependent on them for survival. The girl's eyes were wide with fear.

Grace took the girl's hand. 'Jan, how are you feeling? I'm Grace Hogan, one of the doctors here.'

'I'm all right,' she said in a tiny voice. 'It hurts.'

'Your back?' The girl nodded weakly. 'Well, I'll see what I can do to organise some pain relief,' Grace said. She patted the girl's hand and nodded to Alice on the way out.

Grace went to the tiny office off the ward desk, rehearsing what she'd say before she phoned Clive Markwell at home. With another doctor, it would be more straightforward.

'Markwell,' he answered on the third ring. She could hear a radio or television in the background.

'Clive.' Grace made herself use his Christian name. 'Grace Hogan. I just happened to be on the ward,' she said, not wanting to tell him Alice had come to her, 'and one of your patients needs something for pain. I'm going to give her some gas and a shot of peth.'

He asked her the patient's name. She told him. 'She doesn't want anything,' Markwell said. He was chewing as he spoke.

'She does now. She's a mess.'

'Have you examined her?'

'I popped in when I heard the racket she's making. I really think we need to help her now to avoid a larger problem later. You know how it can go. She's still OP.'

'I'll drop by later and see how she's going,' Markwell said. 'I saw her earlier. She's got a long day ahead of her. Still a bit frisky when I saw her.' Markwell owned horses and used his observations of their mating and gestation in his descriptions of women. Some liked the comparison, felt it located human birth in nature where it belonged. Others, including Grace, found it objectionable.

'Maybe you ought to come in and have a look at her if you don't trust me to—'

'I know what the patient needs,' he said, 'and I'd thank you to remember that.' He hung up.

Alice was right. He was punishing the girl, for having sex, for getting pregnant, for being a girl, he was punishing her. Grace felt angry but also anxious. If she acted against his direct advice, she put herself at risk. On the other hand, he was denying a young girl pain relief to teach her a lesson. And somehow, to Grace, it was worse that he was denying the girl pain relief when she was giving the baby up. Surely their job, hers and the other doctors, was to make this experience as painless as possible. The girl was sixteen years old.

On her way back to the delivery room, Grace passed Margaret Cameri's room. The family was there now, the father telling the other children in a soft, deep voice about their new baby brother, holding the infant in his big hands, the grandmother stroking Margaret Cameri's forehead. They were perfect, just as they were, Grace thought, any domestic trouble stilled, any unhappiness banished, just for this moment. New life was indeed a miracle. Sometimes, Grace thought, but not always, hearing another cry from the delivery room further along the hall.

Alice was holding the girl's hand and stroking her brow. 'Okay, Jan, we're going to give you a mask to breathe into that will help on the contractions,' Grace said, 'and an injection to dull the pain.' To Alice, she said, 'Give her nitrous as needed and fifty milligrams peth two-hourly.'

'How'd you talk him round?' Alice said as she went to draw up the drugs.

'Some docs will only listen to docs. Call me if there are any problems. And mark me as the attending.' Alice looked at her. 'It'll be fine,' she said. 'Dr Markwell will be in by nine.'

'By then it will be over,' Alice said. 'We're doing better now. But the pain relief will be a big help.' Just then the girl had another contraction, bellowing like a cow through it. 'That's the way, darling,' Alice said. 'We're nearly there. Help's on the way.'

Grace smiled. 'Good. Call me if you need me.'

Grace left the hospital and drove home through Auchenflower and Milton, Neil Diamond's *Hot August Night* blaring out of David's five-hundred-dollar car stereo. Grace sang along to 'I Am . . . I Said', blithely at first, no one hearing at all not even the chair. He had a warm voice, Neil Diamond, but lonely too, at its core. It soothed Grace for some reason. She stopped singing and let out a sigh. Nights like this, called into the hospital late, an emergency she might or might not handle, that was the thing you never knew, she wondered how long she could keep it up. Sometimes she felt as if at any moment, something might give way. The kids needed more not less as they grew older – she'd thought it would be easier now that they were all out of nappies but it was just that their needs were different – and work was like a bottomless pit. They never told you that in medical school. She was tired all the time, tired to her bones. And every now and then, you had an emergency like Margaret Cameri where what you did made the difference between life and death. It didn't matter if you were tired, if the kids needed you, if you had no one to lean on. You had to be there and make sure your patient's care was the best you could do. It was more than difficult. Sometimes, it was terrifying.

* * *

61

She crept back into the house just before five, Tolkien having heard the car, wandering out to greet her sleepily, realising she wasn't David who the dog preferred, flopping back down in a sulk. She checked the children again. Henry was in the same position, bedclothes flung again, so she covered him. Phil was sleeping quietly now. Grace crept in to her and David's room, took off her clothes, spooned her body behind David's. Sleep was the last thing on her mind now. 'Did I wake you?' she said softly, and then again, a bit more loudly.

'What? No, that's all right. Everything okay?'

'Yeah.' She snuggled closer, kissed the back of his neck, ran her fingers down his chest and belly.

'Now?' he said sleepily. 'It's the middle of the night.'

'It's morning,' she said, reaching into his boxers, finding his penis already hardening. 'Truth to power my friend.'

He turned around and kissed her gently, his breath sour and oddly exciting. She kissed him back, full on the mouth, and felt his body waking up, his strong arms around her. She ran her fingers through his hair; it needed a cut. David kissed her neck, breasts and belly and started to move down but she took his head in her hands and brought it up to her face. 'Let's just fuck,' she said softly. She only swore in relation to sex. He'd liked it when they were first together but now she thought it made him slightly embarrassed, as if she was middle-aged and wearing teenage clothes.

'You sure?' he said, reaching his hand down.

'Yes,' she said, irritated. She was too wired for slow sex. Emergencies always left her like this. She loved and hated the rush. David absorbed stress, calmed any situation, including Grace.

She wanted to be on top – story of my life, he used to say. She moved her hips in time with his but lost the rhythm again and again and finally stopped moving, felt the power of his thrusts deep inside. He came quickly, moaning softly, opening and closing his eyes.

Afterwards she lay on his shoulder and cried. Hey, he said gently, as if she was a child again, and he was Iris comforting her in some major loss, a tooth, a girl who'd left the class, the end of holidays. Hey. David was like Iris in that way. He always knew exactly what was needed, even when Grace herself didn't know.

By the time she emerged from the shower, David had made coffee and they sat out the back watching the morning sky take shape. She could hear kookaburras singing together in the distance and a butcherbird over towards Iris's place in full song. Middle of winter and the birds were everywhere. Grace loved that about Brisbane. In Canada, it's what she'd missed most, the birds. There were birds in Banff but far less brash, more reserved. You had to really listen for them.

David was wearing checked shorts and a white T-shirt with his old wool cardigan over the top, his blond curls a soft wet mess now, his face more vulnerable without his glasses. She told him about the case.

'Did you tell Andrew he shouldn't have used the Pit?' he asked. Pitocin was needed in a post-partum haemorrhage to make a floppy uterus contract quickly and stop bleeding. But in Margaret Cameri's case, it made the uterus harder to manipulate. Relaxants had been needed.

'I told him afterwards,' Grace said. 'I thought he did well to realise it wasn't right and call me in.'

'How come you let him off but not others?'

'Like who?'

'Me?'

'Well, if you made a mistake like that I'd be worried. You ought to know better. He's a trainee.'

'He's a bloody registrar. He ought to know what he's doing.'

'If we're going to go head to head about each other's registrars, your guy Michael Whatsisname has done some pretty funny estimating lately. I had a forty-two-week caesarean last week. Baby was smooth-skinned and pink as a piglet.'

'Mastin, Michael Mastin. I know. There's something not right with that guy, but he's in with the chaps.' David looked over at Grace. 'Are you okay?'

'What? Oh, I saw a patient of Clive Markwell's on the way out tonight, a kid. He wouldn't give her any pain relief.' Grace told David what she'd done.

'Speaking of the chaps, Markwell's not going to like you.'

'So what's new? He already doesn't like me.'

When Grace had done a term at St John's as a resident years before, she'd been called into a birthing room by one of the registrars who said it would be an opportunity to see a high forceps delivery. Grace didn't know Clive Markwell then but the scene that greeted her and the registrar was grotesque. There was a tall rakish man with one foot up on the end of the bed, using it to provide traction. He was hunched over what Grace quickly learnt was a barely conscious woman. He was swearing at the midwives. 'You bloody idiots. We have to get this baby out now!' It wasn't panic on his face, it was fury, or perhaps his panic had manifested as fury. The midwives looked terrified.

'Dr Markwell,' said the registrar who'd come in with Grace. 'Are you all right?'

'Just get out of the way,' Markwell said. He said afterwards he'd saved the mother's life. At the time, Grace didn't know the background, why he hadn't attended earlier. Later she learnt that his poor judgement had put him in the situation in the first place. He should have done a caesarean. The midwives had contacted Markwell four times in the course of the evening but he didn't come until it was too late. The baby suffered brain damage. In the review that followed, the registrar had been the one to speak out. The attending anaesthetist and paediatrician had lined up behind Markwell but Grace joined the registrar and told the truth when they interviewed her. It won her few friends, although David, recruited to the hospital as a consultant earlier that year, made a point of coming to see Grace and telling her she'd done the right thing. He'd reviewed the case for the investigating panel. 'I told them you were courageous,' he said, 'but it won't be enough. They'll back the chap.' Grace had been surprised at his forthrightness and said so. 'What do I care?' David said. 'They can't sack me. I'm the wonder boy.' David had come from England where he'd worked in one of the new team-based maternity care models. He'd been brought in to revise the hospital's care. He was right. He was invulnerable in those days.

Grace, on the other hand, was completely vulnerable. She missed out on a registrar's position the next year. But now she'd gone against Clive Markwell's direct orders. 'I think he wanted to teach her a lesson,' she said to David. 'I think that's what it was about. She's young and unmarried and had sex so he wanted to teach her a lesson.'

David shrugged. 'I wouldn't worry too much. He's never going to change and everyone knows what he's like. And anyway, she might have been better off. There's research coming out of the Netherlands that suggests labour pain has a purpose, that while we're getting better at blotting out all pain, women in the Netherlands are getting better at giving birth without pain relief. The pain is like a marathon. It makes a woman feel good to get through it.'

Grace laughed bitterly. 'What next? I bet the researchers are all blokes.'

'I don't know.'

'How about if insemination meant we crushed a guy's testicles between two panes of glass.'

'Youch, how did you think of that?'

'I just mean that if men had to go through the kind of pain women go through to have babies there wouldn't be studies in the Netherlands about the usefulness of pain. It would be a given. It's the curse of Eve by another name, that study. And at any rate, if you're arguing that Clive Markwell was denying a sixteen-year-old girl pain relief because he's read a study, I'd have to take issue. I don't think Clive reads studies.'

'Touché,' David said. 'But you did the right thing.'

'I can't abide that generation of docs. They're just so . . .'

Grace heard a noise inside the house. She turned and saw Henry standing at the bottom of the stairs. His hair, curly like David's but dark red, flopped into his eyes. He was holding up his pyjama pants, a pair of plaids they'd bought for Mia, Grace thought now, that were well past their time. Henry refused to give them up. At three, he was already a hoarder. 'Did you wake up, sweetie?'

'My legs hurt.'

'Same place?'

He nodded.

'Did you get that referral?' David said.

'No I didn't,' Grace said, flashing him a look. 'It's probably just those growing pains,' she said to Henry. She put down her coffee and went inside and scooped up her small son. 'Who are you today, Spiderman?'

'No I'm Superman.' He rubbed his eyes, looked as if he might cry. 'I've been Superman for ages.' He pulled open his pyjama shirt, revealing the red *S* on his chest. Grace remembered now that Spiderman had been retired some months before when the suit split in the crotch. When Grace had suggested it be replaced, Henry told her no because he was now the man of steel. David had put the kids to bed the night before. The suit had obviously been non-negotiable.

"Course you are. I'm so sorry. How could I forget that?' Grace sat Henry on the bench while she filled up a hot-water bottle from the kettle. She took him upstairs, put him back in bed, wrapped the hot-water bottle in a pillowcase and put it under his little legs. 'Better?' she said. He shook his head, looked again as if he might cry. 'I'll rub your legs. You try to go back to sleep.'

'But I'm not tired,' he said.

'Yes you are. You just don't know it,' she said in a soft sing-song voice.

'You always say that.'

She smiled. 'And I'm always right.' She pushed his hair back from his face and then sat down on the bed and massaged his calves, stiff as boards. She watched him drowse back off then curled in beside him, taking his tiny thin body into her arms, careful to make sure the heat of the hot-water bottle stayed on his legs. She stretched out around him. Within minutes, she joined him in sleep.

She heard voices downstairs, David making breakfast.

'Not pancakes.' It was Mia, home from across the road, complaining as usual. Grace realised she was in Henry's bed not her own and remembered the sore legs. She'd fallen asleep. Henry himself had gone now. Grace pulled herself out of the bed, still tired but knowing she had to get on with the day.

'I slept,' she said when she got downstairs. 'What time is it?' David was wearing a pink floral apron over his work shirt and slacks. 'Eight. I can take the girls and Henry today. I'm going over to the Mater for ten.'

'Okay,' Grace said. 'I'll pop in to see Iris. You look ridiculous.'

'That's not something you say to the man you woke at 5 a.m. who's cooking breakfast for your children.'

'The man who's their father, incidentally,' she said. She went over and kissed him. 'Sorry. But you do look ridiculous. Where's Phil?'

'Upstairs getting dressed.'

'Where's my pancakes?' Henry, who'd been sitting patiently at the bench, began chanting as he banged his knife and fork together. He'd poured a pre-emptive load of maple syrup onto his plate.

Grace looked at him. 'Henry, is that too much maple syrup?'

He looked down. 'No.'

'Good then. Legs still sore?'

He shook his head.

Grace poured coffee from the pot and sat down beside Henry, his legs dangling from the stool. 'Where's my pancakes?' she chanted along with him.

Half an hour later David was in the car, fiddling with the stereo and calling the kids. Henry was sitting in the lounge, playing with blocks. He hadn't moved on to the girls' Lego yet, couldn't get his hands to make the little pieces fit together. 'Time to go, Henry the superhero,' Grace said. She saw he was rubbing his calves. 'You can have some paracetamol if your legs are still sore?'

'Not sore.' He looked afraid suddenly. She realised he'd heard the concern in her voice. 'Am I doing something wrong?'

'No Hero-man. Of course not. You're doing everything just right. Off you go now. Daddy's waiting. Make sure he's got your bag.'

'Did you put in my suit?'

'What suit?'

'My Superman suit.'

'Where is it?'

'I don't know.'

Grace went upstairs and checked Henry's cupboard. No suit. Dress-up box. Not there either. She checked under the bed, in the toybox, nothing. She went into Phil's room, looked in the cupboard there, no luck, and then saw Superman's deflated boot poking out from under Phil's bed. She grabbed the suit and cape.

At the door, she hugged each of the kids in turn and waved to David down at the car. He leant his head out the window. 'Neil Diamond?'

She smiled. 'Yeah, Neil Diamond.' She started singing 'Cherry, Cherry' and dancing in the doorway, moving her hips and rolling her arms.

'No wonder you woke me at five.' She smiled and blew him a kiss.

After they drove off, Grace went back into the house to get ready for work. She surveyed the kitchen. It was a mess but she had no time to clean it up now. Her eyes rested on Henry's hot-water bottle in the sink where she'd left it earlier.

David was convinced there was something wrong with Henry. He'd been going on about it for weeks. Maybe he was right. But something in Grace resisted. She could just imagine them going down the track of diagnosis, spending years finding some developmental delay that Henry would have outgrown by the time they could name it. Meantime they'd have poked and prodded and tested the poor kid. 'And what's the point?' Grace said out loud. 'He'll still be Henry at the other end of it.'

Iris

The invitation was still sitting on the cane table in the front hall. I'd meant to hide it before she arrived. I'd meant to hide my walking stick too, but there it was, hooked on the hat rack where I'd left it. She'd hardly kissed me before her eagle eyes found the invitation. She picked it up and read as she strode into the house. She missed the walking stick though. She missed the possum too although she sniffed and registered the smell and made a face. But before I could explain she was off down the hall, turning to me as she read.

'What on earth is . . .' She looked at the invitation again. 'Royaumont?' Before I had a chance to answer, she said, 'You're not thinking of going,' a statement rather than a question.

'Perhaps I might go, Gracie,' I said, doing my best to keep up with her. She turned and gave me a look; she hates it when I use her baby name. 'Perhaps I should go before I die.'

'Oh, for goodness' sake, you've been talking about dying for twenty years, and it hasn't happened yet,' she said. 'But this really would kill you, Iris. Where is it? Near Paris? Even with a stopover, it's hours and hours in the air. Your heart would never make a flight like that.' She'd charged down the hall and into the kitchen. When it's not clean, she talks about the nursing home at Marycrest and how lovely the staff were the day she visited. She put the invitation on the table and sat down. I took a chair opposite. I could see the gilt script glinting in the sunlight.

Grace is almost as tall as I was at her age – I've shrunk into my bones now – but she's slimmer than I was, verging on skinny. She's more like Tom than me, lean and athletic, but not as relaxed in her body as Tom was. She's sharp-boned in the face too, cheeks and chin. Tom was softer. But she has chestnut hair that looks red in sunlight and the green eyes of my father's family, eyes that make you think a soul has been here before. I'd have to say that Grace doesn't have the nature of a soul who's been here before. She's become a difficult adult in her own way. As a child, she was particularly curious and perhaps more serious than most. I always felt it couldn't have been easy for her as an only child with Al and me so much older than the other parents. I was still running Al's surgery when she was small so most days she'd come down with me and we'd look in the microscope together or set a broken bone if Al happened to be out. She was as naturally drawn to science as any of the pathologists I knew at Royaumont. Obstetrics was the last specialty I expected her to do. To me it seemed to be the area of medicine that needed to tolerate the most ambivalence and Grace had always liked certainty.

Al used to say that Grace felt more like his daughter than Rose had. He didn't mean it unkindly to Rose, whom he loved dearly, but he and Grace had a special closeness. Rose was

71

all passion. She could only learn by doing and seeing how it felt. Grace was much more circumspect but, like Al, she was never one to prevaricate. Al's world was black and white. You diagnosed and then you prescribed or excised or hospitalised. He wasn't without kindness. He just liked a definite world. It was a good quality in a doctor. Grace was the same. As a youngster, she'd been fascinated by any living creature, torn between wanting to love them and wanting to see how they worked, pulling wings off butterflies and then crying when the butterflies were dead. As she grew older, she became less inclined to cry about their deaths. She became tough in a way I wasn't and I must say in a way I didn't truly understand. I used to wonder if it had something to do with losing her mother at birth, that perhaps she could never really feel nurtured by me and therefore had trouble loving other creatures. I read an article that suggested losing a mother could scar a child for life. I thought of Tom, but I thought of Grace too. She'd lost her mother, however much we'd tried to make up for it. Al said it was all nonsense and that Grace was just like any scientist – she cared about the creatures but she was also endlessly curious about their innards.

'But I'll be right one day,' I said to Grace now. 'I will die.' I smiled. 'Do you know, I think I'd like to go.' I smoothed the tablecloth around the invitation.

She looked at me and frowned. 'Iris, when will you start acting your age?'

'You look tired, Grace,' I said, hoping to change the subject. And she did look tired. Grace hadn't even finished her training when she and David were pregnant with Mia. I'd been angry with her when she told me. I'd told her it was too soon. She'd told me to mind my own business. She'd been right. It wasn't my business and afterwards I regretted saying it to her and told her so. But she did look tired, all the time. How did she manage it all?

'I was called in last night,' she said. 'Don't try to change the subject.'

'Is that all it is?'

She went to answer but held a breath instead and then let it out. 'Do you think Henry's all right?'

'He's very cheeky, if that's what you mean. Tom was like that too at his age. Is that what you're worried about?'

'He's slower than the other two on some things. David thinks there might be something not right.' She stood up and wandered over to the kitchen, surveying the sink and benches, looking for evidence of poor housekeeping. 'Is Henry cheeky?' she said.

'When you were young and so skinny I thought you had tapeworm. At one stage you wouldn't eat anything but ham sandwiches. Al said I was silly to worry.'

'That's what I think. I think David's overreacting. He wants to see a paediatrician.'

'It can't hurt to check. Give David peace of mind.'

'I don't know. You go looking, you find things you wish you didn't know.'

'Like what?'

'It's medicine. We pull people apart, put them back together but we know so little. I'm still skinny. It's just how I am. It didn't make any difference what doctors you saw.'

'David really is such a sweet man. Tell him not to worry so much. But are you sure you're not worried too?' She looked at me and didn't answer. I said, 'It can't hurt to check.'

On the way out, I showed Grace the possum. 'I'll drop in

after work today with the kids and take it out to uni,' Grace said. 'The vet school will know what the problem is.'

'He's just tired and hungry, Grace,' I said, 'and lost from his mother. I can keep him here.'

'I find myself constantly amazed by you, Iris. And you managed to change the subject after all.' She smiled. 'I do want you to think twice about this trip. It's unwise.'

'There's nothing unwise at my age,' I said.

'By the way,' she said, 'exactly what *is* Royaumont?' She was nursing the tiny possum in her hand. 'He's so cute,' she said, 'reminds me of the prems in Vancouver. You get to the stage where a full-term baby seems obscenely big.'

'It was a hospital I worked in,' I said. 'In France, during the war.'

'I didn't even know you'd been to France,' she said, distractedly. 'You mean World War I? You've never mentioned it before.' She put the possum back in the box gently and then looked at her watch. 'You were a nurse.'

'I was assistant to the hospital's superintendent,' I said. 'She was the most marvellous woman.'

'How come I don't know about this?' Grace said.

'The sum of things you don't know about me is vast, my dear girl. It all happened such a long time ago. Now, get off to work and let me get on with my day.'

'Milk and sugar in an eye dropper,' she said, looking at the possum again.

'Good idea,' I said.

'And I'll pop by this afternoon and take him out to uni.'

'We'll see how we go.'

When I'd sold Sunnyside, Grace and David helped me buy a house two blocks from theirs in Paddington. Grace asked if I wanted to move in with them but I'd said no, I liked my independence, and I do. Then she suggested I should buy a unit but I couldn't stand the thought of living in a box within a box. I was happy to move, though. All those I knew in the Valley had died or moved away, making way for shops. Even Al's practice had gone, now a café. Mine was the last house. I sold to Mr Stinson who'd owned the garage in front for most of the years we'd been there. He wanted to pull the house down and use the yard for cars to park. I didn't mind that – the house was old – but I made him promise to leave the fig tree. It died not long after I left and he had it chopped down. David was the one to tell me. 'I'm sorry, Iris. We should have had something written into the contract. He wasn't honest.'

Grace couldn't understand why I was so upset. 'It's a bloody tree, not a person,' she said. 'He can't help it if a tree dies. Trees do die, you know.'

David looked at Grace. 'It was an important tree to Iris,' he said, 'and to you.'

David said he thought Mr Stinson might have poisoned the tree. 'I don't think so,' I said. 'Surely not.'

'Oh, for God's sake,' Grace said. 'It's a *tree*.' And that was the end of it as far as she was concerned. But I mourned the tree. When we first moved to Sunnyside and it was just a sapling, Al wanted to pull it up but I said no. I'd been right. Its branches spread wide rather than tall, shading the house from the harsh summer sun and making a home for hundreds of birds. One year, my father came up from Risdon and helped Rose make a fort up in the tree. Later, when Grace was tiny, I used to sit out under the tree and think my thoughts while she slept. When she was older, she made a home up in Rose's fort, installing her chemistry set and microscope and calling it a laboratory. At ten, she slept out there with Al and they called it their first camping trip. In the morning they cooked breakfast for themselves on the gas stove. Possums often visited the house because of the tree. They made me feel safe after Al died and I was alone in the house. The tree's passing, much more than the house, was like the end of something for me.

Those old memories are so clear in my mind now. I see things from the past and it's almost as if they're happening in front of my eyes. They come back so fresh, with a taste and smell, whereas the recent past is simply gone. The day Grace was born, John Henderson coming out of the theatre, his mask down, his cap half-off, knowing something was wrong from his gait, his right leg resisting, him telling us it's a girl, trying to smile, looking down at his leg, me thinking of course it was the baby, something wrong with the baby, only to learn it was Rose, gone in those moments, the smell of his aftershave, the strange metallic taste on my tongue when he said they'd been unable to save her. Al fell back as if the wind had been taken out of him and John had to hold him up. It might have happened just a moment ago. There's that taste now of metal, that smell of aftershave. I remember these things but I forget the children's names. I forget where I put my purse. I said this to David last time he came to mow the lawn. It had been worrying me and I didn't want to talk to Grace who would have me seeing a brain surgeon quick as look at me. 'I don't remember what grade any of the children are in, or even if Henry's at school yet. He is, isn't he?' David shook his head. 'See? But I remember a grapevine we grew up a trellis at Risdon, the sour taste of those grapes, Daddy calling the sheep, the strong smell of the rye bread we used to get from the German baker. Those memories are clearer than ever. I talk to people who've been dead for years.'

'I think that's how memory works,' David said. 'You remember the important things.'

'Not just important. It's the old things. Last week I was just about to post a letter to a woman I'd known fifty years ago in Stanthorpe when I remembered she'd died. I'd gone to her funeral here in Brisbane three years ago but it completely slipped my mind. It's as if not just memories but the capacity to remember is going. One day I won't know who you are, David.'

'Maybe,' he said. 'But if that happens, I'll just tell you who I am again, Iris. You're doing well. I don't think it's your mind that will go first.' He looked at me.

'Heart?' He nodded. 'Good.'

David is like the heart doctor Grace took me to, except David's kinder. 'I'll die soon,' I'd said to the heart doctor, after Grace had left the room to take a call at the desk, and he'd nodded yes and raised his blond eyebrows with what I like to think was a tinge of sadness, even if it was contrived. I suppose that's why he gets paid so much, for being able to contrive a tinge of sadness as he nods. With David, there was such genuine sadness in his eyes. It was nice to know he'd mourn my passing.

When I moved to Paddington it was a lot like the Valley in our early years, people on the streets, families, shopkeepers, and my new house was not unlike Sunnyside, a timber frame on stumps, with an enormous jacaranda in the backyard that would make a good climbing tree once the children were a bit older. Grace didn't want a place with stairs but I said it would do me good and it does. I can still walk to the shop, as long as I take it slowly, and the neighbours on the downward side, Suzanne and Isaac and their five children, are just as you'd want them, friendly without being overbearing. The uphill neighbours only moved in a few months ago. Grace said they were Christians as if this explained something and I said we're Christians too but she just looked at me. Grace insisted on engaging someone to do the heavy cleaning, and Meals on Wheels to come five days a week with dinner.

'I'll call by this afternoon,' Grace said as she backed out of the driveway.

'Only if you've got time,' I said and waved her off. I hoped she wouldn't come back. I love Grace dearly but it always feels like there's too much electricity in the room when she's here, like I need to be careful and behave well. I'm not sure what might happen if I don't, but I don't want to find out either.

I called the surgery to make an appointment with my doctor. The woman who answered made me spell my name twice. I've been going to the same surgery for twenty-five years, the only one I could find in Brisbane where the doctors were women. I've lived through three doctors and my surname is Hogan. You'd think they'd know me by now and even if they didn't, how many ways do you spell Hogan? In Al's surgery, I knew the name of every patient, their children, their medical histories.

After I got off the phone, I realised I was still holding the invitation in my hand. I checked the possum was still sleeping peacefully, draped a rag over the top of the box, and went out to the front stairs to watch the day.

Water under the bridge, I'd told Violet. What a stupid thing to say.

We worked with three orderlies to unload the mattresses from the truck and carry them up the two flights of stairs to the room in which we would all sleep. Miss Ivens had offered any who wanted it their own room but everyone felt there was safety in numbers. Who knew what ghosts lurked in the dark corners of an old abbey? Violet and I went back down to the kitchen and talked for a while longer with Marjorie Starr and Vera Collum. By the time the other three girls were ready to retire, I could barely keep my eyes open and make it up the stairs to bed.

I woke with a crescent moon through the long window above us and Violet kicking me in the head in her sleep. There hadn't been enough mattresses to go around and so while the seven doctors and Cicely Hamilton each had their own mattress at one end of the large room the rest of us doubled up at the other. I say mattress but really they were no more than mats, calico roughly sewn around straw. Compared to the prospect of another night on the cold stone floor, they were heaven according to Miss Quoyle who confided in me she suffered from chilblains and piles, neither of which was aided by the cold.

Out of shyness on my part, Violet and I had gone to sleep end to end. When I moved to the other end to avoid her kicking feet, I faced my back to her back, but the mattress was small, hardly a single, and the cold . . . I'd dressed in everything I had, only drawing the line at boots because they were so filthy, and still I was cold. Stanthorpe might extend to frost in the middle of winter and we'd keep a fire burning all night but Royaumont had decades of cold in its stone walls, the sort of cold that eats through skin and muscle and bone to your marrow. Even my hair was cold. I woke again when I rolled over onto the icy floor. I moved back onto the mattress, curling in behind Violet this time, warmer as two halves than two singles, and fell into a deep sleep.

I dreamt I was at Risdon and Tom had climbed into my bed like he used to when he was small. I woke some time later and found my arm around Violet. She slept on and I lay there, warm and snug. Suddenly I thought of Tom as he might be now, without a mat to lie on or roof over his head. I shuddered involuntarily.

The first time I got up to Tom in the night he would have been just a few months old, crying loud enough to wake the neighbour's rooster and set it crowing. I lay in bed a few minutes more, expecting Daddy to get up as he had the other nights, but the crying went on. I went into Daddy's room where we'd put Tom's crib. Daddy and I hadn't known much of what to do with him when we brought him home and Daddy said that's what my mother had done with me and it had worked all right. It was the first time since she'd passed that he'd mentioned her name without leaving the room immediately which I took for a good sign.

I stood by the crib for a moment, still thinking Daddy might wake, but he'd been up since four that morning working at the far edge of the property and he remained asleep despite Tom's wailing which was getting louder now that he sensed me nearby. I peered into the crib. Tom was concentrating pretty hard on crying. I tried patting him on the belly but that just made it worse. I stroked his little bald head and on he wailed. So I picked him up and spoke softly and that calmed him somewhat which gave me confidence. But then he was wide awake and his eyes remained open despite my singing 'Go to sleep little baby' as I'd heard Daddy do in the evenings. Tom was making a kind of sucking noise with his mouth and so I figured he must be hungry. I carried him out to the kitchen, thinking to warm some milk. I lit a lamp and went to put him in his little crib by the stove but as soon as I put him down, the cries resumed, so I picked him up again. Holding him in one arm I managed to get the stove lit – Daddy had fuelled it before going to bed – to heat the water to warm the milk. I put the warm milk in a cup – we had no bottles with nipples in those days. He guzzled it down, burped so loudly I thought I must have killed him, then relaxed into a drowse.

Every time I tried to put him back in the crib, by the stove first and then in Daddy's room, he cried again. I knew it was the middle of the night although I hadn't looked at the clock. I'm not even sure I knew how to tell the time. I sat with Tom awhile in the kitchen chair. I was tired myself and cold but the only place he was content was in my arms. Finally, I took him back to my bed and he nuzzled down beside me and went off immediately into a deep sleep and then so did I and neither of us woke until late the next morning.

The morning after that, Daddy helped me move Tom's crib into my room. It was a mistake, I soon realised, for after our mother died, if Daddy was moving forward at all, it was only Tom needing him that kept him on his feet, and once he saw that Tom had me and I had Tom, he drifted into a deep despondence. He still got up in the morning and went off to work as he always had. But he worked and ate and slept like a man condemned. When he spoke, it was as if he was a long way away, talking to a stranger. In the night, I'd hear him talking softly to himself in his cups. One night, after I'd settled Tom, I crept down the stairs and listened. He wasn't talking. He was singing, 'Put on your red shoes, put on those red shoes I know so well.' I knew nothing of the world, but I knew he was the only one left and I'd lost him, and I didn't know quite how to get him back.

Some nights, after he'd graduated to his own little bed, Tom would come into my bed after a bad dream. By the time he climbed in and warmed up, he'd be well and truly awake and we'd lie there facing one another in the dark and he'd tell me things to try to wake me up too. I still remember the outline of his face in the dark, moonlight showing his smile, his hand on my head, pulling my ear around to his mouth to 'tell me a secret'. It would be something nonsensical, something designed to get my attention, generally involving poos or wees. And we'd remain like that and sometimes he'd fall back asleep in mid conversation and sleep on for hours while I lay awake. Other times he'd chat until we'd hear the kookaburras on the water tank and I'd give up on my efforts to get him back to sleep and we'd climb out of bed and start the day.

Tom and I managed as well as could be expected. In a way, losing my mother so young, which everyone said was a terrible tragedy, especially for a girl – imagine when she's older – was softened by being needed for some task other than grief, that of caring for Tom. And he was a grand boy, never bothered by my many incapacities, never even noticing the failure on my part to impose a routine, as Mrs Carson had told me to do on her first visit to the house, and sooner rather than later, she said through a small mouth. She was good to me, Mrs Carson, and I don't mean to sound ungrateful for her advice. She did her best in those first weeks to call in. She showed me the basics, changing a nappy, cleaning bottles and burping a baby. She had strong views about the discipline needed to raise children successfully. She even went as far as to say to Mr Carson, within my hearing, that how could I be expected to discipline a child when I'd been allowed such free rein myself for so long, without meaning to speak ill of the dead, but really, that woman had no idea.

After a time, I had no memory of my mother, although I often told people I remembered her well, repeating others' stories about her, because I felt disloyal forgetting her. But I had forgotten her. I looked at the photograph we had, the one I'd seen a thousand times, taken the day she married Daddy at Risdon – she's sitting at the dresser smiling up to the camera like she knows a big secret – and it was as if I was looking at a beautiful stranger, her red hair and lips coloured in after the photograph was taken, her dress sheeny in black and white. It was a most unbalancing experience to see someone I knew so well and not know them at all.

Mrs Carson's suggestions were beyond my understanding or experience. All the boys had tasted their daddy's belt, Mrs Carson said, and it did a power of good. Perhaps because it was foreign to me, the notion of beating or being beaten, I didn't take any notice. Over time, Mrs Carson stopped visiting. The house became more of a mess, she seemed less inclined to stay long and Daddy didn't much like her coming, and had a way of making it known. To be honest, I was relieved. I didn't understand much of what she told me I had to do, but when I did understand, I was horrified at the thought of purposely inflicting pain on little Tom. We struggled on as best we could until Daddy married Claire. And now Tom had grown into a fine boy who could decide on his own undertaking to go to war.

My thoughts were interrupted when I heard someone get up at the other end of the room, the big door creaking open.

As gently as I could, I rose from the mattress, donned my coat, pulled on my boots and followed, using the coming light of dawn through the windows to guide me. I descended the great staircase. I couldn't see where the other early riser had gone but I managed to find my way to an unlocked door. Out in the cloisters, the world had turned to white. The snow had stopped falling now but that just made its presence on the ground more extraordinary to my eyes. I spoke my name and it came back to me changed, deeper and more resonant. The world was indeed quieter and louder all at once, just as Miss Ivens said it would be. I ran out into the centre of the yard where there was a fountain, frozen now, surrounded by stone benches. All was covered in snow. I picked up handfuls of the stuff, tasted it on my tongue. One or two brave songbirds fought their way through the cold.

I took the route Violet had taken the night before to the abbey lawns and found the stables, Violet's car in its spot, two others beside. I ran along the outside of the abbey, the path now covered in snow, snow up to my ankles, my breath making the steam that as children we pretended was tobacco smoke, the sun appearing and turning everything gold. I looked back at the abbey buildings and was touched once more with a sense of something beyond me. Surely if God was anywhere, I thought, He was here. I knew no French history then, none of poor Royaumont's vicissitudes, but if you could have seen the dawn cradling that beautiful stone structure in its soft fat arms, if I could have painted but a poor cousin of its absolute perfection, you'd know what I mean. I was filled with the spirit of Royaumont and just for a moment experienced myself as nothing more or less than a tiny part of that holy morning.

As is the case when one is overcome by the beauty of the world, perhaps just to reassure us that God has not only might but a sense of humour, just then I was interrupted by another of His creations. A stream that had been the source of fresh water for the monks ran alongside the abbey. Beside the stream on the snow, I spied a creature that at first I took for a rat, until I saw its head was too large. 'Ah, you have become acquainted with M Ragondin,' one of the groundsmen from the Gouin household told me later in the day when I asked if France was populated by giant rats. 'He is cleverer than M Rat.' The ragondin is a rodent but much more appealing than a rat. When he saw me, the ragondin slid into the water and dived under. He looked just like a tiny swimming wombat. I laughed before I realised I was shivering with cold. I ran back the way I'd come, kicking up snow with every step, ran a circle about the cloister to warm up, leaving mine as the first footprints on the world that day.

In the kitchen, I found Miss Ivens, her hair messily pinned up, her greatcoat not quite covering a floral nightgown. She turned to me. 'Thought I'd get some tea on for the girls,' she said. 'They've not had an easy time of it these last few days. Do you know much about fires?' She'd stuffed the little stove so full you couldn't fit in another thing. She was about to set alight the mess she'd made.

'As a matter of fact,' I said, 'I know an awful lot about fires.'

'Oh good. Well, let's get it started.' She gave me the matches. 'You're bright this morning.'

'I've been in the snow,' I said. I must have been grinning because Miss Ivens smiled too, as if she understood, or found my joy infectious. I set the matches down and carried the kindling to the open fireplace Miss Quoyle had used the night before. I spread it out as I'd learnt, leaving room for breath. I lit a fire whose flame quickly grew. I fed it well and it kicked the room into life.

We sat down at the long table together while we waited for the kettle to boil. 'I didn't quite tell you the truth about the abbey, did I?' Miss Ivens said. She looked tired this morning, as if she hadn't slept well. 'It needs a lot of work. Thank God you've joined us Iris. I'd be lost without language.'

'Well, you see the thing is, Miss Ivens, I'm not sure I'm quite the person to help you. I'm . . .' I'd fully intended to tell Miss Ivens the truth, that I shouldn't stay at Royaumont, that I was really here to find my brother, but in her floral gown and with her messed-up hair, I felt sorry for her. I found I couldn't tell her, not quite yet. 'I'm not sure I can help you. I've never built a hospital.'

'Do you think I have? I need your French, Iris, not your building skills. None of us would have chosen it this way but it's what we have and we must do our best.'

Miss Ivens and the first contingent – five other doctors as well as the nurses, orderlies and drivers – had been at Royaumont three days, she told me. When he'd offered his abbey to the Croix-Rouge for use as a hospital, the impractical M Gouin was not entirely forthcoming about its state. Then, in December, with the staff already embarked, M Gouin wired Edinburgh to inform the committee that the abbey wasn't ready for them.

'We were well on the way by then,' Miss Ivens said, 'and I felt it impolitic to delay. It was rash, I realise now. From Dieppe, I wired M Gouin that I would come straight to Royaumont from Paris.

'I think he was afraid I'd turn up on his doorstep with the whole group – I had half a mind to – and he told me the worst, no water, no electricity, no drainage, the first-floor rooms are filled with rubbish and the horses have been here. What's more, he said, I have no bedrooms and no beds for your women.

'I told him not to worry. Our equipments were expected any day and my colleagues and I were of stout heart. I didn't talk to them too much about my discussion with M Gouin. I saw no point. Instead, I got the rest of them here, thought that was best.'

Each day the equipments didn't arrive and each day they found some new way of accommodating their circumstances. Quoyle with the borrowed cutlery and crockery and utensils. Miss Ivens with the straw mattresses. Cicely Hamilton with the makeshift lamps.

As if I'd said something to ameliorate her concerns, Miss Ivens was soon cheering herself with the list of jobs for the day. We had to see the architect, she said. 'Did I tell you about the inspection?' She hadn't. We couldn't be accredited as a field hospital until the abbey was inspected by the health service of the French military and the Croix-Rouge. This would happen some time before Christmas, Miss Ivens said.

'But today is the fourteenth of December,' I said. 'How can you be ready? You don't even have beds for patients.'

'*We*, Iris,' she said. 'How can *we* be ready? Of course we'll be ready. We're women. We do things.'

I looked up from my little fire and saw, out the window beyond us, the heads of manicured pines poking through the snow that now covered the abbey grounds. Back in the kitchen was Miss Ivens in that silly floral gown she'd probably carried all the way from her Warwickshire youth. It was a champion fire I'd set, even Daddy would have said as much. I could be useful here, I thought. I could help. Suddenly, in my deepest heart, I knew I would have to stay at Royaumont, at least a little while. Violet was right. I could write to Tom from here as well as anywhere. The war, as much as I'd seen of it, wasn't as Daddy had described it at all. If he'd been wrong about that, perhaps he was wrong in worrying so about Tom. If Miss Ivens really did need my help, it couldn't hurt to be useful while I searched. Lord knew it could take weeks to find one fifteen-year-old boy among all those soldiers who'd come to France. At least I could feel I was doing something while I waited.

Miss Ivens took the kettle from the fire and as she made the tea, the kitchen filled. Bids good morning were muted; it was too cold for more. Violet was the last to arrive, in her boots and striped flannel pyjamas, her blonde hair falling loosely over her shoulders. 'My friend's,' she'd said of the pyjamas the night before. 'Warm as toast.' As I learnt later that day, she'd also brought his coat, his driving goggles, his glasses and his cigarette case. Must be a good friend, I said. Past tense please, Violet said. He's been moved on now.

Miss Ivens called us to order. 'We have beds of a sort, a working kitchen and seven hours each day in which we have enough light to work. We must all muck in on the first task which is cleaning.'

After a quick breakfast – bacon and eggs with toasted bread – I don't know how Quoyle managed – Miss Ivens told me to go with Berry and address the plumbing problem. 'It's the drain,' she said. 'There's a blockage.' When I tried to protest that I wouldn't be much help, she just smiled. 'You're from a farm,' she said. 'Initiative.' She asked the doctors to stay behind for a few moments and dismissed the rest of us. I went upstairs to dress. I walked into the room just as the sun reached the long windows. The light came across the stone floor suddenly. I stood there transfixed once more by the beauty of the place, until others came in the door behind me and broke my reverie.

Boarding school had accustomed me to dressing in front of others but I felt strangely shy with these women. Their mattresses were neatly folded, their things packed up, all except for Violet's and my bed which was a mess of her clothes and the jumpers and coats we'd slept under. I tidied up – Violet was still in the kitchen finishing her breakfast.

Just as I was about to go downstairs, she came in. 'Let's make sure we work together today,' she said. 'I don't want to be with Cissy Hamilton. Oh Iris, you made the bed. Aren't you a darling girl? It's a bit early for me.' She stretched and let out a long yawn. 'I'd like nothing more than to get back in and sleep for a few more hours. But we can't have that, can we? After all, we're women, we do things,' she said, in her perfect Miss Ivens.

'I have to go and meet the plumber first,' I said, rolling my eyes. 'Apparently, growing up on a farm qualifies me in drainage. I'll find you.' I went to the tap downstairs in the kitchen, the only one in the abbey that was working, and splashed my face with the freezing water. I met Mrs Berry in the foyer. She'd dressed and washed before breakfast.

Miss Ivens had sent me along to interpret but the plumber who arrived soon after turned out to be English, married to a Frenchwoman. 'Don't tell Frances he speaks English,' Mrs Berry said to me when he went out to get his tools. 'She'll be down in a shot.'

'I think she'd want to be here,' I said.

Mrs Berry looked sternly at me. She had those large brown eyes and long thick hair parted exactly and pulled back loosely so that it was like two sides of a heart coming off the part. 'Just trust me, Iris. Frances is wonderful. We love her to death, but if you are to help her, you must know her strengths.'

'And what are they?' I said, surprised at her frankness.

'She's good at what matters,' Mrs Berry said. 'She's an inspired doctor. I've never worked with anyone who has her gift with patients. And she's a good leader for us, the medical team, but she doesn't know about the drains. Do you understand?'

I could hardly run and fetch Miss Ivens now without angering Mrs Berry. On the other hand, if Miss Ivens found out the plumber, who had climbed down into the drains to see what was happening, was English, she'd be furious that she hadn't been told. She nearly came with me anyway, on the basis that I could interpret. But then Dr Savill was complaining that Cicely had ordered the wrong equipment and Miss Ivens had gone to calm her down. Even so, Miss Ivens told me I needed to provide a report.

'I'm afraid you will have to trust me on this one, Iris,' Mrs Berry said.

In the event, Miss Ivens was as wrong-headed as a human being could be about the plumbing. There was no blockage in the drain, as she claimed, and all my attempts to put her view to the plumber were met with a gentle smile, rather like one might bestow on a small child who is not managing a drink of milk. He might be retired, he said, and not much good for anything, but the one thing he knew was grease traps. He and Mrs Berry got along famously, sharing an interest in matters sanitary – Mrs Berry had specialised in public health – going down together into the drains. 'It's the trap,' Mrs Berry said when she emerged. 'Just as we thought. They'll have to dig.'

I duly reported to Miss Ivens that the plumber said the grease trap was not working and it would take at least a week to repair. She had no choice but to accept his opinion but she still asked me what I thought. 'I thought him an excellent plumber,' I said. Mrs Berry, standing behind Miss Ivens, smiled warmly at me. Miss Ivens said very well and didn't mention the problem again.

Miss Ivens had a meeting with the architect. Before he arrived, she took me on a quick walk through the building to show me what she was planning. The theatre and X-ray would be on the first floor, she explained, and a large room on that floor, originally the monks' library, would be a ward. It had deep windows to the north overlooking the cloister and the south overlooking the abbey vegetable gardens. The other ward would be set up in two rooms directly above us on the second floor. When she asked me what I thought, I said the first-floor room was beautiful but those on the second floor would be a long way from everything else except the pathology laboratory. 'Well, yes they are Iris, but where else can we go?' she said. We had been through several other rooms on the first floor but she'd ruled these out because they were filled with the detritus of years, not just furniture but heavy masonry and other building materials. I could see why Miss Ivens came to the decision she did and I had made my point. I didn't think it was my place to make it more strongly.

But when the architect saw the rooms Miss Ivens had picked on the second floor for a ward, he laughed out loud. Too far from the rest, he said, and they're not as well ventilated. When she told him she didn't have a choice, he looked at her above his spectacles. 'My dear woman,' the architect began.

Miss Ivens, whose spoken French was as appalling as she claimed, understood the sentiment if not the words when it came to dear women. 'Tell him I am a surgeon who needs to run a hospital. If he cannot provide us with what we need, we will find an architect who can.'

The architect was a gentle man with soft grey eyes and cared-for nails who reminded me of our parish priest at home. Perhaps because of this I couldn't be stern with him. He could no more understand Miss Ivens than she him and not just because they spoke different languages. And he would do good work, I felt. I couldn't repeat word-for-word what Miss Ivens had said. 'Miss Ivens really feels we ought to do our best to make this area work,' I said. 'Logistically, this is an ideal place for the laboratory.'

'Is that what she said?' the architect asked me with a wry smile.

'Roughly translated,' I said.

After we finished with the architect, Miss Ivens said I could go and help Violet who we'd seen working in the large room on the first floor Miss Ivens had selected as a ward. 'We'll name it for Blanche,' Miss Ivens said to me after the architect left. 'We'll call it Blanche de Castille.' The second ward, on the floor above, would be called Elsie Inglis, for the Scottish Women's Hospitals foundress. By the time I got back to the room, Violet had been joined by a couple of orderlies who were clearing out the junk while she scrubbed the floor. I set to work on the large windows, using a tea chest as a ladder. Layers of dust covered dirt and grime and I must have cleaned those windows three times. Later in the afternoon, warm from our work, Violet and I sat down on the floor to take a break.

The sun emerged from behind a cloud and shone through the windows suddenly, revealing in all its glory the stone Violet had been scrubbing all day, bringing the whole room to life.

'Look, Violet,' I said, for we too were quite suddenly clothed in gold.

Violet smiled. 'You could almost believe in God,' she said.

'You don't believe in God?'

'Oh Iris, you are quaint. Of course not. God's a ridiculous notion.'

'Violet, you mustn't speak like that.'

'Why not?'

'You'll go down for blasphemy.'

'God God God,' she said. 'If that's all it takes to get to Hell, I'm already there. You surely can't believe in God, Iris.'

'Of course I do. If there's no God, who made all this?' Just as I spoke, the sun disappeared behind the clouds and the room dimmed.

'The Cistercians,' Violet said drily.

'Well, what do you believe in?' I said.

'I don't believe in anything,' she said. 'It's all codswallop.'

'Oh Violet, we'll have to work on that,' I said. 'I couldn't stand you going down. I like you too much for that.'

'How do you know you won't be keeping me company there?' She sighed heavily and threw her dish towel into the bucket of water. 'No, I don't suppose you will go to Hell. You're too good.' She lit up a cigarette and walked over to the window. 'Unlike me.

'So what have you decided about your brother?' She stood looking at me, smoke surrounding her head like a silver halo.

'I thought I'd write him and find out where he is first. It's not going to be easy.'

Even if I found Tom, I'd realised, he wouldn't come home willingly. Tom was belligerent sometimes. Daddy always said it was because he'd been so small for so much of his childhood, only shooting up in the last year or so. I thought but didn't say that it was more likely inherited. Daddy himself could be belligerent on occasion and Tom took after Daddy. 'I rushed over here because my father was so worried. But now, I don't know what to do,' I said to Violet. 'I'm not sure my father really understands the war and why we must help. Australia's so far away. But the Germans invaded France and I believe it's our duty to do our bit to stop them. Maybe it will be good for Tom to think he's been part of that. I just don't know though.'

'How old is he again?' Violet said, blowing perfect smoke rings into the winter air.

'Fifteen,' I said.

She whistled. 'How did he get away?'

I remembered Daddy's words. 'You've no idea what you've done, Iris.'

'You couldn't have stopped Tom,' I said to Daddy, trying at defiance. 'He'd made up his mind.'

Daddy looked at me. 'I'd have shot your brother in the leg to keep him here, Iris. You're too young to understand what I'm trying to tell you. I'm going to get him back.'

And that's how it went for days until I got the idea that I not Daddy should go and he agreed, because it would be easier for me to find Tom as I was a nurse and would have a legitimate role to play. And Daddy and I both knew that if anyone could have stopped Tom, it was me. But I'd not only failed to stop him; I'd helped him go.

* * *

It was the twenty-third of September. I remember the date because it was the weekend of the show and Tom and I were both home on account of it. Al was up for the weekend too. He was in his last month at the Mater and things between us had become difficult, from his side not mine. There was a girl back in Sydney. He'd never lied to me about her but for him our friendship was becoming more than friendship and he felt he needed to make a decision about what he wanted. You couldn't have two sweethearts, as Matron had told him when he'd asked her. I only knew Matron had said this because she told me later, over a cup of tea in her room. She also told me to stay away from Al while he sorted himself out and that if I played my cards right, I'd land myself a doctor. Don't fall for the old line, though, she warned me. It's what doctors do best. She smiled and I saw the gold fillings in her teeth. I had no intention of playing my cards in any way at all. Al and I were friends and I truly believed we would remain so whatever happened with this girl in Sydney. I worried about the talk among the nurses – they kept asking me if we were promised to one another – but I wasn't sure what I wanted.

The thing that had attracted me to Al when we first met was his quiet but sure nature. Al was Al no matter who he was with and no matter what they thought of him. We met in the operating theatre at the Mater and the surgeon that day, a difficult little man from England named Jonathan Barton, loved nothing more than to belittle trainees. He criticised everything Al did, although anyone could see Al had a gift for surgery. Daddy always said Al could have been a pianist if anyone had thought to put a piano under his hands. Dr Barton rode Al that day, told him to use the long knife and then told him he got the wrong size, told him he was fumbling when he wasn't, told him to hurry up. Al apologised when Dr Barton told him he'd done the wrong thing, looked squarely at Dr Barton as Dr Barton became increasingly exercised. This infuriated the surgeon who wanted to crush Al, to reduce him to a snivelling mess or make him lose his temper. But Al did neither. He just kept on in the same even way he'd begun. In the end, Dr Barton was yelling, 'You've got no idea what you're doing, you young fool. You think you're better than me? Let's see you find your way through this gut without help,' and stood back, so Al was left to do the operation – I can't remember what it was – all by himself. This he did with the same quiet confidence.

Afterwards, Al had seemed brave to me and I realised only much later that it wasn't bravery. He was simply without guile. He could no more change his nature than a leopard could change its spots. He told me years later that he was terrified of Jonathan Barton but that he'd kept his eyes on me. I was smiling at him, apparently, and it made him feel he could do anything. I really think he made that up because I don't remember him looking at me at all, much less us smiling. I was more frightened of Dr Barton than anyone and dreaded being in the theatre whenever he was on. And we were all wearing masks, so how Al could see a smile was beyond me.

'What about this war business?' Tom said to Al on the train.

'What about it?' Al said over his glasses. He was reading the paper.

'They're calling for volunteers.'

'And?'

'Are you going?'

'No,' Al said. 'You look tired, love,' he said to me.

'They want doctors,' Tom said.

'They'll get doctors,' Al said.

'Not you?'

'Not me.'

'Why not?'

'Not interested.'

'You scared?'

'Yes and no.' Al took off his glasses and rubbed his eyes and then replaced the glasses, a gesture he used his whole life to give himself time to think about a thing. 'If none of us go, they've no one to fight.'

'And then the Germans take over,' said Tom.

'Not if the German people refuse as well.'

'I think I'll go,' Tom said.

Al and I both laughed at this, a terrible mistake I realised later. Tom's face fell. 'Why shouldn't I go? Not everyone's a coward,' he said. His voice had started to break and he lost the last part of coward, had to repeat it. He looked straight at Al who to his credit understood, in a way I didn't, how foolish we'd made Tom feel, how young. Al didn't rise to Tom's challenge. Instead he looked at Tom seriously. 'It's one of those things each man must decide for himself. You do have courage in spades, Tom. But you mayn't have your chance this time around, in any event. They're saying it will all be over by Christmas.'

I looked over at my brother and remembered when he first started school. He cried when I left him at the door of his classroom. I thought he'd settle in but by lunchtime, he'd created such a commotion that his teacher sent for me to come and sit with him for the afternoon. By the time I got there he was sobbing in between sharp panicky breaths.

'Oh, Tom Crane, what's the matter with you?' I'd said to him. He ran to me and grabbed on, not caring a fig what the teacher or the other children thought of him. I stayed with him that day and the next and the next.

'Afraid of his own shadow,' his teacher said to me after the second week.

'He's only young,' I'd said to her. 'Just give him time to get used to it all.' And now, here he was, wanting to run off to war and fight.

'You don't have to be of age,' Tom said to Al. 'There's a seniors boy who's gone. You can just lie about your age.'

Al shook his head. 'Then you'd be a young fool, and if you came home, that is, if you didn't die there, you'd still be a young fool.'

Tom wasn't his usual self that weekend, easily offended, quick to anger. On Saturday afternoon, he broached the subject with Daddy. We were out on the western boundary mending the fence that the neighbour's cows had come through again. 'I'm big for my age,' Tom said. 'Robert reckons they'd take me no worries.' The two older Carson boys had already gone off, with Robert, a year older than Tom, planning to follow them as soon as he could. Mr and Mrs Carson were all for it.

'Answer's no and we're not discussing it,' Daddy said. 'We're just not.' I could see by the look on Tom's face that he was hurt and that the conversation wasn't finished, not for him. Daddy saw it too. 'If you were of age and you told me you were going, I'd advise against it. You're certainly not going now.' Tom tried to protest again. 'We're working, Tom,' Daddy said, 'not talking, working.' I think Daddy thought that would be the end of it.

That night at the dance, Tom drank beer and instead of

becoming giggly and silly as he had the few other times he'd had drink, he became loud. He picked a fight with a boy from Warwick who found a fight at every dance I ever saw him at. Tom should have known better. They were facing up outside and Al and Robert Carson took one each to calm them down. When I asked Tom what they were fighting about, he said it was about who'd walk out the door first. I looked at him. 'Well, how stupid was that?' I said.

On Sunday Al got the early train back to Brisbane because he had to work. Tom and I took the afternoon train. He told me of his plan. 'I have to tell someone, Iris,' he said. 'I don't want bad blood behind me.' He said he and another boy from school were joining up. 'I wanted the old man's help but we're going anyway. I already decided. I got money saved from last Christmas to get me to Sydney.' He grinned with the thought of it. 'They reckon down in Sydney they don't even check you've got two feet. They take anyone.'

And I did nothing to convince him otherwise. I disregarded Daddy's strong advice and Al's view.

I looked out the window of the train. 'What an adventure that would be,' I said and felt a thrill. When I think back now, I can't believe I said that. Was I ever that young? I think. I used to tell myself I had no concept of war so how would I have known to deter him? I used to tell myself I had a romantic view of Europe, especially France, and that in my mind, going to France could never cause harm. I told myself these things in order to soothe myself, to feel better. But in truth I simply cannot understand the twenty-one-year-old self who looked out the window and said to her brother, as if she hardly cared, what an adventure that would be.

I had raised Tom. I had raised him as any mother raises

a son, even though I'd been much, much too young to be his mother and perhaps, after all, that's my only excuse, my youth. Claire had done what she could to help Tom and me. She was good to us when she didn't have to be, but we were motherless children, me the child-mother with no example of mothering to work with, he the child of that child-mother. Tom stuck with me and I stuck with him. And then, at fifteen, he was planning to run away and go to war and I failed to see the only danger I needed to foresee in his whole life.

If I am to confess here, I must confess all. I wasn't even worried. I wasn't worried when the school telephoned to say that Tom had gone. Because I knew where he'd gone. He'd gone to war. I wasn't worried when Daddy sent the wire to the Mater, calling me home to Risdon, calling me to account. In fact, I wasn't worried until I saw Daddy himself in the kitchen, when he stood to greet me. Distraught is how I'd describe Daddy's response when I walked through the door, distraught when he learnt not only that Tom had gone but that I had let him go.

'I thought it would be an adventure,' I said to Violet now. 'But when Daddy was so upset, I panicked. And now I've come over here and seen for myself, I don't know what's right.'

I left Risdon in October. Al and I had become engaged the week before – it was more rushed than either of us probably wanted but it felt important to be anchored in some way to home. Daddy came as far as Brisbane on the train. He didn't bring Claire or the boys and while I was glad at first that we'd have the time to ourselves, later when I saw him at the Breakfast Creek docks I was sorry. He stood there holding his hat, squeezing it and rolling it the way he told Tom not to. I was on the ship by then and high above him. I could see the curve of the river and beyond that the city of Brisbane, the market gardens of the Valley where later I'd live, the convent where I'd gone to school high on Duncan's Hill. Now I even imagine I saw the Story Bridge with its two peaks but that can't be right because it wasn't built until the thirties. But let's leave it there. It's a pleasing bridge. And let's build the cathedral planned for the space across the road from All Hallows', a large sandstone affair with soaring towers to rival St John's down in Ann Street. Oh, that looks better, to have the bridge, the church, and people in carriages on their way to town or the market gardens, and children and dogs down by the river swimming. That looks like a place to which no harm could possibly come.

'You find him and bring him back home, you hear?' was the last thing Daddy said because then there were the three whistles which meant we were leaving. 'Bring him home,' I think Daddy repeated. I couldn't hear for the whistles. His mouth looked tight, as if he might cry, and I wished Claire and the boys had been there to distract him.

'I think Claire's grand,' I called but I don't think he heard.

I don't remember much of the sea journey except that there were hundreds of us keen to see the war and half were seasick and half were not. I was among the second group; I felt like I was on a difficult horse. London was dark when we berthed and dark when I left two days later for France. It was the dirtiest place I've ever seen and that's all I've got to say about it. The Channel crossing was rougher than the open sea and the passengers now were soldiers or nurses and I knew then there was no going back.

I really did believe then that I was going over to bring Tom home and that it would be easy. We'd simply leave the war and come back to Risdon the way we'd gone. I'd marry Al.

Tom would marry Jessica Carson and we'd build houses at Risdon and have our babies and stay together.

'It was a lot easier in theory,' I said to Violet now.

She nodded. 'You are your brother's keeper, Iris,' she said. 'I don't envy you that, not one bit.' The look on her face was hard to read, a flash of sadness or perhaps anger. I didn't feel welcome to ask.

It was later that evening before I had a chance to pen a quick note to Tom. The light had gone for the day and I sat alone in one of the rooms we'd been clearing with a single candle for light. I was exhausted.

We'd had a letter from Tom, just before I left Brisbane. He'd disembarked first in Egypt intending to join the Light Horse, following our neighbour Ray Carson, he said, but he'd met 'some sterling chaps' in port who'd talked him into going on to England instead where, he wrote, 'if a bloke can shoot or run fast, he can join the British Army'. He thought it funny. Our mother was Scottish, our father the great-grandson of a convict. And, yet, they'd have our Tom serve in their army. He was in Southampton now, he said, en route, he thought, to Amiens, where the British were in trouble. He didn't mention his running away and his letter read as if he'd gone off to war with his father's blessing.

Ray Carson had been the lucky one, Tom said. Ray had joined the Light Horse and was already over in Egypt fighting. What Tom didn't know and we did was that Ray had been killed on his first day in Egypt. I didn't see Daddy cry, not even when our mother was dead and he had been the one to tell me, the one who took that role upon himself when someone else might have. But he cried as he read Tom's letter, swallowed, squinted, handed the letter to me, and while we had already agreed I would go and find Tom and bring him home, I was left with a fear caused not by my brother's being at war but by my father's tears. And it was my father's tears that came back as I sat down to write in that candlelit room of Royaumont.

Dear Tom, I wrote, *Where are you? I have joined and am at Royaumont near Asnières-sur-Oise. Write me there urgently. Keep safe. Your loving sister, Iris.*

I wanted to scratch out *urgently* and replace it with *soon* which seemed less frantic but didn't want to mess the paper. Instead I added, *so we can catch up*, which seemed to lend an appropriate air of casualness. But when I read it back over, it just seemed silly. I started again.

Dear Tom, I have joined the Scottish Women's Hospital at Royaumont. Write me there soon, dear brother. I would love to see you. Do keep safe, your loving sister, Iris.

Grace

Iris was still holding the invitation in her hand. 'But I'll be right one day,' she said to Grace, her bright eyes brimming. 'I will die. Do you know, I think I'd like to go.'

Grace looked at her grandmother's hands on the table, mottled brown and purple, old lady's hands. She looked up at Iris's face, heavily lined but full of hope. Grace took a breath in, out, felt a pull of tenderness so strong it stopped her from responding for a few moments. What she wanted to say was, I love you.

What came out instead was, 'Iris, when will you start acting your age?'

When did they swap roles, Grace becoming the parent, Iris the child? It had been the other way around, Iris always there to make sure Grace got up after every fall, and later pushing Grace to work harder at school, to do her best. But now Iris was old. That's all it is, Iris used to say to Grace. I'm just old. Stop fussing so. But Grace couldn't help herself. She was a doctor for a start, taught to her marrow that her job was to fix what was wrong. And if she felt responsible for Iris, wasn't that what you were supposed to feel when your parents aged?

The invitation had upset Iris, Grace could see that, and this talk of flying to France for a reunion was ridiculous. What was Iris thinking? And why on earth would she even want to go? What was at this Royaumont that made her willing to risk a trip like that at her age?

After she left her grandmother, Grace took Milton Road and narrowly missed a collision with a cement truck when she flicked a right back up to Paddington. She had to get to the hospital but realised she'd forgotten her pager. She hoped no one had been trying to get in touch.

Back at the house, the pager had had a minor fit, with three messages from the maternity ward desk. She called in. It was Andrew, finishing ward rounds. Nothing to worry about, thankfully, just wondering where Grace was. 'I'm on my way,' she said. She ran back down to the car and drove straight to the hospital.

Margaret Cameri went to take her baby off the breast.

'Stay there,' Grace said. 'Let's not upset the apple cart.' She pulled the curtain around the bed. The baby was slurping loudly. 'Lusty little tyke, isn't he?' Margaret Cameri looked worried. 'No, I meant that's a good thing,' Grace said. 'Healthy appetite.' Grace scanned Margaret Cameri's chart. 'I just want to check your stitches and tummy.' Grace lifted the covers. 'Legs wide. Good good.' She palpated Margaret Cameri's abdomen gently, moving around the baby. 'And you're doing very well, Mrs Cameri. I think the physio will be in later today or tomorrow. They'll give you some exercises to do when you go home. Any pain?' Margaret Cameri shook her head. Grace made a note on the chart and put it back at the end of the bed.

'The doctor said they might have to take out my womb,' Margaret Cameri said, her face barely controlled.

'No Mrs Cameri, that was me, I was the doctor, that was last night, after the baby was born. We were able to avoid that. You'll make a full recovery, just like with your other children. Have the other docs been round yet, Dr Martin and the team?'

'Yes, they came about an hour ago. Can I . . . if we want more children . . . Can we?'

'Oh yes,' Grace said. 'I would probably be recommending a caesarean next time, just to be on the safe side. You don't want the same thing happening again. But there's no reason you couldn't have more children, no reason at all.' Grace sat down on the edge of the bed. Andrew should have gone through this with her. Grace didn't know if he'd failed because he was a man – a woman would know this was one of the first things a female patient would be concerned about, up there with the health of their baby – or because of inexperience, or both. Maybe that's why he'd called her. Grace would talk to him.

'Have you named him yet?'

'Benno,' Margaret Cameri said, 'after his grandfather.'

'Nice,' Grace said. 'Now, you rest. We're going to keep you in a few days more.'

'I really need to get back to the other children. My husband has to work.'

'I know, but it's more important you get a chance to heal. Isn't your mother with them?' Grace's pager went off. David. 'I need to answer this. Take care, Mrs Cameri. I'll see you tomorrow.' Grace made a mental note to ask Alice what the Cameri household situation was. It wouldn't do Margaret

Cameri any good to be worrying about the other children, and she'd need help when she went home. If there wasn't help, they'd keep her in for the rest of the week.

Grace called David from the office. 'How's your inverted uterus?' he said.

'Fine. She'll be home in a couple of days.' Grace told David about the morning with Iris. 'You don't suppose she's going batty finally, do you?'

'Iris? We'll be batty before she is. France? Which war?'

'The first, she said. She was a volunteer at a hospital. She's never mentioned it before. I still don't really know the story. It's some sort of reunion. God, they'll all be on respirators.'

'Does she want to go?' David said.

'It's out of the question.'

'But does she want to go?'

'Of course she wants to go. You know Iris. She's as stubborn as a mule.'

'I know her granddaughter.'

'I was short with her. I wish I could . . . She's just so old now.'

'Why don't you go with her?' David said.

'That's ridiculous. How could I get away?'

'It might be the last chance she gets. She doesn't ask much.'

'What if she dies on the way?'

'Well, then she dies on the way. But to tell her she can't go; that's pretty tough, Grace. I don't think I could do that to her.'

'What about Henry?'

'What about him?'

'I can't just leave him.'

'Take him with you. Anyway, I'm on so I gotta go. I just wanted you to know I called Ian Gibson. He can fit Henry in at ten tomorrow.'

107

'There's nothing wrong with Henry.'

'He fell over this morning on the way up the stairs at day care.'

'Is he all right?'

'Yes, but he was just standing there and his legs gave way beneath him.'

'Did he trip?' Poor little Henry, she thought, an image of him falling in her mind.

'No, he just went over. You can't keep your head in the sand, Grace.'

'What's that supposed to mean?'

'I just think you're arguing with me when you know as well as I do that something's not quite right. With a lot of these things, it's better to intervene early than wait.'

'What things? We haven't talked about this.'

'We'll talk tonight. Gotta run.' He was gone. Grace held the phone to her ear for a few moments. She was tired, tired to her bones, four hours sleep at most last night, three the night before and no more than five a night all week. It was the same for David. And now he wanted to open up whatever was happening with Henry. It was the last thing in the world she wanted right now. She wished she could curl up in one of the private rooms and sleep for a month.

Grace herself was called to theatre then, an emergency caesarean because a baby was two weeks overdue and was induced and now in distress. Came out a perfect pink and healthy. Grace checked the chart to see who'd dated the pregnancy. It was David's registrar, Michael Mastin, on a consult. There must have been a query about dates early in the pregnancy if it was bumped up to the perinatal team. 'If that baby was forty-two weeks, I'm twenty-one,' Grace said to Alice afterwards.

Grace went down to the special care unit and found Michael

Mastin asleep in the treatment room. She shook him awake. 'Dr Mastin,' she said. He raised a bleary head. Grace ignored his sleepiness. 'Get up. I just delivered a baby. You were out by a month dating the pregnancy and it means we've done a caesarean we didn't need to do.'

'What the hell are you talking about?'

Grace handed him the chart. 'Don't speak back to a consultant like that. This is not the first problem we've had. Instead of sleeping in your spare time, can I suggest you learn how to measure a fundus.'

'Can I suggest you stop telling me what to do,' he said, unrepentant. 'I'm not in your programme.'

'More's the pity,' Grace said. 'Because I wouldn't let you on your own with a patient until I was confident you knew what you were doing. Don't worry. I'll be talking to your boss.' She flicked on the examination lamp above the bed and turned and left Michael Mastin blinking in the light before he could make some snide remark about pillow talk.

After lunch, she called the antenatal clinic and told them she'd be down to help at some stage. Before going down, she phoned the veterinary school at the university. 'Yes, a possum,' she said when the woman who answered the phone asked. 'I think it's a baby that's fallen off its mother's back,' she said.

'Could be,' the woman said.

'Can I bring it out there?'

'We don't really look after wildlife here. Maybe call National Parks.'

'Thanks anyway,' but no thanks, Grace thought. They were a vet school. What else did they do but look after animals?

Grace checked the labour ward, authorised pain relief for a woman having her first baby and agreed with a midwife to try some Pitocin on a labour that had stalled. Then she went down to the antenatal clinic to help finish up. It was like a cattle yard, at least three dozen patients still waiting to be seen by a doctor and only two doctors rostered on. Grace saw four patients in quick succession – all straightforward antenatal check-ups and the midwives had already seen them. She decided to take one more before going to pick up the kids. She wanted to call David back too before she had the kids with her. He was convinced they should see Ian Gibson. Put David's mind at ease, Iris had said, or words to that effect. But what if something really was wrong, something they couldn't fix? Would knowing help?

The woman who waddled over was in her late thirties, possibly close to term but overweight so it was hard to be sure. Thirty-six weeks according to her file. She'd already been to see a midwife who'd written CONSTIPATED!!! and the date. Why three exclamation marks? Grace thought. These young midwives were so unprofessional. And if it was only constipation, why did it need a doctor? It wasn't even a routine antenatal check – the woman had been in for that the day before. She'd seen a doctor then, Michael Mastin, David's guy. Surely he could do an antenatal check without someone holding his hand. Why was she seeing a doc again? Grace wondered.

The woman came into the cubicle and Grace didn't even look up as she washed her hands from the patient before. 'Mrs Wilson, I'm Dr Hogan. Have a seat. Did you ask to see the doctor again?' The woman didn't answer and Grace turned around and looked at her.

She was sitting down, looking uncomfortable in the white plastic chair. Her face was flushed. Big baby, Grace thought.

'Grace Hogan? Is that you, Grace?' the woman said. She put her hand to her chest as if she had indigestion.

Grace looked at her more carefully. The face was vaguely familiar. 'I'm sorry. I know you?'

'Grace Hogan. Oh my God, it is you. I heard you were a doctor. Wow. Grace Hogan. How are you?' The woman smiled. Grace still couldn't place her. 'It's me, Jennifer, Jennifer Bennetts. I'm Wilson now. We were in high school together.' The woman shifted her weight and took a short breath, holding her belly.

Once she heard the name, Grace remembered. Jennifer Bennetts, Deirdre Macklin and Janet Dalton. Year ten, the three girls who'd decided Grace was the 'it' for the year. They were the A group, popular, funny, smart. Grace was never one of them. They turned her interest in science and maths, her tall athletic frame, into something abnormal. Lezzo, that's what they called her, a lezzo. Grace was amazed at how much the description could still make her feel deeply ashamed, as if her body itself was in the wrong. The nickname was taken up by all the other girls for a time and Grace became the class joke. But the initial three fed it and continued long beyond when the others would have stopped. Grace started telling Iris she was sick on school days but Iris got wise to that. So then Grace took to truancy, changing out of her uniform in the Valley public toilets and spending the day on trains or wandering the city. It was this she was finally caught for. The principal's office rang Iris and called her in for an interview.

Before they went to see the principal, Iris asked Grace why she hadn't gone to school. Grace tried to explain, told Iris the name the girls had called her, how they went through her bag, putting boys' underpants in there, how they took pictures of her in the changing room and drew male genitalia and facial hair on them and put them up on the walls. Iris shook her head and said that life would bring harder things than three stupid nasty girls and when would she learn that women had to be tough to survive. Grace had felt even more at fault.

And then the principal's office. She could still remember the tirade. 'Your mother was one of our students, and your grandmother. And you are besmirching their heritage here.' Grace always remembered the word besmirching. It sounded like a little bird, the spotted besmirching. She made herself focus on this and not the yelling. And then Iris, asking Grace to wait outside while she spoke to Sister on her own, listening at the door but not hearing exactly what was said, Iris coming out, looking even more furious than she had when Grace was in the room, putting her hand up in a stop sign saying, 'Don't speak of it. We just won't speak of it. I'm too angry.'

Grace had assumed Iris was angry at her, Grace, for playing truant. Not long after, Iris took Grace out of the school and sent her to a smaller school they had to drive to. There were no boys' schools nearby for her to finish chemistry and physics so she had to have private classes and sit the exams on her own. Grace was sure she'd disappointed Iris terribly.

'Jennifer,' Grace acknowledged her now, as evenly as she could. 'Would you prefer to see one of the other doctors?' For no reason she understood, Grace's heart was racing.

'Oh no. That's fine. I don't mind at all.' Jennifer smiled, a beseeching kind of smile. Please like me, it said. Grace found it hard to reconcile that smile with the cruel girl Jennifer had been.

Grace helped her up onto the bed. 'You can keep your gear on. You saw Doctor Mastin yesterday for your thirty-six-week check-up. No problems?' Grace was doing a quick physical examination as she spoke. Fundus was low.

'I didn't like to say I'm constipated in front of a man,' she said. 'So I came back today and saw one of the midwives.'

'Yes, it says here you're having trouble with constipation.'

Jennifer nodded, looking uncomfortable. 'You sure you wouldn't rather talk with one of the other doctors?' Grace didn't even think of the fact that she herself would rather not see Jennifer Bennetts.

'No, it's fine really, good actually,' Jennifer said. 'I've often thought of you.' She'd had a habit of screwing up her nose, a nervous tic. It was still with her. 'I was terrible to you at school.'

'Water under the bridge,' Grace said and did her best to smile. 'First baby?' It was. 'Constipation's very common. Nothing to worry about. How long has it been?'

'Three days. I just can't seem to go.'

'We can give you something to help.' Grace thought of doing an internal examination, but decided against it. She could have asked one of the other consultants in but she didn't want to tell them why she wouldn't do it herself, that she'd spent years feeling somehow wrong in herself as a result of this woman's ridiculing of her. What she wanted was to get out of the consulting room as quickly as she could and get down to school, to the girls.

Jennifer was sitting up in the chair again, clearly uncomfortable. Grace was cuffing her arm. 'I really am sorry,' Jennifer said, that beseeching smile.

'We were young,' Grace said. She couldn't bring herself to be kind. 'Your blood pressure's a bit elevated. You have high blood pressure normally?' Jennifer shook her head no. 'Doctor say anything yesterday?' Grace was checking the chart. BP normal at the antenatal visit. Whether Michael Mastin actually checked it was a moot point. Grace couldn't see which midwife had seen Jennifer. Still, it wasn't very high and her urine test was clear for protein.

Jennifer put her hand on Grace's arm suddenly. Grace had an urge to pull away. 'No I was terrible. Your grandmother wrote a letter to my mother. My mother contacted the other mothers, Deirdre's and Janet's, but you'd left the school by then so there was nothing to be done about it. My mother was disgusted with me. I can still remember her asking me if we'd done the things your grandmother said we did and me saying yes as if they were nothing. But when they came out of my mother's mouth, when I knew they came from your grandmother, I could see what it would have felt like to be you, how I'd have felt if it had been me, and even now, after all these years, I've wanted to find you, to say sorry. And here you are.' She looked at Grace, as if forgiveness would be forthcoming.

'The past is long gone,' Grace said. 'I don't think about you any more, not ever.' Iris had written to Jennifer's mother. Grace never knew that. She found herself feeling strangely light in her chest, as if a weight had been lifted. She made herself focus on her patient.

Grace looked at Jennifer carefully, thought of ordering a twenty-four-hour urine just to be on the safe side but decided it was too soon. 'I want you to come back again at the end of the week and have your blood pressure checked. It's probably nothing but we want to make sure it stays normal. And if you get any swelling in the ankles, headaches, I want you to come back straight away.' Grace was writing up the file. 'And now, I'm going to find a midwife to come in and go through the medication with you. All the best.' Grace left without saying anything more, didn't even look at Jennifer Wilson.

As she walked to the desk, Grace thought of Iris. Although she hadn't let on to Grace, Iris had held the three girls, not Grace, responsible. She'd moved schools not because Grace had failed but because the school had failed. Iris had taken Grace's part after all. She just hadn't told Grace as much.

Grace found one of the midwives in the treatment room. 'Can you finish up in Three for me? I have another appointment. You just need to give her a suppository.'

'Sure. Are you all right?' the midwife said. 'You look a bit pale.'

'Huh? Fine,' Grace said. 'It's just, I once knew the woman. I don't feel quite comfortable.'

'Knew how?'

'We went to school together.'

'Were you close?'

'More the opposite.'

The midwife, Karen was her name, Grace recalled, walked over and looked into the cubicle and smiled at Jennifer and said, 'I'll just be a minute.' She came back to Grace. 'She looks like a thorough bitch,' she whispered.

Grace smiled. 'I guess. I need to go.'

'Ah well, you're the one who's laughing now. Why don't we do a manual evac?'

Grace was horrified. 'I don't think . . .'

'I'm kidding, Grace. Get a life, okay?' Karen smiled. 'See you tomorrow.'

Milton Road was crawling so she turned off and went up to Birdwood Terrace, beautiful old homes on large blocks looking straight to the city. She thought again about Jennifer and the other two girls in year ten. They had been horrible. But Iris had stuck up for Grace.

Growing up, Grace had never liked trying new things. She still remembered taking her first ever aeroplane flight at eighteen. She felt silly for being so nervous; other girls she knew had flown without even thinking. But it was all so new and the idea of voluntarily boarding a tin can with wings, as Al had always called planes, made her fearful.

Iris and Al took her to the airport and waited with her in the check-in queue. In front of Grace in the queue was a girl about Grace's age, on the same flight as Grace, who'd lost her ticket. The girl was panicking, Grace could see. When it was the girl's turn to go to the desk, Grace could heard the airline staff member telling her she'd have to buy a new ticket. 'She won't have the money for that, Al,' Iris said. 'It's just not right.' They watched for a while more, until Iris, followed by Al, marched up to the girl's side and demanded 'to see the station master'. Grace's turn in the queue came and she went to the next available staff member on her own. Iris and Al were still waiting calmly with the girl. They waved Grace off and later, on the plane herself, Grace saw the girl getting on, looking much relieved. It was the essence of Iris to help someone in trouble like that, and to leave Grace to fend for herself, Grace realised now. At the time, Grace had felt hurt that her grandmother had abandoned her. But it wasn't that Iris didn't care for Grace. It was that she'd always favour the one in most trouble. Grace was rarely the one in most trouble.

Iris had been so tough when Grace was growing up. She made Grace do science even though none of the other girls did. When she was at All Hallows' Grace had had to go over to St James's for classes with the boys. When she complained, Iris had said, 'You'll need science to get into medicine.'

'Who says I want to do medicine?' Grace said.

'Of course you do.'

'Did you do this to my mother, too, push her into medicine?' Grace was fifteen.

'I never had to push Rose to do anything.'

'No, she was a saint, unlike me.'

'I didn't say that. But Rose wanted to be a doctor from the

time she was little. She used to help me in the surgery.'

'I used to help in the surgery too.' Grace had memories of being at Al's work with Iris, Al called out to a home visit or the hospital and Iris doing all sorts of things with patients, setting a broken bone, diagnosing an illness. Grace was fairly sure Iris had even prescribed drugs, forging Al's signature. Many of Al's patients had been coming to the surgery their whole lives. They'd grown up with Iris. Like Grace, they thought that's what nurses did. Later, it had come as a shock to Grace in the hospitals to see that nurses did very few of the things Iris did in the surgery and to realise that Iris shouldn't have been doing some of them.

'Yes you did help me in the surgery,' Iris had said. 'See? Of course you're going to be a doctor.'

And Iris had been right. Grace had wanted to do medicine. She just hadn't known it.

She arrived at the school at ten past three, pulling into a spot as someone else pulled out. She watched Mia walk slowly towards the car, her bag on one shoulder. 'How was your day?' she said.

'Crap,' Mia said. 'And you're late again, Mummy.'

'Don't say crap, Mia.'

'I hate school,' Mia said. 'I want to leave.' They waited until Phil came out, laughing with her friends.

Mia was having a tough time with her year two teacher, Miss Hilsenstein, who found Grace's eldest child too smart for her own good, as the teacher had told Grace and David when they went for an interview at the school. Grace had said that she really didn't know what the teacher meant, how it could be possible to be too smart. Grace was due at the hospital and the meeting with the teacher had run late.

David kicked her under the table but she continued. 'Being

smart can only be good. Surely it's stupidity and ignorance that are the problem here.' The teacher looked confused momentarily and then smiled and went back to the work she was explaining. Grace got up soon after and left as noisily as she could, leaving David stranded.

'Well Mrs Hilsenstein won't be your teacher forever, Mia. She just doesn't know how to manage children. Next year, you'll probably have a better teacher.'

Mia was almost in tears. 'We had to do neat writing all afternoon,' she said. 'Mrs Hilsenstein said I'm the messiest girl she's ever met and that I'm too rowdy for a girl. She said I should have been a boy. Because I'm so rowdy, the kids had to stay in from our run. And they were all mad at me.' Mia burst into tears.

'Oh darling, I'm sorry.' Grace wanted to march into the classroom and scream at Mrs Hilsenstein. 'Well, she's wrong. When kids are restless and making noise, that just means they need a run. You poor love.' Mia sat sobbing. 'Let's go see Iris after we pick up Henry,' Grace said, hoping to cheer her up. She'd figured she could drop the kids with Iris and go home to call David.

Mia smiled through her tears and nodded. Phil started hip-hurraying and leant over to hold her big sister's hand. The girls loved Iris. She always had something fun to do and she was endlessly patient with them. Was she like that when Grace was small? Grace couldn't remember. Craft, she did remember doing craft with Iris in the front room at Sunnyside, the light coming through the timber slats on the verandah onto their work. Grace had wondered what the point of craft was. She remembered Iris trying to teach her to sew too but Grace had no interest in that either. The girls loved everything about Iris, even the floppy skin that hung under her arms, Mia told Grace once. 'It's soft like when Henry was a baby,' Mia confided. 'It makes me think Granna's not very strong.'

'She's all right,' Grace had said, 'just old,' although Grace had been in the room when they'd seen Mark Randall, more like a chorus of angels than a heart murmur he'd said. It took Grace a while to understand what he meant. Mia was right. Iris wasn't strong.

When they got to Henry's day care Grace went inside, leaving the girls in the car. Henry was still lying on his cot from rest time. Grace asked one of the workers if he was all right. 'He's just tired,' the girl said. 'He sometimes stays asleep.'

Why hadn't they told Grace this? She thought back. How long had it been since she'd picked Henry and the girls up? Two weeks? Four? David often started early so he did the pickup, or Mrs Franklin, who babysat if David and Grace were both at the hospital. Still, they should have phoned Grace, surely. 'Do other kids stay in bed after rest time?'

The girl looked at Grace. 'Sometimes. He's just tired, I think.' The girl was all of seventeen. What would she know about paediatrics?

Grace went over to Henry and gathered him up. 'You tired, honey?' He nodded, half asleep. He was wearing the Superman suit over his clothes. 'Well, come on, Superman, let's get you home.'

Grace put him in the back with his sisters. Mia recognised immediately that he wasn't quite awake. She put her arm around him. 'There there, Henry,' Mia, all of eight, said. 'We'll get Iris to fix you up with some nice biscuits and a drink of milk and you'll feel like new.' Henry smiled. Thank God for Iris, Grace thought, not for the first time. Where would we be without her?

Iris

The children came up the stairs, the middle one in front, what was her name, the eldest, Mia, behind, helping the little one, Henry. I called out to Mia to let Henry come up by himself and held out my arms. 'Come and hug your granna.'

'Where's the possum?' the middle one said after a perfunctory hug, her eyes wide. Phil, that was it. Phil was the easy one, Mia already much too serious, just like Grace, bursting with opinions, argumentative. Phil was full of joy, just like my brother Tom at six, wanting to experience everything now.

'Come quick,' I said at the top of the stairs. 'It's time to wake him up.'

Phil was there first. 'Ooh,' she said. 'Can I hold him?'

Mia wasn't far behind. 'No, Philomena, they're dangerous.' Phil looked at me and rolled her eyes as if she'd learnt to expect this from her big sister.

'Who told you possums are dangerous?' I said. 'They're not dangerous, Mia. They're just creatures like you and your sister.'

Mia looked at me as if I were a slightly naughty child. 'Granna, you shouldn't touch wild animals. I would have thought you'd know that. Of all people.' When she'd been little, I'd been to the school to talk to Mia's class about life on a farm. The children, all around six years old I suppose, couldn't believe you might only need to go to a shop every couple of weeks and then only to buy rope or oil, that everything else you'd be able to find or make on your own land. They stared. I think they saw me as something akin to a dinosaur exhibit at the museum. It was all they could do not to poke or prod me to see if I roared. When she thanked me afterwards their teacher told me it was really important that children knew where food came from. I suggested she might start a vegetable garden and she looked at me as if I wasn't all there.

Henry was at the top of the stairs finally. 'See, Mia, he can make it on his own. He just needs encouragement.' But the poor boy looked exhausted. What was it Grace had said about him? 'Young Henry, shall we go and find the possum?' He nodded enthusiastically, catching his breath. 'Do you feel all right?'

'Yes please,' he said. He smiled. Henry has the red curly hair and blue eyes from my mother's family but his smile belongs to my brother Tom and I had a moment where I couldn't quite place him, where instead of Paddington and Grace's children, I was at Risdon and Henry was Tom.

'Are you all right, Granna?' It was Mia's voice. 'You look scared.'

I came back to myself and looked at the boy, momentarily still not quite sure who he was. And then his name came back. 'I'm fine.'

Grace had dropped the children off and backed straight out of

121

the driveway. 'Just going home to make a call,' she'd said. I tried to tell her I had a perfectly good telephone but she'd already wound up the window and didn't hear me. I looked up the street. No sign of her yet. I took the children into the front hall.

I lifted the cloth over the little possum's umbrella box home. He was staring right up at us, blinking in the sudden light. 'I think he's hungry. Let's feed him.' They fought over who'd go first. I said we'd do it by age, youngest to oldest. We warmed some milk and put plenty of sugar in. Henry concentrated carefully as he put the dropper towards the possum's mouth. The possum knew by now what it meant. He slurped hungrily. 'He's a little piggy, Henry,' I said, 'not a possum at all. Now give Phil a turn.'

When they finished feeding the possum, I said we needed to let him sleep. 'Let's go out the back. We'll make some biscuits and have some apple and milk.' I watched Henry get up. He stood slowly, with considerable effort. 'Are you all right, son?' I said.

'I'm super-duper,' he said. 'Can I get some chocolate?'

I smiled. 'There's nothing wrong with you, Tom Crane.'

'Who's Tom Crane?' Mia said.

'What?' I said. 'Tom Crane's my brother. Why?'

'Oh Granna,' Mia said. 'What would you do without us to look after you?'

'I'd be lost in the long grass,' I said. 'But let's not think about that. Let's think of pleasant things.'

At first, when I heard the porter's horn, I thought it was just another rehearsal. We'd been ready for almost a week. But when I saw the cars making their way up the icy drive and then the inspector general from the health service in Paris, the other two, in the second car, emerging and coming towards the doors, I realised it was the inspection at last. I rushed downstairs, joined by Miss Ivens and Mrs Berry coming out of our operating theatre on the first floor. This was it, we knew, the inspection that would make us a working hospital, or not. 'Once more unto the breach,' Miss Ivens said. We went together to the entry hall.

It had been such a busy time and the cold had been awful. I'd never felt anything like it. We rose from our beds and it wasn't until we'd worked for two or three hours that we'd have feeling back in our fingers and toes. I got to where I couldn't stand to wash my hands and face on waking, cracking the ice in the bowl. It seemed better to feel grubby. We had no warm water for a bath. We had running water in the kitchen but nowhere else which meant we carried bucket after bucket up the three flights of stairs for cleaning, and for the first week, we continued to work by candlelight or used one of the makeshift lamps we'd created with rags. Then one dark afternoon, Quoyle and I were looking for something in the kitchen, too lazy to light the lamps, but realising we'd need to soon, and suddenly, there was Mr Edison's electrical light. A great cheer went up through the abbey. A few days later, we had running water and the abbey cesspits were back in business. Still no bath for the staff though.

We were so proud of how much we'd achieved in such a short time but as the inspectors walked towards the door, three of them, I had a sinking feeling. The general, knowable for the plume on his hat and the fact he emerged from his own car, a Mercedes, was short, a foot shorter than Miss Ivens and me, shorter even than Berry. He came through the door before the others and Miss Ivens took his hand, leaning down in that way she had, and I knew we were in for trouble. Miss Ivens and I towered over him, and no matter how I tried to make myself smaller, I could not remove a foot or more to make him feel taller. Later I wondered had Drs Savill and Courthald, of much more reasonable female stature, shown him around, would it have been different? The general was accompanied by a young Croix-Rouge doctor, tall and willowy, who said little, other than that the wards were large and the operating theatres appeared well appointed, and an architect, who took copious notes. None of the three spoke English and so I translated. As Miss Ivens took them through room by room, I could see the general was looking for problems. Some of the X-ray equipment was still to arrive and so we were making do. An old fish kettle had been commandeered as a cistern for developing films. The general picked it up, made a dismissive *hmph* and placed it back down. Wires hung out of the ceiling in the operating theatre – we were waiting for a lamp from Paris. At one stage the general turned to me and asked, 'Where are the WCs?' I assumed he needed to use one so I took him upstairs to the doctors' quarters. 'How will you expect the wounded to climb these stairs?' he said.

I apologised. 'I made a mistake. The patients' WCs are downstairs.' He thought I was an idiot.

The day after the inspection, Miss Ivens received the news by wire from Paris, the full report to be delivered later in the day. She read the telegram in silence, looked up and to the left, narrowed her eyes, read it again and folded it and placed it neatly on the desk. I wanted to ask her what it said but thought it best to wait. Finally she said, 'It seems you were right about the wards, Iris.' She had the softest facial features, Miss Ivens, and while she was as strong as an ox, any upset would write itself all over her face. I hated to see her like this. She handed me the telegram. Our second-floor ward was deemed unsuitable, too far from the entrance to the abbey, too dark and with inadequate ventilation. The general had intimated as much following his inspection tour but this confirmed our worst fears. The report, when it came, was more of the same, highly critical not just of the rooms but of those who'd chosen them. 'It would be obvious to any competent surgeon that the layout of the hospital is totally impractical.' The report listed other problems, unfinished work, a requirement that we prove our doctors were appropriately qualified. It must have stung Miss Ivens to be so criticised although she didn't show it. They'd failed the hospital. They'd failed us and the only option was to make the changes they were proposing – changes that made our earlier work completely wasted – and undergo a second inspection.

Miss Ivens sat behind her desk and looked at me as I read. When I looked up, I saw all the desperate feelings in the world written on her strong face. 'It's not the end of the world,' I said. 'They haven't said no. They just don't like our choices.'

Miss Ivens laughed then, back to her old self suddenly. 'Exactly, Iris. They don't like our choices, damn them to Hell. You'd better call the troops together. We'll meet in Blanche at four. I think I need a little walk first. Get Cicely to spread the word.'

Before the meeting, all the other women knew the outcome and we'd privately or in groups of two and three inspected the rooms we'd now have to clear and clean. One was simply dusty and dirty and full of furniture but the other you couldn't even get into because of the leftover building materials. It was no surprise we'd avoided them.

Miss Ivens came in to Blanche smiling broadly. 'You'll

all have heard by now that the Croix-Rouge is not ready to accredit our hospital. The major concern is the second-floor ward, which is in the wrong place, it seems.

'I would like to be able to say they are wrong but they are not. The first floor will be far more practical for wards, closer to the reception area and the theatre. The good news is that once we establish the new wards, Royaumont will surely be accredited and we will have wounded. I know many of you are disappointed. I was myself at first. But if we take a longer view, our work upstairs will never be wasted. I think some of you are wondering if we'll ever have our patients, but I assure you we will work day and night to that end. We must forget about the Croix-Rouge and its complex machinations. We must forget about our own beliefs that brought us here.' There had been unrest among the women – some had joined in the protests for the vote before the war and others were anti those who'd protested – and Miss Ivens was worried it would erupt into more open conflict. 'The only thing any of us should have to exercise our minds in the next few days is the thought of those wounded soldiers who currently die and lose limbs for want of Royaumont Hospital.'

Of course, we worked hard once more to clean out the first-floor rooms. After Christmas – we had that one day off; Miss Ivens shouted everyone champagne and smoked trout and in the evening, led by Cicely Hamilton, we put on a pageant called 'Le Générale Inspecteur' which was funnier after the champagne than it would have been otherwise – we returned to work and in a relatively short time, managed to clear and clean the new rooms. The chapter room in the eastern wing which opened on to the cloisters became our Millicent Fawcett ward, named after the president of the National

Union of Women's Suffrage Societies, from where the idea for our hospital originated. And the two wards running north and south became Jeanne d'Arc and Marguerite d'Écosse.

I had news from home after Christmas, a letter from Daddy. He said the twins were into mischief now, just like Tom as a boy, and Claire could hardly keep up with them. Daddy was off to Toowoomba the next week for the show and Mrs Carson had offered to come and stay with Claire but Claire had said she'd be all right. I bet she'd said that, I thought. Claire couldn't stand Mrs Carson, who snooped around for any shred of gossip she could take away with her and gossiped about our other neighbours. Daddy asked me to write soon, to give him news of Tom. I realised I'd hardly given Tom a thought since I'd sent my note. I felt guilty, wondered what I'd write to Daddy in reply, put the feelings away.

By New Year we were ready once again. This time they sent a team of four, the same architect, a different chief inspector from the Zone Nord de Paris rather than the general from the Service de Santé, and two Croix-Rouge officers – different from last time – who might also have been doctors. I wasn't sure as I missed the introductions – held up trying to get the stove in the new Jeanne d'Arc ward alight – only catching the rear of the group as they headed up the stairs to the wards. The inspector, who spoke English, and the architect walked with Miss Ivens and Mrs Berry while one of the Croix-Rouge officers went off with Cicely Hamilton to check that our doctors' qualifications were in order – a request after the first inspection. We'd had to send to the British Medical Society for qualification bona fides. The second Croix-Rouge officer remained with me. He was a tall slim man with dark hair combed back from a high forehead so that it stood up slightly. He had piercing blue eyes, quite close together, which, combined with the hair, gave him the look of an eagle. His face was pink where he'd shaved that morning and he smelt fresh like soap.

'Is there anything in particular you want to see?' I said in French.

'I'll just wander around with you quite happily,' he said. His body moved as he spoke with nothing like the grace of an eagle. Gangly was the word that came to mind, perhaps an eagle going for a walk, as if his limbs had only recently grown and he was still getting used to them. 'I understand General Foveau gave you troubles.'

'We've addressed all the concerns he raised in his report,' I said carefully.

'So you have,' the officer said. 'So you have.' He smiled suddenly and his face softened. 'And tell me, what is your name?' I told him. 'And what exactly do you do here?' I said I was assistant to the chief. We were crossing the cloister on the way to the kitchen, following Miss Ivens and the others.

'Weren't you just a little annoyed after our last report?' he said to me quietly. I said no, I wasn't, that the report made some good points and that we should have addressed them. He nodded. 'Good answer,' he said. 'Well, I would have been annoyed at a report like that. I thought it was arrogant of us to assume we might know more than your doctors.'

I was taken aback by his frankness. 'We want to be the best hospital we can be,' I said. 'I would assume the health service has much more experience than us with these matters. We would be fools not to heed their advice.'

He stopped to light a cigarette, after first offering me one which I declined. 'I suppose you would,' he said, 'but it's you

128

not us who have created all this. I want you to know I for one didn't like the report we gave you. It won't happen this time.'

He remained with me for the rest of the visit. He was oddly familiar to me. Not that I thought I'd met him before. I knew I hadn't. But I felt at home with him. I kept having to remind myself that he was a member of an inspection team, that I needed to be careful what I said lest I ruin something for Miss Ivens.

At the end of the tour, the Croix-Rouge officer I'd been with joined the rest of the team with Miss Ivens in the foyer while we waited for the second Croix-Rouge officer who soon came with Cicely Hamilton, smiling and chatting. The inspectors discussed the abbey's history then, the architect speaking French, with me translating for Miss Ivens. The officer who'd accompanied me continued to speak in French and I translated for him too. They seemed less interested in whether or not the abbey was now suitable as a hospital and more interested in passing the time of day. I didn't know what to make of it. When we came to the front door to say goodbye, the officer and I were behind the rest again. He gestured for me to go in front of him and put his hand on the small of my back to usher me through. I felt a strange warmth up my spine, like a static shock. I turned to look at him but his expression betrayed nothing.

The inspectors thanked Miss Ivens for her patience and said they'd have their report to her that same afternoon. The wire came, as promised, granting us full accreditation. 'Just like that,' I told Violet an hour later. 'It was as if they didn't even need to carry out a second inspection.' I told her about the young officer I'd met. 'I wonder why he stayed with me instead of talking to Miss Ivens and Mrs Berry.'

'Knows where the real power is. Or maybe he just liked you.' I found myself blushing. 'Oh, Iris. Iris has a sweetheart! Are you going to see him again?'

'Violet,' I said, 'he's not a sweetheart. I just thought it was nice of him to stay with me, that's all.' I hadn't told Violet about Al. I hadn't told anyone at Royaumont. If I'd thought about why I hadn't, it was that my old life, my life in Australia, already seemed far away.

I realised I didn't even know the young officer's name. I went down to Miss Ivens's office and asked to see the report. The chief inspector's name, Jacques Pireau, was at the bottom along with his signature. I already knew the architect, M Pichon, whose name was listed along with the Croix-Rouge officers Jean-Michel Poulin and Dugald McTaggart. The officer who went to check qualifications spoke English. The officer I was with only spoke French. He must be Jean-Michel Poulin, I thought. When I asked Miss Ivens, she said she couldn't remember which one was which but weren't they a marvellous trio.

Although we'd been awarded full accreditation, there was one caveat in the written report that reached us the next day. The inspectors were recommending 'in the strongest possible terms' that we engage a French chef as the French soldiers couldn't be expected to eat English food. Miss Ivens said they were the living end and they hadn't even tasted Quoyle's shepherd's pie so how would they know about our food. The next day she and I went to Paris to try to work out how we could meet their request and still open the hospital on schedule. We took the train in the morning but we were held up because one of the other lines had been blown up. When we finally arrived, it was late afternoon so we stayed for a night in a hotel near the Croix-Rouge offices. We ate together in a little café on the Left Bank. Miss Ivens said we must get an ice-cream after dinner but it being midwinter and there being a war on, the ice-cream place was closed.

Although I didn't say it to anyone else, I'd hoped I might see Jean-Michel Poulin again the next morning but when we arrived at the offices it was another Croix-Rouge officer who met with us. And it seemed there was no room to negotiate the matter of a cook.

'Oh for God's sake, man,' Miss Ivens was saying to him. 'We're opening a hospital not a hotel.'

'Miss Ivens wonders whether we really need a chef,' I translated, 'since the patients will be injured and will not eat much.'

'My dear madame,' the officer said. 'We must have French food for our French wounded.'

I turned to Miss Ivens. 'Perhaps we can find someone suitable among the villagers left in Asnières,' I said. 'I don't think they can bend on this one.'

'On this one?' she said. 'Which ones *do* these officious fools bend on?'

'You may call me officious if you like, madame,' the man said in accented English. 'I am not a fool. The French don't make those distinctions you English make between the officers and the men. All Frenchmen eat well.'

'I am Scottish and not English,' Miss Ivens lied, without a blink of embarrassment at being caught out calling the fellow officious. 'And I am trying to help your soldiers as I'm sure you are. Please do not get in my way. I implore you.'

The man sighed. 'Very well,' he said, nodding and closing the file in front of him. 'You keep your English cook for now.' He stood up for us to go.

In just a few more days our first patients would arrive and we would be a war hospital. Another pageant, more champagne, and then hospital mode, shifts in the wards, theatre at the ready, X-ray, pharmacy, waiting for wounded.

After Grace left with the children, I felt too exhausted to heat the dinner the Meals on Wheels had left me. I put it in the freezer with the others and ate two more wheat biscuits. I was tired but knew I wouldn't sleep so early. I went out to the verandah to clear up the plates from afternoon tea. My knife was there on the table where I'd peeled an apple for Henry. Once the knife had saved my life, I thought to myself. Don't be dramatic, Iris, I heard Violet saying, so clearly I turned around to see if she was there. We were never in danger, she said. Oh but we were, Violet, of course we were. We were always in danger. We just didn't know what the danger was.

I took the knife and wiped it on a cloth and closed it. What had I told Grace about Violet? I couldn't remember. There was a saying about lying, something about lies only making more lies. I couldn't remember that either.

After I cleared the things, I went and sat out on the front verandah to watch the evening fall. It might fog later, I thought, but for now the air was warm and dry.

Before long I saw them, the mother possum with her remaining baby, along the wire between the house and the road. 'Aren't you upset?' I called out to the mother. 'You've lost one of your babies.' She turned and looked my way before scurrying off, making the leap from the wire to the tree outside Suzanne's effortlessly, despite the load she carried. Suddenly, a boy was there at the bottom of the stairs. 'Who is it?' I said, fear in my voice, for I was sure it was Tom.

'It's Matthew,' he said, 'from next door.' The boy I'd seen this morning.

'Ah,' I said. 'Did your mother let you come over?'

'I said I was going out to play.'

'Well, come up now and see what I found.' I stood up slowly. My legs were so tired they could hardly carry me. I took Matthew inside and showed him the little possum. 'He's sleeping so we won't worry him for now. I just saw his mother out on the wire.'

'Why didn't you tell her to come and get him?'

'I'm afraid she might not remember him.' Matthew nodded as if he understood that from personal experience. 'Tell me something, do you like chocolate?'

'I'm not allowed.'

'Not allowed chocolate. Your mother?' I asked. He nodded. 'Well, I like chocolate. How about you keep to your mother's rules in her house and my rules in my house?' He nodded again, carefully this time. 'Want some chocolate?'

'Yes please.'

'What beautiful manners.' I took him out to the kitchen and showed him the chocolate jar. 'Take your pick,' I said. 'And any time you visit, you can have whatever you want.'

His eyes were big as saucers. 'Thank you!' he said.

After he'd eaten more chocolate than was probably wise, he asked to see the possum again. I took him out to the hallway. The possum was awake now and blinking again. I let Matthew feed it some milk. 'Not too much,' I said, 'or he'll be feeling like you do.'

Matthew smiled. 'You're old.'

'I am.'

'My mum says you might die.'

'I might.'

He nodded. 'Will you die soon?'

'Probably,' I said.

'Are you ready?'

'For what?'

'The Saviour's voice in your ear.'

'I think so,' I said, 'although my hearing's not what it used to be.'

'I'm scared.'

'What are you scared of?'

'God.'

'God's nothing to be scared of. He's not like your mother, you know.'

'How do you know?'

It was a good question. 'Well, I suppose I don't. But he made this little possum for us to feed. And he made the beautiful sky tonight. So I just don't think he's the angry kind. Jesus said the Kingdom of God belongs to children. He saw children as the main thing. And I think he was right there. I think children might be the main thing.' I ruffled his hair. 'But it took me an awfully long time to know that. When I was young, I thought other things mattered.'

'Like what?'

'I wanted to be a doctor actually.'

'Why didn't you?'

'Well, that's a good question. You ask lots of good questions, Matthew. I like that.'

He smiled again and then we heard his mother's voice, yelling for him to get in here now. 'Off you go,' I said. 'Thanks for coming over,' and he was gone.

I sat out on the verandah a while more to watch the

evening. Soon the birds were silent, night was fallen and I heard a hound baying in the far distance. This afternoon, after the girls had run off to climb the tree, Henry stayed with me on the verandah. He sat on the bench beside me and put his hand, his hot little hand, on my arm. Grace said she was worried about him. Jesus had been right about children. Grace was the true blessing, she and Rose before her, although it took me some time to know it. For so long with Rose, I thought my life had come to nothing. I spent my days running after this bright child and helping in the surgery. It seemed meagre, deadening, compared with what I could have been doing. Rose was a difficult child, there's no doubt about that, but perhaps it was because I was a difficult mother. My days were filled with despair or dread, depending whether I looked back or forward. Nowadays I'd be medicated, but back then there were no remedies, just the implacable face of one of Al's colleagues who said it was only to be expected, those bloody women filling my head with nonsense. He must have had a word with Al who worked fewer hours and hung about the house casting furtive glances my way every now and then which only brought on tears. Finally I said to him that I was feeling much better, just to get him out of the house.

'It should have been me not Tom,' Al said once. 'I should have been in France.' I didn't have the good grace to disagree.

While we had been accredited as a field hospital, we would not receive patients without approval from the head of the *gare régulatrice* at Creil, Dr Couserges, who made a point of ensuring that all the hospitals in his zone – north-east to Soissons, Reims and Noyon – were up to his standard. He had told the Croix-Rouge, in no uncertain terms, that they could accredit whomever they wished but he wouldn't be sending patients to Royaumont until he'd come to have a look for himself. So we were to be inspected once again. We waited.

Violet and I took the opportunity to explore the local Lys forest. We found a quiet road that ran to Chantilly past a few little villages. I liked mornings best, the soft sunlight shining through any lingering mist. We visited the tiny villages of Baillon, Boran and Lamorlaye, all three mostly spared from the war so far. We walked miles and miles each day and longed to start finally as a hospital.

On 10th January, tired of waiting, Miss Ivens thought to send one of our ambulances to Creil so that Dr Couserges could see how well prepared we were. Violet and I went with Dr Savill. Creil was a journey of twelve miles and the road, still in fair condition in those early days, wound through forests, now lightly covered in snow. From the crossroads, we climbed steeply for a few miles to a glade of leafless poplars, the sun shining through the branches of the trees and glistening on the snow, and finally drove down into the valley in which the *gare* had been established on a bend of the Oise River. Violet did marvellously well driving in the snow. Although we had a few tricky moments when we slid around, she kept her head and got us safely through. The bridge across the river had been destroyed when the Germans were approaching and so we were forced to take a wooden bridge which had been put up hastily after the Germans retreated. It was quite rickety and made Dr Savill sick, she said. We passed another car near the bridge and arrived at the *gare* only to discover that Dr Couserges had already set off for Royaumont; the car we'd passed on the road. So we turned around and went back, getting home just as Miss Ivens was showing Dr Couserges our Blanche ward. She was doing very well – the beauty of the abbey spoke for itself – but was relieved when I came back to translate for her. Dr Couserges was perfectly happy with the hospital's wards and said he'd soon be sending patients. Mostly sick, he said, until he'd been back to observe our surgeons at work.

Again we waited. And then, on the evening of 13th January, Marjorie Starr called out that a car was coming up the drive – it must be *blessés*, she said – and those of us up in the wards rushed down to see, putting on coats and veils on the way, just in case. Before long, everyone in the abbey was awake and down in the hall where our electric lamps were doing their best to illuminate the large space. We were all accustomed to low levels of light – we'd only recently given up our oil lamps – but to these first patients, it must have seemed strange for a hospital to be so dimly lit. Soon I spied the small group of men shuffling along the long cloister towards us. As they came closer, I saw their faces, grubby, some still blood- or mud-spattered, all walking, no stretcher cases among them. They stopped when they reached the abbey entrance, sitting on the long bench or collapsing to the floor, not speaking, looking around furtively. They were ragged and filthy and exhausted. And they looked afraid. They spoke not a word as the doctors and we nurses moved around them, checking their papers and injuries. Orderlies were dispatched to bring hot soup and bread. The ambulance driver from Creil, a bright-eyed young Frenchman, looked as doubtful as the men themselves that they'd arrived at a hospital.

'It's all right,' Miss Ivens said in English as she strode out to greet them, smiling broadly. 'We are going to help you.' I translated for her and soon, with more reassuring smiles

137

from doctors and nurses, the men began to smile and speak themselves. Those first half dozen were soon bathed, dressed in pyjamas and put to bed in Blanche. I assisted one of them – he looked too old to be fighting – who was sick with a fever and a cough that might turn bad in his chest. His uniform was full of fleas and stinking of mud. Bathed and dressed in our pyjamas, he saw the beautiful ward, warmed by the stove and lit by lamps. I gave him more soup and bread. He climbed into bed between clean sheets and said he was sure he'd come to Heaven and I was an angel. When I replied in his native tongue that I was no angel, merely a nurse, he said then nurses must be angels and French angels at that. He was soon asleep.

The ambulance driver came himself to see the wards – insisted in fact – and looked pleasantly surprised to find his charges now comfortably resting in bed. He explained to me that by the time they reached a hospital, the men had often undergone long painful journeys. They were collected by ambulance from the field and taken to the nearest railhead. From there, they travelled by train to the *gare régulatrice* at Creil where they were assessed and given basic treatment before being evacuated to surrounding hospitals. The patients dreaded going to an unknown hospital – and they'd heard this was a hospital run by English women – and while he'd tried to reassure them, he himself didn't know us and couldn't give them much information. 'But now I have seen for myself, I will be able to let them know.' I don't know what he imagined we might have been planning to do to his charges but I hoped he'd take this experience of us back to Dr Couserges to convince him that the Scottish women really were all right after all so that we might be entrusted with more seriously injured patients. I wouldn't have to wait long.

We quickly realised that the soldiers who came to us needed much more than medical care. The French Army didn't replace worn or torn clothing and so the men's uniforms were not only stinking and pestilent, they were often at the end of their useful life. Initially the bagged clothes were taken up the stairs to the top floor for storage until the soldier left us, but within a week we made an arrangement with a washerwoman from Asnières who fired up her boilers and prepared while we packed the pile of stinking uniforms into ticking mattress cases and transported them to her for laundering. We cleaned and aired coats and boots. A woman from Viarmes, a Madame Fox, took on responsibility for mending. She was quite ingenious at getting the best from a pair of trousers or a jacket that really ought to have been retired. The Royaumont *vêtements département*, as we named our service, was unique in French hospitals, we learnt. We fed the soldiers as well as we could in the time they were with us – albeit English food, which would continue to bother the Croix-Rouge – and we gave them toothbrushes when they left. We would quickly become coveted as a destination for French soldiers who, returning to the front, would be better dressed, better fed and cleaner than their compatriots.

For another two weeks, Dr Couserges continued to send us only sick patients and those with minor wounds. Then he came back to Royaumont – by arrangement this time – and watched Miss Ivens perform an operation, an appendectomy as it happened, and said he was now comfortable with our surgical capacity. Finally, he would send us wounded. During those two weeks he also agreed that our drivers could collect patients from the *gare* rather than using his own ambulances – Miss Ivens had been right about our women being allowed to drive in a war zone – and Violet had been to Creil several times to pick up patients. The two men who'd been sent over specially from Edinburgh to drive for us – just in case – had been sent home. Miss Ivens was adamant we shouldn't keep the men on our staff although some in Edinburgh had thought we should. Miss Ivens wrote to the committee that when Croix-Rouge officers visited and saw two young men of military age doing very little, it was 'awkward and humiliating, as if England is not doing its utmost. And worse, it looks terrible for us to call ourselves a women's hospital and yet have men here.'

Initially Creil would telephone to let us know *blessés* were ready for collection and the ambulances would be dispatched. But this system was cumbersome so by the end of their first week, we agreed that our drivers would go to Creil each evening at six to take evacuees to the *gare* for return to their units and pick up new patients for Royaumont. Also in that first week, we developed the system for receiving patients that would last for the duration of the war. The hall porter – the orderlies shared this responsibility to provide twenty-four-hour cover – would blow her horn as soon as she saw the ambulances coming up the drive from the road, the number of blows indicating the number of cars so we'd have an idea of how many wounded were en route. One nurse and all the orderlies from each ward would go down to assist with triage and stretcher duties, leaving only a sister.

The day we saw our first badly wounded soldiers had dawned crisp and clear. You'd never have believed a war was all around us. I'd been in Blanche the evening before. Miss Ivens had told me that although eventually I would be full-time as her assistant, for the moment, until we had our

140

full contingent of staff, I would continue nursing in the wards. I was due to go off duty but when I heard the porter's horn blow three times I rushed down to meet the ambulances with the rest.

As I descended the stairs, I thought I might faint just from the smell. There was the foul mud I was already becoming used to, but under that the reek of rotting flesh. I pinched myself hard on the arms because I knew I was needed to help these men, not to require help myself. Violet – who'd been to Creil – had tried to prepare me – 'Iris, it's more terrible than you can imagine; how can they do this to each other?' – but nothing could prepare a person for this. There were two dozen, mostly on stretchers, most quiet, some moaning softly, one blinded boy screaming who would not be quelled, at least half of them black as night and calling out in neither French nor English. These were niggers, Dr Courthald told us, from the French colonies of Algeria and Senegal. I'd never seen skin so dark, not even among the blacks in Australia, with such white teeth and eyes by contrast. To a man, they looked terrified.

I looked across the flagged floor. The state of their ragged frozen clothes, their young smashed bodies, beggared belief. How did an army let this happen to its men? The nurses and doctors hardly spoke, except to point out urgent cases. We were all in shock. Closer up, I saw that the wounds were awful, some without even a field dressing. I couldn't help but think of Tom. I'd made what enquiries I could through the drivers who went to Creil or Chantilly or Soissons. No one had heard anything thus far. In truth, I hadn't looked terribly hard; I'd been too busy and, if I was honest, too happy at Royaumont to worry about Tom.

I triaged my first patient, a young Senegalese soldier

with an obviously infected wound in his right arm up near the shoulder, and chest wounds awaiting X-rays, as well as wounds to his face. He understood neither French nor English. I took swabs as best I could – frustratingly, I couldn't tell him what I was doing – and sent them up to the laboratory for testing. The X-rays were soon done and the boy went off to theatre. As I was leaving him, he grabbed my hand with his left hand, his right the more badly injured. I smiled with what I hoped was reassurance. 'It's all right,' I said. 'We're going to make you well.'

After the patients were allocated to wards or theatres and operations were almost done, I worked with Miss Ivens in the office to clear the mounting correspondence and check the equipment orders and then – after a two-hour break during which I slept solidly – I was on duty in the ward again.

My Senegalese boy from the morning had come down from the theatre. Miss Ivens had worked to save his left arm but had had to amputate the right and then discovered that his chest wounds were more serious than they looked. At first I thought he might need further surgery but the chest was too severe, they'd realised, and we would not save him. I found myself dreadfully upset that we couldn't help this boy, this otherwise healthy boy, to survive. I knew I should be strong. I was a nurse. It wasn't as if I was unaccustomed to death. But this boy, it occurred to me, was dying for nothing. Perhaps he knew himself he was dying, for the fear in his eyes was almost unbearable. He wanted his arm back, he signalled to me, his severed arm, in the bed with him, as far as I could make out. We couldn't agree to that, of course. Perhaps he wanted his arm to take across to the other side with him. Perhaps it was his religion. I have no idea but wish I'd simply found a limb and put it in his bed. Matron told me I was to care for him. I sat by his bed and did the best I could, his eyes following me wherever I went.

Another African soldier who'd had a shell wound in his thigh was on the ward. He spoke French as well as the boy's language and he told me the boy was from a village not far from his own. 'His father has given him to France to spare the rest of his family,' the soldier said. 'He is the second son.'

'What do you mean?' I said.

'The French cannot get enough of us to fight their war, so they make arrangements with village chiefs. In my village, twenty young men, in this boy's village twenty young men. The chief must find the young men or be penalised. The men don't want to go. They know they are going to die a long way from home.'

The boy looked at his countryman suddenly and said something I didn't understand.

'He says he wants to go home, to see the sea once more from his beautiful country.' The boy's eyes closed again then.

'You didn't have a choice?' I said, horrified.

'We have not had a choice for many years,' he said. 'Most of my countrymen don't even know why France is at war. They come here to save their families not the French.' The boy opened his eyes again and the soldier spoke to him in his language.

'I am the son of a chief,' the soldier said after the boy had slipped off again. 'My father did not want me to come to France to fight. He told me to run for the hills like the other boys in my village. But my father is a warrior and the son of a warrior. I was disgusted to see the young men of my village flee when the French came. I decided to volunteer so that those who ran would know that men in our family are warriors and proud to fight. My brothers did the same.

'At first my father was angry. But when I returned to my village in my uniform to say goodbye, he told me he forgave me and that it didn't matter any more because now I was in the hands of Allah. I didn't know then how mad this war of yours is. The bombs that explode and send pieces into our bodies. My two brothers have died here. I failed to protect them.' He looked confused suddenly. 'We are not warriors here, just pieces of meat to put before guns.'

'In my country, no one is forced,' I said.

The soldier smiled then. 'You are very white,' he said and put his warm hand up to touch my cheek. I took his hand from my cheek and held it for a moment.

'You should go to bed now,' I said and smiled. 'Thank you for helping. I'll sit with the boy.'

After the soldier went back to bed, I looked at the boy's face. He couldn't be more than fifteen, Tom's age. Tomorrow, I thought, I would get a message up to Amiens. I would find out where Tom was and decide from there what needed to be done. I felt better to have a plan.

Whenever the boy opened his eyes, I tried to communicate peace but I know I failed. I was good at some things – the business of nursing, the practical part – but never one for compassionate care, a nurse's truest virtue. I knew he didn't understand me but I sat with him, the rest of the ward silent around us, and spoke softly in French. At midnight I fed him a little egg yolk mixed with milk – you see what I mean about the practicalities; what was the point of that? Most of it slipped out of his mouth and onto the pillow. He moaned softly and came in and out of consciousness. I said the rosary, which achieved about as much as you might expect for an African Muslim. Neither French nor English would soothe him. I sang; I sang 'Nearer My God to Thee' and 'Just a Closer Walk with Thee', funeral songs I realised when another patient asked me to hush lest he too die in the night.

And then, at about 4 a.m., Miss Ivens came. She'd only just finished in the theatre again – we'd had more wounded come in. She leant over to him and spoke so softly I couldn't hear what she said. But his eyes closed and the moaning stopped.

'I'll sit with him,' Miss Ivens said to me. 'You go off now and get some rest.'

When I came into the ward later in the morning on my way to reception, for still more wounded were expected, another was in the boy's bed. I saw Miss Ivens on her way back to the theatre. I asked her what had happened and she said the end had been peaceful. 'Sometimes that's all you can do,' she said. She must have read the sadness in my face. 'It's enough,' she said. 'Sometimes you can't even give them that. And that's the hardest of all.'

The reception area was much like the day before, if not worse, stinking infected wounds, men in ragged clothes, most of them in shock, unable even to say their own names when we spoke to them. While we worked, a dozen more came in with Violet and another driver, all wounded, most septic. I noticed a man on the other side of the room, moaning low. I looked across. I went to him first.

He was dying, I knew, as soon as I saw him, shrapnel filling his belly on the X-ray, his fingers blue from lack of oxygen. If he'd been moved from the field sooner perhaps he'd have had a chance but the wounds were septic to a large degree. We didn't need laboratory results to know that. The smell that came from them told you immediately. I thought of how he'd spent his last days, lying somewhere in mud by the look of him, cold and alone. '*Maman*,' he said quietly. I looked at his face for the first time. I saw that he wasn't a man at all. He was just a boy, another boy, with dark red curly hair like Tom's. I confess I looked at the boy again to assure myself that he wasn't my brother.

I took his hand. 'My beautiful boy,' I said. 'Are you cold? Would you like something warm to drink?'

He tried to smile. His eyes were closing and opening slowly. I called for blankets. An orderly came over. I'm sure she wondered why I'd stopped. I was supposed to be assessing the patients.

'Get Sister Jackson to finish the other patients,' I said. 'I need to stay with this man. I need some warm tea and a straw.' The orderly looked at me as if I'd lost my mind. 'Hurry now. He's cold.'

I sat with him and looked over his poor torn body. Tom. I couldn't stop the thoughts now of Tom. I was tired, I knew I was tired. Tom. Was he out in the cold, lying wounded, or in some British hospital holding the hand of a stranger while he breathed his last? This boy was rounder in the face than Tom and with a smaller frame. But he had that same dark red hair that would shine in sunlight, a rare enough colour that it made you turn your head when you saw it. And his eyes, oh his eyes that beseeched me. They were darker, brown not green, but now everything about him reminded me of Tom. I felt helpless as he struggled to breathe. I wanted to stay with him and give what comfort I could even as I wanted to run from him and go and find my brother. I knew there was no point calling a doctor. They were all too busy and there was nothing to be done for this boy other than what I was doing, helping him breathe his last. It took perhaps fifteen minutes. He didn't speak again in that time but he held my hand, tightly at first, and then relaxed his grip until he closed his eyes for the last time, drew a breath in and held it there forever. I breathed out myself, as if it might start him breathing again. I sat for a few moments more, unable to move. Tom.

I put down the boy's hand and rushed up the stairs, two at a time, my heart thumping, my view clouded by tears, sadness and fear vying for dominance and both threatening to take me over at any time. For it had hit me, finally and fully, that this boy, this boy who had just died with a stranger as his only comfort, could have been my brother Tom. Oh Iris, you young fool, I thought. Your father was right. When will you learn?

I found Miss Ivens outside the theatre. Before I had a chance to speak, she told me that the electric lights were out again so they'd been using candles in the wards. 'We'll have to get the workmen back. We can't be working in the dark . . .'

I knew Miss Ivens had been operating through the night and that now she'd want me to come to morning rounds with her and then see to the office work. I took in her tired eyes, her slumped shoulders, but I knew also that I must speak. 'Miss Ivens, I need to go to Amiens. I need to find my brother and make sure he's all right.'

'What? What's happened, Iris?'

'Please, Miss Ivens. My brother Tom. He's just a boy. I don't know how I've missed . . . how I've gone so wrong. I had no idea. There's a lad downstairs with red hair.'

Just then Violet came along the corridor. She was wearing her goatskin coat and held her gloves in her hand. I don't think I've ever been as relieved to see someone. 'Violet, would you drive me to Amiens? It's Tom. We must find him.'

'Iris, has something happened? You're white as a sheet, darling.' Violet put her gloves down on the table and took my cold hands in hers and rubbed them.

'I was down in the hall. There was a boy. He looked just like Tom. Violet, it's terrible. I didn't know. We have to go and get him and bring him back here.'

Violet looked at me and narrowed her eyes and then she looked at Miss Ivens. 'It's all right, Frances. You have things to do. I'm going to take Iris to the refectory for a hot drink.' She smiled warmly at both of us. 'And then, with your permission, Frances, I do need to go to Creil and pick up some trays for Agnes. We could go on to Senlis, where there's a command post.'

'Go,' Miss Ivens said. She was about to say something more to me when our newest recruit Dr Henry came out of the theatre behind her.

'He's bleeding from the suture,' Dr Henry said. 'Come quick, Frances, I need help,' and she was gone.

Violet's version of a hot drink was something resembling tea that tasted foul and smelt of rum. She put more sugar in it when I complained and made me drink deeply. 'Breathe,' she said after I'd taken a few swallows. 'And then we'll talk.'

I felt the warm liquid pulse through me but it didn't dull my fear. 'We must go, Violet,' I said. 'We must find Tom.'

'First you need to try to calm down just a little, Iris. You have more colour now. So tell me what happened.'

I recounted the soldier's death as quickly as I could. 'Don't you see, Violet? He could have been Tom.'

'Well, no he couldn't. For a start, he's an infantryman in the French Army. Tom is with the British Engineers. They build things and then blow them up I think. That's all we know. And to speak plainly, Iris, if Tom were dead, your father would know and he would have made sure you knew too. Are you sure Tom's in Amiens?'

'No, but that's where we heard he was going and I've heard no more. I wrote him and I haven't heard back.' I looked at Violet. What she said didn't make sense. Why would I know if something had happened to Tom? No one seemed to know anything. He could be wounded, or worse. 'Why does everyone keep looking at me as if I've got two heads?'

'Because right at this moment, you're acting a bit that way.' She looked at me, took my hands in hers and rubbed them again. 'I understand you're worried about your brother. I understand it's been hard these last days, seeing what we've had to see. But you need to realise that what we can do is very small and we must go on doing that. Understand?'

I didn't but I nodded yes, willing to do or say anything if it meant Violet would take me to find Tom.

Grace

As she backed out of the driveway, Grace wound down the window and held up her pager and told Iris a lie. 'Just got to run home and call the hospital.'

She was already winding up the window when Iris said, 'I have a telephone, dear.'

She waved and continued backing out.

At home, she realised they'd forgotten to hang the morning's washing. It would be stinking in the machine. And the kitchen. You'd think a bunch of gorillas had got ready, not three children and their father. David was a good cook but the messiest person Grace had ever met. She started rinsing plates and stacking the dishwasher while she dialled his number, the phone nursed on her shoulder. Henry's blocks were strewn all over the living room. 'I'll just put you through,' David's new secretary – Naomi? Nerrida? – said.

'I dropped the kids with Iris,' Grace said when he came on the line. 'She found a possum this morning. Don't ask. When will you be home?'

'Late,' David said. 'I've got a case review at the Mater that's sure to run on. I was just heading there now.'

'Well, we won't get a chance to talk again then. David, I don't want to see Ian Gibson yet. I want to wait.'

'Why?'

'Beyond the fact Ian will think we're overreacting if nothing's wrong, we'll have unsettled Henry for no reason. He's a sensitive child. You know that. They'll run bloods and other tests he won't like. And if there is something wrong . . .'

'If there is something wrong, we might be able to correct it. I just can't understand you on this, Grace. We have to know.'

Grace couldn't quite understand herself either. 'I want to wait a bit longer.'

'No,' David said. 'I won't.'

'Let's talk about it tonight, then,' she said. Grace couldn't remember a time he'd done this, gone against her wishes about the children. 'Is there something you're not telling me?'

'No. No, of course not. But I want to find out what's going on. And I'm pretty sure something is. We'll talk tonight.'

By the time Grace joined them at Iris's, the two girls were out in the backyard, climbing the jacaranda tree. Iris was sitting at the table, peeling an apple, Henry sitting almost on top of her, watching the long curl of apple peel form itself. When Grace was little, Iris had sent her to school every day with pre-peeled apples or oranges. All Grace had to do was lift the long curl of peel and voila, there was the fruit ready to eat. And slices, Iris always made slices for Grace's lunchbox, lemon meringue, chocolate-coconut, napoleon. Grace couldn't remember the last time she'd made the kids' lunches, let alone including home-made slices. She'd never made a slice in her life.

Grace leant over and kissed Iris. 'I know I said I'd take the possum out to uni. But the vets there don't care for wildlife so I'm going to take it up to the Red Hill vets once I've called them.' She rubbed her forehead.

'He's fine, Grace. He just needs a rest and something to eat. He can stay here. Are you all right?'

Iris was so stubborn. 'I've been thinking. If you want to go to this Royaumont place, I could go with you.'

'I've been thinking too, dear, about what I need to do,' Iris said. 'I will see the doctor and make sure she doesn't think there's any problem. That's a good idea you had, to see the doctor. And then I'll get one of those shopping bags on wheels. You know the ones you can pull along? But I won't need you to come. So long as I don't take too much—'

Grace interrupted. 'You can't go by yourself. Let me come. We can go to Paris on the way.'

'Take café au lait at Les Deux Magots?' Iris smiled and ruffled Henry's hair and gave him a little squeeze.

Grace wondered how on earth Iris knew Les Deux Magots. Must be from a novel. 'Something like that.'

'I think I really am too old for Les Deux Magots,' Iris said. 'But I would love to see Royaumont once more before I die.'

'What's Royaumont?' Henry said.

'It was a place Granna worked during the war,' Grace said.

'Did you kill anyone?'

'No,' Iris said. 'We saved lives. I worked in a hospital, Henry, like where Mummy and Daddy work, but a hospital for wounded soldiers.'

'Did they kill anyone?'

'Henry,' Grace said. 'Let's not talk about killing. Granna was a nurse.' Henry looked puzzled then, as if he didn't know what to ask next now that killing was off the agenda.

'I saw Jennifer Bennetts today,' Grace said.

'Who's that, dear?'

'You remember. She was at All Hallows' with me.'

Iris shook her head.

'Yes you do. She and two others were mean to me. I changed schools because of it.' Iris was still shaking her head. 'Anyway, she said you wrote her mother. I never knew you did that. You told her mother all the things they did to me.' Iris nodded but didn't say anything. 'But you didn't tell me you did that. You told me I had to toughen up, that I shouldn't let three nasty girls get the better of me. And then you told her mother what they'd done to me. You took my side.' Grace felt tears in her eyes. She blinked them away.

Iris didn't answer immediately. She took Grace in, narrowed her eyes, and Grace wasn't sure if her grandmother didn't remember or didn't want to say she remembered. 'We all have to atone, Grace,' Iris said finally. 'No matter how long it takes, we all have to atone.' It was an unsatisfying answer but it seemed Iris wasn't willing to say more.

Now she was making a mess of the apple after all. The peel had broken and she was hacking into the side of the fruit without realising. Grace resisted the urge to take the knife from her and finish peeling the apple. The knife was an ancient thing. Iris had owned it as long as Grace could remember. It only had two attachments, a blade and a can opener. It was battered metal, silver in colour, not red enamel like the knife Grace bought when she went to Europe after she finished medicine. It didn't cut like Grace's knife either. The blade was so blunt you could run your finger along it.

On a camping trip when Grace was a teenager, she'd asked

Iris how long she'd had the knife. 'Since I was a girl,' Iris had said. 'It's been everywhere with me.'

'Where did you get it?'

'A friend gave it to me.'

'Who was that?' Grace had said, surprised she didn't know the story already. She thought she knew all Iris and Al's stories.

'Her name was Violet Heron. We were very great friends for a time. We were the flower bird girls.' Grace looked a question. 'Our names, Iris Crane and Violet Heron. The flower birds.'

'But where did she get the knife, Iris? I've never seen one like that.'

'A fellow gave it to her,' Iris had said, 'during the Great War.'

'So where is she now?'

'Dead,' Iris said. 'She was thinking of emigrating but she went back to England instead.'

'How did you meet her?' Grace had asked, still curious.

Iris had looked vague and said she couldn't remember. Then she said, 'Oh yes, through Al. We were still in Stanthorpe but he'd started back at the Mater ahead of moving to Brisbane. Violet worked at the hospital. Rose was just a baby.'

It hadn't made sense to Grace, even at the time. Iris had said she'd got the knife as a girl and then she'd said she'd got it when Rose was a baby. But Grace couldn't get more information from Iris, no matter how hard she tried. Iris just changed the subject. Whenever she saw the knife now, Grace remembered the way Iris answered questions. It was as if she wasn't telling the truth.

Grace went back into the house now and picked up the invitation. Violet Heron. That was the name inside, Dame

Violet Heron. This friend, Violet Heron, whom Iris said she'd met in Brisbane and who was supposedly dead, had not only been at a place called Royaumont during the First World War with Iris but was alive enough to speak at a reunion Iris was hell-bent on attending.

Grace went back outside with the invitation. 'That's the knife your friend Violet gave you,' Grace said, feeling triumphant finally.

Iris looked at the knife as if she'd only just learnt this. 'So it is,' she said.

'You also said you knew Violet Heron here in Australia.'

'Did I?'

'You did. And you told me she'd died. But she's the person on this invitation. Was she at Royaumont?'

'She was,' Iris said. 'I'm so muddle-headed.' She squeezed Henry again and smiled. Grace knew there was more to it. 'I'm like that muddle-headed wombat in your book, Henry. Come on, let's see if our biscuits are ready.'

Iris

Senlis was the last town taken by the Germans in September 1914, just before their failed assault on Paris. Many houses were still in ruins and we couldn't drive the streets because of the holes left by the bombs so we parked outside the town where soldiers had set up a barricade. We quickly found the command post, such as it was, a *tabac* converted for the purpose. A British soldier was standing at the counter. I went up to him. 'I'm looking for my brother Tom Crane who's with the Engineers up north,' I said. 'Can you help me?'

The soldier looked at me as if he thought I was mad. 'Calm down a minute,' he said, one hand raised. 'Now who are we looking for?' He looked at Violet.

'Hello there,' she said. 'I'm Violet Heron and this is my friend and colleague Iris Crane. Iris is quite worried about Tom and so we're looking to see if you have records of where soldiers are.'

'You don't want us,' the soldier said. 'We're just signallers. You need to go back to Chantilly. That's Command HQ now.

They've got more chance of finding your man. Else you can write to London. There's an office there finds soldiers.'

'He's in Amiens,' I said.

'He'll have been in the thick of it then,' the soldier said. Suddenly he looked worried and this more than anything frightened me. 'Really, all we do here is get advice from the French and pass it up to our officers.'

I felt faint and had to bend over and take a breath.

The young soldier was not unkind. 'I just can't help you,' he said to Violet. 'The Royal Engineers are everywhere. I can't find one. He might be in signals. He might be a sapper. I can't just find a fellow like that.' He clicked his fingers. 'But you girls really ought to get back a bit further behind the lines now,' he said. 'It's volatile at the moment. We're evacuating Senlis tonight.'

'Thank you anyway,' said Violet. 'Come, Iris, we must get away.'

I stood and followed Violet. We walked back outside. It had started to snow, just softly, tiny flakes that fell to the ground quickly. 'What now?' I said.

'Now we go back to Royaumont,' Violet said. 'And we don't delay.'

'No, Violet, we must find Tom first.'

'Iris, you need to get a hold of yourself. We will find Tom but it's going to take some time. There's just nothing you can do right now and we need to get out of here quickly. We'll wire Command HQ in Chantilly from Royaumont. We can even stop there on the way back if it's safe. I should have thought of that before.'

'I could have been finding him before this. Here I've been—'

Violet took me by the shoulders and shook me gently.

157

'You've been making an important contribution to a war hospital. There's no better thing to have done. There would be no Royaumont right at this moment without you. Do you understand that? Do you have any idea? I know you are worried about your brother. But your job right now, Iris, isn't to look after him. It's to stay at Royaumont, to get back there safely so you can keep doing what you're supposed to be doing. Are you on in the ward tonight again?'

I nodded yes. 'Are you sure we should just go back?' I said.

'Absolutely,' Violet said.

I wasn't convinced but knew there was nothing else to be done. As we headed for Violet's car, I continued to have an awful feeling of foreboding, a feeling that I had gone wrong now, so wrong, and nothing could make it right.

We were on the road to Chantilly, about three miles out of Senlis. The snow was still falling but the sun was out, it shone brightly on the white all around us, and Violet began to sing 'It's a Long Way to Tipperary', not a song I knew but as I listened to her beautiful voice I started to feel a little calmer. Violet had a quality in her singing voice I've never heard since, a warmth combined with a sadness that made the listener feel the song, in this case all the sad longing in the world for home, and yet feel at peace, almost happy about yearning.

We came upon a convoy of trucks heading in the opposite direction, back towards Senlis. We passed marching soldiers too, their ragged blue coats and muddy boots and hopeless faces telling a story. Before long, we were flagged down by a young French officer. 'What's your destination?' he asked us. Violet told him we needed to get back to Royaumont Hospital and might stop in Chantilly.

'You carry wounded?' he said.

'No. We've been in Senlis,' she said.

'You can't get through this road,' he said. 'The Germans are behind us. You'll have to go back.'

'Don't be ridiculous,' Violet said. 'This is an ambulance.'

'Tell that to the Kaiser. You can do as you wish. But we've been ordered back.'

Violet thanked the officer and drove on a while and then pulled off, stopping at the crossroads where she could turn around. 'We have to get back, Iris,' she said. 'What will we do?'

'He said the Germans are on the road in front.'

'But if we go back to Senlis and the line changes, we might be cut off for weeks. We need to think.' She tapped her fingers on the steering wheel. 'What about the forest road?' she said. 'The Germans can't be everywhere. Surely they'll keep to the main road. It's worth a try.'

'Can we can get there from here?' I said.

She nodded. 'This is the turn-off. It's the same road we walk on near Royaumont. I took it once to Senlis. It's a bit rough for a while but then we'll be back towards Royaumont. We need to get out of here, darling.'

Violet was right. Royaumont was already short-staffed. We must get back if at all possible. 'Go,' I said. 'We'll have to wire Chantilly when we get back.'

'Good girl,' Violet said. We turned right and drove towards the forest. For the first few miles, it was quiet and I felt we'd escaped the danger. We saw no other vehicles and I was relieved. Before too long though, we started to hear the guns, so much closer than they had ever been so far at Royaumont, where we'd heard only occasionally what sounded like distant thunder. I didn't know if the guns were from the Germans or the French but they were very loud. 'The fighting must be close,' I said.

'I suppose so,' Violet said. 'Here we go.' She put her foot down and we bumped along as quickly as we might.

We met no soldiers on our back road but the noise of the guns became louder and louder and so either it was getting closer or we were driving towards it or both. I started to feel a tight knot of fear in the pit of my stomach. We were driving into the Germans, I felt sure. Every bend became a nightmare. I expected to see a company of men marching towards us. It was my fault we were here, looking for Tom. I could see now what a mad quest it had been. But if we were captured, we would never return to Royaumont. It would be my fault.

'Oh goodness, Violet,' I said finally. 'I'm so sorry.'

'It's an adventure, Iris. We'll be all right,' she said. 'After all,' she grinned, 'we're women.' I couldn't help but laugh.

Suddenly Violet started singing 'It's a Long Way' again. She smiled across at me, encouraging me to sing along with her for the chorus. This I did and as we sang, Violet's beautiful voice, on that winter afternoon in the dark of the forest, the knot in the pit of my stomach unwound itself and I began to feel strangely safe. We drove into evening, the sky around us flashing white now, the noise of the guns sometimes closer, sometimes further away. Violet sat at the wheel peering ahead, not speaking. The road was terrible, and as we hit bump after bump I wondered if the car would fly apart. We slid around bends in the snow which was falling again now. I thought any minute a shell would hit us. In our favour, the road we were on was hidden by trees, but that just meant that whether we got hit or not would depend on pure luck.

At nightfall, we came upon the village of Baillon that we'd

visited once or twice on our walks from Royaumont in the early days. 'Can't be far now, Iris,' Violet said. 'But we should stop and rest.' No lights shone in any of the houses – they were in blackout – so we went to the first house at the edge of the village and knocked on the door. An older woman answered. I explained our situation.

'Royaumont,' the woman said and smiled warmly. 'You are the crazy Scottish women? Come in, quickly.'

It was a small house, kitchen and two bedrooms, and the woman was on her own with two children, her husband away fighting. I could see they had little food yet they shared what they had with us, a soup that made me think of home, wine and bread. The bombs continued through dinner. The woman jumped every time we heard a loud boom but the children played happily enough. Their father was a brave soldier, they told me.

The woman put Violet and me in the main bedroom and slept on the floor of her children's room. I tried to tell her we'd be fine on the floor but she insisted. Through the night the guns pounded. I thought of the children's father, somewhere out in the middle of it. I thought of my brother Tom. This was lunacy, pure lunacy.

Violet lay awake next to me. 'What's that you've got?' I said. She was gripping something in her fist.

'It's my knife,' she said. 'If they come near us, I swear, Iris, they can have me, but I'll kill every one of them if they try to touch you.'

I looked at the knife, glinting silver in the moonlight. Its tiny blade couldn't even kill a rabbit, I thought, let alone a troop of German soldiers. I laughed then, a picture in my mind of little Violet defending my honour against an army. 'I think they'll prefer you, Violet. I'm not much of a spoil of war.'

'I'm serious, Iris. I won't let them have you. I won't.' But she started laughing too, and then we were both giggling and for some minutes, we couldn't stop, releasing the tension of the day into the forest night.

Eventually our laughter subsided and we said goodnight. I fell into the easy sleep of one too young to know what danger she might be in.

But when I woke in the morning, all was quiet. I knew we weren't far from Royaumont. I woke Violet and we got up and dressed quickly. I made the bed.

We thanked our host – she tried to send us off with the rest of the bread and soup but I explained we were nearly home – and made the journey in perfect weather with nothing but the sound of birds for company, almost as if the terrible attacks of the night before had never happened.

As we pulled along the final drive to the abbey, I expected they'd be waiting, out of their heads with worry about where we were. But we didn't even have a welcome home when we returned. The fighting had led to more wounded than Royaumont could manage. The French had held at Senlis but not without human cost. Violet went off to the garages to grab her things and head to Creil and I went up to the ward. 'You're late,' was all Matron Todd said.

Grace

David was waiting for her just before ten in Ian Gibson's rooms in the private wing of the hospital where there was better carpet, softer lighting, nicer smells and more pleasant muzak than in the public. 'Where's Henry?' he said.

'I didn't bring him.'

'Oh for God's sake, Grace. How can you see a paediatrician without the child?' He was talking in a whisper so the receptionist, who was looking at them, wouldn't hear but it was a loud whisper because he was annoyed, so she probably heard anyway.

'I thought we could talk to Ian first and see what he thinks,' Grace said, without lowering her voice. 'We're both clinicians. We can describe the symptoms.'

'Not in paediatrics,' David said. 'This is crazy.'

'No it's not. I rang Ian and he said it would be fine. Unlike you, he actually understood how unsettling this would be for Henry.'

Just then the door to the office opened and Ian Gibson

came out. He was a small, slight man with a quiet, thoughtful nature and a playful side that only emerged when he was with children. He'd been there when Mia was born. With Phil, he was away and another paediatrician attended. Grace made sure Ian saw her as soon as he got back. He'd seen Henry too when they returned from Canada. Grace trusted him. Ian and David shook hands and turned it into a hug, slapping each other on the back. He went to embrace Grace but she'd already held out her hand to shake his and then realised and ended up putting her hand into his belly and fumbling from there to a clumsy hug.

'How are you both?' he said, gesturing them inside. They sat next to each other. He sat behind his desk, spotless except for a photo of his wife and four daughters and several small but thoughtful toys – a Lego truck, a top, a pull-along car and a puzzle.

'Good,' David said. 'You?'

'Fine,' he said, nodding. 'And Henry.' Not one for small talk. Grace had always liked that about him.

'We're a bit worried . . .' David started. 'He's three now and slower than the other two with his milestones.'

'I don't think that's quite right,' Grace said. 'He crawled earlier than both of the others. He was crawling at six months. I hardly think that's delayed. I think he's fine. You've seen him, Ian. He's just different.'

'He hasn't been here since he was one, I think, Grace, so that's quite a while.' He looked up at her. 'But if nothing's wrong, what are you doing here?'

'David?' Grace said.

'I don't agree he's fine, and I'm sorry that Grace and I are not together on this. I know it makes things tricky for you.

Henry gets exhausted from day care and can't stand up from a seated position sometimes. There's either something going on developmentally or in his musculature that's just wrong. It will need correction.'

Ian listened to them argue back and forth for a few minutes and then held up a hand to stop them. He said, 'David, nothing you've described is out of the ordinary necessarily.' Grace looked across at David as if to say, I told you so, until Ian added, 'But Grace, I can't tell you Henry's well until I see the boy himself. I do think we need to do that. I think David's right. If one parent is worried, especially where you're doctors, we need to rule some things out.'

'You think there's a problem?'

'Asking me that question is like asking whether you think there's a problem with a pregnancy after talking to the patient's husband.'

Grace said she wanted to give it another six months. 'He'll be four by then. Is that okay?'

Ian Gibson shook his head. 'I think you two need to decide this. It's not really for me to say. I'm happy to see Henry any time. I'm much better with his age group than yours, to be honest.' He smiled. 'Maybe sooner rather than later, though,' he said.

As they were walking out, Ian Gibson asked Grace if they had her medical history. 'I think so,' she said. 'I think I provided it when we brought Mia for a post-birth check.'

'Well, I know David's, so if I've got yours, all we need now is to see the boy himself. I'll look forward to it.'

Iris

I saw Tom this morning, out on the back verandah. He was about six, Daddy's face already showing through the simple youth of him, his long limbs and torso, the way he stood. I was beating the hall rug – I'd had Geoffrey lift it out there for me – and one minute Tom wasn't there and the next he was, standing by me, watching what I was doing. I was still the old woman I am now but also a girl, which made sense in the way it does in dreams, and Tom took my hand in his to pull me down beside him and he brushed my hair behind my ear and put his mouth close and whispered, 'There there, Iris,' like I might have done to him. He stood back and looked at me and smiled. 'Haven't we had a grand time of it? And aren't we the lucky ones?' he whispered again. And then he turned away from me, still smiling.

'Wait,' I said.

He turned back. 'Whatever do you mean, Iris?' A little laugh, a blink from me, and he was gone. All that was left was the rug and the lines of winter sun on the verandah.

It was Tom's child self that would come to me like this in the first days after I arrived home from Royaumont. His child self would come and we'd be back in our childhood together, sitting on the leather chair on the verandah at Risdon where we read stories, the smell of summer grass, his arms around my neck. When it would hit me that Tom was gone, that those little arms, those arms that had carefully grown their man's muscles and tendons and veins, would never move again, I would fall on the floor and hard bitter tears would come from me unbidden. I would hear noises, barely human, that were my own. They would pass, those fits of grief, and I'd move on in a fug until the next time I'd see him.

But after I saw him this morning, I've thought of Tom and they've been pleasant thoughts, a whole wasted day we had along the creek at Risdon. He would have been that six-year-old boy I saw. We caught tadpoles in a jar, I recall, and fought over whether we could take them home. They always died, I knew, but Tom refused to accept the fact. We happened upon a group of ducks that were sure we'd brought their lunch. They wouldn't leave us alone. Claire had made corned-beef and pickle sandwiches, Tom's favourite, and fruit cake for after. It was winter – do you remember, Tom? – and you were wearing that blue coat you wouldn't give up. You'd pulled the hood up over your head and you looked up and I thought of that picture of the monk, the one who died, and it sent a shiver down my spine. But the day was sweet and when I told you to take off the hood you did and the image was soon gone.

Having told Grace I'm going back to Royaumont, I can hardly not go and in truth it's not the journey that unnerves me. It's what I might find there. Life reaches a point where you no longer wish to dig about in the earth of the past to find what might have made you grow the way you have. Or how you might have been different. There's no going back at my age.

After he'd shifted the rug, Geoffrey told me I was looking tired. You'd be tired too if you had this little possum to care for Geoffrey, I said to him. Yes he supposed he would, he said. He said if I was travelling in November, I should make sure I bought some long underwear. He said a brand called Antagonia was the best – at least I think that's what he said – and I could buy them at a store he knew in the Valley. I'd never discussed underwear before, let alone with the postman, and I wasn't sure it was quite the right thing to do, even if Geoffrey was a friend. 'Have you travelled a lot, Geoffrey?' I said, thinking to change the subject. He was standing in the dining room, his little satchel over his shoulder, his hand resting on it, keeping the mail safe I liked to think.

'My nephews and nieces have travelled,' he said. 'But the long underwear's the ticket, Iris,' he persisted. He'd taken off his cap to move the rug and he looked quite different. Geoffrey has dark brown hair in the style of Adolf Hitler if he'd let it grow out a little, the same pasted-down, parted-at-the-side cut. He has a moustache too but kind eyes and shoulders that slope so severely they're nearly non-existent. He's not overweight but he's more or less pear-shaped, as if the base of him was always meant to be heavier than the apex. Geoffrey is young, no more than fifty, I'd think. He's never married and while I wouldn't say he lives for work, I'm not sure quite what he does live for. I asked him once was there anyone special and he said there had been once but it hadn't worked out. I waited in the hope he might say more but he stood there silently, hand on his mail satchel.

'Now that the possum's feeling better, he's too big for the box,' I said, hoping to move away from the subject of underwear. I started walking towards the front door, intending Geoffrey to follow. 'I think it will be time for him to survive on his own soon.'

'You'll miss him, Iris,' Geoffrey said. I nodded. 'But it will be cold over there come November,' he said. 'Might even snow.'

Certain he was planning to start on underwear again, I opened the door. 'Lovely of you to pop by, Geoffrey, but I really must get on with the day.'

'All right, Iris, I'll see you tomorrow.'

Geoffrey was right about one thing. I was tired. I'd been out early to see the doctor. She's a lovely young woman, Dr McKellar, and I was late for the appointment, having muddled the time before I called the taxi. The girl at the desk was rude, said since I was late I'd just have to wait for them to fit me in, but Dr McKellar called me as soon as she was free again. She always comes out with a big smile on her face, as if your visit is the highlight of her day. She does it for all her patients and she can't feel that happy about seeing everyone.

When we sat down, I told Dr McKellar about the trip. I didn't mention Grace's concerns. 'And what did you do there, Iris?' she said, still smiling. I must have looked confused. 'At the hospital in France, I mean,' she said, genuinely interested.

'I was assistant to the hospital's medical chief,' I said. 'I trained as a nurse.'

'I never knew that. Aren't you a marvel?' One of the other things I like about Dr McKellar is that she doesn't patronise me, and although her comment might sound patronising,

I can imagine her saying aren't you a marvel to any number of her patients, not just the octogenarians.

She picked up her stethoscope and began to fiddle with it. 'Iris, I'm not sure a long flight is a good idea,' she said. 'Your blood pressure's not great. And it's a long time to be in a depressurised environment.'

'What effect does that have?'

'That's a good question. We don't know exactly. But it's a change and we don't much like change. And your body's old. It's up to you. I'm just saying it's a lot of stress to put on your heart.'

As I was leaving, I asked Dr McKellar had Grace been in contact with her. She smiled sheepishly. 'As a matter of fact, she did call to let me know you'd be coming. I told her I'd need to be sure you wanted me to discuss your health with her before I could do that.'

'Did she tell you to say I shouldn't go?'

'Yes she did. But that's not why I'm saying it, Iris. I'm saying it because I think a trip like that would be an enormous load on your already tired body.' She stopped and smiled and looked at me. 'But it's up to you and if I were in your shoes, I'd probably want to go too.'

I had intended to tell Grace that the doctor hadn't been concerned at all about my travelling but now it would be difficult as Grace would probably check with Dr McKellar. I could imagine the pair of them talking about me, saying what a crackpot I was becoming, and difficult to manage. All the same, Dr McKellar's words had shaken me. I started to wonder if Grace was right after all, that the flight would be a risk. I phoned David at the hospital. The girl on the switch didn't know who I meant at first. I couldn't remember his last name but eventually we sorted it out. He's the only David in

170

perinatology, fortunately. Ravenswood, the girl said, I think you must mean Dr Ravenswood. Very well then, I'd said, still not sure. When I told him, David said it was funny I could remember the name of his discipline but not his surname.

I asked him if he knew what I'd need to do in order to travel. He said he'd be coming over to mow at the weekend and he'd find out before then. He asked me if I had a passport. I did, I said, but it would have expired in 1920, I thought. He laughed and said he'd phone someone in the government and find out what I needed to do but I should find my old passport if I still had it as that would be a good place to start. He didn't ask me why I hadn't asked Grace about all this and I didn't say but he and I both knew why and that neither of us would breathe a word to her. It was the only way, as far as I was concerned. She'd just fuss.

'David, the GP said she thought it might be unwise to travel,' I said.

'Why?'

'My blood pressure, I think, although I'm not sure.'

'Well, Iris, it's probably unwise to walk up to the shop every day too. And it's probably unwise to get excited about anything so maybe the kids shouldn't come over any more. But you won't live forever even if you do all the things that don't raise blood pressure. It's up to you but I think it would be very difficult to live safely at your age. Life's the hazard.'

I laughed. 'You make me feel marvellous, David.' I gave him the details from the invitation and asked him if he could wire for me and find out who else might be coming. 'And tell them I'll be there. Tell them I'll be there for certain.'

'I'll call them today,' he said.

* * *

171

After I rang off, I went into the bedroom and sat down on the floor and reached under the bed and pulled out the box I kept there. It had come from my mother's family. It was made of a dark wood inlaid with ivory and when I was a girl Daddy would bring it out to show Tom and me, telling us he'd killed an elephant to make the box. Even Tom didn't believe him. I used to try to feel with my eyes closed where the wood stopped and the ivory started but found I couldn't. I closed my eyes and ran my fingers over the box now, and found, to my surprise, that the two materials were quite different to the touch. In places there was a faint line where inlay met wood, and the ivory was cooler and smoother. It gave nothing back to my hand, as if it still felt the insult of its making.

I brushed off a layer of dust and opened up the lid of the box. It smelt musty, as if the possum had spent some time in there. On top was the little piece of damask I'd cut and hemmed from a serviette with a gravy stain that wouldn't scrub out. Under the damask was the stack of letters, the first envelope tattered in the corners, worn from its long journey across the world and since. My address, my old address, written in that elegant hand: *Iris Hogan (née Crane), Risdon, Warwick Road, outside Stanthorpe, Queensland, Australia.* I don't know how she got the address. I certainly didn't give it to her.

I remember when that first letter arrived it went to Risdon and Claire kept it until she saw me alone, handed it across the next time I was over with Rose to look after René and André. They'd been wild toddlers who'd grown into wild boys and Claire appreciated having someone to watch them while she ran errands. When I saw the handwriting on the envelope and knew the letter was from Violet, I felt a sharp stab. I waited to open the letter until I was home that night, Rose asleep, Al called out to a childbed.

I took the envelope from the box now and carefully slid out the two sheets of paper.

My dearest Iris,

It seems an age and I thought I'd write with news from this end, and hope to hear from you. I've settled on digs with two others. One is in her final year. Her name is Iris too, which is a funny coincidence, isn't it? The other one, Patsy, has been ill with a fever for a few weeks. It's just like having a live specimen the other two of us can work on, trying this and that cure, seeing how she responds. Perhaps if we manage not to kill her, we'll make good enough doctors after all.

I miss the girls at Royaumont. I miss the freedom most, I think. Now every day is filled with lectures and tutorials and study for the examinations which, although some way off, are going to be hard work, or so the teachers keep telling us with glee. I'd give my eye teeth for half a day of the boredom I used to complain about in the quiet times at R. Remember the afternoon we had cocktails at Asnières, and Cissy Hamilton's face when she saw us stumbling in for dinner? She was furious. I've never told you this but we were nearly sent home. It was only that they couldn't very well send you all the way back to Australia that they let us both off. You wouldn't think us grown-up women at all in some ways. I suppose we hardly acted grown up.

Frances has a fellow who calls on her, or so I've heard. She has a house in the country in France now, and spends a good part of the year there. That's where she met him. He's French. We don't see as much of her as you would have if you were here. When she's in Edinburgh, she has plenty of calls on her time. She has a group of doctors who she's training to take over her practice. Not me, though. She never comes to see me. I think she'll marry this fellow and move to France. What a lark, Ivey loose in France without you as an interpreter. Ha ha.

We had a lovely holiday near Cannes with Agnes Savill. You remember Agnes? She and Elsie Dalyell stayed on after the war and did some research in Vienna. Do you see Elsie at all? I hope you do. I hope you're happy, Iris, and wish you'd tell me.

I remain, yours sincerely,
Miss Flower Bird

Dr McKellar had told me I shouldn't go back to Royaumont because of my heart. I didn't say to her, I didn't even know until just now, that my heart was the very reason I had to go.

I'd been twenty minutes coaxing the stove in Blanche to life, only to walk away for half a minute and have the thing go out again. It was a special anthracite stove, the newest thing, hopeless compared to the old Kooka at home but supposedly good for warming our large wards. I couldn't get the correct amount of air inside to sustain the fire. It kept going out like this and as I'd let myself become the resident fire expert, they'd call me back to relight it. I had been to the Croix-Rouge offices in Paris often with Miss Ivens since the hospital opened but I hadn't seen the officer I'd met when the inspection team visited the abbey to accredit us at the beginning. I saw the name Jean-Michel Poulin on reports occasionally but I didn't see Jean-Michel Poulin himself and found myself disappointed each time I returned from Paris on the train. I didn't mention this to anyone, least of all Violet, who had teased me for weeks after the inspection, even implying to Miss Ivens that the officer had been sweet on me and that's what led to such a positive report. By the end of February, the Croix-Rouge were so impressed with Royaumont that they were asking us to open more wards. This we did, using not only the rooms we'd originally intended on the second floor – our Elsie Inglis ward – but also the monks' guest hall down on the first floor's west wing. During the winter, we had used it as a general storeroom but now, as our Queen Mary ward, it would provide an extra fifty beds.

'You've a visitor, Iris,' Quoyle said, and at first I confess I wondered if it might be him, Jean-Michel Poulin, although I knew that would be ridiculous. 'An Australian,' she said. 'A handsome one.'

I threw the lump of anthracite I was holding into the little stove and ran to Miss Quoyle and kissed her. Then I rushed from the ward, took the stairs two at a time and heard her yelling behind me, 'In the cloisters, dear.' I'm sure she thought me fresh. I couldn't have cared less. I went outside without coat or hat. There was no one in sight. I looked left and right. No one. And then he emerged from behind the pillar right in front of me. A sound came from me and my heart thumped against my ribs.

It was Tom, all right, as large as life. Taller, thinner about the face perhaps, looking more man than boy in the greatcoat, but with Tom's grin and eyes. 'Jesus, Iris, you'll crush me.' I had my arms around him without even realising I'd put them there. The smell was his smell, his oily sweet apple smell, but he was a good two inches taller than me now. He'd started shaving; I could see the shadow on his face and I felt the roughness when we embraced. He'd stretched into manhood and I'd missed it.

'Oh Tom,' I sighed, wiping tears from my cheeks.

'Hell, Iris, what's the matter with you?' he said, holding me at arm's length, smiling, which only set me off again. I couldn't tell him what I'd feared, could only look into his face and cry. He hugged me close then, held on as I sobbed.

Violet and I had sent the wire to Chantilly when we returned from Senlis. A sergeant at the new Allied Command Headquarters had wired back that they'd do their best to locate Tom. And then I'd waited. I'd told myself I mustn't worry, but my dreams were full of fear. Many of the women knew I had a young brother who'd gone to war. Others had brothers or cousins who were fighting too, though none as young as Tom. I looked at the way they went on regardless of the danger their own relatives were in, and I wanted to be as brave as they were.

Tom took my arms from around his neck and looked at me and smiled but when I tried to smile back, I just cried again. Orderlies walked past, each carrying a lump of anthracite for the stoves, and Mrs Berry, who looked as if she wanted to speak to me but smiled and kept going instead. News of my visitor would be all around Royaumont within the hour.

'I hadn't heard,' I sniffed. 'I thought . . . I don't know what I thought. Are you all right?'

''Course I'm all right,' Tom said, noticing the glances and smiles from my colleagues. 'I got your letter, Iris. I was going to write and then my captain said a mad young woman had gone to Senlis when they were under attack, looking for me, and that sounded pretty familiar – the mad young woman bit. I think you saw a corporal there. He was pretty worried about you apparently. Anyway, he asked if the captain knew me. The captain asked had I upset a young redhead. I thought I'd better come and find you.' It was Tom's slow drawl, though his voice was nearly as deep as Daddy's now. 'You know what happens? The letters go to England and then come back here. It's still pretty quick, considering. What about this place, Iris? It's a palace. God, it's good to see you.'

Eventually I stopped crying. 'Are you well, Tom?' I said, holding on to both his hands.

'I'm grand,' he said. 'I'm a proper soldier.' He grabbed at his hat to show me. 'A British soldier, can you believe it?'

'But where are you?'

'I'm just at Chantilly. I'm with the post office, believe it or not.'

'The post office?'

'Officially the Royal Engineers – Special Reserve, Postal Section. We do the mail for all the soldiers.'

'You're safe.'

'Safest job in the war,' he said. 'I work out from the lists where the soldiers are then sort the mail into bags. And soon I might even get to deliver it. You're the most popular bloke around if you're bringing letters from home.'

'When we didn't hear, I thought . . .' I didn't go on for fear I'd start crying again. 'Come in and we'll have a drink.'

He followed me inside and we went into the staff dining room – the monks' refectory – where we kept a pot of hot tea. I made Tom's tea, half milk and three sugars, and black for myself. We sat down at one of the long tables. Tom had taken off his hat when we went inside and with that mess of dark red curly hair he looked more like the boy he'd been when I last saw him.

He told me about his boat trip to England, and signing up with the Engineers. 'When I got here to France, I was supposed to be going up to Amiens, with an infantry company. At that time I didn't know the battles from the bush. But one of the officers asked me what work I'd done back home. I said I'd been a postie, not knowing that's what I'd end up doing.'

'But that's a lie, Tom.'

'Not completely. Remember last Christmas I delivered the post?'

'For two weeks, and you only carried the extra for Garth.'

'Well, I had to say something. He asked me how old I was anyway, the bugger. I said I was nineteen and he asked me was I sure. No one else had doubted me, not in Sydney, not on the ship. I told him I was and he sat there a while just looking at me.

'There was another bloke with him, Captain Driscoll, who was recruiting for his own unit, the postal unit that is, and he said to the first bloke, just put him in with me. Turns out there's quite a few of us in Captain Driscoll's unit who aren't nineteen. He has a thing about it. I don't mind, other than I feel a bit useless. The unit's mostly made up of retired posties and some of the old blokes look at me and I know what they're thinking. The blokes I came across with, they're in the thick of things. And I'm sorting bloody mail,' he said.

I wasn't listening to Tom. I was elated. Tom was safe. If I could have met right then that wise Captain Driscoll who gave my little brother a safe job, I'd have thanked him with all my heart.

When we'd finished our tea I grabbed my coat and scarf and we went back outside. We walked across the abbey grounds.

It was a fine clear afternoon. I showed Tom the remaining stones that marked the outline of where the church had been. I'd read the abbey's history now. Royaumont was completed in the thirteenth century for Louis IX as his summer palace. During construction, the sixteen-year-old king visited each day to work with the stonemasons and monks. He'd kneel down with them and pray so that God would reside in the very walls they were building. 'King Louis was about your age when he built this,' I told Tom. The abbey's church, more ambitious in design than any that had been built before, was demolished during the French Revolution. The abbey was sold to a cotton miller who installed the paddlewheel for the mill. After the miller moved out, the Sisters of the Holy Family of Bordeaux planned to establish a novitiate but the nuns too gave up and sold the abbey to M Gouin's family. 'And M Gouin donated the abbey to us.'

I told Tom all about Miss Ivens and the other women. 'At first I thought we couldn't do it. You should have seen the place, Tom. And some of them don't have a lick of sense. But we have done it,' I said. 'Miss Ivens is the most marvellous person. She has a way of believing in you that makes you think you can do anything. The British Red Cross didn't want anything to do with us but the French jumped at the chance. I can hardly believe it.'

We had walked across into the forest. The leafless trees made lovely forms against the blue of the sky. It was late already, the light fading into evening.

'It's great you came over,' Tom said. 'We'll never forget it, you know. It will make us.' It was strange to hear Tom talking so seriously. I was always the more serious when we were younger.

I didn't tell Tom I'd come to France to take him home. I didn't want to scare him off. Not yet, I told myself. We'd been asked to extend the hospital, which would mean creating new wards and recruiting more staff. Miss Ivens would need me there. At any rate, I thought, the war would be over soon. Tom was safe in the postal service so we may as well stay.

'How's the old man?' Tom said then, looking me in the eye, not with defiance, as I might have expected, but with fear.

'Has he written you?' I asked softly.

'Only about ten times, telling me to come home.'

I chose my words carefully. 'He's frightened. I'll write and tell him I've seen you and you're in a safe job. He'll come round.' But even as I said it, I doubted its truth. *You've no idea what you've done, Iris.*

We'd walked for two hours and hardly noticed the time but soon darkness would be upon us. 'We should get back,' I said. 'I'm on nights.'

We came out of the forest and onto the road that would take us back to the abbey. Before long I heard a motor. It was Violet in her ambulance. She tooted and blew me a gloved kiss and pulled up a few yards down the road. 'Who's he?' Tom said, looking put out by the familiarity.

'She,' I said. 'Violet Heron. I told you about her. She's my friend. Come on, we'll grab a lift.'

Violet was dressed in a wool coat and her long pants and boots. She wore a leather cap and goggles and gloves against the cold. 'Hullo,' she called as she jumped down from the ambulance. 'Want a ride, honey?' She pulled off a glove and offered her hand to Tom. 'I'm Violet,' she said. 'You must be Tom.' She turned to me and smiled. 'You found him, darling!' I nodded, grinning.

'I am Tom,' he said. 'But how did you know?'

'Iris doesn't have time for a suitor. She's mentioned her handsome brother.' Violet pulled up her goggles. 'She wasn't kidding. You can sit by me, sweetie.'

Tom blushed. 'She's mentioned you too,' he managed to say.

'Want a lift?'

'Rather walk,' he said, clearly annoyed at himself for being embarrassed.

'Forget it, Tom,' I said. 'It will be freezing in about half an hour. Violet's saved our bacon.'

'Can you take me to the station then?' Tom said. 'There's a train back at six.'

'Of course,' Violet said. 'Iris, I've just been to Creil. They say we'll have another rush. The word "imminent" was used.' After the first busy time when the hospital opened, we'd had a lull. Now, it seemed, we'd be back to double shifts. But even the prospect of days and days without rest couldn't take the shine off my day right then.

We climbed into the car, me in front, Tom on one of the benches in back. Violet started up and set off along the track. 'Iris tells me she's going to send you home,' she called back to Tom.

I turned around to see him glaring at me. 'Is that true?' he said with fierceness in his eyes.

'I told you Daddy was worried,' I said. 'And so was I until I saw you.'

'But is it true?'

'Yes,' I said. 'Yes, I'm supposed to take you home.' Oh Violet, I thought, I wish you hadn't said anything.

'I don't want to go. I won't,' he said, sounding like he had as a child of six, refusing to go to school if I didn't sit in his classroom.

181

'Oh pet,' Violet said. 'Aren't you a baby boy? I told Iris she should let you stay. But now I think she ought to take you home and put you into bed. You might need a little nap.' She glanced over my way, a little smile on her face. I shook my head slightly to try to get her to stop but I don't think she noticed.

Tom was embarrassed again and it made him angry. 'This is none of your business,' he said to Violet.

'Tom, that's enough,' I said.

'No, he's right, it's not my business,' Violet said. 'But, Tom, you had your sister worried as heck a week ago. And it's jolly rude to be angry at her when she's only trying to look after you.' Violet turned around and looked at Tom. 'You're just a boy, that's the truth of it. She's right. You should be home and in school.'

We arrived at the station and Tom jumped out. Violet wished him well. He didn't respond and I got out and gave him a hug. 'Don't mind Violet,' I said. 'I've been very worried about you, and she's just upset for me. She really is very nice.'

'She doesn't act it,' he said. 'I'm not a baby.'

''Course not. You're taller than me now!' He smiled then and we hugged again. 'Stay safe, Tom.'

'You too, sis.'

I thought I might cry so I turned and got back into the car without watching him walk into the station.

On the way back to Royaumont, I told Violet about Tom being with the postal service. 'But I really wish you hadn't teased him,' I said.

'Why?' Violet said. 'I thought he was a bit rude to you to be honest.'

'He's already said he doesn't feel he's doing enough. He wants to go and fight.'

182

'And you think that because I teased him a little he might actually do that?' Violet looked at me, incredulous.

'No . . . Yes, I do think that. He's always been a bit sensitive and you treated him like a baby.'

'He acted like a baby.' She smiled. 'He was furious with me though, wasn't he? He's actually rather sweet when he's angry.'

'I think you were thoughtless and callow if you want to know,' I said. My voice faltered as I said it. Daddy had been so worried about Tom and now today I had found out he was as safe as he could be. I didn't want him getting in harm's way just to prove himself.

Violet pulled over to the side of the road. She turned to me, looking contrite now. 'I'm so sorry, Iris, dear. I didn't realise you were so worried. He's in the postal service. He's ended up with the only officer in the British Army who seems to understand it's a mistake to make children fight in a war. That's great news, wouldn't you say?'

'Yes, it is,' I said. 'I just want to keep it that way.'

'So do I. I'll be a good Violet from now on. And to celebrate our finding Tom safe and snug, I am going to buy you a drink.'

Violet turned off the road back to the abbey and took us to Asnières. She jumped down from the car and marched into the bar with me in tow. She greeted the woman behind the counter as if they were old friends and ordered champagne with cognac, sugar and lemon. After we got our drinks – in beautiful long-stemmed glasses – we sat at a little table in the window. 'To the war,' Violet said, clinking hers against mine, and then, leaning in, more quietly, 'may it never end.'

'Violet,' I said. I was still angry with her.

'Ah,' she said. 'I'm just having fun. I don't mean the war's fun. I mean, all of this, you and Frances and Royaumont. We'll look back on this and wonder if it was all true.' I could see she'd forgotten completely about what she'd done with Tom.

I took a sip of my drink and it was delicious, going down my throat smoothly and making my middle feel it had a flame under it. The woman behind the bar looked at us as if we were naughty children. 'Good stuff,' Violet said to her, and ordered a second round. Before too long, I was feeling quite light-headed and merry, relieved to have found Tom safe, happy in truth that I could stay at Royaumont.

'So, Iris, tell me about the men in your life.' Violet looked at me, a wicked smile on her face. 'Not counting the baby brother.'

Violet was never afraid to ask embarrassing questions. She'd taken a lover too, she'd told me. More than one, in fact. It wasn't all it was cracked up to be, she'd said, a lot of fuss and noise. Afterwards is nice, she said, when you're all soft and gooey-eyed. I'd smiled and nodded, as if I too knew the feeling, relieved when we were interrupted in our conversation by Cicely wanting me to find a letter Miss Ivens had mislaid. But as Violet had spoken, I'd had the same feeling I had when she talked so offhandedly about her family, as if it was all so unimportant, when somehow it mattered a great deal. Still, I was fascinated by how much she knew about men.

'Violet, why is it that whenever you talk about your men, you look sort of sad?' I said now, without answering her question about the men in my life. Al. Al was the men in my life. He seemed uninteresting compared with Violet's stories.

'I do not,' she said casually. 'My eyes may glisten with the fond memory of love. That's all.' I could see she was forcing the smile.

'But what's it like to have a lover?' I said.

184

'Don't you know, Iris? Haven't you ever?'

'I'm engaged to be married,' I stammered.

'Don't tell me. He's a boy you grew up with from the farm next door. A great big farmer and you'll have twenty-five children and call them all after dead people.'

'As a matter of fact, he's a doctor at the hospital in Brisbane.'

'Even better,' Violet said. 'You're a nurse. He's a doctor.'

'What's wrong with that?'

'You can spend your whole life doing what you're told.'

'Well, at least I'll be happy.' I felt hurt by what Violet had said.

'Will you?' Violet said. 'Will you really? I don't know, Iris. I can't say I know what makes people happy.' She looked wistful.

'Finding out Tom's safe. That makes me happy,' I said. 'I'm sorry I snapped at you before. It's just that Tom's so young and I've always looked out for him.'

'It doesn't matter,' she said. 'Let's forget about silly old Tom. We're the flower bird girls. Let's flit.' She downed the rest of her drink in one go and got up. I remained sitting there looking out on the country night. 'Seriously, Iris, we'd better get back. You're on duty and I bet Creil is beckoning. Cicely will have our heads as it is.' She took my arm and pulled me up out of my chair. 'You're a good friend, Iris. I'm glad you came to Royaumont. It would be awfully dull without you.'

'I love you, Violet,' I said and hugged her clumsily. The words had come out before I'd thought about them. When I'd first met Violet, I'd seen her as so sophisticated, so experienced in the world. But right then, I wanted to take her in my arms and tell her we would all be all right. There was something wounded about Violet, I realised, something she was at pains to hide.

We drove back to Royaumont in falling snow, singing our hearts out. I laughed so much my stomach hurt. Tom was safe. I could stay and help Miss Ivens and the women of Royaumont. I couldn't think of a thing that would make life better.

I was still sitting on the floor of my room, the letter from Violet in my hand. What was I doing here? David, I'd been on the telephone to David and then I'd come to find my passport. I looked at Violet's letter. *Do you see Elsie at all?* she'd written. Violet really had no idea. Elsie Dalyell had been our bacteriologist at Royaumont and the only Australian other than me, although Dr Lilian Cooper, who trained in England before moving to Australia, served in one of our Serbian units. Dr Dalyell and I weren't particularly close at Royaumont. Like most of the doctors, she didn't socialise with nurses. After Vienna though, she came home to Australia and worked in Sydney in the public service. She wrote me a couple of times, perhaps after what happened, but I didn't respond. When Al and I went to Sydney I'd thought to look Elsie up but I never did. I never looked any of them up. I couldn't stand the thought of looking back like that. I could only look forward.

Underneath that first letter were all the others. I hadn't looked at them in over fifty years. I'd thought I might go through them now but found that after all I couldn't bring myself to go any further.

Years after the war, I remembered, Vera Collum wrote me. She'd been an orderly at Royaumont who trained as a radiographer and later studied medicine. She wanted my advice, about Violet of all people. Collum was worried, she wrote.

She's not like the girl we knew any more. I can't put my finger on the difference and say, there, that's what's wrong, but do you remember how Violet was friends with everyone? She had that special skill of making you feel right at home.

When any of us gets to see her now – and it's rare that we do – it's as if she's not there, Iris, as if that strong girl has fled her and left nothing but a shell. I sat in on a consultation with her. She'd asked me to give an opinion. There was a growth and the woman won't see another summer. Violet knew this, I am sure. But she was inexplicably cold to the woman, cruel in the circumstances, and when I tried to talk to her about it she looked away from me and I could see tears come into her eyes. It was a puzzle and I thought that if any of us could help Violet, it would be you.

If any of us could help, it would be you. These people had no idea. Rose was fourteen when I received Collum's letter. Violet could be tough, I thought. Collum just didn't understand that.

I took out the bundle of letters and papers and found my passport and put it aside. As I was putting the sheaf of papers back a photograph fell out onto the floor. I picked it up. A group of women standing in front of a truck in the snow, thick overcoats, gloves, boots, all smiling. One of them is me, I realise, but I don't remember the photograph being taken. And while I peer at her from less than an inch away from her face, I don't remember her either, the girl I was at Royaumont. There she is, all the same, at Miss Ivens's side, standing in front of the lorry she's just managed to buy, legs slightly apart, head held high, as if someone has just told her to stand up straight. They needn't have bothered. Miss Ivens and the girl tower over their colleagues, Marjorie Starr, when I look closely, and Cicely Hamilton. There they are, the chief and her assistant, pleased with their latest acquisition.

Until the end of our first winter at Royaumont, the drivers had had to drive to Creil to collect loads of coal for the stoves in their ambulances. They would make the journey, only twelve miles, but the road deteriorated as time went on and they couldn't drive quickly. They'd return with as much as they could carry, enough for a day for just one of the five stoves. I suggested we needed a lorry to carry things back and forth and Miss Ivens agreed so I drafted a request for her to the committee in Edinburgh for funds. A week later, I found a lorry for sale in Chantilly. I asked Tom to look it over for me. He sent a message back: *Buy it. It's a beauty.* I sent the request for funds which was referred to the equipment committee in Edinburgh but they responded by wire that it was too expensive and we probably didn't need a lorry anyway.

Around this time, we were also in trouble with Edinburgh about uniforms for the doctors. The uniform committee was chaired by a Miss McIntosh, an elderly woman who had donated more money than anyone else to the cause so far. Her committee had designed uniforms for the doctors in a dark grey flannel with tartan facings and then sent material and patterns to a seamstress in Paris. Miss Ivens had taken one look at the design and material and instructed the seamstress to make blankets for the staff from the grey flannel, telling Miss McIntosh by wire that we needed blankets more than we needed baggy suits. She'd already engaged Nicol of Paris, she said, who wasn't charging as much, incidentally, to design more suitable uniforms. 'If they think my doctors and I are going down to Paris in that hideous flannel, they can jolly well forget it,' she said to me. 'And I'll be damned if we will wear tartan.' Miss Ivens was given to swearing when she was annoyed.

While Miss Ivens's Paris tailor ran up the new uniforms – light grey twill with red velvet *caducées* in the lapel and a heavy dark blue for winter – we received a wire. Miss Ivens didn't mention it to me at first but kept picking it up and throwing it down as if this might make it go away while we went through the correspondence. Eventually, realising it wasn't going away, she passed it over to me. 'Damn them to hell,' she said. 'As if any of this matters. Now that stupid woman has dragged Elsie into it.'

The wire was from Dr Inglis, the Association's president.

'NAVY BLUE DEFINITELY NOT APPROVED STOP,' it read. 'PLEASE USE GREY WITH TARTAN AS AGREED STOP'

'Leave it with me,' I said. 'I'll do what I can.' Miss Ivens went off on her rounds. As I sat there looking at the telegram, it occurred to me that Miss McIntosh, the uniform committee chair, might be in a position to help us with procuring the lorry we so badly needed.

I found Violet and told her my idea. 'What if we write to Miss McIntosh that we're getting the uniforms made and then tell her the trouble we're having with the lorry and ask for her help?'

'Oh yes,' Violet said. 'And it's not really an untruth. We *are* getting the uniforms made, just not her uniforms.'

'Excellent, Miss Flower Bird,' I said. 'Should we tell Miss Ivens?'

'Oh God, no,' Violet said. 'What the chief doesn't know . . .'

'The chief doesn't know.'

'Exactly.'

Miss McIntosh did better than intervening with the equipments committee on our behalf; she funded the lorry herself. I felt a little bad that I'd lied to her, even though she was in her seventies and unlikely to come to Royaumont and see that her uniforms had never materialised. Violet assured me we were doing a small wrong in order to do a large right. Miss Ivens, who knew nothing of the scheme, said she'd send me to Edinburgh next time to negotiate her annual budget.

The lorry could carry five times as much coal as one ambulance. As for the uniform, by the time Dr Inglis came to visit us again, the doctors were already clothed in grey twill the Paris tailor had made and the nurses in plain white with blue trim, red for the sisters. The drivers wore no uniform at all. They got about in men's pants and shirts and whatever else was comfortable and clean. In truth, we were so busy during the rushes that no one had any time to notice whether we were wearing official uniforms or not. Most of us hardly had time for sleep. What we wore was the least important thing in our lives.

I looked at the photograph again, those strange women bursting out of the snow in front of the lorry. Even in the greatcoat, you can see my youth in my slim legs and face. I was so young, I tell myself now. I was twenty-one, only recently farewelled by childhood, although at the time childhood seemed like ancient history. I was so young, with so little experience of the world. How could I have taken so long to see that, to understand that I was not my brother's keeper, that I was simply a child who had made an adult decision? 'Oh Tom,' I said to myself now. 'I loved you so.'

* * *

Early one evening in March, we heard a loud buzzing overhead and switched off all the lights in the abbey. Violet was out in her ambulance, she told me later, thankfully not with a full load of wounded. When she heard what she thought must be enemy planes, she pulled over on the side of that treacherous road between Creil and Royaumont and waited.

I'd been in the kitchen lighting the stove – I remained the resident expert. I gave the order to turn out all the lights and lamps and then I walked out into the cold, no hat or coat, and saw, far above me in the winter sky, the two zeppelins. They seemed such jolly machines I almost waved, relieved it wasn't planes from Germany come to drop their bombs. We later learnt the zeppelins were just as deadly. They went on to bomb Paris.

They could have bombed Royaumont just as easily, Quoyle said the next morning when we were in the kitchen making up the order for supplies.

'Why ever would they do that?' Cicely Hamilton said. 'We're not a target, Quoyle. We're a hospital.' Cicely didn't much like Miss Quoyle, who was close to Miss Ivens.

'Seems to me everything's a target,' Quoyle said. 'I don't like it.'

'Dissatisfaction registered,' Cicely said. She'd taken to wearing a beret on the side of her head, for suffrage Quoyle had told me. The beret was too far to the side, though. It looked as if it might fall off. I wondered if she'd pinned it there.

Despite Cicely's cavalier attitude about the bombs, we became more cautious. The front was now just twenty-five miles from Royaumont; sometimes we heard the guns, and the drivers found shell holes along the road to Creil. We realised that while we all felt safe within the abbey's cradling walls, we would not be immune to the bombs of the Germans. Soon after the zeppelins flew over, we started blackout drills.

Tom came to visit me again that week. He walked from Chantilly and went to the kitchens where Quoyle had just finished making custard for the patients. He had a dog with him, a stray he'd found, a pretty little spaniel with no brains at all, and he asked Quoyle if the dog could stay at the hospital as he wasn't allowed to have a pet in his unit. When I came in, summoned by one of the orderlies, Quoyle had put out a large bowl of the custard with a pile of biscuits for Tom and a bowl of water for the dog. Tom was sitting at the counter, eating happily, listening to Quoyle's various complaints. The dog, for its part, was lying in front of the stove. 'Bingo's his name,' Tom said when I asked. 'He's your new dog.'

When I objected to the custard and biscuits she'd served up for Tom – the staff weren't fed like this – Quoyle simply said a man had to eat. And as for the dog, Quoyle said it would cheer the poor patients.

'"A man has to eat",' I said to Tom as we walked over to the stables. 'How come you always charm people like that?'

'I don't do anything.' He grinned. 'It's just my nature, Iris. They see how nice I am.' An affable chap, Tom's school reports always said, but without drive or motivation. *Charming, by all accounts, but one wonders how far charm can take him*, his latest had said. Well, it had taken him all the way to France and hot custard and biscuits.

I punched his arm. 'I'd have liked some custard too.' Until the abbey vegetable gardens produced, we were restricted to what supplies we could get and the patients always came first. I felt like I'd eaten nothing but bread and soup my whole life. 'And what do you expect us to do with a dog?'

'It can be the hospital mascot,' he said. 'I have a cat too, in my room, and a couple of birds, but my officers don't know about them. There's strays everywhere, pets whose owners have gone.'

We walked together in the grounds, taking a seat in the cloisters near the little fountain that had thawed out now and chattered happily all day. It wasn't sunny so we had no patients out in the cloister but it was warm and the rain was holding off. I told Tom things had settled with Edinburgh somewhat – the committee was always complaining about our equipment orders.

'How they expect us to run a hospital without wound dressings is beyond me,' I said. 'Even beds for staff have been slow to arrive. I'm sleeping on the floor this week.' We'd been told extra beds for the new staff were on their way across the Channel only to learn they'd not even been paid for and would be another three weeks. Meantime the patients' beds, which had been bought as cheaply as possible, were falling apart. Miss Ivens, never one to let a patient suffer, would be the first to give up her own bed for a patient. So I'd give mine up to Miss Ivens and share with Violet again but then Miss Ivens would give mine away to a patient too and someone else would offer her theirs, until none of us had beds again.

Tom had become very quiet as I spoke. 'Are you all right?' I said finally.

He took my hand. 'Iris, I have to tell you something.'

'What is it, Tom?'

'I've been up to the north this past week. Captain Driscoll said I could do a mail run up there. I thought it would be fun, visiting the blokes, bringing their mail. I went in a truck with some other posties, got dropped off near the companies I had to deliver to.' Tom had become very still. He was staring at the water in the fountain, as if it had something to tell him. He gripped my hand tightly. 'Iris, if you could see what it's like . . . They live in these holes they dig in the ground. It was quiet when I was there but at any time the big guns might start firing on them, from the other side, or even from their own side when they get the calculations wrong, one young bloke told me. They just get blown up. They never know when it will happen. They're just so brave. I really want to go up and help them. If you could talk to Captain Driscoll, I'm sure he'd let me.'

I knew I had to respond carefully, not bring up Tom's youth, which would only make him feel more strongly he should be fighting. I kept hold of his hand. 'I can understand how you feel. I really can. It's helplessness. I feel it too.' Soldiers had told us stories about the conditions they fought in and we saw the state of them when they arrived at Royaumont, wet dirty uniforms, dreadful infections and their feet were often in a terrible state from standing in water. 'We do what we can at Royaumont but for every soldier we save, hundreds die, some for want of the most basic care. But what you're doing, although it doesn't seem much, *is* important. When you gave them mail, were they happy?'

Tom nodded. 'They sure were, poor bastards.' He cheered a little then. 'I suppose you're right. At least we're doing something.' He took away his hand. 'You can't keep me under your thumb forever.'

I was going to argue with him but stopped myself. 'Just until you reach your majority,' I said lightly. 'Then you're out on your ear.' Tom wanted to do more than just deliver mail, I could tell. And I had an idea of just what that could be. 'Come, let's go over to the garages and see if we can make use of you.'

We walked across the lawns and found two of the drivers in the garages. I introduced Tom – 'My brother's a mechanic,' I said, and asked them if they needed any work done on their cars.

'We do them ourselves,' Kathleen Parnell said, eyeing Tom. She was a surly girl from Liverpool and had been involved in the Cause before the war, Violet had told me. 'We don't need a man to tell us how to fix a car,' she said now. She showed us her hands, covered in dirt and grease. The two girls left the stables soon after, as if Tom brought some sort of illness with him. Oh dear, I thought. This hadn't been what I'd wanted at all. It would only make Tom feel even worse.

'You can fix my car.' Violet emerged from the little kitchen we'd set up for the drivers. 'Tom, it's you. How are you?' She took him lightly in her arms and kissed each of his cheeks in the French way, her eyes on me, letting me know she was going to make up for their first meeting. I beamed at her.

She was wearing her goatskin coat. Most of the drivers had put their furs away in favour of woollen greatcoats now for the spring, but Violet felt the cold and held on to the warmer coat. It made her look like a little round bear. She must have just come in. 'You look the part at least,' Tom said.

'What part is that, dear?' she said.

'Aren't you all suffragists out here? That's what the fellows in Creil told me. "Don't cross the Royaumont chauffeuses."' He softened his voice. 'When I met those first two, I was pretty sure the chaps were right. But you're more difficult to work out.' He grinned.

'You have it in one,' said Violet. 'I'm a suffragist and we wear the skins of animals and sacrifice the male of the species at the full moon. Which is this week, my friend. Come look under my hood. There's a rattle.'

'A rattle,' Tom said. 'Is that a mechanical term?'

'Yes,' Violet said. 'A mechanical term. Come on now.' She took his hand and led him across the garages to her car. I was grateful to Violet then, for I knew the more useful Tom felt, the less he'd think about trying to get among the fighting. And Tom – well, any man really – seemed to brighten Violet's day, which needed brightening. It wasn't easy driving to and from Creil and seeing what she had to see.

I left Violet and Tom to their machine and went to the office to go through Miss Ivens's mail – she hadn't had time this week and there were sure to be urgent matters to attend to. I approved expenditure on new X-ray films, responded to a telegram from Edinburgh querying our equipment order again, and drafted a letter from Miss Ivens to the Croix-Rouge about our new wards. Then I went to the doctors' dining room to see if Miss Ivens needed anything. All of the doctors were there seated at the large table except Dr Dalyell, who was in her lab, and Dr Savill, who was away. Cicely was at the far end of the table.

'Oh good, Iris,' Miss Ivens said to me. 'Would you translate this for us?' She handed me a clipping from a newspaper.

I knew Cicely would prefer to be the one to translate for Miss Ivens but I couldn't suggest it without looking as if I was shirking so I sat down where Miss Ivens gestured, near her at the head of the table. Cicely scowled at me for the entire time we were there.

'Listen to this,' Miss Ivens said to the group as I quickly scanned the article.

'These ladies are suffragettes,' I read out loud. 'They do not belong, it behooves us to say, to the revolutionary, or better, rowdy, element of that federation. We have been present at operations and wish everyone could see the minute precautions and the delicacy with which the feminine hands of the doctors, and the qualified nurses who assist them, tend to the often frightful wounds of our brave combatants.' I looked up.

'We've made the news, girls,' Miss Ivens said.

'Minute precautions and delicacy. That's you they're talking about Frances,' Mrs Berry said. She sipped her tea thoughtfully.

'I think it's your feminine hands they mean, Ruth. I'm more likely the "rowdy". But what this article means is that people are noticing. We are the women of Royaumont. There are nurses and orderlies and drivers but it is this team of doctors that has made the greatest difference to our success.'

After the meeting broke up I went back to find Tom still underneath Violet's car.

'Oh, Iris, your brother's a whiz,' Violet said. 'He's cleaned the engine, fixed something in the wheels I don't quite understand but that might have killed me if he hadn't come along, and he's tightened up my brakes. Not that I use the brakes much, I must admit.'

I laughed. 'I can vouch for that.'

Tom came out from under the car. 'All done,' he said. He stood up and wiped his hands on a cloth hanging out of his pocket. He looked grown suddenly, like the mechanics who came to work on the tractors at home. 'I'll just take her for a test run.'

'Tom, you don't have a driving licence,' I said.

'So? Neither does Violet.'

'Did I say, don't tell Iris?' Violet said to him, mock-angry. 'Did I say she'll just worry? And what do you do? Tell her straight away.'

'Violet, you don't have a licence?' I said.

'I have a kind of licence,' she said slyly.

'What does that mean?'

'I know how to drive. Oh, Iris, don't tell. Please don't. As soon as you do, they'll send me home to miserable old Cornwall and Mummy staring into space. Don't. Please.'

I sighed. 'Violet, you are the living end.'

'Well, let's just focus on the living part and not the end. Come, Tom, take us for a spin around the neighbourhood.' We climbed into the car, Tom behind the wheel, and went for a quick run to pick up some more mail for Miss Ivens from the post office in Viarmes. We farewelled Tom at the station and Violet and I drove back to Royaumont.

'Thank you for being so kind to Tom today,' I said. 'He had a lovely time. I could tell.'

'So did I, my dear. My God, Iris, I didn't get a good look at him that first time with all our coats and scarves. I thought him handsome. But he is absolutely beautiful.'

'What?' I said.

'I know beauty is always more than physical and he has a way with him as well. But frankly he could have said not a word and I'd still be swooning. In fact, he should have kept his mouth shut. He looked better before he spoke. He even smells good.'

'Violet,' I said, becoming uncomfortable. 'He's fifteen years old.'

'So how long do I have to wait?'

'Violet!'

'Sorry, sorry. To you, he's the little brother. To me, he's a man, or near enough that I could care less. Those eyes. They pierce a soul. Oh oh.' She mocked a swoon. 'And he's nothing like the baby he was when he first came. He's growing up so fast.'

'Violet, he's a boy.'

'Believe me, honey, I know the look. He is most definitely a man.'

'You won't be the first to be all ogle-eyed over my brother. He has no interest in girls.'

'We'll see about that,' Violet said.

'Violet, you cannot talk about my young brother as if he's one of your stupid lovers.'

'I'm not. And they're not stupid. I'm just saying . . . Oh, come on, Iris. I'm not the only one. Every orderly in the place came over to the garages this afternoon, to drop off milk or pick up fuel or see one of the drivers. Half the nurses too. That boy's a man waiting to happen. Who knows who the lucky girl will be?'

I looked at Violet. She was right. The other women at Royaumont looked at Tom too. I'd not really thought of him as a man. He'd always been just my little brother. Once he'd needed nappies and bottles, then milk and biscuits, then a good talking to about his school results.

Something about Violet's attitude to Tom made me queasy. We had become great friends now but the way she talked about men – her lovers, she called them – they were like chocolates she'd eaten and enjoyed. I wouldn't want Tom to be one of her sweeties.

'Violet, you mustn't talk about Tom that way. You're a woman. He really is just a boy. I mean it, Violet.'

'Very well,' she said. 'I'll leave off. We're almost home now. Let's see if we can't steal a bit of that custard from the kitchen.'

Over the next few months, Tom established himself as an honorary woman of Royaumont although none of us told him that's what we'd decided. 'You want to watch that one,' Quoyle said to me after his first spring visit. 'He's a cheeky young fellow.' But the next time he came he fixed the kitchen table with the wonky leg Quoyle had been complaining about and he put in another light for the kitchen. Then he helped the orderlies clear blocks of stone from a downstairs room we planned to use as an extended reception area. Before he left, he showed Miss Ivens how to tie a reef knot.

'He's a lovely boy, your brother,' Miss Ivens said afterwards, practising the knot without success.

'He's always been a handful, to be honest,' I said. 'But that's what brothers are for.' I took the rope and fixed Miss Ivens's knot.

'Of course they are,' Miss Ivens said, looking at the rope with a puzzled expression. 'He's going to make something of his life. You mark my words. He's got the same good heart as you, Iris. Your father must be very proud.'

I hadn't told Miss Ivens much about myself at all. Not that she hadn't asked. But we'd been so busy that I'd kept our conversations to the work mostly and now, we knew each other so well, it would seem silly to tell her about my background. She'd told me her mother had died when she was twenty and so I'd told her about my own mother's death. Miss Ivens's father had remarried too, but unlike Daddy he'd moved his old family, as he termed Miss Ivens and her older sisters, into another house and his new wife into his old house. 'We were eating bread and butter pudding at the time he told me,' Miss Ivens said. 'I've never been able to stand it since.'

Not long after Tom's spring visit, I received a letter from Daddy, the first I'd had since I'd written to tell him the good news that Tom was not only safe but gainfully employed in the postal service, that I had found a position in a hospital, and that with this in mind, I thought it best for Tom and me to remain in France.

Daddy's reply started innocuously enough, talking about

Risdon and the long dry summer. *The twins are into all sorts of mischief*, he wrote. *Claire says they're good boys, but they remind me too much of Tom when he was a tyke, built for trouble.* And then it started. *I had a letter from him, Iris. This business of being in a safe job. I can't see there can be safe jobs when blokes are running around shooting each other. Every week the list of dead and wounded gets longer.*

When I wrote back, I told Daddy more about Royaumont, the soil, the weather, the people I'd met. When I mentioned Tom it was only to say that he was safe and that I was keeping an eye on him as we'd agreed. In his next letter, Daddy responded that there's no such thing as safety when men have guns for shooting and Tom was a boy who should come home. *All I've got in the world that matters is my family, and the thought I might lose either of you I can't abide.* So I continued to write, telling Daddy about the things I discovered, the bird that sang in the evening rather than the morning at Royaumont, the light so soft in the middle of the day with nothing I'd seen in Australia to compare it to, Mr Ragondin the shy rodent. Daddy wrote back, pleading with me to see sense. I didn't give him any more thought than the flowers I started finding in the fields around Royaumont as spring found the fullness of summer. And of course, the longer I stayed and ignored Daddy's pleas, the more convinced I became that Tom and I had been right all along and Daddy had been wrong.

Late in the summer of 1915 the weather unexpectedly turned cold. The drivers were in their wool coats, there was sleet on the roads and there was even a suggestion we'd have snow. Violet returned from Creil about two one morning. I'd come off the ward at eleven and was sound asleep. She was noisy coming into the room, bumping into things, not like Violet at all.

'I'm sorry, did I wake you?' she said when she saw my eyes open.

'No. Are you all right?' She was still in her boots, still wearing her wool coat and gloves which she'd normally have left downstairs.

'Tonight, I was driving a chap, died on the way. The others did their best. It never stops.' We'd had a busy few weeks and Violet had been under considerable strain as we'd lost one of our drivers who'd had to go home to nurse her sick mother.

I got out of bed. Violet's skin was pale and sheeny. I'd left the window open a crack when I went to sleep but there was quite a chill up now. I put my palm to Violet's forehead. 'You've got a fever,' I said.

She was standing in the middle of the room and she started to sway. I went to grab her as she fainted. I half-caught her, forced to let her down onto the floor.

'Someone, come quickly!' I called and in a moment Marjorie Starr was at the door in her nightdress. 'Violet's taken ill.'

Together, we lifted her onto her bed and took off her coat and boots. She was sweating underneath all the layers. There had been an outbreak of typhoid around Creil and I feared the worst. Marjorie went to find a doctor. It was Mrs Berry who came and I was relieved – she was our best physician. She examined Violet, who'd woken by this stage and was feeling much better, she said. Just a little faint, she said. She might get up and go back to Creil, she thought. I told her to stay where she was.

'You need to rest,' Mrs Berry agreed.

Violet tried to get up and fell back on the bed. 'But I have to go back,' she said.

'No, you don't. Violet, you're sick,' I said. 'You have to stay here with me.'

When Violet had settled down again, Mrs Berry took me outside. 'Her throat's inflamed, glands are up and her chest doesn't sound good. Iris, you need to stay with her. I don't like the look of it.'

'It's not typhoid?' I said, terrified suddenly.

'No, but it's a nasty infection. And Violet's not strong.' Mrs Berry put her hand on my shoulder and this more than anything worried me. Everyone knew Violet and I were inseparable. We spent every spare minute in each other's company. If Mrs Berry was trying to offer me comfort she must think Violet gravely ill.

Matron Todd came in then. She took one look at Violet and said to Mrs Berry, 'I rather think we ought to send up to Paris for a man, don't you?' Mrs Berry stared at her and didn't reply.

To me, Mrs Berry said, 'At least we know she'll have good care here. Iris, you need to stay with her. The fever's sure to go up again.' She shook her head. 'It's little wonder frankly,' talking to herself now. 'We're not eating properly, not sleeping. And the drivers are out there night after night. Even in the summer, it can be cold. It's no wonder poor Violet is ill. I'll go and find Frances and get Quoyle to make up a broth. Tomorrow, I'll tell Edinburgh this must stop. They must send us the resources we need.'

Miss Ivens came up later that night, the front of her gown covered in blood. She'd forgotten to take it off on her way out of theatre. Violet's fever had gone up again and come down, I told Miss Ivens. 'I sponged her when she was hot and resisted the urge to cover her too much when cold.'

'Poor little flower,' Miss Ivens said, putting her hand on Violet's forehead. 'Iris darling, I'm still operating,' she said without looking at me. 'We'll be going through the night again, I should think. Will you stay with her?'

'Of course.'

'And will you . . . will you come to see me if there's any change?'

'Yes, Miss Ivens.'

'She's young,' Miss Ivens said. 'That's in her favour. But she's not strong. She's never been strong.'

To me, Violet was so strong. I said, 'Do you think not? Oh Miss Ivens, Violet's a champion. She'll be all right.'

Miss Ivens didn't reply, instead putting her hand on my head and leaving it there for a moment. She looked kindly at me and I realised that Mrs Berry must have communicated something to Miss Ivens she hadn't communicated to me. They really did believe Violet was gravely ill.

After Miss Ivens left, I sat by Violet's bed and cried silently. 'No, Violet,' I whispered. 'You mustn't leave me, do you hear? We're the flower bird girls.' I realised how much she'd come to mean to me. She stirred in her sleep, grabbed for my hand. I took both of hers in mine.

I sat on the wooden crate we had as a bedside table in our little room and waited for morning to come. I said decade after decade of the rosary. I added extra Our Fathers and Glory Bes. And then, just before dawn, the priest from Asnières appeared at the bedroom door. Father Rousselle had become a key part of our life at Royaumont. He often sat and prayed with the soldiers, or said a mass. He was particularly helpful to those who suffered mental problems following their ordeal. It was kind of him to come out in the cold, I said, and he could come and bless Violet but she was not to be anointed. She didn't believe in it anyway, I knew, and for my part I would not accept that she was near the end and requiring anointing. Father Rousselle was such a sweet man; he came and did as I asked and no more.

As dawn made its way into the room, Violet became delirious. She kept saying the name Peter and whoever he was, he disturbed her mightily. No, Peter, no, she was saying. Peter might have been the one who'd given her his car and cigarette case, I thought. He'd been older than Violet, she said, 'and terribly sophisticated, darling' until 'I got bored. I always get bored with them.' Even at the time, I knew she hadn't been telling me the full story. Her confidence was marvellous – it shone from her – but it was also somehow brittle, so that even as she dazzled everyone around her, including me, I knew I was the happier person. I was ever the quiet one, the observer, the dependable plain Iris Crane, but Violet was amazing. And even if her brash confidence masked another Violet, this frightened girl I nursed through that long, long night, strangely, it didn't make me love her less. It made me love her more.

As if the priest's blessing had spoken some stern words to her soul, little Violet returned to us. By lunchtime on the second day, her fevers were less severe. By nightfall, she had improved further. Miss Ivens came again, with Mrs Berry, and they said it was my dedication that had saved Violet but that now I must rest. I was fine, I said, relieved to my very bones. I stayed by Violet until she was awake and had taken some broth and then I sponged her and changed the bedding. It wasn't until she slept again that I crept in beside her, spooning my body around her as we had that first night, and fell into a deep sleep myself. We remained there, sleeping peacefully, until morning.

Violet spent the rest of the week in bed on Mrs Berry's

orders. I popped in to see her when I could. I was just so relieved to have her back. 'Oh Violet, don't you dare get sick again.' I had made much of the priest's visit. 'I'm sure you're for Heaven now,' I said. 'Father Rousselle has blessed you. You're going up not down after all.'

'Stop it,' she said. 'I'm going straight to Hell and the old curé is coming with me.'

'Don't talk about Father like that. He's wonderful.'

'He is,' Violet said. She grabbed my hand. Her green eyes were shining and her curls fell about her face. 'I heard you wouldn't let him anoint me, darling.'

I'd confided in Mrs Berry my decision about the priest. She must have told Violet.

'Of course not,' I said. 'He said he could anoint the sick even if they weren't dying and that if you died without anointment, he couldn't vouch for your soul. But I couldn't let him do it. I decided I'd vouch for your soul if it came to that. I felt it would be like giving up on you.' I swallowed hard. 'Oh Violet, just don't get sick again.'

'Of course I won't, darling,' she said. 'Perhaps if I never drive to Creil ever again I'll be healthy as a horse.' While I knew she was joking, I could see that the horror she faced was taking its toll on her.

If ever I felt upset or worried about the awful things we witnessed at Royaumont, I walked through one of the wards, and the light coming through those long windows, the red blankets over the beds, neatly made, the soldiers as comfortable as we could make them, it truly was as if Royaumont could protect all under her roof. We were a haven in the forest, in the midst of chaos. But Violet was daily in the chaos itself. Violet, who drove that long rough road to Creil, who saw those poor men who never made it to Royaumont, brought from the trains already dead or so close to death there was no point moving them, the horrors she witnessed were much worse than I could imagine.

We had a concert at the end of 1915 to celebrate our first year and Miss Ivens shouted us all champagne and a wonderful supper of smoked trout. Cicely created another pageant, a musical this time, and if you could have seen the wards lit up for Christmas, the orderlies in their costumes, elves and sprites and fairies, the candles, the men clapping and laughing and singing along, you'd have thought there was no war on at all. Violet, with her beautiful voice, had always played a key role in our performances, but she said she wasn't well enough and despite all our pleadings she didn't join in. I could see her in the audience. She sat, unmoved. It wasn't until they started on Christmas carols – six of the girls had got themselves dressed up in the blue capes the sisters wore and came through the wards with candles singing – that Violet agreed to get up and sing with them. She sang a solo of 'They Didn't Believe Me'. As I listened, I let tears run down my cheeks unashamedly. I doubt there was a woman there who wasn't crying and as for the patients, they clapped and clapped when Violet finished and then when she sang the chorus once more, they gave her a standing ovation of sorts, those who could stand standing and the rest sitting up as well as they could.

'You see, Violet,' I said, wiping my eyes as she came past me. 'You *are* giving something important.'

Early in 1916, Miss Ivens spent a day and a night in Amiens to visit the British hospital there. I'd taken the opportunity to tidy her desk and now we were back together on her morning rounds. We'd had another problem with provisions for soldiers.

The army had decreed that every French soldier was to be provided with a daily ration of wine, the precious *pinard*. The hospital was expected to pay for the wine. The committee in Edinburgh couldn't see the need. I was wondering how I would broach the matter with Miss Ivens without angering her further.

She was unwinding a bandage around a man's calf. She'd been quiet since she'd been back and I missed her usual chatter. I even wondered if she was offended that I'd tidied her office. I watched as she changed the dressing, taking such care it might have been a tricky amputation.

I was about to ask about her visit to Amiens when she said, 'When I finished medicine, I wanted to be a surgeon to make people's lives better. I mean, I knew the College wasn't admitting women but I believed they would change. They'd let us sit their examinations and slowly, as we showed them our hands were as nimble as theirs, our minds as deep, they'd capitulate and admit us as Fellows.'

The man had fallen asleep by this time. They often did. Miss Ivens always spoke in low tones around the patients and her voice was so calming. This man was from Algeria, with skin as black as night, and he couldn't understand a word Miss Ivens said, but he'd listened all the same until his eyes were too heavy to remain open. It was as if she hypnotised them. Dr Henry once joked that if Miss Ivens had been born in another century, she'd have been burnt for a witch. Miss Ivens said it was no joke, we'd all have been burnt for witches. It's what happened to women healers.

Miss Ivens sat back and surveyed her work and looked up at the sleeping man and smiled. 'But do you know, for the first time, I'm not even sure I want to be one of them.' She pinned the bandage and stood up and smoothed her coat and we walked together from the ward, having finished the day's rounds. She nodded towards the ward sister on her way out the door and the sister, a new recruit from Canada, looked as if she might be about to salute, but Miss Ivens raised an arm to stop her. 'All's well, Sister Courtney,' she said. Miss Ivens always called the staff by name. Sometimes she was even right. Not this time though. This was Sister Jackson not Courtney. Sister Courtney had come from Liverpool not Canada. I never corrected Miss Ivens and most of the staff took her forgetfulness about names in good humour.

'You know I went to Amiens yesterday to meet the surgeon there,' Miss Ivens said on the way down the stairs. 'The folk at Creil suggested it, told me the surgeon was a good chap I should get to know.

'His name is Roger Crampton and I'd heard of him. I'm sure Berry knows him. I must ask her. Well, he was pleasant enough and happy to have me there. But as we moved from bed to bed, I saw that between one patient and the next he wouldn't use antiseptic – wouldn't even wash his hands. God knows what he does with his instruments because when I said are you not sterilising he said, "Don't tell me you've fallen for that Lister nonsense. You'd do better to cut deep around infection than worry about those so-called germs."

'I can't believe there could still be a doctor on God's earth who doesn't know or respect bacteria. It puts us back fifty years. He's in charge of the surgical group and he has no idea.'

We'd reached Miss Ivens's office and she unlocked and opened the door and went in, still speaking, assuming I'd follow. She went to the desk and looked wearily at the pile of papers, neater but no less overwhelming, hung her coat on the hook behind the desk and wound her stethoscope around the same hook.

'We went to the wards then. Sepsis was everywhere. He gets

away with it because they're closer to the front. You expect higher mortality but even the most rudimentary analysis would probably show him up.

'I tried to speak to him again, told him the successes we've had with gas gangrene and Elsie's lab, invited him down to spend some time with us.' She sat down in her chair and shook her head. 'He thought I wanted him to come down and teach my surgeons. "I would love to Frances," he said, "and I know you girls are struggling but I'm needed here."'

I could see Miss Ivens was tired and needed to talk. 'So what did you do?' I said.

'When we'd finished the rounds, I was blunt with him. I told him he must find a matron trained in Nightingale's methods who could manage his theatres properly. I told him he must start washing his hands and make his surgeons do likewise. I told him he must don a mask, boil instruments. Such basic care, Iris. I couldn't believe I was having to say it. For if you don't, I said, you are killing patients of sepsis. Look around you.'

'What did he say?'

'He asked me was I questioning his practice. I wanted to avoid a confrontation but more than that I wanted to see something done. I said, I am pleading with you to consider what you're doing. I will send you some papers. He laughed. "Papers," he said. "What on earth do I need with those? Chaps who've never seen the inside of a patient telling me how to operate. Pah. Mr Lister and his idiot germs. I've got more important things to worry about."

'Do you know the awful thing was that in another context I'd have liked him? He's a jovial man, quick to laugh, more accepting than most of women in the discipline.

'I didn't know what to do then. I should have felt proud

of Royaumont, of how different we are, what we've achieved. But I just felt sick and I've been feeling sick ever since. For surely I'm guilty of just as much arrogance and I'm making similar errors. Not with hygiene, perhaps, but something else. Something I don't know, some ignorance.

'It suddenly occurred to me as we said goodbye outside the hospital – we were curt now and far from friends – that we'll never know all things, that we'll do more harm despite our oath because of ignorance, or arrogance.'

Thinking back later on poor Miss Ivens's worries about the state of medicine, I knew the things I might have said. *You'll never be like him. Your humility shines through all you do. You have no arrogance.* Tens of things I could have said but didn't. I just started going through the day's mail and said, 'I'll draft you a letter to the Service de Santé. For you must write now and lodge a formal complaint.'

About half an hour later Mrs Berry joined us. Miss Ivens had cheered herself up by talking about what happened, first to me and then to her dear Berry who knew just how to jolly Miss Ivens out of any bad mood. The cesspits had caused problems again. It was repairable, Mrs Berry had told us, but the terrible stench around the entrance to the abbey would continue for at least another day. 'But fear not, dear chief,' Mrs Berry said. 'Your faithful servants Berry and Iris have the matter in hand, so to speak.' We had the plumbers in again, fixing the cesspits, and the electricians, trying to give us more lights. It was never-ending, the work to keep the old abbey functional.

Now Miss Ivens was back onto the topic of surgery, completely cheered and ready to expound on why it was the best discipline. 'You can do all the treating on the earth, spend weeks and months monitoring your patient, altering a dosage, changing a regimen. But with a single cut, you can transform someone, save a limb, stop a growth. Nothing else does that.'

I felt, as I often did among the doctors, that they'd forgotten I was there. It was not an unpleasant feeling, for I learnt much and was rarely put on the spot to respond.

'Obstetrics,' Mrs Berry said, taking a sip of her tea. 'You should have stayed with obstetrics.'

'Miracle of life, you mean?' Berry only shrugged. 'Obstetrics is to surgery what ping-pong is to tennis. Surgery is power to change a life. I hate admitting that I want it, especially after I saw Crampton, but I do.' Miss Ivens noticed me then. 'Listen to us going on, Iris. You'll never want to be a doctor if I keep this up.' Miss Ivens had started to tell me I should be a doctor. I never took it seriously, but I was glad she'd cheered up and I smiled.

'Iris will be all right,' Mrs Berry said. 'Women in her generation won't have to worry. The battle will be over. They'll be doctors and barristers and scientists and no one will think twice. Did you know, Iris, that Frances was a gold medallist at London University, and still they wouldn't let her do surgery at first?'

'Even so, I wouldn't have lived in any other time than my own,' Miss Ivens said. Mrs Berry looked as if she might disagree, but Miss Ivens looked beyond us, out towards the cloisters. The sun was gone for the day and the orderlies were helping the patients back inside. Miss Ivens smiled. 'How many women will ever have the opportunity to go from nothing to this?'

'It wasn't nothing,' Mrs Berry said.

'What?' Miss Ivens said.

'What I had, nor you, I'll warrant. We have families and

lives back at home. They predate medicine. They're worth something, Frances.'

'Not like this,' Miss Ivens said. 'Nothing in my life will be like this. Did I ever tell you that when I first registered, the medical board told me to forget surgery?' Mrs Berry shook her head. 'It's not for women, one of the physicians said. You need to be stout of heart. He was nothing like as good as you, Ruth, with no idea of a woman's fitness to practise. I looked him in the eye and said, I will be a surgeon, as if my saying it might be enough.

'Well, the College refused me that year and the next but finally, after three years, they let me into the surgery programme.

'And once in, I had to wonder what on earth he'd meant. Surgery was different from general medicine, but stoutness was not the requirement. It was flight you needed, lightness and faith and nimble hands. I had none of those to begin with but nor did any of them. We watched the surgeons and cultivated the skill of flight as best we could. I'd never do anything else. But of course, they never wanted us to practise. They let me into the programme but told me all I could do was women's health, never general surgery.'

A breeze came through the window. We could smell the cesspits. Miss Ivens sniffed and smiled. 'You did say they were fixing the problem, didn't you, Iris?' she said.

Just then Violet came in. 'Frances, why is the Queen of Serbia in the front hall?'

'The Queen of where?' Miss Ivens said.

'Serbia.'

'Oh yes, Elsie wired to say she was coming. Iris, I forgot to tell you. I don't know what I did with the wire. We're starting up another hospital in Serbia and the Queen wants to see Royaumont. I hadn't realised it was today. What date is it, Iris?' I told her. 'Oh dear, she's here on the right date unfortunately.'

'What should I do with her?' Violet said. 'This place stinks.'

'I don't know, find one of the doctors to take her round.'

'Frances, you can't do that. You're the chief,' Violet said, exasperated.

'Very well, I'm coming.'

'Just before you go, Miss Ivens,' I said. 'We've had advice from Paris after the last inspection. It concerns the *pinard* for the soldiers. The committee has written . . .'

'Yes, Iris, thanks for reminding me. I fixed that.'

'How do you mean?'

'Well, the committee decided to give me a raise in salary since Royaumont is doing so beautifully. A hundred pounds, Iris! And it's just enough to cover the cost of wine for the patients. So that's settled. I couldn't be bothered arguing with them this time, dear. Problem solved.' She smiled.

Miss Ivens and Violet went off to deal with the Queen of Serbia and I went to collect the day's mail, holding my nose as I passed the plumbers at work.

Grace

She was in theatre when her pager went off. One of the nurses went to check it. Alice. 'She'll have to wait,' Grace said.

A few minutes later, Alice herself turned up. 'We've got a failure-to-progress,' she said from the door.

'So why are you coming to me?' Grace was supervising a D&C. She looked up briefly, saw the set of Alice's jaw.

'I want you to see her.'

'I'll be twenty minutes more here. Get Andrew.'

'They don't listen to him. It's a tricky one.'

Grace sighed. 'What makes you think they'll listen to me? Who's the midwife?'

'Chantelle Dupont.'

Grace flicked her eyes at Alice again. 'Tell me I didn't get up this morning.'

'You didn't get up this morning. Will you come?'

'Give me fifteen minutes. Get Andrew to work it up first. Failure-to-progress?'

'Or something,' Alice said.

Grace finished up in theatre and stopped at the office to call the medical library, hoping that by the time she finished they'd have sorted out the failure-to-progress. 'Grace Hogan returning Katie's call.' Grace had asked the library to do a search on the doctor named on Iris's invitation to Royaumont.

'Hi, Dr Hogan. I've found out what I can about Violet Heron,' Katie said. 'Dame Violet, I should say. She's quite well known in Scotland, graduated University of Edinburgh Medical School in 1924, then did obs and gyn. She was a big advocate for reproductive rights for women, started the first birth control clinic in Scotland, got into lots of trouble with the churches.'

'A woman after my own heart,' Grace said.

'Well, she was still practising until recently, mostly reviews and reports for government on women's health. The biggest was a national inquiry into abuse of children in care five years ago. Very outspoken. We've got some clippings from the inquiry if you're interested.'

'That's great, Katie.'

'She's pretty full-on,' Katie said.

'How do you mean?'

'Imagine a little old lady walking at the front of a major protest march carrying an "Our Bodies, Our Choice" placard and you'll get the idea.'

'Thanks, Katie. I'll drop over when I can and pick up the clippings.'

Grace left her pager with the desk staff and crossed the corridor to the birthing centre, a new maternity care unit run by a group of midwives. To preserve calm, doctors weren't supposed to come in unless invited. They weren't to bring their pagers. Grace opened the door of one of the rooms a crack and peered in. There was music in the background and the lights were dimmed. Andrew was there. 'I just need to examine this woman quickly,' he was saying calmly.

Grace opened the door fully and strode in purposefully. 'Chantelle,' she said.

Chantelle Dupont was a small middle-aged woman who always managed to make Grace feel inadequate, as if Grace was missing some key piece of information that would enable her to truly understand women and birth. Chantelle turned to Grace, then swung around and glared at Alice.

'Failure-to-progress?' Grace took a pen out of her top pocket and put it back in.

'We prefer to call it normal labour,' Chantelle said. Some midwives hated the term failure-to-progress because, they said, it implied the woman was failing. As far as Grace was concerned, it implied labour was failing, and sometimes it did. They talked about birth as a human experience. Grace had given birth twice. There was nothing human about it. She'd felt like an animal and not a cuddly one. 'Alice asked me to review this case,' Grace said. She couldn't see the chart anywhere.

'This is Grace Hogan, Jen,' Chantelle said to the patient. 'She's a doctor.'

'Talk to me,' Grace said, looking at Andrew and not Chantelle.

'Elderly primip, failing to progress, she's been at six centimetres for two hours. Foetal heart's not great.' He flicked a look towards the head of the bed. The husband was sitting forward in an armchair holding the woman's hand. He looked nervous.

Just then one of the other midwives poked her head in the door. 'Dr Hogan?'

Irritated at the interruption, Grace went over.

'You just got a call from the office at Milton State School.'

'What about?' Grace said.

'Didn't say.'

'Tell the desk to call them back. Give them David's number at the Mater.'

'I didn't even know you had kids.' The young midwife smiled. Grace had only told a few people at work about the kids. In her last job, at the Royal, so many people had been critical of her for working at all, let alone for pursuing obstetrics, it was easier to pretend she was childless.

'Actually, it's a bit tricky here right now.'

'Sorry.' The girl left, the birth centre doors swinging closed behind her with a swish.

Grace walked back over to the husband, still sitting at his wife's side.

'I'm Grace Hogan, one of the obstetricians,' she said. 'We're a bit concerned about your wife's and particularly your baby's condition. Can you tell me how long she's been in labour?'

The husband stood up. He was wearing track pants and a T-shirt. 'Craig Wilson. The pains came last night. They said the baby would be born by now. She's not herself. I keep telling them.' He looked towards Chantelle who was smiling back at him.

'Has your wife had any sleep?'

'Nup. Me neither.' Men during labour. With some of them, you'd think they were the ones having the baby.

'Excuse me.' Grace took the husband's place at the head end of the bed. The woman was turned away from her, Chantelle on the other side of her. Grace spoke calmly to the woman. 'Mrs Wilson, can you hear me? We're going to transfer you to the hospital and get you comfortable so we can deliver your baby. Do you understand what I'm saying?' Grace went to the other side of the bed to face the woman, forcing Chantelle to move out of the way.

It was then that Grace realised.

It was Jennifer Bennetts. Wilson, that was her surname now. Jen, Chantelle had called her. Jennifer Wilson. Grace felt her heart beating. Yesterday, in the clinic. Constipation. They'd given her suppositories. Did that bring on the labour early? Grace looked more closely. Jennifer Wilson appeared barely conscious. Grace checked carotid pulse, fast and weak. 'Something's wrong here,' she said. 'Jennifer, can you hear me? Give me a torch.' Alice handed her one.

Chantelle had moved around to the other side of the woman's head now, level with Grace again. 'We're doing just great, aren't we, Jen?' she said in Jennifer's ear. Just then there was another contraction and Jennifer Wilson moaned.

Andrew took the opportunity to check the foetal heart. 'Not recovering well after the contraction,' he said evenly, looking at Grace. She knew he was keeping his voice calm in front of the husband but a foetal heart that wasn't recovering after each contraction was worrying and the look on Andrew's face said it all.

Jennifer Wilson moaned. High blood pressure. That's what it was. Grace remembered now. Jennifer Wilson had high blood pressure. There was no protein on a stick and Grace had ummed and ahhed over a twenty-four-hour specimen. Protein – indicating pre-eclampsia – they might have found it with a twenty-four-hour urine specimen.

Grace turned to the husband again. 'I won't pull any punches, Mr Wilson. With more warning, we'd have moved to a caesarean an hour ago. We need to act now. I need you

to consent to this on behalf of your wife. *Now*, Mr Wilson.'
Chantelle went to speak and Grace said, 'Chantelle, step out
right now.' There was no time to explain.

'Jen,' Chantelle said, 'they want to move us to the hospital,'
as if Grace hadn't spoken. Jennifer Wilson didn't respond.

Grace said to the husband, 'Your wife is no longer capable
of providing consent. I implore you to understand. I saw your
wife yesterday. You need to say yes right now.'

'Craig, you have a right to—' Chantelle began.

He looked away from Chantelle and towards Grace and
nodded, almost imperceptibly.

'We're moving,' Grace said. 'We're moving now. Alice, get
a gurney, let theatre know, get another consult and paeds.'

Grace headed to the door and flicked on the fluorescent
lights and then two things happened at once. Chantelle started
coming towards Grace, speaking too loudly for the room. 'This
is a woman, a woman with feelings and views.' Grace turned
and was about to respond by asking Chantelle to leave the room
when Jennifer Wilson became rigid on the bed, fists clenched.

'Where's maternal BP?' Grace said to no one in particular,
as she walked quickly back to the bed and pushed the button
that called in the code.

Alice was shepherding Craig Wilson towards the door. 'In
about thirty seconds, there will be about ten more people in the
room. You need to wait outside.' Then, louder, 'Mr Wilson,
we need to work now.'

Chantelle sobbed quietly in the corner. 'I can't see where
they've recorded BP,' Andrew was saying as Grace moved to
clear the airway.

'Can someone help me lift her?' Alice was on the other
side. They rolled Jennifer Wilson onto the gurney.

'Last BP was on admission twelve hours ago. It was normal,' Andrew said, cuffing the patient's arm to take a measure. He looked at Chantelle. 'You haven't checked it since then? Hang on, yesterday it was one thirty over ninety. What was she doing here?'

The crash team arrived as they were wheeling Jennifer Wilson out of the birth centre, across the wide linoleum corridor towards the theatre.

As Grace left the theatre to go and talk to the husband, she was already thinking about what had gone wrong. The blood pressure wasn't all that high when Grace saw Jennifer Wilson, and stress could have accounted for it. It had been normal the day before, it was normal on admission, if it had actually been checked, and then the birth centre midwives hadn't checked it again, not wanting to interfere in the labour. None of it mattered. There was their history, hers and Jennifer's, and there was Grace's tiredness, chronic though it was these days, and her keenness to get away. And she couldn't be sure. They hadn't even confirmed Jennifer Wilson was pre-eclamptic, and foetal heart had been fine right up until those last minutes. You might not have picked it.

But none of it mattered. If Grace had done an internal examination yesterday, she would have confirmed Jennifer Wilson was already in labour and should be admitted. She'd have seen Jennifer was a birth centre patient and transferred her to hospital care. If Grace had referred Jennifer Wilson on, another consultant might have picked it up. If Grace had ordered the twenty-four-hour urine specimen, they might have recognised pre-eclampsia in time. Hindsight is easy, David always said to her, but she felt completely washed out. She'd failed her patient. She'd failed a child.

Clive Markwell found her in the scrub room. He'd been in one of the other theatres. He'd come in at the end. Grace saw him speaking with the paediatrician. 'Dr Hogan,' he said, the emphasis on the doctor. 'I hear you missed this yesterday at clinic.'

Grace was still shaken. 'I'm sorry, Clive. I need to go and tell the father now.'

He snapped off his gloves and put them in the bin. 'Of course you do,' he said. 'But mark my words, Doctor. This is another example of your failing to follow protocol. It won't finish here.'

'I'm sure you'll do whatever you think's best,' Grace said. She bit her bottom lip to keep back tears. She could taste the blood in her mouth. She sucked hard on it.

She found Craig Wilson in the waiting area. He was slumped in a chair, no idea what she was about to tell him. He stood to greet her, eager.

'I'm so sorry,' she said. 'We did everything we could. We were able to perform a caesarean section and we're confident your wife is going to be fine. But we were too late, Mr Wilson. We lost the baby.'

He fell back onto the chair. Moments passed. He kept beginning to speak and then closing his mouth. He stood and sat and stood again. 'Was it a girl or a boy?' he said finally, standing now.

'It's a little boy,' Grace said, taking his arm to support him. 'He's in there now and you and Mrs Wilson might want to . . . There's a social worker coming up soon. They'll talk to you about what to do now.'

'But what happened?' His face was ashen.

Grace thought of Henry suddenly, when they'd brought

him home from the hospital, the two big girls excited they had a brother who'd appeared magically, like a new doll to play with. She felt a hard lump in her chest and pushed it back down. She was supposed to be careful in what she said but she told Craig Wilson as much as she knew. 'I think your wife developed pre-eclampsia, a reasonably common complication in late pregnancy, but I think there was a rare further complication which meant your baby didn't have enough oxygen during labour. And he died.'

Craig Wilson stood there, not moving, willing Grace to stay too, as if while they talked he could make what she'd told him not so. She registered the pain on his face and something else too, the beginnings of blame. He kept going to say something and stopping himself, taking a breath, trying again. He didn't cry. He was too shattered to cry. 'A boy,' he said.

Grace nodded. Her pager went off. 'I have to go now.'

By the next day, Craig Wilson would be asking hard questions. He'd be demanding answers, why they didn't admit his wife the day before, why they let her remain in the birth centre, why they didn't move to a caesarean sooner. The hospital would review the death. The coroner might even be involved. Grace didn't know for sure what they'd find. The only thing she did know was that she'd be there when Jennifer Wilson woke up to tell her that her first baby had died.

Grace went to the desk to pick up the message. She walked slowly, felt the weight of the world on her shoulders. You couldn't do everything. She knew that. Doctors are fallible. But if only she'd . . .

The page was from the antenatal clinic asking if she was coming down. She was the doctor rostered on for the day. Then she remembered. There had been an earlier message for her. The school had called. The school had called when she'd been in the birth centre. 'Give me the phone,' she said to the girl on the desk. 'What's the number for Milton State School?'

'Hi, it's Grace Hogan here. Someone called me.'

'Grace Hogan?' The woman sounded vague. 'Oh yes, it's your daughter. She's had a fall. We couldn't get you. She's gone to the hospital.'

The hospital. Which hospital? 'Is she all right? What's happened?' Phil was the most accident-prone child in the world. Grace felt her heart thumping in her chest.

'I'll put you through to the deputy principal. She talked with the ambulance folk.' Ambulance? Grace steadied herself on the counter. What on earth had happened?

Grace waited several minutes while they paged the deputy. She almost hung up and drove to the school but they said Phil had gone to the hospital. She needed to know which hospital.

'Grace, hi, it's Jenny Nearing. Mia fell from the verandah. I think she was trying to get a ball for one of the littlies who'd thrown it up there. She came down on her back and we weren't sure it was a good idea to move her.' The woman was speaking too carefully.

Mia? It was Mia not Phil. 'What? How? Where is she?'

'Royal Children's. It's the closest. We couldn't get you or David. We rang your GP. He said straight to hospital. I thought that was best.'

'Tell me again. The fall, the nature of the fall.'

'Maybe twenty feet, onto her back onto the grass.'

'Skull?'

'None of the teachers saw how she landed. We don't think so.'

'What did the ambulance do on site?' This would give Grace an idea of injury.

'They confirmed she's broken her arm.'

God, Mia, at eight, with a broken arm, and taken to the hospital in an ambulance by herself. Grace forced back tears. At least she'd put her arm down first. Better than her head.

'Her spine. Spinal injury. Did they think . . .' Grace could hardly form the words.

'She had movement and feeling and she was conscious.'

'Okay, okay. I'm on my way. Call the Royal, tell them I'm coming now.'

'Fine. We did everything right, Grace. Everything we could.'

'I know you did. I should have . . .' Grace hung up the phone, looked at the clerk. 'Call David at the Mater. Tell him to meet me at the Royal Children's.' The girl was making notes, looking at Grace. She had no idea what Grace was talking about. 'Oh for God's sake, get Alice Jablonsky. She'll explain.'

Grace arrived at the Royal Children's fifteen minutes later, parking in a doctor's bay and throwing the keys at the gate officer on the way in. She went straight to casualty. There was a long queue at the desk. She took in the clerk, stick-thin, lipsticked, slow. Grace went to the front of the line, said to the woman next in the queue, 'I'm sorry. My daughter is eight. She's been injured and she's alone.' Grace thought she might cry. 'They only just found me.'

'Of course,' said the woman. 'Go ahead.'

'I'm Dr Hogan,' Grace said. 'My daughter is here, Mia.'

The clerk looked flatly at Grace and then at the file on her desk, running a polished fingernail down the list. Mouth like a deflated balloon end, a smoker. 'We don't have a Mia Hogan.'

She looked past Grace to the next person in the queue.

'Ravenswood. Mia Ravenswood.'

'Well, why didn't you say that in the first place? Mia Ravenswood.' The clerk consulted the next page of the list. Grace saw she was in treatment room seven. 'I'll get a nurse to come out and take you in.'

'Thank you,' Grace said.

She went to the waiting area and as soon as the clerk's attention was taken by the woman who'd let Grace go ahead of her, Grace went through the push doors. It took her several minutes to find room seven, but finally there was Mia, all alone on a gurney, head collar, arm twisted crazily in front. Grace rushed to her daughter, careful not to bump the arm. 'Oh honey, I'm sorry. I'm here now. Does it hurt?'

'Hi, Mummy. A little bit. They gave me magic medicine.'

'Magic medicine.' Grace saw Mia's pupils were way too small. Had they morphed her? She was eight and they'd morphed her. Grace might have told them not to do that. She looked at the arm. Fractured ulna, radius, possible shoulder. Grace couldn't remember how bones were different in children, only that they were.

Just then she heard David's voice outside. 'I managed to get a Cherry Ripe and a Mars bar but no Kit Kats. The machine . . . Grace, hey.'

'David, you're here! The school said they couldn't get you.'

'Mick Dalton called me as soon as he saw Mia. Mick's here now. He'll be back soon. Do you remember him? He did paediatrics at the Mater. He was going to go into orthopaedics. Remember? Ended up in paeds. Big career change. Great for us. Couldn't get better for a fracture.' David was calm, even chirpy. Grace didn't know if she wanted to hit him or kiss him.

Grace put her hand on Mia's forehead, checking her temperature, as if she'd have a fever. She couldn't believe how casual David was. 'Just the forearm?' she asked. 'The collar?'

'It'll be off soon. They've X-rayed. Nothing to worry about. She'll have a cast for a month or so but that's it.'

Grace felt her heart slowing down for the first time since she'd left the operating theatre.

David picked up Phil and Henry and they had fish and chips at home. Henry drew a big *S* on Mia's cast and told her she must have been exposed to white kryptonite. Why white? Grace had asked. She's lost the power to fly, Henry said. Silly, David added. You should have known that. Later, the kids in front of the television upstairs, Grace and David were drinking tea at the kitchen bench. Grace said, 'I'm not sure we can keep going like this.'

'Like what?'

'Mia today. The school called me. I was in the birth centre. I didn't even take the call.' Grace remembered Jennifer Wilson suddenly and put the thought away.

'Well, you can't stop and drop everything in our line of work. It was just lucky I was in a clinic. And Mia was fine.'

'She was all alone. In the ambulance.'

'No, she was with the paramedics. They know how to treat kids. They gave her pain relief and one of them stayed with her until I got there. Lovely guy. I must pen him a note.'

'But one of us should have been with her. I told the school to call you.'

'Maybe they don't have the Mater number. I'll get Naomi to call it through tomorrow. But it didn't matter. Mick called. I met Mia at the hospital. It really was all right, Grace.'

But Grace continued to feel uneasy. What if the attending hadn't been someone David knew, if he hadn't got David, if Mia had been all alone in the hospital system? What if the injury had been worse? And while Grace had been in the birth centre initially and then in theatre, she'd forgotten about the call. Sure, they'd had an emergency to contend with. But what mattered more than her own children?

She couldn't bring herself to tell David about Jennifer Wilson. She'd tell him tomorrow. Jennifer would be awake, she realised. Grace had wanted to be there. 'I have to go back into the hospital,' she said. 'You're okay to wait here?'

'Sure, but do you really have to? Mia might want you.'

'I'll be back as soon as I can.'

Jennifer Wilson and her husband were in a private room. The hospital had managed to give them that much. He looked so soft sitting there on the little visitor's chair holding his wife's hand. Grace told them how sorry she was. They weren't even beginning to come to grips with what had happened. Grace knew she shouldn't tell them she felt responsible but she did say to Jennifer, 'I wish I'd known yesterday you were in labour. I should have done more tests.'

'It's not your fault,' Jennifer Wilson said. 'I wish I'd known too.' Grace found herself biting back tears for about the third time that day.

She was driving home from the hospital at about ten. Fog had descended over the city and she was listening to Cat Stevens's 'Wild World' on the cassette player.

Grace had joined the Medical Women's Society when she was a student. The president was a middle-aged paediatrician, married, no kids. Grace's was the generation of hope, she'd said to them, the luckiest ever, because things had changed, there would be no stopping women now, they could have everything, a career, children. What a crock it had turned out to be.

Before Grace left the hospital, Andrew Martin had told her that Jennifer Wilson didn't want an autopsy. Grace couldn't blame her for that. Now they weren't sure whether pre-eclampsia had contributed to the death, Andrew said, but Clive Markwell was going to make a complaint.

She'd called David then to see how Mia was. She was sleeping peacefully now he said. Neither Grace nor David mentioned the morning's appointment with Ian Gibson and when Grace thought of it, it seemed a million years ago. But Ian had said that they needed to bring Henry in. He hadn't said it was urgent but he hadn't agreed with Grace that it could wait. He'd wanted her family history. Why would he want that if he wasn't thinking anything? Grace had done a paediatric term during medical school. Leukaemia, that was the one you dreaded, but Henry wasn't bruising any more than you'd expect. There was cystic fibrosis and spina bifida but he didn't fit the profile for those either. And, at any rate, the inherited conditions weren't in either family.

Henry had been the easy baby, that was the thing. Grace didn't even labour to have him. They'd been in Canada for David to finish his perinatology training. She and the girls were living in Banff for six months while David went back and forth from Edmonton. They were planning to have Henry in the hospital in Banff.

Grace had just dropped the girls at school. Walking back through town to their condo, she'd slipped and fallen and hit her head hard on the ice. She fell into unconsciousness briefly and then woke and felt what she thought might be blood oozing onto the ice. She imagined it freezing there and her hair sticking to the ground if she tried to get up, then imagined her tongue stuck to an ice cube, then noticed the side of Mount Rundle looked like a series of faces, Banff's Mount Rushmore, except the faces wore sunglasses. The blue sky. A single cloud. Grace tried to focus. Heavily pregnant and prone on the ice, she knew she shouldn't move. It was a cold morning and the streets were quiet. She lay there for several minutes more watching her smoking breath until a boy walked by on his way to school. 'Are you asleep?' he said, backing away from her, thinking to go around her. Somehow Grace managed to convince him to go to the nearest house for help. By the time the ambulance arrived, Grace was in and out of consciousness. She grabbed the paramedic's shirt. 'The girls are at school,' she said. 'Tell them to ring Nan Hughes to pick the girls up. Mia and Phil. Their names.' The paramedic, who'd responded by asking her what her name was, what the date was, where she was, told her everything was okay; they were going to lift her one two three, as if he hadn't heard what she'd said. She grabbed his shirt again. 'You're not hearing me. My daughters are at school. They're babies. Please.'

'Nan Hughes,' he said, 'I got it, it's okay, I know Nan. We'll call the school right away. But for now I need you to keep calm and don't try to move.' Nan Hughes was the mother of a girl in Phil's class and a singer. They'd met in the corridor and agreed to have a coffee. Later, Grace had heard her sing at a concert at the Whyte Museum at Christmas. The feeling she could put in a song. Nan was the only person Grace knew in the town. Someone who could sing like that would look after children.

The next thing she remembered was waking up, David in

a chair beside her, talking to someone's baby in his arms, the smell of a hospital. She remembered thinking how sweet he looked holding a baby, how much she was looking forward to having another baby. Grace closed her eyes and when she woke again, he was still holding a baby but it was screaming in his arms now. David had stubble on his chin and looked a mess. 'What are you doing here?' she said.

'Oh Grace, Grace it's you. You're back.'

'Whose baby is that?' she said.

'This is Henry, Henry our son.' David was crying for some reason. 'And he's pretty keen on getting a feed.'

'What?' she said. She couldn't understand. Totally unaware of what she was doing, she took the baby David was holding – whose baby was it? – and placed it at her breast. Immediately, it became focused on feeding. She noticed her breasts were engorged.

'You had a fall,' David said. 'You've been unconscious.'

Grace felt a stab of panic. 'You have to pick up the girls. They're at school.'

He smiled. 'No, they're still in Banff. One of the other mothers picked them up. They're staying with her. Everyone's been wonderful.'

'Where am I?'

'Calgary. You had a brain bleed. They delivered Henry to reduce your blood pressure.'

'I've had a caesar?'

The baby continued to suck happily as Grace shifted position, sitting up. She looked down at him, and then it hit her. 'This is Henry? Henry our son?' David nodded, tears streaming down his face again. And then Grace was crying too. 'He's got your forehead,' she said finally.

David tried to smile through his tears. 'He's very glad you're awake too. The nurses keep coming up here from the nursery with bottles of formula. He's pretty hungry.'

'How long have I been out?'

'Two days.'

'You let him go two days without feeding?'

'I've put him on the breast now and then. You wouldn't be producing milk before now anyway.'

'I need to see the girls.'

'Yes,' David said. 'We'll get them today. You're all right. That's what I can't get over. You're all right.'

Grace had recovered fully and Henry had been fine. They'd escaped potential tragedy, both of them, she'd thought later. And then at two, Henry had fallen off their first-floor verandah onto the driveway. Grace had seen it happen, had seen him climb up the balustrade and was going out to stop him when he went over. He'd fallen face up and been knocked unconscious. Grace saw immediately that he'd stopped breathing. Looking back, she couldn't say how she'd done what she'd done. She rushed down to him, cleared his airway and started to breathe air into his tiny lungs, counting out the seconds. A neighbour emerged from his house. 'Get an ambulance!' Grace called. 'Get an ambulance now!' She kept count of the breaths, remembered exactly how to perform CPR on a young child, how often and how much pressure on the chest, how much breath into the lungs. By the time she heard the ambulance siren in the distance, her little son was breathing. His eyes were wild with pain. We need to stay very still, she was saying, not knowing if he'd broken his spine. We're going for a ride in an ambulance. But right now, we need to stay very very still, nodding as she held him down. Grace heard something behind her and looked up and around. There was Mía, all of six, looking terrified. 'It's all right, honey,' Grace said. 'Henry fell over. He's going to be all right,' as if saying it would be enough. It wasn't until she'd seen Mía's face that she realised she'd just resuscitated her own son and felt the terror.

Henry had surgery to repair a kidney – he'd hit a wooden garden stake on the way down. It had probably saved his brain by breaking the fall. Ian Gibson had been the paediatrician. He'd come across to the hospital specially. Grace liked about him that he didn't pull punches on that occasion, told them the truth that even the surgeon had been unwilling to tell them, the blow to his kidney, the possibility it wouldn't heal. But it had healed and Henry had been fine.

She thought of these things now as a fog settled over the city. What if she'd harmed Henry, when she fell, when she let him fall? What if there had been some damage to his foetal or two-year-old brain that was only now coming to light? She realised that this was what she was dreading, why she hadn't wanted to take Henry to see Ian Gibson. She would blame herself. This is what she was avoiding. It wasn't enough.

She went into the house and telephoned Ian Gibson's rooms from downstairs, leaving a message. 'Ask Ian if he can fit Henry in.' She was about to hang up when she realised she hadn't given a name. 'It's Grace Hogan here, I'm Henry Ravenswood's mother. We need to see Ian as soon as possible.'

Iris

It was before seven o'clock in the morning when Grace turned up at the door, knocking loudly enough to wake the entire neighbourhood and calling my name. I hadn't slept well, having fallen off the afternoon before and then up half the night with my silly old thoughts. When I heard her calling, I closed my bedroom door – the contents of the box still spread all over the floor – and went out.

Grace charged in and said she wanted to know what the GP had said about travelling but she was agitated, couldn't sit still.

'She says I'm fit for anything,' I lied, but my heart wasn't in it. I was exhausted. I couldn't even muster the energy for the shop, and the idea of fixing breakfast was impossible. I wasn't hungry anyway, I felt as if I hadn't been hungry for months.

'I found some two-for-one flights to Paris in November,' Grace said, walking from the kitchen to the dining room and back. Where did she get the energy? 'If I came with you, we've got a better chance of getting you there and back alive.'

'Have a cup of tea, dear, for goodness' sake. You're making me nervous.' And then a strange thing happened. Grace burst into tears. And not just tears. She started sobbing, rather loudly. 'Oh my Lord, Grace, whatever's the matter?' I couldn't remember a time she cried like this, not since she was small.

She continued to pace around the kitchen sobbing. I'd have got up to her if I could but I was just too tired. 'Iris, I think I killed a child.'

'What do you mean?' And I was confused then. I thought she was talking about Tom. 'You didn't do anything to him.'

'What? No, at the hospital. I missed something I shouldn't have missed. It led to a baby's death. And then Mia broke her arm, and I wasn't even there.'

'Mia?' It took me a moment to remember who Mia was.

'Yes, she fell off a verandah at school. She was all right but I wasn't there. And the baby. I should have seen . . .' She looked as if she might fall over on the spot.

'You come here,' I said. I must have said it loudly and sternly for she came immediately and sat down opposite me, sobbing all the while. I put out my hands and waited until she gave me hers. 'Grace, one thing I know for sure. You've always been too hard on yourself, right from when you were little. If something didn't go your way from the beginning you threw it across the room and called yourself stupid. I never knew how to help you develop patience and compassion towards yourself and I still don't know.

'But one thing I do know better than you is that doctors make mistakes just like everyone else. Even Miss Ivens, Grace. Now, did you mean to kill a baby?' I thought that's what she said she'd done. She shook her head between sobs. 'Will you know next time?' She nodded yes. 'Then stop your silly crying.

Won't do you any good anyway. I'm certainly not having tears if you're coming to Royaumont with me.'

She sniffed and wiped her nose with her arm. 'Do you mean it, Iris? Do you mean I can come?' She was taking the short breaths of a child.

Get a hold of yourself, I wanted to say. 'I suppose,' I said. 'As long as you let me do what I need to and don't organise me and as long as we don't have any more outbursts like that.'

'Of course,' Grace said. She wiped her face, produced a tissue from somewhere deep in her jacket, blew her nose loudly and proceeded to do exactly what I'd asked her not to do. She was organising me. 'We'll fly first-class so you'll be more comfortable. And we'll have a stopover on the way. It'll be fun – and I can find out what you were like when you were young.'

Here was Grace crying about a death for which I was almost sure she couldn't be held responsible no matter what had happened, cheered by the fact she could chaperone an octogenarian on a trip to France. The poor girl needed an easier life.

And then it hit me. If Grace came with me to Royaumont, I would have to tell her the whole story. I would have to tell her everything. I wasn't sure I'd have the courage to do that. For if she was unforgiving when it came to herself, Grace had always been even more unforgiving when it came to me.

Paris 1918

He looked up towards her. The tilt of his head, his grin, the way the light shone in his hair; she felt as if her heart would burst. She breathed in sharply. What? he said.

Nothing, she said, letting the breath out slowly.

What's the worst thing you've ever done? he said, leaning back on the bed, one hand behind his head, the other holding a cigarette.

The worst . . . She screwed up her nose in thought. She went and sat on the end of the bed and had to look back to him. You, she said finally, I think you're the worst thing, but maybe losing my school blazer? I don't know. Hard choice.

Seriously, he said.

Ah, seriously. She stood up and walked over to the window, pulling the robe around her. Let's not talk seriously.

The war? he said. Is the war what's too serious?

She could see he really didn't understand. But she nodded. The war, yes, now that you mention it. And the drapes. The drapes are just too serious.

He looked even more confused. I have never met anyone like you, he said. I thought I was in love once. But you're like another language.

She turned away from him, looking past the serious drapes out at the Luxembourg Gardens. We shouldn't talk like this.

Why not?

Because. Because we don't know how we feel really. It's all so fraught.

Fraught. How?

The war. That's what I was trying to say. I don't know what I think or feel. And there are complications. I ought to tell you.

I know what I feel, he said. I've known since the very first time I met you.

We live worlds apart.

Only if we decide we do, he said. He got up and went over to where she stood, put his hands on her shoulders. He swept her hair aside and kissed her neck softly. Slowly she turned around to face him. She saw there were tears in his eyes again.

Oh my heart, he said. Oh my heart.

Iris

There's a knock on the door. I seem to have fallen asleep on the floor, the contents of the wooden box around me. His letters are spread over the floor, that sure hand I'd never forget. I pick them up quickly and put them back in the box. There's a line of spit from one corner of my mouth that I quickly wipe off my cheek.

Did Grace come this morning? Is she still here? The sun is streaming in through the window. 'Coming,' I call as sensibly as I can. But when I go out there's no one there.

I am still half in a dream I have just had, where Tom came and spoke to me, like the waking dream but I'm sure I've been asleep this time. Not Tom as he was in France but as a boy, perhaps eight. There's a photograph of him at that age, standing at the side of the house holding a dead snake he and Daddy have just pulled from the water tank. Tom's head is at an angle, and while his eyes are as bright as ever and shine straight out at you, it's this tilt of his head that lends him an air of uncertainty, impermanence, as if perhaps he knows he's not here forever. I look and want him to tell me, did he know, did he know he would die so young? And was life, the life he had, enough? That's what you come to eventually. When you've got through the guilt and the rage and the blaming. You just want them not to have suffered, to have lived enough. The snake is longer than Tom and he holds it up to show it off, and perhaps it's this rather than some deep life knowledge that tilts his head. 'Wasn't it grand, Iris?' he says in the dream. 'And didn't we have fun? Don't you think, Iris? Well, don't you?' I can never answer. I try but my voice fails me.

In my groggy state, I see Tom again, as large as life, standing in the hallway, Tom as the young man I knew just before he died. But when he speaks, I realise it's only Geoffrey. He must have been down getting my spare key from under the house when I went to open the door. He looks worried. 'Where were you, Iris? I've been knocking for ages.'

'Oh, I was out the back,' I lie, my face all bent out of shape – I could feel it – and my hair all over the place when I touch it.

In June of 1916, we received word to evacuate as many patients as were ambulatory and expect severe casualties. For three days, the hospital was almost empty. We'd already increased our capacity again in response to requests from the Croix-Rouge and now we had four hundred beds, including an emergency ward we set up in the refectory, originally intended to be temporary, moving the staff dining room out into the cloister. Goodness knows what we'll do when winter comes back, Miss Ivens said about our new dining arrangements, but we can't worry about that now. We knew the wounded would come soon as the pounding of guns grew more frequent. We remained twenty-five miles from the front and unlikely to be attacked at Royaumont, but we were near enough to Paris – a key target for the Germans – that Miss Ivens continued to make us carry out occasional drills, blacking out the hospital and moving patients and staff to the cellars under the abbey.

I'd seen Tom every few months. Either he came to Royaumont or I went to Chantilly on an errand. He'd remained in the postal service and seemed to have resigned himself to his role, much to my relief. He lost weight as he grew even taller, so much so I worried at times he wasn't eating enough. When I could, I took something from Royaumont, biscuits, cakes, a lemon tart. He told me I had to stop worrying. He was fine, he said. Violet said she thought I was driving him mad.

As soon as we received the advice from the Croix-Rouge I went to the kitchen to let Miss Quoyle know we were expecting more wounded and we should check our stores and reorder whatever might be needed. When I walked in she and Cicely were arguing. I knew what it was about before I heard their words. A new doctor, Louisa Martindale, had joined us that week. When she'd offered her services to the Scottish Women's Hospitals, Miss Ivens had snapped her up. But Dr Martindale had brought her husband across with her and she wanted a job for him. Miss Ivens had said he could be a driver. Some of the drivers were happy enough – as happy as they ever were about anything – but because he was a man some of the others were exercised about it. They'd been the same about Tom. Whenever he visited, he helped out in the kitchen – he was a favourite with Quoyle – or shifted furniture for the sisters. He worked on the cars, too, for any of the drivers who let him. Most of them were used to him now. But Cicely on the subject of men working at the hospital. You'd think Dr Martindale had brought the Devil himself to work with us at Royaumont.

'Listen to yourself,' Quoyle was saying to Cicely now. 'What's he ever done to you?'

'It's not him,' Cicely said. 'It's all of them, what they've done to all of us. He comes here and we simply let him in. It's only because he's the husband, not the wife. If he was a woman, what do you suppose would happen?'

'Well, I imagine you wouldn't be making such a fuss,' Quoyle said. 'You'd put her straight in. I know your type. You hate men, don't you?'

This was the wrong thing to say to Cicely if Miss Quoyle had hoped to calm the waters. 'And I know yours,' Cicely spat. 'You're ignorant.'

Quoyle burst into tears – not an easy thing even for Cicely to achieve – and left the kitchen. I looked at Cicely. 'This Cause of yours can't be much chop if all it does is upset someone like Miss Quoyle. Have you no respect for age?'

'Shut up, Iris,' Cicely said. 'You're so stupid you don't see what's right in front of you.'

I thought about Cicely for the rest of the day. She struck out at everything like a cat that had been mistreated as a kitten. Sometimes you just had to wait for it to subside with people like that. Sometimes it never did. But in the evening, I went over to the garages to find Violet. The truth was, even though it had been a frequent topic of conversation during my time at Royaumont, I didn't really understand what all the fuss was about with the Cause and why it was a source of tension among the other women.

'Suffrage,' Violet said. 'They want the vote. Aren't they doing the same in Australia?'

'Women already have the vote in Australia,' I said.

Violet nodded. 'Well, in England there are those who want the vote and those who will go outside the law to get the vote, the Pankhursts and their friends. Royaumont was started by the national union. Elsie Inglis was for the hunger strikes, or at least, she didn't come out against them. The war's put a hold on it all anyway and I've no idea why Cicely's so upset about old Jack Martindale. He wouldn't hurt a fly. And he's good at poker.'

When Violet mentioned the name Pankhurst, I remembered my aunt Veronica, who visited us from Scotland when I was eight. The first I knew of her was when Daddy showed me the letter saying she was coming, '. . . to meet the wee bairns.' I didn't even know I had an aunt and when I asked Daddy, he said he hadn't thought to tell me. He'd only met her once before he married our mother. When I asked Daddy what she was like he just said, 'She's like your mother, only younger,' which didn't help.

'Your mother's sister is a suffragist,' Mrs Carson told me the day before Veronica was due to arrive. She said it delicately, as if I might be offended. I think Mrs Carson came over especially to warn me, to make sure Tom and I weren't going to be in any moral danger. 'You'd do well to be polite, but not listen to what she has to say. She's in cahoots with Pankhurst and her crew.' Mrs Carson left a rhubarb and apple pie, which was kind of her, and then scooted off when she saw Daddy's horse approaching from the western boundary. I wondered what cahoots were.

Daddy shaved and changed his clothes and told me to bath Tom. He cleaned up the bottles from the table and helped me wash the linen and make the beds. He swept. Then he took me and Tom to the railway station in the trap. Before the train had quite stopped, a woman jumped down and I knew straight away it was Veronica. She had a huge grin on her face and red hair like mine that fell down her back like a long rust waterfall, a wild thing, and she had my green eyes and milky skin but not my freckles. She was tall and long-legged and looked as if she might like to get on a horse and ride pretty fast right then. And she wore pants. I'd never seen anything like her before. She was amazing.

Veronica was five years younger than my mother, my father had told me, twenty-eight when she visited us. I was big for my age and awkward. The only models of womanhood I had were Mrs Carson, who was large and slow-moving, and the nuns at the convent who were impossible to fathom. I knew enough to know that clothes were part of being a woman and that my clothes were never quite right – the hems, the pressing, the combinations – but not enough to know how to fix them.

'You must be Iris,' Veronica said, picking me up in surprisingly strong arms and swinging me around onto her hip and then scooping Tom up in the other arm on the turn. 'Aren't you both gorgeous?' At first Tom held onto my hand as we swung around but soon he was giggling. I'd never seen him as comfortable with a stranger.

Daddy was shy, pulled at his hat, couldn't seem to get his big hand around Veronica's to shake it, then couldn't seem to let go. Back at home, the trip punctuated by Veronica's chatter and Daddy's meagre responses, he couldn't make tea in the pot or get the bread cut for sandwiches. He kept dropping things and forgetting what he was doing. He'd set up a camp bed in my room so that Veronica could have his bed and he managed to tell her so. She told him not to be silly. 'I've come to see them, Jack,' she said. 'At least let me share their room.' And so my aunt slept in the room with Tom and me and it was the best month of my young life.

For here was another kind of woman altogether, different from Mrs Carson and the nuns and the whole sex as I'd known it to that date. I wondered was this what my mother had been like? Veronica didn't care a hoot what anyone thought of her and when I told her what Mrs Carson had said, that she was a sufferist, she laughed for a full minute before she said, 'That's a good word for it. I'm a sufferist.'

The sufferist brought gifts, a little Eiffel Tower for Tom she'd picked up in Paris, some drinking chocolate from Belgium for me that tasted heavenly when you whipped it up with fresh milk and put extra sugar in, toys for both of us that were just perfect.

'I have met a suffragist,' I told Violet now. 'My aunt from Scotland was in the movement.'

Some of the suffragists at Royaumont wore trousers like my aunt Veronica. Some smoked pipes and acted like men. Violet made fun of them, had to explain to me so I'd get her jokes. Dykes, she said, after the boy who put his finger in one, and giggled. They like each other the same way you like your Al. How do you mean? I asked, although I understood immediately. They sleep together, do things with their hands. I giggled. What things? I'll leave that to your imagination, my dear.

When I thought about it, I'd met girls like these before, at school, in nursing. At Royaumont they were more open about their man–woman-like relationships. I wanted to ask Miss Ivens about them but I was too shy. Was it normal? Did she know before they came? Mostly both had jobs, one as

245

driver, the other as orderly, one as doctor, the other as nurse. Was it sinful? On this last count, I'm sure it was. Most things I wasn't told about were sinful, I often later learnt.

They fascinated me, these women, the way they strode about like men, the openness of their smiles, like they'd found the secret of life. I wanted to be like them, or to be a boy, with a boy's straight body and a boy's easy laugh. For some of them, especially the doctors, it might have been a convenient arrangement. How could a woman have a husband, even the most understanding husband, and lead the kind of life a doctor of Royaumont led? There would be children and then what would she do? For others, though, it was the only way they'd live. These were the ones I admired most, the women who had chosen this life because they wanted it. It was their courage, their certain knowledge that they were not wrong just misunderstood, that I loved in them. I suppose it came from having had to be different, likely suffering jeers from others, shunned by some. They were truly brave, I always felt.

When I told Violet that I felt admiration for and even an affinity with these women, she didn't, as I feared she might, recoil. 'Who wouldn't be a boy given a chance?' she said. 'That's the country where all the real living is, after all.'

Veronica had been staying with us for a week when I heard her talking with Daddy late one night. Tom and I were in bed, him fast asleep, me listening intently.

'He has your sister's temper,' Daddy said. He was talking about Tom, who had his father's temper as far as I was concerned.

'Then he'll get along just fine as soon as he learns how to use it properly.'

'Well, Sarah sure knew how to use hers.' They both laughed. There was a pause. 'I don't know,' Daddy said. 'He lost his mother and I haven't been enough. If it weren't for Iris . . .'

'He's a boy, Jack, and boys are forgiven much. I wouldn't worry about Tom but I think you need to do something for Iris.'

'Iris? She's a brick.'

'Exactly. She's eight and already she acts like a mother, chasing after Tom. She needs more support. I'd like to take her back to Europe with me.'

My stomach went to butterflies. I couldn't imagine leaving Daddy and Tom but Europe, where the chocolate had come from, the Eiffel Tower, the Europe where it snowed for Christmas morning, that would be amazing.

'No,' said Daddy. 'She's needed here. It wouldn't be fair.'

'Fair? Listen to yourself, Jack. She's a child but she's like a wife and mother. Talk about fair. It could be just until after Christmas and then I could bring her back.'

'I said no,' Daddy said. 'And that's the end of it.'

I don't believe Daddy said no because he felt he needed me. He and Tom would have managed. I think Daddy was afraid I wouldn't come back. Whenever I did well at school or noticed something Daddy had missed, he'd say I was clever just like my mother. I knew she'd been a zoology student, interested in the monotremes, Australia's strange egg-laying mammals. Daddy had met her when he was hired to show a group of students the bush around Canungra, south of Brisbane, whose creeks were populated by platypuses. She and Daddy fell in love and married and that was the end of her research career. She'd always been more interested in the platypus than

247

in Daddy, Daddy said to us, despite his best efforts. Mostly when Daddy said I was like her, I knew he was proud of me. But she was also headstrong, he gave me to understand, and he could say you're just like your mother and mean it in a different way. And now I'd seen her sister Veronica, this wild woman from the north of Scotland. These were the women I came from. I wouldn't say I was proud exactly, but I situated myself differently, realised I came from different people from my father's people, and I might be different too.

I lay in my bed, Tom's breathing slow and even in the bed beside mine. I didn't know if I was disappointed or relieved that Daddy had refused to let me go, and perhaps I was a little of both.

A few days later, I was trying to change a bandage on Tom's leg. He'd come off his go-cart and a branch had made a deep gash. Really it needed stitches but Dr McLeod's wife was sick after their fourth was born and no one liked to call him out unless it was an emergency. Tom didn't much like me changing the bandage. He liked to do everything himself and I had to keep him still so he didn't bump the wound. 'No!' he yelled and ran away, the bandage trailing along behind him. I caught up with him and dragged him back. He was pinching me and pulling my hair. It wasn't that hard a job – I'd had to do much more difficult things – but his resistance and the sight of the wound, puckered red with what might be infection – I just felt hopeless all of a sudden, completely incompetent to the task. I think I was yelling at him when Veronica came in. 'What's the matter, Iris?' she said and her voice was so kind I felt even more angry, as if she were pitying me.

'Nothing.' I was barely holding back tears. 'I'm just trying to do this.'

'Here,' she said, 'let me help, Tom.' He was watching me carefully, terrified I think that he'd finally sent his sister mad. He became perfectly quiet now, of course, and let Veronica reapply the antiseptic and gauze and rewind the bandage without a peep. I could have killed him for making it so easy on her.

The next day Veronica took me to Brisbane on the train. We went to TC Beirne in the Valley and she bought me a frock in a beautiful blue gingham with a satin sash and a matching ribbon for my hair. We had tea and scones at a teahouse. I'd never been in a teahouse before and I remember being amazed that they made the scones; you didn't have to bring them yourself. We stayed in a hotel in the city and in the morning we had breakfast on a tray with starched linen napkins and little pieces of crisp toast in a silver holder.

I kept that first gingham dress Veronica gave me and I wore it every chance I could. By the time I put it away for good, wrapping it in tissue and cheesecloth and packing it in a box, it was faded to grey and the sash was the only thing still vaguely bright. To me, the dress still looked as it had when new.

When Veronica went home a week after our shopping trip, it left a gap something like the gap left by my mother's death. I suppose my aunt had reawakened in me some notion of what a mother might be like. Not that she was motherly; a much better aunt, with her expensive tastes and indulgences, than a mother. But it was true what Mrs Carson had said, when she visited the first time after Mummy died, that a girl needed a mother figure especially in those between years, and if I ever wanted to talk, well, Mrs Carson had her own daughter, and was more than willing to do her best to fill the breach for me. I had to ask Daddy what the breach was, and he said it was the hole left when two things were torn apart. And that made sense. But Mrs Carson could never fill that breach whereas in her way Veronica already had.

A year later, Daddy solved the problem of how to manage his children by marrying Claire. It did take a load off me for a time, although I always felt responsible for Tom, a responsibility I certainly wasn't willing to give up to Claire. But even after Daddy remarried and for the rest of my young life, Veronica sent me clothes, every Christmas and every birthday. Beautiful clothes, enough of them so that I would never feel out of place among the other girls. When I think back now, it was such an act of kindness on her part, suffragist or not.

'Were you in the Cause?' I asked Violet now.

'Goodness me, no. I don't care about voting. Governments don't change my life. And as if women would ever vote as a bloc. I'd rather have other things.'

'Like what?'

'Like I'd rather not feel I'm being watched all the time.'

'What do you mean?'

'I don't know, just that men watch us. I don't like it.'

'Oh Violet,' I said. 'If you don't like it you'll have to stop being such a flirt.'

'Not that sort of watching,' she said. 'Waiting for us to do the wrong thing so they can blame us. Don't you feel it?'

I shook my head no but I knew what Violet meant. At Royaumont, where we didn't have a man in charge, where we had Miss Ivens, it was different, as if we'd all breathed out a sigh and could relax.

Towards the end of that week the casualties we'd been waiting for started to flow in, slowly at first and then like a river. I was back on the ward again – we were constantly short of staff – and when I finished my fourth night in a row after the first influx, I went to bed but couldn't sleep. So I got dressed and went up to the roof. I sat overlooking the cloister and watched the sun ease into the sky over the poplars of Lys. And I felt such simple joy, the same joy I felt as a girl when I'd see Tom dressed and ready for school, his trousers pressed, his lunch packed, his hair combed. Necessary is what I felt. Useful.

I'd told Matron I'd come back later in the morning so I went downstairs and washed and went out to the cloister tables for a quick bite before going back to the ward. Cicely Hamilton was sitting at a table by herself. She looked upset and I went over and asked if I could join her. I'm not sure I did so out of concern for Cicely, I'm afraid. More likely, I looked forward to telling Violet some bit of gossip. I was fairly sure Cicely had been crying. The iron maiden crying? as Violet might have said. She ought to watch she doesn't rust.

'Where are you working?' she said, pleasantly enough.

'Blanche.'

'How many in?'

'We're full,' I said, 'with seven still waiting downstairs for a bed. They've finished in the theatre for now though. More expected later today. It's the big push, they say, that will end the war.'

'I'll believe that when I see it.' Cicely shook her head slowly. It wasn't like her to be circumspect. She was normally all efficiency and bustle. I noticed an envelope in front of her, postmarked from England. She had tea and toast she hadn't touched.

'Have you news from home?' I said.

'My mother died,' she said flatly.

'I'm so sorry.'

'Don't be. I'm not.' She forced a smile.

'Why ever not, Cicely?'

'My mother,' she started, then stopped. She looked up and away to the left, her mouth clamped shut, tears threatening.

'Let's take a turn around the grounds,' I said. 'I could do with a walk to shake off last night.'

To my surprise Cicely acquiesced. We collected our raincoats – the clouds were heavy and looked likely to give forth – and crossed the cloister to the back lawns. As I'd hoped, the movement of walking made it easier for her to talk and talking was what she needed to do.

Cicely's mother had been excitable, or that's the word Cicely had heard used to describe her mother's strange behaviours. To Cicely, of course, her mother was just her mother. If she stayed up all night baking for one of the children's birthday parties, ran around decorating the house and cleaning in a frenzy, only to tell all the other children to go home almost as soon as they'd arrived for there wasn't enough food, Cicely thought nothing of this. She had no mothers to compare her own to, so this was what mothers did, she supposed. 'Looking back now, I think we were too much for her,' Cicely said. 'She wasn't frail exactly. It was just that she experienced too much of everything. She was too open to it all, if that makes sense. Like the whole world was in her head.'

'What was your father doing?'

'My father was in the army – *is* in the army. He was away most of the time. And when he came home, it was like having a boarder.

'My mother made my life difficult,' Cicely said. 'She came to school and told my teacher that someone was stealing my things. She described shoes I'd never owned, a pair of mittens, a necklace. I stood there and let her do it and never said a word. I don't think the teacher suspected, not then. But when the visits continued – she was sure someone put nits in my hair, she'd found a dead rat in my school bag – my teacher began to understand. She asked me to stay behind one afternoon. Your mother's worried about things, she said. Sometimes, yes, I said. You've no idea, Iris, how you lie for them. No matter what they do, you defend them because the alternative, that they could somehow be wrong, is unbearable. Is everything all right? this teacher said and she put her hand on my shoulder. Of course everything's all right, I said. The next day I went to her and said, Miss Jenkins, you must understand that my mother is excitable, and when someone's excitable you just have to know which parts are true. She nodded. That's very wise, Cicely, she said.'

Cicely's mother was taken from her children in Cicely's thirteenth year, not long after her conversation with Miss Jenkins. It wasn't Miss Jenkins who acted though. It was Cicely's father, who came home and found their mother had shaved the children's heads and shredded their clothes, searching for the nits that continued to elude her. The next day she was gone, no tearful goodbye, not even strong-armed orderlies in white manhandling her into a black car, at least not in Cicely's view. Cicely's view was her father's eyes narrowing, sweat beading on his forehead as he told the children, in a line, that their mother had gone on a nice holiday. One morning they'd woken and their mother was there. The next she was gone. They were going on an adventure, their father said, and he divided them up, three boys and three girls, and sent them off to charitable institutions. He sold the house, moved into the barracks and never saw his children again.

We'd walked twice around the outside of the abbey and our pace was slowing now. 'I saw my mother once,' Cicely said. 'I found out where she was from my grandmother. It was an asylum in the country not far from my school, strangely enough. She'd loved beauty, but the light had gone out of her. She was wearing a stained nightdress with her breasts on show. She didn't know who I was.

'I can't help but think that there was something I didn't do that I should have. I used to go and sleep in her bed if she was scared, and I think sometimes if only I'd gone to her bed that night, I'd have stopped them coming, she might have been saved, mightn't she?'

I was naïve in the extreme, I see now, with no understanding of how guilt worms its way into a heart and festers there. 'You can't blame yourself, Cicely,' I said stupidly. 'You were young.' As if the reality of Cicely's youth or her poor mother's condition could possibly compete in Cicely's mind with her mother's warm body in the bed and her thirteen-year-old sense of responsibility for it. 'Poor Cicely,' I would say now that I have lived my life. 'What a cross to bear.'

For two weeks after that, we had a constant stream of wounded. I was working sixteen-hour shifts, having a four-hour break and then working again. At some stage, the ward sister told me to go off for eight hours and I went up to the room and fell into bed without changing or washing. The ambulances had been back and forth from Creil all through that day and the night that followed. I came to dread the sound of the porter's horn. It haunted my dreams. I'd wake thinking I'd heard it and fall back into a fitful sleep only to wake minutes later. No sooner did we clear the front hall of patients than another load arrived. I worried about Violet.

The stories the men told beggared belief. The shells had made deep holes in the trenches. The soldiers were living in mud up to their knees and so now it was impossible to see where the deeper holes were. One man told me he fell up to his chest and waited five hours to be pulled out. Another man right next to him drowned. And we were all terrified by the new weapons of war, the horrid gas that poisoned eyes and lungs for which we had as yet no treatment. We watched them die in slow agony and any of us who had once thought the war was righteous knew that what was happening to these men and boys could never be related to justice. Now there wasn't a woman in Royaumont who spoke in support of war. No one thought the Kaiser had done right but when you saw the soldiers on both sides, for we treated German prisoners, you knew it should stop. All we could do though was keep treating them. We had no power to intervene in any other way.

The surgeons operated constantly through the first week of July. We set up a second theatre at one end of Blanche. The laboratory was working through the nights to keep up with the surgeons. Swabs were taken of wounds on admission and Dr Dalyell had to sort those with gangrene from those without immediately so that we could prioritise. Vera Collum had trained as a radiographer, and now worked with Dr Savill in the X-ray room. She and two others worked day and night too. Nearly ninety per cent of the wounds we saw in those weeks were gangrenous, and the surgeons needed films in order to know what to excise. Mostly they didn't stop to look for shrapnel, just to clean or amputate to stop the gangrene spreading.

The Senegalese soldier I'd met on one of my first nights at Royaumont, the one who'd known the dying boy's village and had spoken the boy's language, returned to us, this time gravely wounded. He'd lost both of his brothers to the war and now he too would die. I stopped at his stretcher and said a prayer. Allah was the name of his God so I said it to Allah. 'Take care of this poor man who will never go home,' I said. He opened his eyes and looked at me. I don't think he remembered me but I stayed with him as long as I could and I held his cold hand. I don't know why they'd bothered to move him from Creil. Dr Henry came up behind me. 'This one's dead, Iris,' she said. 'Move on to the next.' I looked up at her and there were tears in my eyes but she failed to see them. 'Come on, Iris. We don't have time to tarry.'

Later that day, a group of two hundred soldiers, underfed, tired to exhaustion and ragged, walked by Royaumont. They asked if they could sit on the lawns for an hour or so. We did better, giving them fresh straw to sleep on overnight, a hot meal and fixing what we could of their minor scrapes and dirty uniforms. Where were their officers? Where was their canteen? These poor boys hadn't eaten a meal for over a week, hadn't slept. What we could do for them, for any of them, was so meagre compared with what was happening across France.

After I finished on the ward again, I went up to my room and lay on my bed but couldn't sleep. I spent a long time staring up at the ceiling without thoughts, just wide awake. Finally I fell into a fitful sleep but woke after less than an hour feeling worse than when I lay down. I'd never felt so tired and yet I knew I had to go back to the ward. I dragged myself up, washed quickly, and dressed and went down.

Miss Ivens had operated for eighteen hours straight the day

before and had had less rest than me, I was sure. There were no shifts for our surgeons. They just worked whenever we had urgent cases, and right now we had a constant stream of urgent cases. Miss Ivens was already back at work, according to an orderly I saw on the stairs. Violet had worked through the night too as more casualties poured in. I found her in the cloister and we shared a cigarette before she went off again to Creil to pick up another load. I'd worked hard to learn to smoke. It had taken time but finally I was as competent as Violet. I found it calmed my nerves.

Violet told me a patient had fallen from her ambulance in the night and she'd had to go back to get him. It shouldn't have been a reason for mirth but as she told it – she'd heard a thump, assumed it was a pothole and had driven on, the other patients yelling at her to stop – we both started to giggle.

'The worst of it is,' Violet said, trying hard to suppress laughter, 'I went on for half a mile before I realised what the din in the back was about.' And then she broke up altogether and I joined her, a picture in my head of little Violet, sitting up straight at the wheel of her ambulance in the way she did, leaning forward, peering ahead into the darkness, intent on getting her wounded to Royaumont, ignoring the noise in the back until she could no longer, then realising what she'd done, turning round, just as intent on getting back to the poor wounded man who'd fallen from the truck.

The man was ambulatory – a minor head injury – and he hadn't been further injured by the fall. All arrived safely at Royaumont half an hour later. But we couldn't stop laughing, and all I can say in our defence is that we were exhausted beyond all reason.

I had continued to worry about Violet's mental state. She was often in a black mood now and more against the war than any of us. I sometimes thought she might just quit and go home. She didn't seem to be able to find any good in what she was doing. I was glad we were laughing again, more than laughing, giggling like the young girls we were, as if the horrors all around us were nothing but stories. 'What's the joke?' Quoyle asked. Even if we could have got the words out amidst our laughter, I knew she wouldn't have understood.

Miss Ivens came out to the cloister then, looking exhausted. She ignored our laughter, which quickly sobered us. 'Iris, I need you with me today. I'm meeting with the Croix-Rouge later and I must have you there. There's trouble again. They want us to open another ward. I can't see how we can.' Her eyes were wet with tiredness and just for a moment, I thought she might fall over or cry. I got up and, without thinking of the breakfast I hadn't eaten, followed her back through the abbey and out into the day.

There were a few women who weren't cut out for Royaumont – you had to be a certain sort, ready to do whatever was needed, ready to muck in, as Miss Ivens termed it. The hardest thing for those who weren't suited was admitting it to themselves. They so much wanted to be women of Royaumont, could see something worthy in it I suppose. Miss Ivens usually let them come to their own decision. Who am I to know their hearts? she would say to me. The first matron, Miss Todd, tried her best to fit in but was too steeped in the old ways. She didn't have the kind of flexibility we needed, not knowing from one day to the next how many wounded would come and how we'd cope. It wasn't always ordered and neat. The final blow had come when Violet was ill and Matron Todd had suggested sending up to Paris for a man. I really thought Miss Todd was for it. But Miss Ivens was kind, she let Miss Todd resign on her own terms and even wrote to Dr Inglis later that while Miss Todd hadn't fitted in at Royaumont, 'it's our fault for asking her to come out in the first place. She wouldn't want you to know that she cried when she resigned.' Strangely, after Miss Todd left, many of the nurses missed her. Later they spoke of her as their mother away from home. I didn't find her motherly but perhaps that was because she saw me as one of Miss Ivens's crew and not one of hers.

The only person I remember Miss Ivens speaking to directly about leaving Royaumont was Dr McCourt, who'd already come to her own decision so it hardly mattered. And I only mention her now because had Dr McCourt not come to Royaumont, had she not awoken in me a feeling about myself I still don't quite understand, other than it had something to do with pride and perhaps wasn't my noblest feeling, had Dr McCourt not done what she did, I probably would never have taken seriously Miss Ivens's suggestions to me and the future might have been different. I might have done what my father had told me to do and taken my brother home.

Dr McCourt came to us highly recommended from one of the Serbian units. It's true she hadn't stayed long in any one hospital but when I raised this, Miss Ivens just said that Dr McCourt might like change and this was hardly a reason to worry. I met Dr McCourt on her first day. She ignored me and spoke to Miss Ivens as many doctors did. She was very sure of herself, I remember thinking.

There was an operative case, a head injury, and Miss Ivens had embarked on a particular course of action, untested but successful with other such cases. War presents so much useful trauma, the same over and over again, and Miss Ivens or one of her colleagues had discovered or read somewhere that if you made a hole in the skull and inserted a drain, the fluid collecting around the brain after trauma would disperse, easing pressure and reducing the mental damage that would render a man useless.

When Dr McCourt saw Miss Ivens drill the already damaged skull, saw her insert a catheter drain into the injured man's head, she was horrified, I think, for she brought it up in the theatre, even though Miss Ivens was leading the procedure and she, Dr McCourt, was assisting. 'Whatever are you doing, Frances?' she said, despite the fact that Miss Ivens had just explained what she was doing. There was silence in the theatre, for our practice was that the lead surgeon – it wasn't always Miss Ivens but whoever it was – made the decisions and others followed and no one questioned the lead surgeon, not during an operation and especially not if it was the chief. I was assisting that day and I knew we were in for some trouble with Dr McCourt.

Miss Ivens was for the most part one of the gentlest souls I ever knew but when you crossed her you were never in any doubt that you had done so. Miss Ivens looked up at Dr McCourt over her mask, her big brown eyes and dark skin a band of energy across her face, and asked her to leave the theatre. Which of course she did.

On another occasion, not long after this altercation, Miss Ivens and I were doing her ward rounds. She asked me to irrigate a wound and change a complicated dressing, normally something a doctor would have done herself. Miss Ivens had often used me in this way, even in the operating theatre. The first time, it had been necessity. One of the young doctors, Dr Henry I think now, collapsed in the middle of an operation. Exhaustion was the culprit. It was during that rush of July when everyone was working an extra share. Dr Henry fainted and one of the orderlies stood down to help her but Miss Ivens had to continue and she needed a second surgeon but none was available. 'Iris,' she said, picking me over more experienced operating theatre nurses. 'I need you to help me.'

To be honest, despite my terrible nerves about making a mistake, there wasn't much to it, cutting and scraping tissue to remove little pieces of metal and infection while retaining as much good tissue as possible, using an X-ray to guide the knife. The trick, I learnt, was to proceed slowly, rather like one does skinning a rabbit so as not to waste good meat. Miss Ivens, busy on a facial reconstruction, left me to my own devices until she'd finished, which eased my nerves considerably and gave me confidence. Surely she'd be watching if there had been a need to do so. When she finished what she was doing, she looked carefully at the man's thigh where I'd been working, compared my work against the X-ray, in the same way she'd do with a junior surgeon. 'This is splendid,' she said. 'Where did you train?' and smiled. I remembered that smile. It was like a bath of warm light in a darkness you didn't even know was darkness but once you'd been in that light you knew what it was to be back in the dark.

By the time Dr McCourt joined, Miss Ivens was using me to assist from time to time. I never felt I was asked to do anything I couldn't manage and Miss Ivens said that my hands were as nimble as a surgeon's. I'd always seen my hands as rather large and I was just glad to have a use for them finally.

So on this day Miss Ivens asked me to change a dressing, it

was nothing out of the ordinary and she did so confident that I would cause her patient less pain than the assisting doctor for the day who, while well meaning and competent in diagnosis, was ham-fisted to a large extent and so nervous about her ham-fistedness that she'd inevitably cause more pain than ease. None of the other doctors took much notice of me or seemed to mind me doing more than my role would strictly permit. I don't know if they discussed it among themselves but no one ever said anything to me until Dr McCourt arrived on the ward that day and exclaimed, in a voice too loud for the space, 'Whatever are you doing, nurse? Let me take over.' Miss Ivens had been called away and I had no choice but to stand aside. I hoped and prayed Miss Ivens wouldn't return before the procedure was finished.

I watched Dr McCourt change the dressing, causing far more pain than I would have, and while it may be conceitful for me to say so, the poor patient's groans were enough evidence that I was right. As she was leaving, Dr McCourt, who looked impervious to the pain she'd caused, looked at me. She must have seen something in my eyes, something of disrespect, for she said, 'I will be talking to Matron about your behaviour, nurse. There is nothing in the world worse than an upstart.' She said it loudly enough that the men around us and the nurses and orderlies heard her. My ears burned with rage and embarrassment but I said nothing. 'Yes, Doctor,' she said. I looked at her, unsure what she meant. 'Say Yes, Doctor,' she repeated.

'Yes, Doctor,' I said, wishing the stone floors of the abbey would rise up and swallow her whole.

They didn't but the next week, Miss Ivens told me Dr McCourt had left. I hadn't told Miss Ivens about that day and the dressing, but for Miss Ivens, anything but total loyalty was unthinkable. Dr McCourt had questioned Miss Ivens's clinical decision-making. She had to go. Dr McCourt left and while it wasn't the last we heard from her, she never again served with the Scottish Women's Hospitals.

What happened with Dr McCourt started me thinking along a path, I feel sure now. Dr McCourt may or may not have been right in her criticism of Miss Ivens. I will never know the truth of that. But she hadn't shown anything of the skill even someone like me had been able to learn at Royaumont which would have enabled her to change that complicated dressing without doing further harm to an already traumatised patient. And yet, she was a doctor. For the first time, I started to think that perhaps Miss Ivens's faith in me wasn't misguided kindness. Perhaps I did have some gifts to offer.

Every year, the Croix-Rouge sent an officer to inspect the hospital and renew our accreditation. The first year they sent an accountant from Paris, a large round fellow who gave us an equivocal report, not failing us but not really lauding us either. But at the end of 1916, they were sending a new auditor, Miss Ivens said, and I was to help.

The rushes of earlier in the year had finally abated and we'd been able to catch up with the maintenance work on the abbey, emptying the cesspits, working out where we might further expand the wards, finalising the plans for a new staff dining room. I went to a Halloween party in Blanche dressed as a kangaroo, using Collum's fur coat and mittens and a scrunched-up hat as a joey for my pouch. The patients loved the parties we had, playing games like musical chairs or find the slipper as if they were carefree children rather than men who'd seen such horror. At the end, Violet sang for us and I found tears in my eyes to listen to her again. The soft autumn sunlight streamed through the big windows and the men were listening intently, their red jackets and blankets against the stone walls, surrounded by staff in all manner of get-up, Berry as a rabbit, Miss Ivens as Father Christmas ('It was all I could find in the costume box, dear'), Dr Courthald as an Argyll and Sutherland Highlander, Cicely Hamilton as a tank, crawling in under her canvas bath.

Violet's voice had come into its own at Royaumont. On All Saints' we commemorated the dead in the cemetery at Asnières. It was awful to see the graves of the young men and to know they were now gone forever. When Violet stood and sang the Marseillaise that day, she herself cried, tears streaming down her face, her voice never faltering.

I had all but forgotten about the Croix-Rouge officer who had accompanied the accreditation inspection team, the one I'd worked out was Jean-Michel Poulin. In fact, I'd seen his name on a report from a hospital in Reims and assumed he'd transferred north. But the new auditor was one of his colleagues from that inspection team, Dugald McTaggart. I went into the room where the inspector was sitting at the little table we'd set up. I could only see his back as he was bent over the desk writing something. 'Hello. I'm Miss Ivens's assistant. I'm to help you,' I said in French.

'Dugald McTaggart. Spy on me you mean?' he said in English and turned around. It was him. He'd only spoken French when I'd met him before and I'd assumed, wrongly, I realised now, that he was French. But he was Dugald McTaggart and not Jean-Michel Poulin. His accent was Scottish-French.

I'm sure I was blushing. 'I imagine so,' I managed to say switching to English, 'if that's what it takes.'

'You have given me a beautiful room,' he said.

'This is the Chapel of Saint Louis,' I said, doing my best to recover my composure.

'Perfect place for confession?' he said and smiled. I remembered his smile, the way his face would change from severe to soft in a moment.

'Or an Inquisition,' I replied.

'Which do you think we have here?'

'Both?' I said. Turning to the task at hand, I gave him the schedule of interviews for the morning. 'Before we start, I'll show you around.' Miss Ivens had told me not to let the inspector wander the abbey unaccompanied and to sit in on his meetings. While I had no intention of spending the day shadowing him if he wanted to work on his own, I also didn't want to let him loose unaccompanied among the orderlies or drivers.

As he picked up his bag from the table, I noticed his long fingers with well-groomed nails. 'So, Iris, are you still working for Miss Ivens?'

I was surprised he remembered me. 'Yes, but I'm also a nurse,' I said.

'Ah, I could have picked that. You have a nurse's eyes.'

'What does that mean?'

'Nurses can communicate everything they need to communicate with their eyes, which is why they are invaluable in the operating theatre.'

The reference made me think suddenly of Al. We had first met in theatre. I felt guilty for no reason I could explain. 'And how do you come to know so much about theatre sisters?' I asked.

'I'm a surgeon. Did they not tell you that?'

I didn't say I'd assumed he was an accountant. 'No, I didn't realise they'd send a surgeon this time.'

As I led him through the abbey, he talked about his work. He'd been a psychiatrist, he said. He'd signed up at the outbreak of war and they'd put him through basic surgical training. 'We do what we can for their bodies but no one is caring for their minds. We'll pay for this.'

It was something Mrs Berry had talked to me about. Many of the men who came through Royaumont, especially the ones who'd been wounded once already, woke in the night from terrible dreams, at once shaking as if cold and sweating as if hot, or didn't sleep at all, smoking constantly through the hours. Some developed facial tics. Many were convinced they would die and could talk about nothing else. Others spoke incessantly with false cheer, or talked of revenge on the Germans. 'We see it here too,' I said. 'Our priest talks with them. I don't know what he does but he calms them.'

'Religion can help,' he said, 'but these men's minds are broken. They can't stop remembering what happened to them. And it's no wonder, because what happened to them should happen to no one.' He looked at me and smiled. 'But this is gloomy talk. Here is your Canada ward, I see. This is the new one?'

The refectory – which had been the staff dining room – was our latest ward, set up during the rushes of 1916 and named for the country that had raised so much money for us. The Canadian girls among us were thrilled to have a little of their own country here at Royaumont.

'It's beautiful,' he said. 'Being here must help the men to heal. It's such a wonderful place.'

'It is,' I said. I didn't tell him that we were still dining in the cloister, albeit in our warm coats now. We'd shifted the tables and chairs for his benefit. Although Miss Ivens and I had worked out where we could put a staff dining room, we could never be sure workmen would be available – most were off fighting. The project was dragging out. 'In the summer, the morning sun comes through the stained glass and you can imagine what it must have been like to be one of the monks here. It's a . . . a holy place.' I reminded myself he hadn't come to hear me talk about the abbey. 'How did you come to work with the Croix-Rouge?' I asked him.

'My mother is French,' he said. He stopped to light a cigarette.

'Ah, that's how you fooled me. I assumed you were French.'

'I am,' he said.

I took him out into the cloister, where a dozen or so cots were lined up along one side, soldiers sitting reading or writing, or lying down sleeping, rugged up against the cold with their wounds exposed to whatever sun was working hard to make its way through the clouds. 'We've found that sun exposure aids healing and helps prevent infection,' I explained. 'Our Dr Dalyell in pathology trained in Vienna.' As I spoke, the sun came out suddenly as if commenting positively on Dr Dalyell's theory, and Dr McTaggart nodded appreciatively.

I saw Violet sitting on the little bench in the middle of the cloister smoking and chatting with one of the patients. Her hair fell in soft curls to her shoulders. 'The sun, Iris. Finally, we have some sun,' she called over. She looked at me and smiled. Violet had been better since the rushes had abated. Miss Ivens had sent her on leave to Paris and she seemed much happier. 'Who are you?' she said to Dr McTaggart, not unkindly, holding her hand over her eyes to shield them. He introduced himself. 'Ah, the auditor. I'm Violet Heron, ambulance driver. What do you think so far?'

'I think Iris is an excellent guide,' he said, looking at me. 'I've hardly noticed the hospital.'

Violet laughed. 'You, my friend, can stay.' The patient beside her cleared his throat noisily. 'How rude of me. This is Henri Michelet. He can tell you about the care here, can't you, darling? You've been here forever.'

Henri Michelet was all but healed from a shrapnel wound in his left leg that had become infected but he'd taken to spending his days in the abbey kitchens and since Miss Ivens had taken a liking to him he'd been allowed to stay. Before the war he had been a chef in Paris and so Miss Ivens had let him cook a few meals for the patients, thinking perhaps this could solve the problem we'd had. Miss Quoyle remained our cook but the Croix-Rouge had continued to press us to find a French cook for the French soldiers. When Michelet cooked, the patients loved the food compared with what we were able to prepare for them, and while none of us said it in Quoyle's hearing, the staff loved the food Michelet prepared too. Miss Ivens had told me she wanted Michelet to stay but the French were going to send him back to the battlefield. We'd already kept him for longer than strictly needed. 'The nurses are beautiful angels from God,' he said now. 'The doctors we worship.' He put his hand on Violet's leg. 'And the drivers? The drivers have hearts of lions and wits of hyenas.'

'I'm not sure I like that last bit,' Violet said. 'Anyway, Dugald, you can ask me anything you like.'

'The front has moved,' he said. 'I believe there is shelling on the road to Creil these days.'

'Occasionally,' Violet said. 'I can't wear my cap any more. I have to wear a helmet which is heavy and ugly and ruins my hair. The noise gets to one sometimes. I wear earplugs. That way, if doom is coming, I'll not know.' She laughed but it rang untrue to my mind.

'The women are not scared?'

'I'm sure they are,' Violet said, 'as are the men.'

I tried to give Violet a look but she couldn't see me. She and Michelet were seated and she still had her hand over her eyes to look at Dr McTaggart. He smiled. 'I am sorry, Miss Heron,' he said. 'I didn't mean to imply you would be more frightened than a man. I don't know you at all but feel I know you entirely. I am sure you are more courageous than a hundred men.'

Violet didn't respond. Michelet said, 'I need to tell you a thing that is wrong with the hospital.'

'What's that?' Dr McTaggart said, moving effortlessly back to French.

'They feed us English food. It is glug day in, day out. They need a French cook.' Michelet grinned.

'I see,' Dr McTaggart said. 'I'll ask the patients about this. It's something we've talked to your chief about in the past.'

'Make sure you do,' Michelet said. 'The patients will tell you.'

We completed our tour and I told Dr McTaggart I would leave him to organise himself. 'I won't sit in on your interviews unless you want me to,' I said. 'Although Miss Ivens has asked me to attend with her.'

'You can sit in on all of them if you like,' he said. 'There's nothing secret about what I'm doing.' He frowned slightly. 'But on the other hand, perhaps the staff will find your presence intimidating.'

I laughed. 'I don't think so. I'm not anyone important here.' I corrected myself. 'I mean, powerful. I'm not powerful. But I am important enough to show you around.' I was blushing, not wanting him to think we didn't see his visit as significant.

'I find you intimidating,' he said, 'or perhaps powerful. Miss Ivens clearly thinks the world of you. She's written us about you.' I wondered what on earth Miss Ivens would have written about me and why I hadn't seen a draft. But I quickly moved on to the arrangements for the interviews and forgot what he'd said. The day went smoothly with everyone turning up on time. Miss Ivens got rather worried when Dr McTaggart asked her about whether we'd had any doctors resign and why. 'It's that bloody McCourt,' Miss Ivens said to me later. 'She wants to do us in.'

I told her not to worry, that even if he had some information about Dr McCourt, Miss Ivens had done the right thing and Dr McTaggart would see that. He met with a group of doctors without Miss Ivens and his questions were about relationships with the chief and how clinical care decisions were arrived at. Mrs Berry told me later that she was fairly sure his questions were because they must have heard something about Dr McCourt but, Mrs Berry said, she saw no reason to worry Frances with the details. I agreed. Miss Ivens would only fret and if Dr McTaggart was going to write something in his report, our bothering Miss Ivens now wouldn't stop him. He also met with a group of nurses and with Matron Simpson and the orderlies and drivers. He asked to interview the cook and I thought back to Michelet's comments. I explained to Dr McTaggart that Quoyle had been with us since the start and was proud of what she'd achieved. 'I'll be fine, Iris,' he said. 'But thank you for the warning. I won't be unkind.' He visited the wards and sat on beds with patients. I went with him but remained at a respectful distance. I watched as he listened to them, nodding from time to time, extending his hand to a brow or arm, smiling, occasionally laughing. By the end of the day he'd collected several letters to post home and various messages he needed to convey for the men. 'Inspecting the hospital is one thing,' he said, 'but this is what's important about what we do.'

'Those soldiers saw you as one of them,' I said.

'*Vive la France*,' he said, holding his hand on his heart. He sang the first two lines of the Marseillaise. He had a lovely tenor voice and I couldn't help but smile. I didn't sing 'God Save the King' in response.

I saw him out to the car that waited for him in the drive. As he was getting in, he took my hand in his and I felt the same feeling, almost as if we were electrified, that I'd felt the first time we met. His face showed nothing.

'Thank you, Dr McTaggart,' I said.

'It's Dugald,' he said. 'Thank you, Iris. It has been a . . . an educational day.' And that's all he said about the visit. He got into the car and spoke to the driver who pulled away. I turned to go back inside when I heard the car stop in the gravel drive. He got out and ran back to where I stood. Running, he looked young, more like a boy than a man, certainly not an auditor who could pass or fail our hospital. When he reached me, he said, a little breathlessly, 'Can I . . . visit you? Can I call on you?'

'Of course,' I said, confused. 'You need more information?'

He shook his head and smiled. 'I want to see you,' he said. 'Iris. I want to see you again.' He grabbed both my hands in his and nodded as if to encourage me to say yes. I couldn't speak, only nodded my head yes. 'Good then. I'll come for you.' I nodded again. He smiled and was gone, turning around once to wave as if to check I was really there. On my hands, I could still feel the warmth of his fingers.

I walked back through the cloister. I found Violet in the garages, getting ready to set off for Creil. 'What a dashing young man that inspector was,' she said. 'I'd like to do a bit of inspecting with him,' she said.

'Violet.'

'What?'

'You mustn't talk like that.'

'You can't tell me you weren't taken with him. The eyes said it all.' She looked at me, saw something in my face. 'Iris, don't tell me he's the one.' I blushed. 'He is. He's the one, Iris. Oooooooh, he's beautiful.'

I smiled. 'He asked to call on me.' I frowned. 'After his report's finished of course.'

'Ooh,' Violet sang. 'Iris has a lover. Iris has a lover.'

'Don't be ridiculous,' I said. 'We simply got on well.'

'We simply . . . got on well,' Violet said, 'and what do you think Major Simply Got on Well is planning for his next visit? A more detailed inspection?'

Now I felt the blush right to my ears and the more I blushed, the worse it got. 'Oh Violet, you go too far.'

'And you, my dear, don't go far enough. If you're not careful I'll snatch him out from under you.'

'Iris, you need a break.' Miss Ivens had invited me to sit down in her office and had offered me tea. This was the second time she'd ever done so and I knew she had something on her mind. It was, it seemed, my mental health.

'I'm fine,' I said, offended at the suggestion I wasn't coping. 'I'm just tired.' Dr Courthald, our anaesthetist, was off birdwatching. She'd dragged me along with her the evening before and we'd spent over an hour discussing the difference between the common nighthawk and the rednecked nightjar. 'They're so alike, Iris,' she'd said, identifying their calls one by one. 'But the nightjar's more of a *kyok-kyok*, wouldn't you say?' I'd been unable to tell which was which and I didn't much care and told her so. I wondered now if she'd told Miss Ivens I'd been short with her and Miss Ivens was worried about me.

It was early in 1917 and so far we'd seen none of the rushes we'd experienced the year before. Miss Ivens and I had continued to be busy, but we were dealing now with a different order of problem, one I didn't much like. Cicely had always made life difficult for the drivers – she had a terrible temper and didn't like that the drivers worked so independently. Miss Ivens did her best to patch things up. Finally, Cicely herself decided to leave us and I do believe it was for the best. She came to say goodbye to me. 'Thank you for your kindness, Iris,' she said, awfully formally. I was about to respond that she'd been kind too – which we both knew would have been a lie – when she nodded her head once, looking for all the world as if she might break down and cry – and turned and walked away.

But the damage Cicely had done with the drivers was irreparable, it seemed, and they had their finances to think of. Like the orderlies, the drivers were all volunteers and while they'd been able to get through a year, stretched to two, without income, no one expected the war to continue so long. They simply had to go home. Even Violet was having trouble staying in terms of money.

Miss Ivens pleaded with the committee to put the drivers

on salary to no avail. She even paid some of their expenses herself but still the committee refused to pay them and told us we must find new volunteers. This wasn't easy. The conditions the drivers worked in were appalling, the roads rutted and sometimes dangerous, shells falling, and the state of the patients they collected sometimes defied belief. They had to get back to Royaumont in quick order and they worked day and night as needed just like the surgeons. Miss Ivens didn't want new inexperienced drivers coming and having to learn what our drivers already knew.

Eventually, we found new girls but they weren't as dependable as those we'd lost, which simply put more pressure on Violet. I worried about her again.

Now Miss Ivens was focused on my well-being. 'It's not today,' she said. 'You've been working under terrible pressure for months. I forget you're only twenty-two. It's not fair.'

'I'm twenty-four,' I said.

'Whatever. You used to be twenty-two. I'm speaking as a doctor now, not as your employer, and I prescribe three days in Paris. Violet can chaperone you, or perhaps you'd better chaperone her. She needs a break too, poor girl. She's never really recovered from her illness. So, chaperone each other. At any rate, stay out of trouble.'

'Oh Miss Ivens, are you sure you can manage without me?'

'Of course we'll manage. After all, we're women. You go off and take a break and come back full of beans.'

I thanked her and went immediately to tell Violet, who was as excited as I was. 'Why don't you ask Whatsisname to meet us, your inspector friend? And the little brother Tom? He's good for a laugh.'

'Dugald McTaggart? Do you think I should?' I hadn't seen

Dugald since the audit visit although he'd been in touch by telephone and message to ask for information. He'd been friendly, said he was looking forward to seeing me again once his report was finished. Secretly I'd been pleased. I thought often of his face, how it changed so much when he smiled.

'Of course you should. Let's have some fun for a change.'

That evening, I sent a note off to Tom – the telephone was out of order again – to tell him I'd be in Paris. He sent a note back that he would meet me at ten at Les Deux Magots, a café on the left bank of the river.

'Quite the poet, is he, your brother?' Violet said when I told her.

'What do you mean?'

'Les Deux Magots is where Rimbaud met his lover,' she said. 'Maybe your major inspector should meet us there too.' I had told Violet that Dugald confided he wrote poetry about the war. He'd promised to send me some. I'd make sure Violet never saw any of it; she'd only have fun at his expense, I was certain.

'Les Deux Magots is not quite what I would have expected from the mechanic.' Violet had taken to calling Tom the mechanic. She would take the car to him in Chantilly or he would come to Royaumont. It was a wreck, he'd confided in me, that had been driven badly. He didn't know how long he could keep the thing going the way Violet drove. Although Violet and Tom had never become close, Violet was doing her best to be kind to Tom and working on the Royaumont cars made him feel useful. I appreciated her help with him. And since now two of the cars had been replaced by purpose-built ambulances, Violet's was one of the only vehicles Tom could work on.

In the end, I couldn't bring myself to write a note to Dugald but I gathered up some statistical reports he'd requested. I'd planned to post them but I thought I could take them to his office while in Paris. If he was there, he was there, I told myself. If not, not. Violet had picked daisies all through the summer. She'd pull their petals off. He loves me, he loves me not. 'Who?' I'd ask. 'Anyone,' she'd say. 'All of them.' After I met Dugald, she'd do it for me. 'He loves you. Iris, he loves you. It came up he loves you. Ooh ooh ooh my dear.'

On the train the following Thursday, we met a group of soldiers on their way back to their units. When we told them where we were from, one of them said he'd been cared for at Royaumont and that any soldier who knew that's where he was going breathed a sigh of relief. He'd keep his legs and arms, the soldier said and I thought how different his attitude was from that of the soldiers who came to us on our first night in 1915. We really had done well. The soldier on the train sang us a song he'd made up, '*Les Dames Écossaises*', in front of the whole carriage. It was lovely.

Another of them tried to give Violet the ring he wore on his finger. 'No,' she said, taking his hand and smiling. 'This is yours.' He pleaded with her but she wouldn't be moved. He was a handsome young soldier with black hair and brown eyes. Violet refused him again.

Afterwards, I asked her why she didn't take the ring. 'It would have made him happy,' I said.

'Oh Iris, you idiot. It's his wedding ring. He's giving it to me because he thinks he's going to die. By refusing it, I'm telling him to stay alive.'

We came out of the station into a bright spring day. As soon as I saw the city again, I realised Miss Ivens had been right, as she so often was. I was exhausted, not just from work, but to my soul, and Violet, while better than she had been a year before, wasn't fully healed. We'd seen so much at Royaumont, so much human suffering. You couldn't keep looking it in the face and not start to sink. Paris, beautiful Paris, refreshed us.

Violet took my arm as we walked the streets. 'Oh Iris, I wish we could just be here from now on and not have to go back to the stupid war.'

'Trouble is, the war will come here eventually, Violet.'

'I suppose it will.' We bought croissants from a little baker we found near the station. We sat outside and ate them. The sun was shining on our faces. A gentle breeze blew towards us. It felt like perfection.

We found the hotel in the Latin Quarter and then went to a bath house Violet knew. The hot bath was heavenly after months and months of a quick sponge or shower under a canvas bag. To lie and soak in warm water was as good as finding a book you could escape into. We slept on freshly laundered sheets. I woke to a fine day feeling wonderful.

We took breakfast in a little café across the street from our hotel. Coffee was available again – it had been rationed – and Violet ordered us each a café au lait and croissant. 'You're so much brighter here,' I said. Violet was wearing a plain green sweater that drew out her eyes. Her cheeks had some colour again.

'You're so sweet, Iris,' she said. 'Like a mother.'

'Am I?' I said. 'I'm going to see Dugald today. I hardly want to be like a mother.'

'No, I don't suppose you do. But I'd give my eye teeth to be like you.'

'In what way?'

'You're just uncomplicated.'

'No I'm not,' I said. 'You just haven't seen my complicatedness.'

'Perhaps,' she said. 'But I think you'll be happier than me.'

'Do you?' Violet was such a bright star. But I knew what she meant. I'd felt it too. There was something not quite real about Violet's brightness.

'Come on, darling,' she said, smiling now. 'Let's take in the sights while we may!'

I saw Tom as we approached along Boulevard Saint-Germain, sitting at a table on the footpath, his long legs extended out in front of him and crossed at the ankles. He stood when he saw me and came towards us. I could feel his ribs under his coat as we embraced, could see he no longer filled it. He'd lost more weight. I could see it in his face too. How long was it since I'd seen him? Perhaps a month, two, even three? I needed to keep a closer eye on him, get him coming to Royaumont more often to help out.

'Violet,' Tom said, and took her hand. He smiled and it was so like the Tom I knew that the anxiety of a moment before faded. 'You have hair again.'

Violet laughed. 'I do,' she said, 'and ears too. Just like the humans.'

Tom laughed. 'I meant . . . Your hair is mostly hidden in the helmet.'

'Yes,' she said. 'Is there something on my face?'

'No,' he said but he kept staring.

Tom had brought a friend, the one who suggested the café, I later learnt, who had also stood and now took off his hat. He was a tall thin boy, sandy hair already receding, pink cheeks and clear blue eyes. Something about him reminded me of fresh cream at the top of a pail of milk. He stared at Violet too. She took her hand from Tom's and looked at his friend. 'Oh, how rude of me,' Tom said. 'This is Hugh, Hugh Passmore. He works in the postal service with me. Hugh, Violet Heron and my sister, Iris.'

'Hello to you both,' Hugh said. His voice was soft like his face. He looked more a boy than Tom.

'Shall we sit, or just stand here all day?' Violet said.

'Let's stand,' Tom said and laughed. He and Hugh both went to pull out a chair for Violet but Hugh got there first and sat down next to her, Tom next to me. We ordered – I'd become partial to the tiny cups of strong black coffee prepared in the mornings by Michelet. Violet ordered the same as me. Tom and Hugh had hot chocolate.

The waiters wore long starched white aprons and treated us with disdain. I don't know if this was their usual demeanour or resentment born of war and invasion. Hugh said it was the way they always were. 'Service is beneath them, and yet they serve. It's a conundrum.'

'So tell me, Tom. How's the postal section?' Violet said, a hint of mockery in her voice.

Thankfully, Tom didn't pick it up. 'They've set up a distribution centre at Le Havre,' he said. 'So a lot more sorting can be done there. It's easier for us.'

'They say the Germans target our postal ships because they know how much a letter can mean to a soldier,' Hugh said. 'We get millions of letters every week.'

Before long, Tom started talking again about the fighting. He said the other blokes in the postal service agreed a young fellow ought to be fighting. 'Most of them are old or injured. That's why they're doing the post. Signals is the ticket, they reckon. They think I'd make a good messenger because I'm fast on my feet.'

'Is that safe, Tom?' I couldn't help myself.

'We're at war, Iris. Nothing's safe.'

'Where are you from, Hugh?' Violet said, changing the subject. He said he was from Tintagel. 'I'm from Port Isaac. We're practically neighbours. Passmore . . . not the McClintock Passmores?'

'That's right,' Hugh said. 'Are you Mrs Heron's girl?' Violet nodded. 'My brother and yours were at school together.' Violet's older brother Ian had died of pneumonia. 'You were at Harry Moore's engagement.'

'Your older brother,' Violet said to Hugh. 'Richard. All the girls were sweet on him at school.'

'He's up in the north fighting,' Hugh said.

'And your mother?' Violet said. 'I remember she made a wonderful apple pie.'

He laughed. 'Still does. She sent me some, but it didn't do too well on the journey. I ate the crumbs. She writes every week and tells me to keep my head down. You know what they're like.'

'I do,' Violet said. 'Iris here is playing mother to Tom. She says he should go home. What do you think?'

'I think mothers and sisters ought to be locked up so we can get on with the men's work,' Hugh said.

Tom laughed. 'Violet likes to point out I'm too young for war too,' he said. 'Tell them your age, Passmore.'

'I know how old he is,' Violet said. 'You wouldn't be seventeen yet, Hugh. Is that right?'

'Sixteen,' he said. 'My dad was happy enough for me to come over but my ma's angry.'

Violet shook her head. 'Where will all this end?' she said.

'Please don't start,' Tom said to Violet. 'Guess what else I'm doing, Iris? Censoring letters.' Tom had told me that in their letters home, soldiers weren't supposed to mention anything to do with battles or troop movements or even the conditions they lived in. Envelopes were opened routinely by officers in Tom's unit, who blacked out anything forbidden. The only way to write openly, Tom said, was to use an honour envelope. The soldiers had to sign a declaration on the back that said there was nothing but private and family matters contained within. 'Boy, people are strange. One chap tells his fiancée he wants to kiss her knees. I felt like blacking out knees so she'd think he was a bit more romantic. Another asks his mother if she can send his girl's underwear which he left behind. I kid you not. They have no shame.'

'They're going to die,' Violet said. 'Shame probably isn't high on the list of things to worry about.'

'Survival's more important, you think?' Tom said.

'Although less achievable,' Violet said.

When we'd first come to Royaumont, Violet was always one for fun. She'd make a laugh out of even the worst situation. But now, while I had become more tender, crying at the drop of a hat, Violet had become tougher. She hated any kind of talk of the war that suggested it was somehow righteous or heroic and if any of the new drivers started that way, she was quick to put them straight. I could see that Tom and Hugh, with their talk of fighting and going up to the front, had set her off. 'I carried a man in my ambulance last year,' Violet said, and took a long draw of her cigarette. 'He'd lost both arms and one of his legs.'

'Violet,' I said, not wanting her to tell this story.

281

'Be quiet, Iris,' she said. 'They want to go to war. Let them hear. He died before we reached Royaumont, as we knew he probably would. I wondered why they bothered transporting him at all so I asked my stupid question when I went back to Creil for the next load. Do you want to know why they sent him to Royaumont?' Neither Hugh nor Tom responded. 'They didn't want to have to fill in the forms themselves. So they sent a dying man on an excruciating journey to avoid paperwork. We none of us should talk of the war as if it's anything but evil. We've lost the right to be called human.'

We sat silently for a moment until Tom said, 'Well, that's cheered me up no end. Thank you, Violet. We're all feeling brighter for that.'

Violet looked at him and smiled bitterly. For a moment, I thought she might cry.

We talked of other things then. Tom asked after Daddy, Claire and the twins. He said he hadn't heard from them. I said they were well and that Daddy had hired some shearers who weren't as good as Tom. I'd had a note from Veronica too I said, our mother's sister, to say she was coming across to Paris and would visit me. 'Do you remember her, Tom? She came to see us at Risdon.' He shook his head. 'You're probably too young. She was grand. It will be nice to see her again.'

Tom looked over at Violet. 'Come on, cheer up. It's a horrible war but look at us. We're happy.' He smiled. I looked across at Tom. He had grown into a handsome young man, Violet had been right, but it was more than that. Tom had a light within him that shone on everyone his life touched. Daddy and I had done well by him, I thought then.

Violet smiled with a sigh. 'Yes, look at us,' she said. 'We really are the lucky ones.'

I looked at my watch. 'We must go, Violet. I'm due at the Croix-Rouge at eleven.'

'Do I have to come?' she said. 'I think I'd rather take in the morning a bit longer.'

'Stay with us,' Tom said. 'We're going sightseeing.'

'Do,' said Hugh. 'It would be so much fun to spend some time with someone who's not a chap.'

'I'll be the un-chap then,' she said.

'All right,' I said. In truth, I was relieved. I hadn't wanted Violet with me when I saw Dugald. And as I often did, I felt surplus to requirements with Violet when anyone of the male sex was around. Both Tom and Hugh hung off her every word.

Hugh had brought a camera along with him and he asked me to take a photograph of him and Tom, which I did, under instruction from both of them about how to hold the camera and expose the film. Hugh then took one of Violet and Tom and me sitting at the table – Violet had just asked the waiter for another coffee and he'd been so very rude she'd given him one of her looks and we all fell about laughing for some reason. Hugh promised to send me a postcard of the picture but he never did.

I said goodbye to Hugh and wished him well. I hugged Tom tightly. 'You take care of yourself,' I said.

''Course I will,' he said.

I told Violet I'd see her back at the room in the afternoon.

The Croix-Rouge offices were in the Latin Quarter. I walked down the narrow streets to a small square fronted by the church they were using to pack up parcels for soldiers. I walked around the side of the church to the door of the Croix-Rouge office and went in and asked for Dr Dugald

McTaggart. Normally he worked in Chantilly at the Allied Command Headquarters, but he was in Paris working on hospital accreditation reports.

A few minutes later, Dugald emerged. 'Iris, you came to see me.' He smiled, taking my hands in his and kissing me on both cheeks. I felt the roughness of his cheek against my own. He smelt sweet like cinnamon. He stepped back to look at me. 'Will we walk?' he said. 'I'll get my coat. It's so good to see you.'

I almost forgot about the reports I'd brought. 'I actually came to give you these. I believe you asked Miss Ivens to provide them. They're our clinical reviews.'

'Ah,' he said. 'And here I thought you'd come to see me.' I blushed for in truth that's exactly why I'd come. 'Let's walk anyway,' he said. I was still holding on to the reports. 'If you give me those, I'll put them in the office and get my coat.' I handed across the sheaf of papers and as I did our hands touched. I felt the same spark of electricity I'd felt before.

Dugald came back in a long grey coat and wide-brimmed hat. As we came out into the day, which had turned sullen, he grabbed my arm and slid it into his and said, 'It won't rain, not while you're here. Let's take the park.' We went to the Luxembourg Gardens. A group of old men played pétanque on the grass and one of them called hello to Dugald who took his arm out of mine and waved back. We went down to the little lake where boys sailed boats and sat awhile to watch. Dugald said he'd sailed boats like these with his grandfather as a boy.

As we walked again, Dugald asked me how Miss Ivens was going. I told him she was well, on my guard given the questions he'd asked during his visit. He sensed my reluctance.

'I know this is a delicate matter,' he said. 'But we have had a complaint about your Miss Ivens, about her surgical practice.'

'Dr McCourt,' I said.

'Of course, I cannot say but I need to know, Iris. If we get a complaint from a senior surgeon, we must assure ourselves. You know Miss Ivens better than anyone at the hospital. I know this is unfair but you must tell me, for the sake of the men, if there is a problem.'

I thought of the day Miss Ivens dressed up as a bear for one of our pageants, jumping across the stage, the patients in fits of laughter. I thought of her with the little Senegalese boy in our first days as a hospital, easing his passage to the other side, her voice when she addressed him, so kindly. I thought of a note we'd received just that week from a lad whose arm she'd saved, *Ma colonelle*, the patients called Miss Ivens, *Ma colonelle, I can write this because of you, and I thank you from the bottom of my heart*. I thought of her standing in front of us all, telling us we'd failed the first inspection and needed now to rally, her brave face, her meddling with anything and everything to do with running the abbey, driving us all to distraction. 'On my honour, Dr McTaggart, Miss Ivens is truly the finest human being I have ever known and as every patient or doctor you speak to at Royaumont would tell you, she is a great surgeon.'

'Thank you, Iris. It is as I thought it would be. But I needed to be sure. I know you would tell me the truth.'

I felt strangely guilty, as if I'd lied to him, which I hadn't, although I had often thought about Dr McCourt since her departure. She was angry with me for doing what she saw as something a nurse shouldn't be doing. And she was right there. None of the other nurses would have been changing a dressing as complex as that. And she had been worried enough about Miss Ivens's actions to question her in the theatre, which she must have known would lead to trouble. Who was I to know whether any particular course of action in surgery would be efficacious? I dismissed these thoughts. Whatever errors Miss Ivens might have made, she was everything I'd told Dugald and more.

We found a seat among the trees. Dugald motioned me to sit and sat down next to me. 'Enough on the hospital. Let us speak of more important matters.' He put his arm over the seat behind me. I did nothing to stop him. 'Time is against us,' he said. 'The war makes me bold. Iris, I have thought of nothing but you since we met up again. I have hardly been able to write my report.' He took my hand in his and I felt a charge.

I had thought of Dugald too but I didn't say so. I also didn't say that I was engaged. I didn't mention Al at all. I sat on the bench and let Dugald kiss me full on the mouth. I looked up at the big fat wet leaves of the elm trees, the sullen sky above them, and felt my heart would burst. Was this love? Was this what love would feel like? I could smell something sweet like perfume on Dugald's cheeks, feel the roughness of his beard. When he withdrew from the kiss, I could see in his eyes – they looked like fire – that he felt it too. I had a sudden feeling of foreboding that I didn't understand and that I dismissed.

A soft rain started to fall. I didn't think to say to Dugald that he'd been wrong. The rain hadn't held off at all.

Two days later his report arrived and was an 'excellent document' according to Miss Ivens. I could feel myself blushing as she read from it. 'Whatever is the matter, Iris? You're flushed to the ears.'

'Nothing, I think I've just been too busy. It's nothing, really.'

'How odd.' She went on reading.

Violet sat beside her, grinning and looking at me. I tried to give her a look to make her stop.

'This is by far the best report we've ever had,' Miss Ivens said. 'I don't know what you told him, Iris, but you're going to show the auditors round from now on.'

'That's a terrific idea, Frances,' Violet said. 'Iris certainly seems to have the touch.' She smiled sweetly at Miss Ivens. I could have killed her.

'Quite,' Miss Ivens said. 'It's champagne for all this evening. Iris, you are worth your weight in gold.'

'Gold,' Violet repeated, a stupid smile on her face. I glared at her.

Dugald had commended the hospital for its achievements while making sure Michelet could stay on for the duration as our cook. Quoyle had been a little miffed to lose her position but happy once Miss Ivens told her she'd be working in the central office with me. Miss Ivens was not a good organiser and seemed to lose everything she touched. Quoyle had a way of watching where Miss Ivens put things and always being able to locate them. It made the office run much more smoothly.

Michelet had begun to tend the abbey vegetable gardens and everyone agreed they'd become much more productive. We'd always produced as much of our own food as possible but Michelet understood the soil and climate in a way none of us did. He resurrected the abbey orchards, pruning trees and telling us we would soon have wonderful fruits. He put away preserves and even planted flowers for the spring and summer. The hens started laying again under his care, and he bought pigs and goats, which were easier to explain to Edinburgh than I thought they would be. He really was a marvel and we were lucky to have him. Having said that, he didn't come without difficulties.

When Michelet took over the abbey kitchen, we had trouble finding kitchen hands who would work with him. We lost two good girls in as many weeks. He wasn't temperamental exactly, but he was particular about the way food had to be prepared. Miss Ivens was always ready to forgive him whenever staff complained. And I supported her in this, for Michelet was wonderful with the patients, sitting with them at mealtimes, feeding those who couldn't feed themselves if he had time, giving the wine from his own cellar. He never baulked at a request for a meal for the many hungry soldiers who passed the abbey and he always participated happily in our celebrations, turkeys at Christmas, cakes for our ward parties, special meals for other occasions. In the evenings after the dinner was prepared I would often go into the kitchen and find him sitting at the window playing a tune on his little flute. Sometimes Violet would be there with him, drinking wine, and she'd sing a song. Other evenings, I'd see Michelet coming from the forest, his jacket bulky, and when I asked he'd show me a pheasant or two he'd shot to cook up for the doctors.

But the kitchen hands who'd worked with Quoyle through the first few years couldn't abide Michelet. They got into a scrape over the kitchen floor of all things. They said Michelet was messy and they wouldn't wash the kitchen floor for him. According to one of the girls, Michelet responded by spreading grease all over the floor and threatening to leave the floor in that state for Miss Ivens to see. Eventually Miss Ivens herself intervened. She sent Michelet away for a break –

he'd been working intensively to re-establish the kitchen, the gardens, the animals, the supply room, and he was exhausted. But then the kitchen hands refused to run the kitchen in his absence so Miss Ivens dismissed them and brought Michelet back and found new people. He was happy with the outcome and so was Miss Ivens, who never liked the kitchen hands much anyway. 'Most of them have no idea how to cook meat,' Miss Ivens said. 'Michelet cooks meat splendidly.'

Violet said Michelet and Miss Ivens were alike. 'They're both skilled and arrogant and hard on everyone around them except the weak. I agree he's wonderful with the patients but kitchen hands are a whole different matter. They're in his zone of expertise so he expects them to respect that. When they don't do things the way he does them, it drives him crazy. And for most of them, this has been the one thing in their lives they've been allowed to run, a kitchen, and here, a man is telling them what to do, shouting when they don't do it the way he wants them to, and getting away with it.'

'Miss Ivens isn't like Michelet,' I said to Violet. 'She's never been angry with me.'

'But you're not in her zone.'

'Yes I am. We work in the same room.'

'But you're not a surgeon. That's her zone. Administration, that's your zone and she knows it. But if you were a surgeon, you'd have to do what she says.'

'The doctors love Miss Ivens.'

'The doctors know better than to cross her.' I thought of Dr McCourt.

The other recommendation of Dugald's report was that the Scottish Women's Hospitals and Miss Ivens in particular be asked to supervise another hospital. We'd known for some time that the French wanted to open a centre closer to the front in order to treat injuries nearer where they occurred. It had become obvious that the original practice of 'resting' an injured soldier before surgery was a recipe for death, giving infection time to take hold. We'd heard talk of the plan for another closer hospital in our zone but didn't think we were to be involved. As a result of Dugald's report, the committee in Edinburgh, reassured about Miss Ivens's excellent management ability, with just a minor concern about her lack of thrift, had agreed to the proposal that *les Dames Écossaises* should set up a sister hospital. We would locate a site close to the fighting that could function as something more than a casualty clearing station but less than an operating hospital.

Royaumont had continued to remain quiet during that first half of 1917 – the fighting was to the north of us – and we were glad to have a new project to work on. I went with Miss Ivens to find the best location. We visited the abbey in Soissons, on the grounds that our abbey was an ideal hospital, but the abbey at Soissons had been too badly damaged by shelling. Similarly, we inspected a large house gifted by a French family and ruled it out. We settled upon an old evacuation centre made up of timber huts at Villers-Cotterêts, forty miles from Royaumont, right on the railway line and only twelve miles from the front. And then we set about creating another hospital for France.

Grace

When she arrived at work, there was a message from Ian Gibson's rooms to say they could fit Henry in early the following week. She called David. 'Good,' he said. 'You're probably right and it's nothing but at least we'll know.' That morning at home, Grace had looked over at her small son, sitting on the floor playing with his tip truck. He was tired even though he'd only recently woken from a night's sleep. It wouldn't be nothing, Grace already knew, but hopefully it would be something they could deal with.

David had left early for the hospital and she still hadn't had a chance to tell him about the incident with Jennifer Wilson. 'I have to talk to you about something that happened here at work,' she said now. 'Can we meet for a coffee?'

'Give me fifteen to finish up here,' he said. 'Ground floor?'

They met in the hospital cafeteria. David ordered coffees and a danish for himself. Grace wasn't hungry.

He sat down across from her. 'I don't know how to say this,' Grace said. 'I made an error.'

'The Wilson baby,' he said matter-of-factly, biting into the danish.

'How do you know?'

He chewed and swallowed. 'I work here. Clive Markwell is telling everyone but me that you can't follow protocols. This is the man who induces labour for every woman under his care just before he goes on holidays. Not exactly protocol, that. But let's not worry about him. He thinks he's just fine.'

'But I saw the woman the day before. Her blood pressure was up. I should have admitted her.'

'For goodness' sake, Grace, any other clinician might have done exactly as you did.'

'But I knew her when I was at school. I should have found someone else to examine her.'

'Did you offer her the opportunity to see another doc?'

'She didn't want to.'

'Well, that's her choice. You know as well as I do you can't just run and get another doctor. We're all too busy to have the luxury of worrying about personal histories.'

'But it did worry me. I think I should have seen it,' Grace said.

He grabbed her hand. 'Hindsight's a great way to punish yourself, Grace. I've got enough real idiots to deal with. I gotta go.' He kissed her on the cheek and got up. Halfway to the elevator he turned around. 'You're just my amazing Grace. I wish you knew it.'

She couldn't help but smile. She wasn't sure what she'd expected when she told David but it hadn't been this. He was such a good clinician himself, careful, meticulous. Grace had thought he would see this as her fault. And yet, he hadn't. She gathered up his coffee cup, half drunk, his danish, half eaten, and threw them in the bin on her way down the corridor.

* * *

She stopped by the medical library. Katie had left the clippings for her at the desk. In the photo, Violet Heron was a sparrow of a woman, bent over with age, snow-haired but with fierce eyes. She wore a beret on her head and large glasses. She looked familiar and Grace thought she might have been one of the women pioneers in medicine they'd studied in med school. Most of them were British, starting with Sophia Jex-Blake who'd had such a difficult time of it that she'd started her own medical school for women.

We have no mercy for these men, Violet Heron was quoted as saying. *We will find them out, make their dirty secrets public and care for their sisters and daughters whose lives have been irreparably damaged, whose bodies and minds bear the scars of what these men have done.* Grace could see what Katie had meant. Violet Heron was certainly out there, unconventional, and completely unexpected as someone who would have been friends with Iris, who'd always been so proper about everything. Iris had this saying. Whenever someone upset Grace, Iris would say you never knew people. 'You never know people. Don't forget that, Grace.' Now, it seemed, it was Iris herself Grace didn't know.

When she got back to the ward, the director of obstetrics was there. 'Can we go to my office?' Rob Ingram said curtly.

They took the elevator back down to the third floor. Although they were alone, he spent the trip in silence, staring at the numbers above them. They walked along the corridor, again in silence, and when they arrived at his office Rob gestured to Grace to sit and sat opposite her, pushing his chair back as if what she'd done was contagious. He wore a neatly pressed short-sleeved shirt with a badly knotted tie.

He put his hands together as if in prayer before he spoke. 'I've had a complaint from a senior clinician.' He frowned slightly as if he didn't quite understand what he'd just said.

Grace nodded. 'I know.'

'Who says you went against his direct instructions in relation to one of his patients.'

'I did,' Grace said.

'Why?' Rob Ingram said, looking as if he wished Grace had lied instead of telling him the truth.

'Well, if I'm right and it's Dr Markwell, he wouldn't authorise pain relief for a patient who needed it.'

'He says she didn't want pain relief.'

'I was with the patient at the time, Rob. He was at home.'

'I'm sure he had good reason . . .'

'Punishment. That was his good reason.'

Rob Ingram looked at his desk. 'And now he's saying you failed to follow protocols in relation to a suspected pre-eclampsia. This is the Wilson baby. Terrible thing.'

'I'm very aware of what happened, Rob. And yes, I wish I'd admitted the woman the day before. In hindsight, that's what I'd have done.'

'Good. Well, we'll have to set up a panel to investigate all this now.' He smiled weakly, tilted his chair forward, found a pack of cigarettes on the desk and lit one up. He inhaled deeply then looked at Grace and shook his head. 'I don't like these things any more than you do, Grace. We'll get it over and done with as quickly as we can. I just wish it wasn't . . .' He sighed. 'I mean, you don't help yourself, Grace.' He tapped ash into the ashtray. 'It wouldn't hurt you to be a bit kinder.'

'To whom?'

'Senior clinicians, the junior staff. I've had a couple of

complaints about the way you speak to some of the registrars.'

Michael Mastin. 'Who's complained?'

He sighed again and stood up. 'I'm just telling you, Grace. It wouldn't kill you to be nice to people.' Grace noticed he was developing a paunch that hung over a tight belt. 'Thanks for coming in.'

Grace called David as soon as she got back to the ward. 'The vultures are circling,' he said. He sounded as if he thought it was funny.

'David, they're setting up an external panel.'

'They have to do that now that Clive's complained. I wouldn't lose sleep. Any clinician worth their salt will see it the way I did. I can talk to Rob if you want.'

'No,' Grace said. 'I don't want that.' David was more senior than Grace in the hospital. She'd never let him speak for her.

'Well, maybe give Pat Barton a call.'

'You think I need advice?' Grace started to feel frightened.

'No, I didn't say that. But if you're worried, just call Pat and ask him what you ought to do. Sorry, love, I have to go. I'll be late,' he said. 'Love you.'

The next day was Friday and she rose early to meet Janis Kennedy. They ran together once or twice a week as their schedules allowed, from the university around the river and back up through the campus to finish at Chez Tessa on Hawken Drive for breakfast.

Janis had been a few years ahead of Grace in med school. They'd met at a women-in-medicine meet-and-greet in Grace's first year and had been friends ever since. Janis was older by ten years – she'd started medicine as a young mother – and she'd helped Grace when Grace had babies and was struggling to maintain her career. Janis had been with David in saying that Iris should continue to live independently after they sold Sunnyside. And when Janis's only son died following an overdose, it was Grace who held her friend as sobs racked Janis's tiny body. 'Psychiatrists' mothering,' Janis had said to Grace bitterly the day of the funeral. 'Fucked like plumbers' pipes and builders' houses.' The loss had punctuated her life since. She was tougher but also somehow softened, Grace knew.

Grace had told Janis about Jennifer Wilson, said she felt responsible for the baby's death. 'I made a mistake.'

Janis stopped running and put a hand on Grace's arm to pull her up. She bent over to catch her breath. Then she said, 'You probably did. But it wasn't the first and it won't be the last. We make mistakes.' Janis narrowed her eyes. 'When Ryan killed himself, I knew it was my fault. Of course it was. Everybody said it wasn't but I knew.'

'It wasn't your fault.'

'Okay, keep that thought in your mind and then look at your situation. It wasn't your fault.' She started up running again. 'Anyway, David's wrong. It's not a lawyer you need. It's a dick.'

'What do you mean?'

'They're doing this because you're a woman, because you're a woman and you're strong. If you were a man, they'd say you're doing great and well done for taking on someone like Clive Markwell, but because you're a woman, and they don't like women anyway, let alone women who have opinions, women who have the audacity to be doctors, and because they know most of their sex feel the same, they're not afraid to express it, they're after you.'

'What do you suggest?'

'Change sex or discipline. I can't recommend being a bloke but I can recommend psychiatry as a discipline.'

'I'm not sure I fit the profile for psych,' Grace said.

'Because you don't have bad enough taste in ties or because you lack a sustainable neurosis?'

'Neither. Both. Seriously, I don't agree this is sexism,' Grace said. They ran more slowly now. Grace had been so worked up she'd been sprinting, she realised.

Janis had become stronger on feminist politics as she'd got older and she and Grace often argued now. Grace had always been of the view that female doctors just needed to be better than the males. Her own experience had been that her colleagues had mostly welcomed her as an equal once they realised she was there to stay and good at her job. Sure there were doctors like Clive Markwell but Grace was certain there were fewer of them. In Grace's mind the problem wasn't men so much as biology. Women bore children and breastfed them. They were in a unique position to care for them. It took them away from their careers in the years they'd get crucial experience. Nothing would change that as far as Grace could see. She had no time for medical students and junior doctors who complained. You have to learn to succeed regardless, she told them. You have to be tough. You have to be better than them.

In her own career, Grace had managed as best she could. Many of her colleagues, even one or two of the males, had covered for her when the children were sick, as she had for them, and David took responsibility for the children more than most husbands. 'This isn't the whole profession against me,' she said to Janis. 'It's just one difficult clinician, a man who will never be any different.'

'For now,' Janis said. 'But mark my words. They're gunning for you, Grace. You put your head above the parapet, and now?' She made a gun with her hand. 'Bang.'

Iris

The possum is looking positively unwell. For the last few mornings, he's been up and out of the box to explore the house. I've tried to keep him to nights so that when he returns to the wild he'll be the nocturnal creature he's supposed to be. But now I think he might have caught cold from Matthew next door. Even milk and honey in the dropper doesn't seem to soothe him. I should have told Grace when she came around earlier but forgot. I called her at the hospital. She said she'd pop by on her way home. She sounded tense.

When I turned to go to the kitchen, there was Tom again, just standing there, tears in his eyes. I can't speak to tell him I'm sorry, to ask him what it's like wherever he is, not even to tell him I long to see him again. He doesn't speak at first either, just does his best to smile through his tears.

'I see your little possum's doing well,' he says and I realise he's not Tom at all but Geoffrey again. They bear no resemblance to each other, Tom and Geoffrey, and it's unnerving to think I would mistake one for the other in the light of day.

'Geoffrey, I think he's unwell,' I say.

'I don't quite know how you'd tell Iris. He's brown as he was yesterday.'

'He seems listless,' I say, 'and perhaps fevered.'

'What's a fever for a possum?'

'Oh I don't know, Geoffrey. He just seems unwell.'

'Fair enough,' he says. 'Do you want me to call someone?'

'I'm perfectly capable of using a telephone, Geoffrey. I just told you because you asked.'

He nods. 'You're out of sorts today too, Iris.'

'What do you mean?'

'You just don't seem your normal self. A bit grumpy perhaps.'

'It's my brother Tom,' I say. 'He keeps turning up unexpectedly.'

'That's brothers for you,' Geoffrey says. 'Whenever my brother turns up all he wants is money. What does yours want?'

'I don't know, Geoffrey. That's the problem.'

'Well, Iris, I never knew you had a brother.'

'Nor I you. What's his name?'

'George. George and Geoffrey Johnson. He's one year younger than me and since our mother died he thinks I'm a substitute. Yours?'

'Tom and he's a grand boy.'

'How old is he then?'

'Eight, I think.'

'Iris, are you sure you're all right today?'

'Well, of course I'm all right, Geoffrey. Now off you go.'

299

'Oh, I almost forgot. I've an international letter for you. Quite the celebrity this month.'

He gets a blue envelope from his satchel. I put out my hand and take it but don't look at it. If Geoffrey thinks this odd, he doesn't say so. When he leaves, I drop the envelope into the possum's box, feeling better to leave it there for now.

I forgot about the envelope altogether until I went with some cut-up apple for the possum. He chewed hungrily. He wasn't unwell, I decided, just moving on from milk and sugar, growing as he should. I found the envelope in the box and wondered at first how it had got there. Then I remembered.

I knew without opening it who the letter was from. Who else would write now? And when I looked, I could see it was her writing, less sure of itself, fewer flourishes but Violet's lovely hand. She hadn't written for over fifty years and now she sent one of those impossible to open aerogrammes where the paper is also the envelope. It took me five minutes to get it open without tearing it and by the end I just wanted to rip it up.

Dear Iris,

I was thinking of you tonight and I can't sleep which is nothing unusual these days but I'm writing in the hope that after all these years, I'll hear back.

Do you remember, Iris, the night we had the fight with the cream? You'd been working in Blanche – it always sent you a little mad – and I'd done nineteen hours without a break or some such. We were in the kitchen, the little one off the staff dining room, and Quoyle had whipped cream for a trifle and I took a fingerful and flicked it at you, just a little really, but you flicked a little more back, and on and on until we were throwing great handfuls of the stuff and laughing like children. We made such a terrible mess. Remember? I don't think I've ever laughed so much in my life as I did when we were friends, Iris.

It was all too serious, that was the trouble. I was too serious and I truly believed it mattered. And all that mattered really were those laughs. That's what I think now.

You weren't made for bitterness, Iris, dear. You were made to be happy, I think. Are you happy? I'd like to think you are. I hope you'll come to Royaumont with me now and we'll laugh again together. It would do us such good, dear friend.

It really was just water under the bridge.

Miss FB

In the years after I came home from Royaumont, I tried to reply to her letters. *Dear Violet*, I started again and again. Sometimes I wrote what I thought I should. *All those things you mentioned happened such a long time ago I barely remember them.* Sometimes I wrote what was in my heart and it pierced through a gloom. *I loved you so, like a sister. I have never had another friend quite like you. But what I did was terrible. I was my brother's keeper. I was my brother's keeper and I lost him.*

In the early days after I arrived home, I'd go some place where noise would drown me out – under the railway bridge at the Warwick Road – and I'd say what I'd done out loud. It soothed me to say what no one else would say. I was my brother's keeper, and I lost him.

'Do you remember when we brought Rose home to Risdon?' Al said the day we came home to Sunnyside with Grace all those years later. I didn't. 'I remember your daddy's face, like we'd brought some disease into the house. He wouldn't go near her.'

I did remember Daddy when I first came home, the look in his eyes. It wasn't like Al said at all. It wasn't disdain on Daddy's face. It was such a mix of pain and joy, I could hardly bear it. I burst into tears, handed Rose to Al and ran to Daddy. 'I'm so sorry.'

He didn't respond for a full minute and I could see his struggle. Then he said, 'Iris, it's good to have you home.' It was me who couldn't bear the weight of Rose in my arms that day, not Daddy.

He could have said I'd failed. I knew it well enough. He could have refused to take me in. But he didn't. A week later, we went out riding together, up the hill to Holding Rock where he thought some lambs had wandered. We stopped for lunch at the top of the rock. We could see Risdon below and the neighbouring farms. Daddy had written Tom, he said, six months before the telegram came. 'I just decided I couldn't stay angry at him any more. He'd always been one to make up his own mind. And by the time . . . he was near enough to manhood. It wasn't up to me any more.

'I told him I was proud of him for sticking to what he believed in. I'm glad I did, Iris. I'm glad I made my peace . . .' His voice failed him.

'This is a roundabout way of saying you mustn't blame yourself,' Daddy said. I didn't reply, wasn't ready for the conversation. 'It was the worst decision he could have made, but he made it, not you.'

We found no lambs that day and I took little comfort in Daddy's words. I had blame enough in my heart for both of us and more.

Violet, do you remember that summer? Do you remember the day, Violet, that we walked from Royaumont to Chantilly? The morning had started with a fine cloud covering the sky and it was brisk. The flowers covered the fields. I couldn't believe they grew on the side of the road although no one tended them. We get nothing like that here. Those are iris, you said, common as weeds. No offence. None taken. By eleven the sun had come out in a perfect pale blue sky, hopeful as I've ever seen the heavens. We sang as we walked.

We met Tom and Dugald in Chantilly and the four of us found a spot under some trees by a little stream for lunch. It was in the forest around Chantilly, those tall stately trees you loved, I don't recall their names now, you would know them. You and Tom wandered off for a walk after lunch – 'to leave you two lovebirds alone,' you said to me. 'Will you walk with me?' Dugald said. We set out through the forest, walked among oak and poplar newly green. The spring had eased into summer, our world lengthening and warming once again. The war always seemed preposterous in summer.

Dugald stopped on the path and turned to me and took my hands in his. 'I will never forget these hands,' he said. 'They are like art.'

I laughed and took my hands from his. 'They are not,' I said. 'They are like a nurse who doesn't use enough barrier cream.' My hands had dried out like raisins, the nails chipped and broken. 'Rough as hessian.'

'Who said art was smooth?' he said, taking one hand again, turning the palm in his own. 'The thing is,' he looked away, 'I'd rather I didn't have to forget your hands, Iris. I'd like a daily lesson in them.' He looked at me briefly, checking my response, smiling gently, looking away again. 'Except . . .' He didn't finish.

I made to move on, to keep walking, and I will never understand what I did instead. I turned to face Dugald and I kissed him and all the passion of my life was in that kiss. And he responded. We moved off the track and down into the forest. I remember the smell of the pine needles which covered the ground beneath us, his sweet grateful face as his hand first touched my breast and the charge that went through me as his hand moved down my belly. I remember looking upwards towards the sky and noticing a cloud drifting quite quickly past us. It was a perfect cloud, fat and white and alone. And here we were below it and on fire.

I used to think of Dugald in the years after the war. He went to America and served again and was killed in the Pacific. He's buried in the sea, nearer my home than his own. I like to think of that, Dugald near me once again. I'd like him back, I'd like them all back, all the people I loved at Royaumont, just for a day so I could tell them how much it mattered, so I could close my eyes and take in the smells – the clean hospital, the spring blooms, Dugald's face – and convince myself that yes, yes, that was me. That was Iris. I was she. And oh, it was wonderful.

My body made its own decisions about what happened that afternoon, almost in spite of me. I suppose I'll never fully understand the Iris who did those things. As we grow old we are given opportunities to let go of our sins. My sin with Dugald hardly deserves the name now. He didn't write me after I went home, and I wasn't inclined to write him.

He would never have taken on the child and we'd never have survived if he had. You don't need much to raise children, as I've learnt, but you do need love for one another that runs deeper than the scent of pine.

But when he kissed me, Violet, I thought my heart would never beat again. It stopped for that moment and oh, I thought I loved him. I already told you that, in the evening of that day, late, when we were sitting up drinking hot chocolate and watching the moon. I was honest with you, Violet, told you everything. We both know that those trees and fields around Royaumont had other secrets they could tell, and they saved more than a few of us from despair. I remember in that awful winter that followed our balmy summer, when we couldn't keep up with the wounded again, that constant stream of raw stinking flesh, of men we couldn't make whole, those fields were a haven where your jangled nerves could be quieted. But that afternoon with Dugald, I felt a recklessness I've never felt since. Dizzy with my own power. Frightened by what it meant about me.

Paris 1918

What will you do when all this is over?

Be with you.

She shook her head lightly, smiled. Seriously.

Seriously. He took a lock of her hair that had fallen onto her face and put it behind her ear. Do you remember the first time?

This is a quaint room, she said. Out the grimy window they could just make out the spires of the cathedral. As they'd made love, she'd opened her eyes and watched.

The first time, she said.

Chantilly, he said. I'll never forget.

She shook her head as if she didn't remember. She turned away, blushed to think of the raw feeling that had taken her over. She'd felt like an animal there among the leaves. But she couldn't stop. Whenever she saw him, she wanted him.

She'd decided she would end it today. She would do the right thing. She booked the room, telling herself she couldn't very well finish it on the street. M and Mme Zabé, the names they'd always used. She picked up the key and went up in the elevator and waited for him.

It was his face, when she saw his face, the trust in those eyes, that she melted. He took her in his arms and kissed her for a long time. She could smell his sweet smell, sense his body moving with hers. He danced her into the room then, like a boy might. I've never been so happy, he said. And when they made love, slowly, tenderly, he cried, his tears falling onto her chest. This is the most beautiful . . . I've never . . . No words, he said.

She'd put a finger to his lips. No words is good, she'd said. And they'd kissed again, a long kiss, not a goodbye kiss. It had been the wrong time, she'd known that. She should have stopped. She should have stopped but she couldn't. It was as if their love was written long before they ever met, as if the child they would make was a star in the heavens that singled them out and said, yes, you and you, I choose you. Too bad if you have other plans.

I'm going to be a doctor, she said.

He laughed. You're too beautiful to be a doctor, he said.

And you're too stupid to be a lover, she said, getting up from the bed and pulling on a robe.

I didn't mean . . .

What didn't you mean? she said. I've had enough of you. I've had enough of the whole bloody lot of you.

Do you ever think . . . he started.

No, she said. Never.

Do you ever think if we died, if we died right here, it would be enough?

I don't ever think. That should be obvious to anyone. I don't ever think.

Iris

I woke to the sound of a bird that at first I thought was the blackbird that sang in the winter evenings at Royaumont. But I knew that couldn't be right. I thought I heard a noise in the kitchen and just for a moment I was sure it was Tom, he'd soon call out for me to get up and come for coffee and after the bitter hot drink – he always made it too strong – we'd ride out together to join Daddy at whatever he was doing. We'd take cheese and rye bread from the German baker and we'd breakfast together on some rock Tom liked and we'd talk about nothing important – the lambs soon to come, the milker who was off again with the moon, which chicken I should kill for Sunday lunch – and we'd part and go about our separate days, as if there was no need to mark this day as anything special, as if the number of days just so was limitless and our lives would go on and on unchanging.

But of course it wasn't Tom in the kitchen. It could no more be Tom than the bird could be a blackbird. I sat up and turned towards the window behind the bed. I parted the curtains and flattened my palm on the glass. It was warm to the touch. I'd expected it to be cold. I should get up and check that Rose was warm enough. But of course Rose was dead too, had been dead for years. Where was I?

Just then, the singer let out another long line of notes. I could see now it was a butcherbird, a male, high in the gum tree in front of Suzanne's house. He dipped his head as if to acknowledge his audience, and then raised it again, up and out, pulling his tiny body to its full height, filling his chest cavity with enough air to bring morning to the world. He made a long sweet song that was answered by a mate in a neighbouring tree. They sang to one another, back and forth, and for no reason I understood, quiet tears filled my eyes.

I thought I heard the back door open and gently close. Was Al up already, going out for the firewood? Poor man had enough on his plate without having to worry about filling the stove. I wiped my eyes with the front of my nightgown and turned from the window to Al's side of the bed. His pyjamas weren't there. Normally they were neatly folded on top of the pillow. I put my hand under the blanket and on the sheet where he'd slept. It was cold, as if he hadn't slept there at all.

I was sure I heard the back door close again, and then the squeak of the old stove door, the chuff of a log hitting the fire, the other logs chuckling their way into the box like disobedient children, Al trying his best to keep them quiet. Then the kettle scraping across the trivet, the puff of the larder door. I turned back to the window. The world was softened by fog suddenly, heavy as a blanket in the low areas. The butcherbirds were quiet for now, contemplating the fog, perhaps their first. Above the line of fog, you should be able to see the iron lace on the top verandah of the Grand Hotel, the clock tower on the post office, the spire of St Joseph's, but they weren't there. These three tall characters, which summarised perfectly the life of Stanthorpe, always seemed lonely in the first fog of the winter. But they weren't there.

I heard Al's feet in socks on the floor in the hall, the house moving under his weight. I lay back down on the bed and turned away from the door and closed my eyes. He'd stop at my door and then at Rose's door. He'd go in there, perhaps pull the covers over her, whisper a goodbye. I heard Rose's door gently close and a few moments later the squeak of the chair on the front porch, Al pulling on his boots with a sigh. As I heard the front-door key turn in the lock, I had an urge to run out to him in my nightdress and kiss him goodbye, or pull him inside to bed to warm each other, but I held back.

I listened for the front gate closing. Again I had an urge to run out to Al, easier to resist this time. I looked at the clock on the wall but the clock was gone. It had been a wedding present from Al's mother. I hadn't wanted it in our room but Mary had supervised Al putting up the hook when she visited and I would have looked ungrateful if I'd said no. Some nights, before we turned out the light, I would see the clock and understand why Mary had wanted it there in our bedroom. It was like a beacon to remind me, should I need reminding, that Al was not mine, not really, that he belonged to Mary and the hospital and the world, and that I would only have little snatches of time when we'd be together. But the clock was gone now.

I fell back into a deep sleep. When I woke again, I was in my bed in Paddington and someone was knocking on the door again. Why couldn't they just leave me alone?

* * *

It was David, come to mow. I went out to greet him and set him to work straight away so I could give myself time to wake up properly. I didn't want to say anything unwise. When I went back inside, there was no one there, no Tom, no Al. Oh, just those minutes. I wish they'd gone on.

The possum was much better, I thought, although still sulking in the box. When David had finished the front he came upstairs. I asked his advice. He looked inside the box and said anything that smelt so much ought to be living in the outdoors. 'I really don't know what to do, Iris,' he said. 'We didn't study much about marsupials in Cambridge where I did medicine.'

I always kept some apple juice for David so I poured him a big glass with plenty of ice. He'd brought some papers with him which he'd left on the table. We sat down.

'I made those enquiries we talked about,' he said. 'We can organise a passport by post, but I need some documents, your birth certificate, a photo – we can get one next week – and a couple of other things.' He'd filled the form out as well as he could, he said. 'I wasn't sure of some things. What was Al's full name?'

'I loved him, David.'

David nodded. 'I'm sure you did. Do you remember his full name?'

'He was Alastair Joseph, the Joseph after the patron saint of a peaceful death. I'm Iris Josephine. I wonder does it mean I'll have a peaceful death.'

'I hope so,' David said. 'But let's get back to the task at hand.'

I gave him my birth certificate, the old passport and our marriage certificate. He looked at the certificates, marking things off on the form. 'You were married just after the war,'

311

he said. I nodded. 'And when was Rose born?' He was smiling.

'After that,' I said without returning the smile.

'Of course,' he said. 'I'll do the backyard now,' he said, putting his hat back on.

Dear Al,

I received your letter this week and I'm glad things are going well. All is well here too but very busy.

Do you remember when you said to Tom that if everyone refused to fight there would be no war? I think they were close to achieving that in the early days. It was the first Christmas, so long ago now, and they stopped fighting, just for that day. Imagine if they'd stayed that way. For if they'd stayed that way the terrible wounds would stop. Oh Al, if you could see these boys, for some of them are younger even than Tom, if you could see what they've been through, what they endure, you'd ask how it can be allowed to go on. The worst are the Africans who don't even know why they're here. It's terrible to see the fear in their eyes.

Among the women, there are a few who still see the war as justified, who say the Germans started it and we must fight them, although most now see the war as wrong and even those who don't would agree the authorities are failing the soldiers. Miss Ivens has been to The Hague where there's talk of an international women's association for peace. We won't join at this stage but Miss Ivens now says it's women who will stop the war. She's been awarded the Legion of Honour, we've just found out. We've had a job talking her into going to Paris for the ceremony. She's so very humble

312

and has only agreed so as not to snub the French.

We are all of us, to a woman, committed to helping these poor men and boys who have been injured through no fault of their own. While I agree with you that without soldiers there would be no war, the Germans are the aggressors here and we must remember that. We hear stories about what they do in the villages. We had a boy in from Senlis, a little town to the north, and he says his parents and brothers haven't enough food. They have German soldiers living in their house and while the Germans eat their bread and potatoes, they are left with a stew made from the potato skins. The Germans have imposed a tax on the townspeople, he said, and if they don't pay up when required the men are imprisoned.

I have been working double shifts – we all have – to cope with the wounded, and still they pour in.

You ask me how long I think I'll be here. I can't give you an answer. I feel I must stay while I'm of use. I have seen quite a bit of Tom these last months. He is happy to be here too, although he wants to see some fighting. He is still with the postal service and looks set to remain with them.

I know you feel strongly that the war is wrong and that by doing anything we are supporting it but on this I cannot agree with you. I am doing something, some little thing, to ameliorate suffering.

Yours, Iris

My dearest Iris,
I think about you daily, and wonder what you're doing.
I am not trying to pressure you to come home.

I just want to know where we stand. When you left Australia, you were returning by Christmas with Tom. Now almost three years have passed and the one thing you don't mention in your letters is coming home.

It's almost as if the war can't go on long enough for you. I cannot understand it.

You know my thoughts on the matter of war. I am sorry if that makes me a coward in your eyes. Perhaps you can join the dozens of people who feel moved enough by my cowardice to send me white feathers in the post. I have a rather large collection I can show you when you do come home.

I know I sound petty, Iris, but I miss you. I miss you terribly.

Come home safe.

Your loving fiancé, Alastair

Dear Al,

I have never thought you cowardly and believe I have respected your right to hold your own views about the war.

As for disagreement, as far as I can tell, the only difference between us is that I have come here and have found myself useful. In the end it doesn't really matter how that has come to be. It just is. Miss Ivens needs me and while ever she needs me I intend to stay here.

I will understand if you are not willing to wait. I don't know the situation with the girl you left in Sydney but perhaps if she is still free she would entertain a proposal from you. If that is the case, you are free to do so, as far as I'm concerned.

Please stop asking me to come home. Between you

and Daddy, I feel I have no friends in the world except the ones I've made here at Royaumont.

Iris

My dearest Iris,
I have written this letter fifteen times over and have decided, instead of relying on the usual niceties, to speak as plainly as I can.

That you would suggest I might want to break off our engagement makes me sick to my heart. You are the woman I love. But if what you are really saying is that you no longer want me, then please make your views plain. I have a life and while it will be less of a life if it is not with you, I would rather know than deal with these shadows that plague my nights right now.

Your loving fiancé, Alastair

My dear Iris,
I have not heard from you in such a long time and when I saw your father – he came down to town for the show last month – I asked after you. He's had letters every month, he said. Hadn't I? I said nothing, of course, or told a lie, actually, that we'd been writing. But we haven't. Or you haven't.

I would never try to pressure you to do something you don't want to do. But I need to know, Iris. I need to know where my life is heading.

Al

A fortnight after Al and I arrived home with Rose, I went to a sewing group with Claire. Mrs Carson was there. When she said, with a gleam in her eye and through a tight mouth, 'You and that husband of yours didn't waste any time, did you, Iris?' there was silence among the other women. They all looked at me. Claire went to speak but I cut across her.

'Add it up, Joan.' I'd never used Mrs Carson's Christian name before. It was a mark of disrespect, intended. 'As I'm sure you already have. Can't be nine months from the wedding to the birth, can it? You've guessed right, the lot of you, so let's just get on with our stitching and stop supposing.'

The other women remained silent and no one looked my way except Claire, who smiled and shook her head slowly in that way she had. On the way home in the trap, she said, 'Iris, you shouldn't have said that.'

'Why ever not? They make me sick with their supposing.'

'But think of the child in years to come.'

'Rose? She'll have to put up with worse. Hang them.' The child giggled at something that tickled her. 'That's right, Rose. If only they knew.' Suddenly, I felt like crying.

Claire put a hand on my arm. 'How are you managing?'

'How do you expect?'

'I expect you know it's not your fault.'

'Oh but it is.' The tears were coming now and I could barely get the words out.

We crossed the Severn River, the river in which Tom and I had learnt to swim, had raced one another from one side to the other, the first day he beat me clear as day in my mind, when his boy's body overtook my girl's. The river under whose bridge we'd both had our first kisses, me with one of the Carsons, I can't even remember if it was Ray or Henry, he with Jessica who would have been his bride, borne his children. The memories flooded back in a swirl like the river water itself and I felt sick to my stomach.

Claire pulled up the horse under a willow and took my hand. 'You mustn't blame yourself, Iris. Your father doesn't, not ever. We can't be responsible for other people. You were a mother and sister both to Tom but you shouldn't have had to be. And even mothers, we only do what we can. You feed them and hold them close and sing to them. But what they do, that's theirs.'

'I could have stopped him.'

'Could you? Could you really have stopped him? Think about it. You might have delayed him by telling your father. But Tom was going, one way or the other.'

'I could have brought him home.'

'Oh Iris, if you keep this up all that will happen is your heart will become hard like a peach stone and you'll never be able to feel anything again. Please don't.'

Three years after we arrived home, Al and I moved to Brisbane. We bought the house in Fortitude Valley and Al set up a surgery underneath. I called the house Sunnyside because in the mornings the winter sun came streaming through the slats onto the verandah on the eastern side. We were a long way from Risdon, the fresh smell of eucalyptus taken over by the pungent smells of mornings in a large town, the boiling hops at the brewery, the smoke from fires, the fumes of motor cars. I was happier to be away from all my memories, happier to be away from the person I'd once been.

Things were better for us after we moved. No more eyes watching me all the time. Of course, there was the question of children. Why weren't there more children? Al and I only spoke of it once. We were blessed with Rose, he said.

'Is it enough?' I said.

'Of course,' he said. 'She's enough for any father.'

317

Grace

She woke to crows rarking across the back verandah. David had bought a water pistol with a view to squirting them every time they did this but they either didn't wake him or by the time he got out there, they'd gone. He wouldn't let the kids play with the water pistol – Philomena was particularly keen – because he was opposed to children having guns as toys. When Grace tried to explain that since Phil's father had a gun as a toy Phil couldn't really understand his logic, he just looked at Grace and shrugged.

On the one occasion he made it outside while a crow was in sight, he missed by miles, the crow and friends rarking their way off as if to say hah hah you fool. It made David angrier than Grace, who never minded being woken and just wished he'd give Phil the water pistol so she'd stop whining about it.

David had already been over to mow Iris's lawn. They could have employed a gardener but he didn't mind he said and if he didn't do it Iris would have insisted on doing it herself to save the money. David told Grace mowing was like praying. 'Good for the soul.'

'Tell that story at the pearly gates,' Grace said. 'I'm not sure gardening qualifies as a novena.'

After David finished mowing, he and Iris would have a cup of tea. 'She said today she's forgetting words. I think the trip is worrying her. She was quite confused when I first got there, thought I was her husband and then poured me a glass of what I'm pretty sure was vinegar.'

'Well, I didn't want her to go on the trip. You were the one who said she should go. What did you do with the vinegar?'

'Down the sink when she wasn't watching. I do think she should go if she wants to but that doesn't mean it won't be stressful. I was thinking we should all go, take the kids, visit the Emersons. They're somewhere in Burgundy I think. Early holiday. It would be great.'

Grace was about to say let's wait until we see Ian Gibson but stopped herself. 'It is a good idea. And then, if anything did happen . . .'

'We'd all be there.'

'What about Henry?'

'Least of our worries,' he said and squeezed her shoulder.

Mia, who'd been watching television rather than listening as far as Grace was aware, wandered over. 'Why are we worried about Henry?' as if she were another adult joining the conversation.

Grace looked at David. He said, 'I wouldn't say we're worried. Henry's not doing things at the same rate as you and Phil. Sometimes that happens. We just want to check that Henry doesn't need any help.'

'What things?'

'You know how he gets sore legs and can't walk far?' She nodded.

'I don't think it's anything to be worried about,' Grace said.

'Okay,' Mia said, looking at them both carefully before wandering back over to the television.

Grace and David exchanged a look. 'She doesn't miss anything,' Grace whispered. She got up to put on the coffee.

'Hey, what was your mother's birthdate?' David asked her.

'Maybe May 1919?' Grace said. 'I don't remember the exact date. Why?'

'Nothing,' he said. 'Do you know when Iris and Al were married?'

'August the year before, I think. I always wondered why they didn't have more children. But you can't ask Iris about stuff like that. She didn't even like me saying "vaginal" when I asked her about delivery.'

David nodded. 'I think she was pregnant before they were married.'

'Iris? Never. She's too proper.' Grace had been so heavily pregnant when she and David married that the ceremony had had to be interrupted for her to do a wee. 'Remember she was pretty quiet when I told her we were having a baby? Asked if we were planning to marry before I "showed", and then later went on and on about my final exams, said I couldn't possibly manage them.'

'Vaguely. But conceivably, if you'll forgive the pun, once she was a girl with passion.'

'What makes you think she was pregnant before they married?'

David went to speak and then stopped. 'I was just thinking. Don't mention it to Iris.'

'I wasn't planning to. She'd hit the roof. Sometimes you come up with the weirdest ideas.'

'I do. But you knew that when you married me. So that makes you weird too.'

* * *

Iris answered the door, looking tired. She'd sounded vague on the phone the night before, calling Grace Rose and talking about Tom her brother but without correcting herself like she normally did. Grace was planning to go into the hospital but after what David said when he came home from mowing, she wanted to make sure Iris was all right.

There was a musty smell in the hall. The possum. 'I forgot about taking it to the vet,' Grace said as she kissed Iris. 'Is it still alive?'

'Of course it's still alive.'

'I'll pop by on the way home and pick it up. I think the vet's open today.'

'No, Grace.'

'What?'

'I said no. I want the possum to stay here.'

'Fine. Care for a sick possum. Is that why you can't come to the coast?' They were planning to go away to Byron Bay next weekend and Grace wanted Iris to go with them. But Iris had said she wasn't up to the drive. How she thought she'd be up to all those hours in a plane was beyond Grace.

'No. I'm just tired,' Iris said.

'When are we due to go back and see Dr Randall?' The heart surgeon who'd seen Iris the year before. Not so much a murmur as a chorus of angels. Grace hadn't laughed along even when she'd got the joke.

'I'm not sure. It's written up on the calendar.' Iris didn't get up to look herself which unnerved Grace. She wasn't a good colour either.

'Iris, are you all right?'

'I'm old,' Iris said without smiling. She didn't resist when Grace went to take her pulse. It was thready and weak.

'I'm not happy about this,' Grace said.

'My heart?' Iris said.

'Oh, never mind,' Grace said. She sat Iris down in the lounge, put on the kettle for tea and went into the bedroom to make the bed, already made, typically Iris. She refolded singlets in the chest of drawers to no purpose. She dusted the dresser, looked around the room, which had a calming effect. On the way back out, she noticed a black and white photograph on the floor and reached down to pick it up. Four women, standing in the snow in front of an old truck. One of them might have been Iris as a young girl, wearing a big wool coat and mittens. In one hand she held what might have been a snowball. On either side of her were women Grace didn't know.

She went back to the lounge. 'Is this you?' she said to Iris.

'I need my glasses.'

Grace fetched them from the bench. Iris really was a poor colour. Grace would call Mark Randall when she got to work.

Iris looked at the photo. Grace didn't speak, hoping Iris might. Finally, Iris said, 'You don't always know the best thing in a situation. You can't really be sure, I mean really sure, of what might happen. He was a good brother. The boys at school used to make fun of us, our hair. They called us names.

'There was a group of boys we often passed on our way home, hanging around the bridge. One afternoon they were rude to me.' Iris paused and Grace could see tears welling in her eyes. 'One of the boys asked me if I had red hair all over, if . . . you know what I mean, and I was so embarrassed.

'Tom heard them and turned around and asked them what they'd said. I tried to stop him, I knew it wouldn't do any good but here he was, all of six, defending his sister against these much older boys. Tom was small for his age and he'd always been so frightened of trouble. But something cracked in him. It took all three of them to wrestle him to the ground. I screamed at them to leave him alone or I'd tell our daddy and he'd come over and shoot them. That stopped them.' Iris smiled. 'My father was a quiet man but he had a temper. He really had taken a shot at someone once. Those boys scattered quick-smart.

'Poor Tom. They'd hit him and kicked him when they'd got him to the ground like the cowards they were. And yet, when he stood up and dusted himself off, the first thing he said was, "Are you all right, Iris? They'll think twice about saying those things to you next time." And while I thought he was wrong, that the boys who'd taunted me and had beaten Tom up would surely only get worse now, they did stop then, as if my small brother's willingness to take them on had convinced them.'

Iris was raving. Grace had got up and was checking the fridge – old milk she'd bought last week, the eggs she'd bought the week before, untouched, jam, butter, also bought by Grace, also untouched. She turned to look at Iris, who was looking out towards the backyard, talking more to herself than to Grace. Grace felt a sudden pull of sadness. She knew Iris was between worlds now, not quite with them any more. The Byron weekend somehow symbolised the loss that would come. 'Come for the weekend,' Grace said. 'The kids love you so much.'

Iris looked at her as if in a dream. 'What? What did you say?'

'Byron. Come to the beach. I promise you can sleep all day. The sea air will do you good.'

Iris looked at Grace as if she was having difficulty placing her. 'I did love him, you know. I really did.'

'Tom?' Grace said.

'Al,' Iris said. 'I loved Al.'

Iris

It was a Sunday morning and I went out to the verandah to tell him it was time to get ready for lunch. Grace was still at the medical school but she'd be home by one. Al looked peaceful enough, sitting there on the chair, book on the table beside him, the bookmark returned, page 347 of a biography of Abraham Lincoln I'd bought for him. He loved the American presidents. Truman was his favourite, although lately he'd said he was becoming a Lincoln man. I like to think he marked his page and put the book down on the table so as to have a little snooze before lunch as he often did of a Sunday. It was a roast we always had, with baked vegetables. I'd called him perhaps half an hour earlier to help me get the meat out of the oven. I'd hurt my shoulder the week before and had been shy of lifting and when he didn't answer and I'd called again and he still didn't answer I thought nothing of it other than that he must be asleep and I pulled the roast out and was quite pleased really because it didn't hurt my shoulder so I knew I was on the mend.

After I turned up the oven to finish browning the potatoes

I thought I should wake him. You don't want Grace thinking you're getting old enough to sleep on a Sunday morning. I heard the chapel bell up at All Hallows', I recall, and I wondered why. A wedding, probably, some past pupil so dedicated to the school she wanted her marriage there.

Al was so obviously dead. His eyes were closed, which lent support to my notion that he'd died in his sleep. His right arm was resting across his chest, his left hung limp by his side. His skin was grey. His lips were dark, blue-purple. His jaw was slack. I wiped my hands on my apron and closed his mouth, which made him look much more normal. His skin was faintly warm to the touch. And then I heard a hound baying in the distance, as if it knew, and that almost undid me.

Later Grace asked, delicately, whether I'd tried to revive him. I hadn't, intentionally. Al had come out to the verandah at around ten. He'd not heard my calls at eleven and it was nearly twelve when I found him. If by some miracle I'd managed to force his poor heart to pump again, what would I have left but the idiot he would never want to be? I thought as clearly as this in those first few moments, however much I regretted not trying to drag him back to life in the days and weeks and months that followed.

I sat down on the floor beside his chair. 'The veggies are nearly done,' I said. I'd parboiled and scored the potatoes so they'd have the crisp skins Al liked. 'And I've done onions, love,' which I knew he'd enjoy even if later he'd suffer with gas. I took his hand, cooling now. I held it in both of mine as if to warm it. I said, 'I hope your soul hasn't flown yet. For I want you to know that I love you. It took me a long time to know it myself, so I hope you know it too.'

325

I sat by Al while sunlight came through the blinds and stretched itself across the coverlet like an old cat. 'Oh Al,' I said, 'how will I go on without you to guide us straight? Do you remember the time you and Tom went swimming in the dam at Risdon in shorts? It was the first time I saw you naked or near enough to naked. You were so complete in yourself, I confess I wanted to touch you, I wanted to put my hand to your breastbone. You felt it sooner, that heat between us. You were young, in love with medicine, in love with life, in love with me, as you've said. You never gave in to despair like I did.

'And you were right. I didn't love you, not then. I liked the square set of your shoulders, the compact power in your chest and middle. I'd have wanted you if I'd known the feeling enough to name it but I didn't love you.

'And if I hadn't gone to Royaumont, hadn't learnt about a world where women sat rather than served at table, I'd never have had cause to complain, never have known what I missed. You bore the brunt of the anger of a million women whose lives were something like mine. And it was never fair.'

Just then I imagined Al stirred as if to protest so I paused with my thoughts but it was just a trick of the light or my eyes.

'I know when I came home I was unkind. And I don't know why you stayed by me. But I'm fortunate you did. Because Al, and this has been a roundabout way of speaking the truth, I came to love you and I love you still and if Tom had lived in the flesh instead of in the dark sadness of my heart, I'd have loved you better.' I was crying as I spoke. I knew this was weakness twice over – to burden Al with my confession in order to relieve my own conscience, and to tell him in death to avoid his response.

'Let me tell you when I knew I loved you,' I said. 'It was

that day at Pyramid Rock. Do you remember?' It was nothing in particular that happened, no great life change. A day for a picnic, Rose at two – a beautiful child – Al with a rare midweek day off, his shirtsleeves rolled up, his strong fair forearms. Rose had been up in the night with dreams. I was tired but not so tired as I'd been, it seemed, for years. I'd woken in the morning in bed with Rose and I'd had a peculiar feeling, something like that after a journey back from somewhere far away when the familiar of home seems bright and new. The smell of eucalyptus struck me as I was hanging the sheets in the morning. I heard a butcherbird high in the dead gum at the front gate. I remember the sun that day as it rose pink and gold on scuddy clouds. It struck me as so beautiful and yet I'd seen sunrises just like it perhaps a hundred times since Royaumont. It was as if I was seeing the world again for the first time.

Al sensed the change. After the long walk up the rock, Rose on his shoulders when she tired, we ate our lunch – cold chicken and potato salad – and lay down together under a tree. We all slept; I woke first, and when I looked across at Al and Rose, their faces so free in repose, I swear I felt I was the luckiest woman alive. Al woke too and something in the expression on my face melted something in him and while Rose slept we held one another and kissed and renewed the bond that made us man and wife. And then in the afternoon, we wandered home at Rose's deliciously slow pace.

It didn't end right there. There were nights still when I woke in a sweat of anguish or fear. There were days when all I could manage to do was go through the motions of being Iris Hogan. But that day was the point at which the life I lived, the life with Al and Rose, became the life I wanted, and the life I had been living, in my fug of guilt and resentment and pain, became the life I wanted to leave behind me.

'That's when I knew I loved you,' I told him now.

When Grace walked in and saw Al, she panicked, or perhaps it was me on the floor beside him that frightened her. We'd been there a good while and we were quite settled. She grabbed Al's wrist and said, 'Oh my God, he's dead. Quickly.'

'Why?' I said.

She looked at me as she had when she was three, summing me up. 'Shock,' she said and ran inside to call an ambulance. I didn't say not to, although I prayed they wouldn't try to revive him even as I wished they would. For the beginning of realisation was with me. Death as the end of someone and I didn't want to let him go. Looking back now, Al, I'm glad I gave you that one gift. I let you go.

I was left to myself, more or less, while Grace and the ambulance men talked in whispers about me. They thought me mad, I'm sure, but I just wanted to sit a while more with you Al, before you went over. I just wanted to be able to smell your dear coconut oil head for a little longer before you went away forever.

I believe that loss brings memories of loss and in the months after Al died I grieved for both of them, him and Rose, as if they'd both just died, even though Rose had died over twenty years before. I suppose I never had time for grief when Rose died, for there was Grace to be cared for and I didn't have much energy left for anything else. And so it was Rose as much as Al I wept for in the months that followed his death.

Violet and I had been in Paris with Miss Ivens the day before. Violet was having some work done on her car and Miss Ivens and

I had to see the Croix-Rouge. I'd seen Dugald in the afternoon – he'd come to the meeting with Miss Ivens and we had to pretend we hardly knew each other – and then we'd met again that night after Miss Ivens retired. I felt awful to deceive Miss Ivens about our relationship and guilty about my feelings for Dugald. They seemed duplicitous, selfish. Miss Ivens and I caught the train back to Royaumont and I know I was distracted. I couldn't concentrate on the figures we were working through, trying to increase the hospital's capacity ahead of opening Villers-Cotterêts. Violet had stayed on in Paris for an extra night as they needed parts to fix her car. I hadn't had a chance to tell her what had happened with Dugald, how difficult it had felt to be in the same room as him and pretend I hardly knew him.

Violet wasn't expected back before morning.

I woke in the dark, from a dream I couldn't remember, unable to shake a feeling of foreboding. In the dream, there was a funeral in Asnières but I didn't know whose funeral it was. Daddy was there and Claire too and the twins but not Tom. As I woke fully, the feeling of foreboding centred itself on Tom. I knew in my bones that something terrible had happened to him.

I was wide awake now, my heart thumping, my belly filled with fear. I looked over and saw in the faint light from the window that Violet had come in after all and was in her bed. I got up, lit the lamp and shook her awake.

'I'm worried.'

'What about?' she said, blinking in the light.

'I had a dream. I can't talk about it. Please will you take me to Chantilly, to Tom?'

'Oh Iris, I only got back three hours ago. Can't it wait?' She turned over to go back to sleep.

'No, Violet. I think something's happened.'

She sat up and rubbed her eyes. 'To Tom,' she said flatly.

'Yes.'

'He's a postie, remember?' She smiled hopefully, blonde curls all over her face. 'Iris, he's all right. How about I tell you I saw him yesterday and he was fine.'

'Did you?'

She looked at me and didn't answer straight away. 'No, of course not. But really, he's all right.'

I shook my head, close to tears.

'Very well, Iris, let's go and get the postie out of bed.' She got up, pulled on her long pants and boots, grabbed her coat, splashed water from the bowl on her face and followed me out into the predawn morning.

On the way to Chantilly she talked cheerfully, as if I hadn't just dragged her out of her first long sleep in two weeks. In the dim light I could make out the huge craters in the earth where shells had exploded. Violet saw me watching. 'He's going to be all right,' she said finally. I said nothing.

We arrived just as the sun was coming across the muddy field, and went straight to the barracks. I found a soldier I'd seen with Tom on one of my visits. 'Where's Tom Crane?' I said.

'He's in bed, I think,' the soldier said. 'He came in late but I'm pretty sure he's not working today.' He must have read something in my face. 'I'll get him.'

What seemed like an eternity later, Tom came into the canteen, half asleep, hair a curly mess, a dark red stubble covering his cheeks and chin.

'Well, Tom, you've had your sister worried again,' Violet said. 'You've got me out of bed, and here you are, sleeping like a baby.'

'What is it, Iris?' Tom said. I couldn't speak. I just looked at him.

Violet got up and poured Tom a cup of tea from the pot on the stove. 'Drink this, sunshine. It'll wake you up.'

Tom took a sip and spat. 'It's got no sugar.' He rubbed his face.

'Oh pet,' Violet said. 'Grown-ups don't have sugar in their tea.'

'Tell that to our captain. This is his second war. He's been injured three times and he has more sugar in his tea than I do. Sunshine.' But he smiled as he said it.

I got up and put milk and sugar in Tom's tea, trying to shake off whatever was left of my feeling of foreboding. Tom held the mug in both hands and looked at Violet. His sweater hung loosely off his shoulders and wasn't long enough in the waist. 'You've not a skerrick of extra weight on you, Tom,' I said finally, as if our dawn visit had no purpose other than to tell him to eat more. 'It's no wonder you're feeling the cold. Do you remember when you were little and wouldn't wear your coat?'

'No.'

'You'd be shivering and shaking, saying you weren't cold. Finally I just stopped nagging and after a while you put it on. I wonder if that's how to get you to go home too.'

'Iris, I'm not going home. Is that what this is about?'

'It's not,' I said. 'Of course it's not. I just had a bad dream.'

He looked at Violet. 'My lieutenant says I'm a good shot, by the way,' he said. 'And a good runner. They need riflemen and messengers up at the front. He's going to see what he can do about getting me transferred.'

'When?' I said, worried suddenly. Was this what the dream was about?

'Dunno,' Tom said. 'Soon I hope. We had a shooting competition among the blokes. I won hands down.' He took his arm from around my shoulders. 'The old man isn't right about everything, Iris. This matters, what they're doing. I want to help.'

'You are helping, Tom.' What could I do? If I tried to push, Tom would only pull away harder. If I did nothing, he might be transferred to a fighting unit. I would have to see his commanding officer, I decided. I would have to tell them the truth. He's too young to be in the thick of the fighting, I'd say. You need to understand he came here as a child. That would fix it. Surely they'd send him home if they knew he was so young. Tom would be furious with me for telling them the truth, that he was not of age, but it might be the only thing I could do.

'Doing the mail isn't enough,' he said, looking at Violet. 'It will never be enough.'

'Oh for goodness' sake,' Violet said, 'you think if you fight you'll be a man? That is just the living end, Tom.'

Later that week, Miss Ivens had a meeting in Chantilly and I went with her. Violet was back in Paris picking up the new part for her car which hadn't come last time and so Marjorie Starr drove us. While Miss Ivens was at her meeting I went to see Tom's commanding officer as I'd planned. Marjorie offered to come with me. I said I'd be all right but thanked her for offering. She was such a good old stick, Marjorie, always offering to help.

I found Captain Driscoll in the tiny office at the rear of the mail room, his oak desk immaculate but for one folder. 'I'm sorry to disturb you,' I said. 'My brother Tom is one of your postal workers.'

Captain Driscoll was approaching middle age, with a full moustache fashionable in those times, a crisp uniform, greying thinning hair. 'Tom Crane?' he said. I nodded. 'I can tell from the hair. And the accent. Yes, I know Crane. Doesn't like doing what he's told.' I frowned. 'Personally, I like an independent thinker but they're not much good to us here. We want sheep.'

'Yes,' I said, 'and he's been very happy working in your unit, sheep or goat. I just wanted to make sure he stays with you. He's not as mature as he looks.'

Captain Driscoll nodded. 'He's not, eh?'

'And the thing is, he's very keen to be more involved in the fighting, and I'm not sure he's . . . mature enough to make that decision.'

'Hmph,' Captain Driscoll said. 'How old is your brother?' I looked at him. 'I'm not going to discharge him, woman. Just tell me how old he is.'

'He's just turned eighteen.'

'I knew he was lying. I knew it the first time I laid eyes on him. He's not the only one, you know. The army's full of them.'

'I was thinking that if I told the authorities his age they'd send him home. He really doesn't want to go and I've been so happy he's here in the postal unit.'

Captain Driscoll smiled. 'The recruiting sergeants couldn't care how old the boys are. They just want soldiers. But I care about it. I have a son your brother's age. One of those sergeants tried to accost him in the street at home, followed him and when he said he was seventeen, told him he was lying and he must be nineteen. When the boy reached our front door, my wife told the sergeant what she thought of him in no uncertain terms. My son's not over here and he won't be over here until he's of age. Then he can decide for himself but for now, he stays home and looks after his mother and sisters.' Tom had told me Captain Driscoll had six children at home, five girls and this one boy. 'I won't be sending your brother anywhere,' he said. 'You have my word.'

I could have kissed his neatly clipped moustache.

In the closing months of 1917, we set up our new hospital at Villers-Cotterêts. While I was involved during the construction phase, Miss Ivens said I wouldn't go with her and the first contingent. Violet would go with two other doctors and a team of orderlies and nurses. I would remain at Royaumont. I am mostly an even sort of a person, with a calm disposition, but I felt hurt not to be included in the Villers-Cotterêts group. For some reason, Violet's going bothered me more than the rest. She'd always been on an equal footing with Miss Ivens in a way I never could be, calling her Frances and joking in a comradely way. They shared a background I didn't. Now I was being left out and I couldn't help but wonder if this was the reason.

I said nothing but Miss Ivens must have guessed for she said, the day after making the announcement, when we were doing our ward rounds, 'I couldn't go to Villers unless I knew I had you here, Iris.' We were on our way between Blanche and Canada. I did my best to smile. 'Oh, the hospital would keep going without us. I know that. But I wouldn't manage. It's as if Royaumont is my child and while there are many here competent to care for her, you're the only one I trust. Does that make sense?'

I nodded for I couldn't be sure my voice would remain steady. Miss Ivens wasn't taking me to Villers because she was entrusting me with Royaumont, her precious Royaumont. It was the greatest compliment she could ever have paid me and even if I felt her faith was misguided – I was never so competent as she imagined I was – I was greatly honoured that someone of her stature would consider me worthy.

Still, I felt lonely in those weeks that Miss Ivens was gone and I missed Violet terribly. There was no one else I could confide in, laugh with, sit up late talking to, and I remained a little jealous that she was in the new place with Miss Ivens. How exciting it must be. I wanted to be there too, back at the chief's side, helping her in whatever way she needed. At Royaumont I kept expecting Miss Ivens to walk through the door. I had come to rely on her in the ebb and flow of my days. The two of us would often walk through the hospital – sometimes with no destination in mind – while she talked. She walked quickly, even when we didn't have to be somewhere. I missed those walks. I missed her marvellous brain with its grand ideas. I missed the notion of my day changing suddenly because she was there.

Villers-Cotterêts was nearer the front and the guns were closer. When girls came back, they said it was awfully thrilling sometimes to hear the shells and not know what would happen next. The local commandant at Soissons had assured us Villers was safe but the shells sounded so near, one girl said, that she felt certain her doom had been coming. Miss Ivens had sent her back to Royaumont. Unsuitable, Mrs Berry told me. We can't have overexcitement. I put the girl to work in the kitchen back at Royaumont and she seemed much happier.

A month after we took patients at Villers, Miss Ivens returned to Royaumont, along with Violet and Quoyle, leaving Mrs Berry in charge at Villers. It had been much easier than Royaumont to establish, Miss Ivens said, at least in part because there was more help from the French military to see the hospital operational and a local commandant keen to care for his wounded. So now we were running two hospitals, and more besides.

General Pétain had taken command of the French Army in 1917 and for the first time since the beginning of the war, the conditions French troops were expected to fight in came under scrutiny. We found out that the reason we'd taken so few wounded at Royaumont through the first half of 1917 was that the French were refusing to attack and now many were deserting altogether. Pétain visited every unit in the field. The conditions for troops were dreadful, and now we were heading into the coldest winter in fifty years. French soldiers not only lived in frozen mud. They weren't rested from the front like their British or even German counterparts so their ordeal just went on and on. They didn't have enough food or even water. They stayed there day after day, hungry, thirsty, frightened and cold to their bones. One boy at Royaumont told me he would have twenty or thirty rats crawling over him every night. The rats ate whatever food he had in his pockets and then started on his clothes. He couldn't sleep for fear they'd start on him next.

When they were returning from leave, French soldiers were not entitled to rations until they rejoined their units, which meant they were at the mercy of people in towns and villages who themselves had too little food. More than once at Royaumont, we took in hungry soldiers, gave them straw to sleep on and a good meal. While Miss Ivens was at Villers, we had a request from our local commandant to set up a canteen in Soissons. The town had only recently been retaken by the Allies and there were few houses that hadn't been bombed. But large numbers of soldiers passed through Soissons on their way back to the front from leave, so we set up kitchens in an abandoned schoolhouse and served two thousand meals in just over a month until more permanent arrangements were made.

I spent that last Christmas at Royaumont. I remember it as if it was yesterday. We'd had sleet, snow and more besides. And yet I was happier than I'd ever been in my life. Here was I, Iris Crane, at the centre of something of such great goodness in the midst of horror. Michelet killed our favourite pig Louisa for dinner. Father Rousselle came to say mass in Canada on Christmas Eve. The ward was full, the men quietly in their beds, candles at the altar at one end as Father gave up the offertory. And then the choir sang an Ave. I knew then that what we had created at Royaumont was the very opposite of the war. It was beauty itself.

In March 1918 the Germans were bombing Paris again and some of the shells fell close to Royaumont. It was louder than anything we'd ever heard but I tried to stay calm as the new volunteers, who'd never heard bombs before, were terrified. We had a rush of casualties as a result of the renewed fighting and so had to keep our wits about us. One shell was close enough to shatter windows in the refectory, thankfully recently emptied to be used to extend the receiving area. The rush of patients lasted through April and most of May, many seriously wounded cases, with infections so bad we were unable to save many. We had sixty beds in the cloisters, even though it was quite cold, and the staff went back to dining outside, sometimes in the snow that hung on with that long cold winter. By mid-May the rush had abated but we were told it was a calm before a storm. We needed more doctors and orderlies but Edinburgh couldn't help. We sent some of the Royaumont doctors up to Villers for a rest – Villers hadn't experienced the rush that Royaumont had because their sector wasn't seeing the fighting we were – and brought some

Villers doctors back to Royaumont. Miss Ivens asked me to go to Villers too in order to 'sort out their administrative problems'. Violet drove me and as we left Royaumont, I saw the shell holes from the bombs frighteningly close to the abbey itself.

'Goodness me, Violet, we might have been hit.'

'Put on your helmet,' she said. 'We might be hit yet.' Her face was grim. We passed many soldiers and guns along the road.

Villers was so different from Royaumont, the six wooden shacks, each named for an ally, joined by duckboards over the dirt. They'd had a steady stream of wounded rather than a rush but the staff were on edge for different reasons. So much closer to the front, the guns were much louder here and more frequent. On my first night, we had pretty constant alarms and we had to black out the lights even in the theatre. On one occasion, Dr Henry was in the middle of an operation and had to finish by candlelight. We even extinguished the candle for some tense minutes while Dr Henry leant over her patient and waited, hoping he would survive.

The administrative problems I was called in for were quickly sorted out. They'd been running out of basic supplies, Mrs Berry told me, and I realised it was only for want of knowing when to order. Within a week, things were running more smoothly, but Mrs Berry asked me to remain with her at Villers and I was happy to feel useful once again although I missed Royaumont.

Violet brought some new staff over late in May when both hospitals were relatively quiet. We went together to the staff canteen, not nearly as nice as the cloister at Royaumont, nor the refectory which for so long had been our staff dining room. But the tea was more like what I was used to at home than the heavy stewed stuff served up at Royaumont under Quoyle's instructions. Violet said Royaumont was like it was in the early days, new staff with no idea what they were doing, and Miss Ivens was going mad without me there to calm her down.

I hadn't seen Tom since I'd left Royaumont and Violet told me she'd seen him up at Chantilly when she'd gone up with Miss Ivens and that he was well. 'The good news is that he's given up the notion that he has to fight,' she said. 'I think he's finally happy with what he's doing.' She took out a cigarette, offered me one which I took, and lit both.

I thought of my treachery, going to Captain Driscoll behind Tom's back, and felt just a twinge of guilt. I hoped Captain Driscoll had managed to make Tom feel useful at what he was doing and that's what had changed his mind.

'Thank goodness he's happy again,' I said to Violet, blowing smoke above her head. 'And you, Violet. How are you?' She looked tired, dark circles under her eyes, and I worried she was in the doldrums again. I could tell she wasn't her normal bright self.

'Oh you know me,' Violet said, forcing a smile. 'Ever one for bouncing back. I can't imagine being anywhere other than Royaumont.'

I knew what she meant. The war intensified everything, as if we knew, for the only time in our lives, how precious a moment is, a stone, a flower, a person. Not that we thought we'd die. I don't truly believe any of us thought we would. I certainly didn't. But death was all around us, death and severed limbs and broken men. You couldn't see that, I mean really see it, and not contemplate your own place in it all, not see you only had this moment to live in.

I smiled at her. 'I think about home, about Daddy and Claire and the twins, and I think I should miss them. But some mornings when I've worked all night and I'm walking in the snow or writing a letter for Miss Ivens or helping with ward rounds, I feel I could die right then and it would be all right.'

'I don't ever feel like that,' Violet said. 'I didn't mean that. And I don't agree at all, Iris. I've so much to do. I'd feel cheated.' She looked at me with a new intensity in her eyes.

'What have you to do?'

'All my life, I haven't cared a fig for anything. I've grown like a chestnut in an orchard, been fed and watered and nurtured, but I don't really do anything. I just stand there for people to admire. The war has made me realise I can't go on being a chestnut. I need to do more.'

'What about chestnuts? Where would we be without chestnuts?'

She ignored my joke. 'Coming over here's been the opportunity I needed. It's been like waking up after a long sleep. I've seen people who need help. More, I can help them.'

'So, what will you do when all this is gone?'

'I don't know. I'm going to talk to Frances.'

'You could come home with me and do your training and we could work together in Al's practice.' Al's practice, I said it automatically, even as I knew that now there was Dugald, Al's practice and the life we might make together were as far away from my heart as he himself was.

For Violet, it was as if I'd slapped her. 'I don't mean nursing,' she said. 'What a waste of time. I'll be a doctor.'

Now I was the offended one. 'Well, I guess you've the money to do what you like.'

'It's not a matter of money, Iris.' Violet never noticed my hurt feelings. I don't know if I disguised them well or she had a blindness. 'It's ability, aptitude. And I'm terrified I don't have it, if you want to know the truth. I mean, there's a reason you're Frances's pet. She thinks you're a wonder. Even if we had the money, my mother would never pay for me to do anything like study. She'd see that as beneath a Heron. So without Frances to provide support, I'm helpless.'

Now I realised what she was talking about. The Scottish Women's Hospitals Association had started up a scholarship fund for one woman from each of its hospitals in France and Serbia to study medicine after the war. At Royaumont, everyone thought it would go to one of the orderlies – Collum or Starr – who helped out in patient care or in the X-ray room, not a driver or nurse.

'Violet, you're twice as clever as most of the doctors at Royaumont and they are the cleverest people I ever met. You'd be a grand doctor. Do talk to Miss Ivens. She thinks you're wonderful too.'

Why not medicine for Violet, I thought. To hear Miss Ivens talk, it was something she herself had never even considered, not until a friend suggested it. She'd spent her early twenties living a life of relative comfort and leisure, tennis, parties, riding. 'My family went into something of a conniption fit when I told them,' Miss Ivens had told Dr Henry, in my hearing. 'I'm the youngest so I had all my sisters to convince. My father was easier. He liked the idea of a doctor in the family. He had children by his second wife and two were poorly. But he worried the medical studies would tax me. I'd be away from home cutting up dead bodies. He wasn't sure it was natural.' She laughed. 'And now, look at me.'

The next day, Violet went back to Royaumont. A few days later, I received a message from Miss Ivens asking me to please come back to help her clear the great stack of correspondence that was 'threatening to knock over my desk, dear' and I had to respond. I promised Mrs Berry I'd be back at Villers as soon as

I could and headed back to Royaumont with one of the drivers.

'Sit down, Iris,' Miss Ivens said before we'd even started on the pile of mail. I was looking for a telegram she said she'd received from Edinburgh the day before. I moved the stack of letters from the chair at the side of the desk and sat down, nursing the pile on my lap lest it get mixed up with the piles on the desk. 'How are you going with all this?' She gestured around the office.

'I'm sure it's here somewhere,' I said, putting the pile in my arms on the floor so I could poke through the tray on the desk again. 'They only sent it yesterday.'

'I meant more generally.'

'Oh, fine,' I said. 'I just wish I didn't feel so behind all the time.'

'I think that's from working with me,' Miss Ivens said. 'Have you thought about what you'll do after?' I looked a question. 'After the war. With the Americans involved, it can only be a matter of time. Mr Wilson is keen on peace, and he seems to be a man accustomed to getting what he wants. You've put Villers back together, you keep Royaumont running. What next?' She smiled at me.

After the war. After the war, I was supposed to go home and marry Al and run his practice and have his children. But now there was Dugald, whom I'd continued to see in spite of everything. I still hadn't told him about Al and now when Al wrote, I didn't reply. And there was Royaumont. It was as if I had taken a final step into my new world and when I looked back I could no longer understand the world I'd come from. 'I'll take my brother home,' I said. The words rang untrue even to me.

'And then?'

'I haven't thought too much about it. There's a fellow in Brisbane.'

'So you'll marry?'

I wasn't used to talking to Miss Ivens about myself. We always had so much else to get through. 'We're engaged. I didn't want to, not until after I'd been over here. But he didn't mind. Doesn't mind. I haven't thought about the future much lately, to be honest.' This wasn't quite right. 'Or I haven't thought about home much.'

'What's the situation with Dugald McTaggart?'

I could feel myself blushing. I had no idea Miss Ivens knew about Dugald. 'We . . .'

'Never mind,' she said. 'It hardly matters. Have you considered medicine?' I smiled. 'It's not a joke, Iris. You've gifts. A good brain, hands. It's much worse to have and squander. The scholarship. They'll take a recommendation from me.'

'I'm sorry, Miss Ivens,' I said. 'You caught me on the hop. You and the other doctors, well, you're another species altogether. I could never be confident I was up to your standard.' Suddenly I thought of Dr McCourt who'd made such a bad job of the dressing that day and then humiliated me. I could do better than her. I knew that much.

'Of course you are. Confidence is like anything else. The more you do it, the more you believe it. Think about it. After the war, there will be no stopping women doctors. We've shown we can do whatever the men can do, that our biology isn't as they say.' She paused. 'I've already sounded out the Croix-Rouge about providing support for you. And the scholarship would cover your living expenses.'

When she said scholarship again, I remembered what Violet had said, that she was going to talk to Miss Ivens. 'I think Violet might be planning to have a word with you about that scholarship,' I said.

'Never mind Violet,' Miss Ivens said. 'I'm talking about you. I look at you and see . . . I fear you'll look back and feel your life's been a waste. You're too bright to do nothing. What does this fellow of yours do? The one in Australia,' she added, as if I had fellows on every continent.

'He's a doctor,' I said.

She smiled. 'And what does he think about women doctors?'

'I don't know that he's ever met one.' Al didn't have to tell me what he thought of women doctors. It was in every line of his letters by its absence. He never mentioned the doctors at Royaumont. He never asked what we were doing or commented on the treatments we used. He wrote about Stanthorpe – he visited Daddy and Claire when he could – and about the Mater. The only things he noted in my letters were things about the place itself, the abbey, the weather, the food and Tom. How was Tom going, when was I bringing him home. The distance between us now was suddenly as wide as it could ever be.

I thought of Dugald too. I had a feeling he would have a different view from Al. He had no problem with Miss Ivens or with any of the other Royaumont doctors. I imagined he would encourage me. I even entertained thoughts of a life where we were both doctors, working on in France.

'Would I have to choose?'

'The right choice is yourself. I want to offer you the place because, of all our staff, I think you will make the best doctor. That's all that should matter.' Miss Ivens patted my leg and stood up, ending our conversation.

After Miss Ivens left the office, I found myself feeling strangely light. Had she really meant what she'd said, that I would have a scholarship to go to Edinburgh and study medicine? She would be in Edinburgh too, I imagined, and we'd continue to work together as we did now, except that I would truly be her protégée. I would be training to become just like her.

Suddenly I thought of Violet again. Had Violet already spoken to Miss Ivens? Was this what had prompted Miss Ivens to speak to me? I wondered too if it had been Violet who told Miss Ivens about Dugald. Violet didn't mention it the next time I saw her and I didn't either and there the matter settled itself, except that now Miss Ivens had planted a seed in me and it wanted to grow. I watched the doctors with new eyes. Berry, whom we all called Mammy – not to her face – because she was so kind, Courthald who'd been a doctor forever, Dalyell who'd studied in Sydney where Al had studied – surely he'd met her – and Henry, of course, the youngest, twenty-eight, with a blaze in her eyes such as I've never seen in a woman.

In our world of Royaumont the doctors were gods, venerated above all the rest. They were courageous and nimble and had strode into the world of men without once looking back. And they would surely change medicine. Even our treatments – new techniques to avoid amputating limbs, fresh air and sunlight for wounds, even mending and laundering uniforms – were exactly the treatments you'd administer to weary soldiers if you were able to get under their skin and feel what they felt. We healed from within, I think, as only women could. Surely Royaumont would pave the way for women to take their place beside men as doctors. To be included among those women would be the greatest honour possible.

I'd been working solidly all afternoon and had managed to clear most of the backlog on Miss Ivens's desk when Quoyle came in and said I had a visitor. 'I didn't know you had a sister, Iris,' she said.

'I don't.'

I went out to the reception area where there was a well-dressed woman in her forties, tall and slim, with long red hair. She held her hands to her cheeks. 'Well, look at you,' she said. 'You've grown just like your mother.' She shook her head slowly and then held her arms out and we embraced.

'Aunt Veronica,' I said. 'How lovely of you to come.' I hadn't seen my aunt since she'd visited us in Risdon. I felt so glad. She was smaller than I remembered but perhaps that was because I was grown. But she still looked like a girl, so free-spirited. I could see why Quoyle might think we were sisters.

She'd been in Paris for the week, she said, and Daddy had written her, imploring her to 'talk some sense into those two', meaning Tom and me. 'Do you need someone to talk sense into you, Iris?' She peered at me over spectacles, new since I'd last seen her. Her green eyes were still so clear.

'Possibly,' I said. Daddy had continued to be uneasy about us remaining in France. He still wanted us to come home and his letters always asked when that might happen. 'He's worried about Tom more than me.'

'I imagine,' she said.

We left Veronica's bag in the office and I took her for a tour of the hospital.

She met Miss Ivens and some of the other doctors, Miss Ivens taking her aside briefly to speak privately, and then Veronica and I walked together in the forest. Late in the afternoon, I walked with her back to Viarmes.

'Your father has asked me to convince you to go home but I've no intention of doing that,' she said on the way. 'Your Miss Ivens says you have a gift, Iris. She wants you to be a doctor.' Miss Ivens had made a point of saying to Veronica, in my hearing, that she had plans for me. That must have been what she spoke to Veronica about.

I smiled. 'Miss Ivens is very kind,' I said. 'I'm glad to have been able to help her just a little.'

'But you've grown into such a fine young woman,' Veronica said. 'I'm so proud of you.' We'd reached the station and were ready to say goodbye. She looked at me, her features serious. 'You know, Iris, your mother loved bugs. In the summer we spent hours together catching all manner of creatures for her collection. She killed them by pinning them to a wooden board, kept records as to date and place of capture. And then she became a scientist. She could have kept on with it. It's not unheard of in our family. You could pursue a medical career. I'd help too, you know.'

'And then my mother had me,' I said and smiled. 'Which wasn't all bad.'

'No, it wasn't,' Veronica said. 'But part of her was like one of those bugs pinned to a board.'

When I woke up Grace had left and I was alone in my chair in the lounge, an unfinished cup of tea beside me. The photograph of the truck was on the table next to my glasses. I didn't remember putting it there. The light was strange, late afternoon. I must have been asleep for hours. I went to stand up but thought better of it and sat back down. Was this death? I thought. Was I dying?

Soissons 1918

He came out of the bathroom wrapped in a towel that looked too small on his frame, the front rising up like a little tent as he stood watching her. On another day, it would make her laugh, but not today. He telephoned down to the desk and ordered breakfast, the tent collapsing as he concentrated. She was still lying on the bed. The sun was coming through the window onto her belly. She felt like a cat, stretching, drinking it in. You make me unashamed, she said.

You should be unashamed. He went over and sat on the bed, brushed her hair from her face, a habit. He took her hand in both of his, studied it. I love you, he said.

The town was a ruin around them, the hotel one of the few untouched buildings. Their room looked out to a small garden and beyond that to the street. She got up from the bed and pulled on the robe from the closet, lit two cigarettes from the pack on the bedside table, handed him one and then walked to the window. Let's not talk about love, she said. It doesn't seem right here.

A knock on the door, breakfast. She told him to go into the

bathroom and she went to the door, gave the boy a handful of coins, brought the tray, put it on the little table by the window. *Merci*, Madame Zabé, the boy had said and she'd turned around and looked, forgetting this was her name. Then she smiled at the boy. *Merci*, she'd said.

After the boy left, she stubbed her unfinished cigarette out in the ashtray, leant against the windowsill, sipped coffee, bit into the croissant. You make me hungry, she said.

He came over, sat beside her on the sill, took her hand again. We're so happy together, he said. He sounded like a child. For some reason, it annoyed her.

I need to tell you the truth, she said. You don't love me.

I do, he said. You can't speak for me.

Well, I can't love you, she said.

Why not?

They took out my love bones.

Who took out your love bones? he said, smiling now, confident.

Oh, I don't know. It's just a thing to say. But I can't love you, I know that. I have to tell you the truth. He kissed her then and it was the kiss that changed everything, always. She felt his rough cheek against hers, smelt something sharp like almonds on his skin.

She thought of telling him then. A child, she would say, there's a child, it changes everything.

What is it? he said, looking at her face.

Nothing, she said, nothing at all. Kiss me again.

Grace

The table in the hospital boardroom seated twenty-four at least, and the panel members were seated facing the door. On the other side, where Grace stood, there was a single chair, a glass of water on the table. The chairman of the panel, an obstetrician from the west, bearded, grey, ursine, gestured for Grace to sit. She hesitated, feeling safer on her feet, flight rather than fight, and then sat. There was a crucifix at the other end of the room, and paintings of former board chairs lining both sides, all old men.

It was a panel of three, the chairman, another outside obstetrician David said he knew, smaller and younger, piercing blue eyes, and a midwife, younger than both the obstetricians, a slight blonde woman whose eyes darted from Grace to the obstetricians, as if she was trying to figure the dynamic. She didn't know the local scene but she'd have been expecting the obstetricians to take Grace's side in any investigation, Grace was sure. She wouldn't be friendly.

They had papers in front of them, the complaint, perhaps

a report, testimonials from staff. The midwife was looking down at her papers now, asking Grace why it had taken her so long to attend.

'It was a busy day. I was in theatre. I told the registrar to examine the woman and come back. By the time I got out of theatre, he'd still been unable to do that.'

'Why had the registrar been unable to examine the woman?' The midwife looked up at Grace sharply.

'There was disagreement between the midwife and the registrar. He wanted to move to a caesarean. She wanted to continue to try for a vaginal delivery.'

'Why didn't you go yourself?' This was the younger obstetrician. 'Was it fair to leave it to a registrar?'

This was a question Grace would have asked. 'At the time, all I knew was that a woman was failing to progress in labour. I had no other information and no way of getting more information until someone had examined Mrs Wilson. The registrar was experienced and highly competent. I was very comfortable asking him to go ahead without me until I could get out of theatre.'

'Now?'

'Now I wish I'd gone earlier. What was needed wasn't a different diagnosis. He was right about the transfer to theatre. But sometimes midwives don't listen to registrars.' The chairman smiled. The midwife did not. 'I could make a decision the midwife might not have liked but she'd have had to go along with.'

'But you stopped to make a phone call,' the midwife said.

'I did.'

'Why was that?'

'I had asked the librarian to find something out for me. I returned her call.'

'And then, Dr Hogan?' The chairman leant forward to study Grace more closely.

'I took control of the situation, moved the woman to theatre and delivered the baby.'

The chairman asked her to comment on the care provided by Chantelle. 'Some midwives have a different view of pregnancy,' Grace said. 'It leaves them exposed when things do go wrong. But I think to hold a particular midwife responsible would be unfair.

'I probably would have been more critical of the midwife for not seeing signs of pre-eclampsia were it not for the fact that I'd examined this woman the day before. At that stage, she'd had marginally high blood pressure but no other symptoms. In hindsight, I wish I'd admitted her there and then.'

'Why didn't you?' This was the midwife again.

'The high blood pressure was isolated. She went into labour that night and presented with normal BP on admission.'

'Surely you would go in with more urgency given that you knew this woman had already presented with high blood pressure,' the midwife said.

'I didn't realise it was the same woman until I came into the room. As soon as I knew, I acted immediately.'

'Dr Hogan, do you think there's a risk your views about the midwives – which are well known – meant the team wasn't functioning effectively that day?' Grace had no idea what her 'well known' views were, but she'd never understood the anger among these midwives. Powerlessness, Janis had said. It has a way of making women angry.

'There was no team to speak of. I can make no comment on the care provided by Chantelle other than to say my experience of her is that she's a competent if passionate care provider.' Grace looked at the obstetrician who was chairing the panel. 'I won't try to make her the scapegoat if that's what you're asking me to do.'

It took more than an hour. They went over and over what had happened. At the end they thanked Grace for her time and said their report would be completed when they finished their interviews. Grace felt exhausted.

David phoned when he finished in theatre to ask her how she'd done.

'I don't know,' Grace said. 'I was honest. I think they want to do over the midwife, Chantelle Dupont.'

'You could see where they might go in that direction. What did you do?'

'I told them the truth. I might not agree with her. I don't even like her. But she was doing the best she could.'

'Mark Laurie's a good guy. He'll put this in the right context.' Mark Laurie was the young obstetrician David knew.

'And what's that?' Grace said, defensive suddenly.

'A mistake, a reasonable mistake.'

'A baby died, David.'

'Babies do die.'

Ian Gibson was a perfect paediatrician, serious and thoughtful with adults but most at home with children. Grace watched him carefully as he examined Henry. 'Show me what those legs can do now. Goodness me, is that all you can manage? Here comes another bang. That's more like it. What about those arms, Mr Muscles? Oh dear, I think you've broken my machine. You're too strong.' It went on like this as Ian tested Henry's reflexes, range of movement, control, motor skills.

Grace couldn't guess what he was thinking, another skill of a good paediatrician.

After they finished, Henry said, 'That was fun.'

'Well, you can come back and do it again but next time don't break my machine, okay?' Ian Gibson said. 'This kid's amazing,' he said to Grace. 'Doesn't know his own strength.'

Henry laughed and pulled open his shirt, revealing the *S* on his chest. 'No, I'll break the machine again.'

'Okay, Superman. You can break the machine next time.' He lifted Henry down off the bed. He looked at Grace. 'I want to run a couple of tests.'

'What are you thinking?' Grace asked, her clinician voice, she realised, as if they were discussing a patient.

'I'm not thinking anything,' Ian said. 'I'm ruling out things.'

'Like what?' Grace knew she sounded tense.

'I'm wanting to run a couple of tests first, blood, urine.' He looked at Henry. 'Muscle man like this, we want to find out where it comes from, don't we, champ?' He looked at Grace again. 'I'll call you later today.' He was nodding to let her know he didn't want to talk in front of Henry which only made her more nervous.

'Do you want me to take the bloods request?'

'No,' he said quickly. 'I'll get Janet to phone it through to the lab when I've worked out what I need. We got your history, didn't we?'

'Will it hurt?' Henry said when they got to the car.

'Will what hurt?'

'The blood. He said they'd take my blood.'

'No,' Grace said. 'They only need a bit.'

After she dropped Henry with the babysitter, she called

354

David. 'He thinks something.' David was silent. 'You think something too.'

'No I don't. I know what you know. He falls over a lot. He has pain in his legs. There's a whole stack of things that could be caused by. We shouldn't jump to conclusions.'

Later in the day, when she got a call from Ian Gibson's rooms to say they'd phoned the request through to the lab, Grace took Henry for the blood test, told him again it wouldn't hurt and then when it did, took him for an ice-cream. She watched as he went to stand, pushing himself up with his hands. 'Why do you do that?' she said.

'What?'

'You use your arms to push yourself up, not your legs.'

'I don't know,' he said. 'Will they have to take more blood?'

'No,' she said. 'I just wondered why you do that.'

'Is it wrong?'

She took him in her arms. 'No way, Superman. It's completely right. Let's go get your sisters.'

Iris

I soon returned to Villers to help Mrs Berry. The guns seemed louder now although I put it down to having been back at Royaumont, further from the front. At Villers, the big guns would pound all night, shaking the buildings so much that the tables in the theatre which held the instruments would hop about the floor. Sometimes I was sure we were going to be hit. Often now we had to operate in blackout mode, but the doctors never mentioned the bombs – I wondered if they even noticed. They just went on working by candlelight, their only concern the patient under their hands. I focused on keeping my own hands steady to hold the candle or assist. Poor Dr Courthald administered her anaesthetic in the dark. I don't know how she did it. More than once, we even had to extinguish the single candle flame that guided the surgeon's hand and wait until the danger had passed.

Soon after I returned to Villers, Miss Ivens arrived with staff from Royaumont and told us we must expect a great rush of casualties. 'I had a call from Dugald McTaggart,' she said. 'I don't know why we weren't advised officially. We must be ready.' Within hours of her arrival, the wounded started to pour in. Miss Ivens remained with us and the extra pair of hands was much needed. That night, medical staff from an American hospital even closer to the front arrived on foot. They'd been evacuated, they said, and so they took up working with us too. Injured soldiers came on foot as well. We were frightfully busy all through that night – the receiving ward constantly full, the theatre never empty – and I was thankful we were so busy, for the sound of the shells and the shaking of the little wooden huts would otherwise have sent us mad, I was sure. Miss Ivens worked tirelessly. She was never afraid and perhaps because of that, we were all able to keep our fear in check.

The wounded continued streaming in through the next day and night. We each took an hour's break when we could. I don't think I slept. The commandant who'd helped us set up Villers arrived on the morning of the third day. 'You must evacuate,' he told us. 'We cannot guarantee your safety. The Germans have taken Soissons again.' After the commandant left, Miss Ivens gave the order to pack up. The commandant had said we were to wait for advice about evacuation of our patients but he returned later in the day to say there was nowhere to take the wounded yet. 'All the other hospitals are closed or destroyed,' he said. 'And the wounded are still coming. Can you stay until we have somewhere for them?'

'Of course we can,' Miss Ivens said, without hesitating. 'After all, we're women. Iris, you must get in touch with Royaumont. Get them to send every spare car and ambulance. Tell the staff we must be ready to move at a moment's notice.' I watched her furrowed brow, her dark eyes looking up to the left in the way they did whenever she was planning, and I loved Miss Ivens with all my heart and soul.

I sent a messenger to Royaumont – the telephone had been cut the day before. I called as many staff together as were free and Miss Ivens explained the situation quickly. 'We must stay here until they have somewhere to take our patients,' she said. 'It is our duty.' Not one woman questioned that we would stay, despite knowing how close the Germans now were. We unpacked what we needed to keep working and set about the task at hand. The wounded continued to arrive all through the afternoon, on foot or stretcher, or in train or car. We were frantically busy, setting up a temporary theatre in one of the wards, using another to extend reception, operating into the night. We fed refugees and soldiers. Any patients who were able helped us with care.

Miss Ivens did nine thigh amputations in a row, wounds foul with gas. We had the lights out at least three times. The men were ragged, some screaming in pain, some dying just as they reached us, brought by comrades left with nothing but hope for a friend, only to have their hopes dashed. And all the while, bombs exploding with a flash in the night sky, the terrible noise of the big guns our constant companion. It was the worst night of my life.

At around 4 a.m., not having had more than an hour's break at a time in three days, I was sitting in the staff canteen. There was an eerie lull in the guns. Miss Ivens appeared out of the darkness. 'Oh Iris, we've seen it all now, haven't we?'

'We certainly have, Miss Ivens,' I said. I didn't know whether to laugh or cry.

An hour later we received word that evacuations should start. Miss Ivens continued to operate until the last possible moment. And then we began to take the wounded to the trains which would take them to Senlis. We ourselves were going to make for Crépy, twelve miles towards Royaumont. At about midday, the shells began again in earnest and now they were so close we heard them whistle overhead and knew we must get out quickly. We were each given a retreating ration of boiled eggs, orange and some cheese and bread. We packed what we could. I didn't have much although some had to leave behind precious possessions.

At two o'clock that afternoon, Miss Ivens sent a group of sturdy walkers out on foot to meet the train to Senlis, including any patients who could walk. They joined the refugees of the towns that had already been taken. A constant stream of women and children, pushing their belongings on little carts before them, as well as soldiers, many of them wounded, came past the hospital all through the day. The town of Villers-Cotterêts was on fire, we learnt, and people had to escape.

Late in the afternoon, as I went outside with Dr Courthald to collect an empty stretcher, I saw a woman and two children walking towards the hospital. A bomb exploded right where they stood and I watched their bodies fly up into the air and land like nothing more than rag dolls. I went to run to them but Dr Courthald stopped me. 'They're dead, Iris,' she said. 'We must do what we can for the living.' Fifteen minutes later a third child was brought over to us by two American soldiers; they said he'd been with his mother and two sisters but had run ahead – it had saved him. Miss Ivens operated to remove a large piece of shrapnel from his chest. His chances were good, she said, but what life now, without his mother and sisters? And God knew where his father was. Miss Ivens put the boy in one of the cars and told Marjorie Starr to take care of him. There were only four staff left now, Miss Ivens, Dr Courthald, our X-ray technician Miss Stoney and me, as well as the remaining wounded.

'Where are the blessed cars from Royaumont?' Miss Ivens said. Just then, we saw them coming along the road, trundling in with a confidence that made us take up a cheer. They'd been held up on the terrible roads. The cars could take the wounded back to Royaumont, making for Crépy in the first instance, leaving any that could be cared for at the hospital there. Miss Ivens and Dr Courthald would accompany the worst cases. We loaded the patients and then rushed back to pick up our knapsacks. Just as we did, two American cars pulled up and told us the Germans were advancing much more quickly than had been anticipated. We heard the scream of shells overhead. I don't know why but I felt very calm.

Miss Ivens went in the last car with Violet. I gave my seat to a wounded boy and said I would make for the train on my own, following the walkers who'd gone earlier. Violet hugged me as she left. We hadn't seen as much of each other since I'd been at Villers. Our friendship had changed since Miss Ivens had spoken to me about doing medicine. I felt I had a guilty secret. I didn't think Violet knew and I couldn't bring myself to tell her. For her part, she was distant with me too. I didn't know why but assumed perhaps she knew something about the scholarship.

'Do you remember when we spent the night near Baillon, frightened the Germans were coming?' she said now. I nodded. Of course I did. 'This is for you, darling.' She put something small in my hand and closed it into a fist. I opened my hand and saw it was the knife she'd had that night in Baillon. 'Take care, Iris. We'll see you when we see you. I love you.'

'Go, Violet, and stay safe.' I gripped the knife in my hand. 'I love you too,' I said to the back of the car receding into the distance.

I could smell smoke in the air and hear not just the thunder of big guns but the rat-a-tatting of smaller fire that couldn't be far away. I went to the railhead expecting I could help with wounded en route to Senlis but they'd all gone. It was chaos now, soldiers who'd become separated from their units – American, French, Canadian – mingled among fleeing French civilians, no one knowing quite what to do. And now, an American soldier told me, a munitions train had blown up at Soissons so the trains had been stopped. 'The Germans have taken the town. They march like the living dead,' he said. The Germans were five kilometres away, the soldier told me. They were burning everything behind them, desperate now to establish supremacy. I held Violet's knife in my fist, a talisman. No one even noticed me, a young nurse on her own in all this mess of people and vehicles. I'd never felt so alone in my life.

I started on the road I knew led to Royaumont but soon saw the folly of this course. The shells were finding their mark less than a mile from me. I wished I'd gone in the car with the others. At every step, fear threatened to overtake me but I knew I must remain calm. I would have screamed if I wasn't so crazed with fatigue. There was nothing to do but go on.

I saw French soldiers on the road, grim-faced, resolute, as if they'd already gone to their deaths and were nothing but spirits. The Americans and Canadians were there too but even they were without hope now. As the sun was setting, I came to a field I knew – we'd walked there earlier in the summer when the flowers first bloomed – and now it was covered in daffodils and cornflowers lit up by the last of the day's light. Suddenly, I remembered the forest road Violet and I had taken four years before when we'd been afraid for our lives. It might serve me now, I thought. It might truly save my life. On top of a rise, I looked back along the main road and saw, to my horror, the German soldiers marching towards their victory.

I veered off across the field and headed west and south towards the forest road. The sun had set now and I was glad to see a clear night would follow that dreadful day, with a full and peaceable moon already risen to light my way. I soon found the road and walked through the night, stopping briefly every hour or so to rest, climbing down into the forest and sitting or lying down where I stopped. I slept in these breaks – I can't say how long – and saw no other travellers, as if all had fled before me.

As the sky began to grow less dark and I knew a day was coming – whatever it might bring – I felt a kind of joy. I was hungry – my rations had run out – and I was tired, but nothing would stop the morning now and the morning brought hope.

Just then my reverie was interrupted when I heard a motor. I scrambled down into the forest and crouched among the leaves. Before long I saw them – well, heard them first. They were singing 'It's a Long Way' and I knew. It was Violet and Miss Ivens and the crew coming back to Royaumont.

Violet saw me first. 'It's Iris!' she screamed. She pulled up the car, at first forgetting to apply the brake so it rolled back as she was getting out but she jumped back in and stopped it. 'It is you! Oh, my dear. We'd heard the trains were out. We thought . . . We didn't know what had happened. We've been searching the road for you. I told them. I told them I knew you'd take this road. And you did.' We were hugging tightly.

'Violet,' I said. I could have collapsed into her arms if she didn't feel so frail herself. Miss Ivens was emerging from the car now and Dr Courthald. I burst into tears. 'Oh my friends. How wonderful to see you all safe.'

Miss Ivens had taken her patients safely to Crépy and had since picked up more wounded to bring back to Royaumont. They were as glad to see me as I was to see them – they'd heard about the railway line and were planning to send a car for me but they'd come to the forest road 'just in case'. They'd had a wild night, narrowly dodging shells on the road. Dr Courthald said they'd had a few sharp minutes. 'I really didn't think we would get through unscathed.' She was very unhappy we'd left so much behind. But she'd picked the last of the radishes from the vegetable patch – to stop the Germans getting them – and so we munched on those. We piled back into the car, Dr Courthald forced to sit on my lap but we weren't about to leave anyone behind. None of the patients was seriously wounded and soon we were back home. We arrived at Royaumont at dawn, just as the sun was striking the abbey walls.

Royaumont remained untouched, although a shell burst in the back fields leaving a huge hole not a hundred yards from the abbey. The staff and patients had spent the night in the cellars, fearing the worst. They were relieved to hear the cars returning staff to Royaumont.

Miss Ivens and I went straight from Royaumont to Senlis, only stopping for a quick wash and coffee and bread. The German advance had been halted and Senlis had been held. We met at the new hastily established Command HQ with the new Allied Health Service authorities, where it was decided Royaumont would replace Villers-Cotterêts and cover the entire zone, collecting wounded now from Senlis as Creil was too vulnerable to continue. Royaumont would be the largest hospital in the region, providing up to six hundred beds. We were all so exhausted I didn't know how we were going to manage it.

Two days after we closed Villers, everyone was safely back at Royaumont. We'd left equipment and supplies behind, much to the consternation of those in Edinburgh, although the X-ray machines and films were saved thanks to Miss Stoney, who risked her life to go back the day after we evacuated and retrieve them. We didn't lose one patient in the evacuation and Royaumont was full again. The town of Villers-Cotterêts was completely destroyed, Miss Stoney told me, but the hospital, on the outskirts of the town, remained eerily untouched by the German advance.

We found out that we were the only hospital that had continued operating in the region – Royaumont was too far from the field to take the wounded – and Miss Ivens said we'd saved lives that surely would have been lost without us. Marjorie Starr was among those who had evacuated to Chantilly. She'd seen Tom, she said, and he was quite safe. The child Marjorie had taken with her turned out to have an aunt in Chantilly and they managed to see him united with family. 'Poor little tyke was so brave,' Marjorie said. 'If we'd not found his people, I'd have taken him in myself.'

'Thank goodness he has someone, Marjorie,' I said. 'Imagine having no family anywhere.' I left Marjorie in the kitchen and went to the office to find Miss Ivens. When I got there, the telephone was ringing. Quoyle answered it. 'Iris, it's for you,' she said. 'A Captain Driscoll.'

My heart was banging in my chest when I picked up the receiver.

'Miss Crane, I'm sorry to be calling you like this.'

'What's happened?'

'Nothing, nothing like that. Of course that's what you'd think. I'm so sorry. I shouldn't have said my name. Young Crane is fine. But I wanted to let you know that I've been transferred to Le Havre to coordinate postal operations there. Lieutenant Michaels has taken over the postal service and I thought you should know. I understand your brother is still keen to transfer to signals. One of the other boys, Hugh Passmore, has already moved out into an infantry division. Michaels didn't stop him. I'm not sure that he'll stop Crane either. I wanted to let you know.'

I hung up the telephone just as Miss Ivens walked in. 'What is it, dear? You've a terrible pallor.'

'I'm not sure,' I said, 'and I'm sorry to ask but can I take the afternoon? I need to go and see my brother.'

'Of course, Iris. Is everything all right?'

'Yes, I'm sure it is. I just need to talk with him.'

None of the cars was available to take me so I had to walk to Chantilly. The fields were in full bloom now as if no one had told the flowers about the days that had just passed.

The only thing I knew for sure was that I didn't want Tom to fight and at all costs I must convince him not to pursue that course.

When I arrived at the mail centre, I had to wait for Tom. The new officer in charge, Lieutenant Michaels, had sent him out with a message. 'He's a fast runner, your brother,' Michaels said. He was not much older than me, with a narrow beaky face, eyes too close together. It made him look nervous. 'Make a very good messenger, and he's keen, wants to join the signallers.'

'He is fast,' I said. 'Comes from running away from me all his life, but he's very young.'

I'd decided not to talk with Lieutenant Michaels about Tom until I'd had a chance to see Tom himself but Michaels raised it. He got up to walk out with me and I saw he favoured his left leg. He noticed me watching. 'Shrapnel,' he said. 'Shredded the knee. Now I'm stuck here.' I went to open the door for him but he opened it and stood back and all but pushed me through.

'Crane's been here the longest of any of the men,' he said. 'He ought to be more involved.'

'Lieutenant Michaels, please understand, Tom isn't even nineteen,' I replied, as calmly as I could. 'He was only fifteen when he came here. He wasn't old enough to decide to fight and I have been thankful that Captain Driscoll has understood that a boy shouldn't be making a man's decision.'

'Driscoll's not in charge any more.'

'I just meant—' I began, but Michaels spoke over me.

'Crane's old enough to make his own decisions.' Just then Tom walked in. 'Ah, the man himself. Your sister's giving me a roasting, Crane.'

'Iris, I wasn't expecting you,' Tom said. He looked as he had when as a child he'd done something he knew he shouldn't have done. But he wasn't a child. He was a grown man now and I realised suddenly I couldn't make him do anything.

We took our leave from Lieutenant Michaels and went over to the canteen. I told Tom what Michaels had said, that

Tom should be more involved. 'He's just talking, Iris. Don't pay him any mind.'

'So you're not trying to move.'

'Of course not. I'm happy here.'

'Are you lying to me?'

'About what?'

'What did Michaels mean? He said you wanted to join the signallers.'

'He didn't mean anything, Iris. And even if he did, mind your own bloody business for a change. I'm not a baby any more.' He'd raised his voice and looked around to be sure no one was listening. 'I'm a man.'

I was angry suddenly. 'No, you listen to me. I've told our father that you are in a safe job, despite the war, that you're making an important contribution without risking your life. He was ready to come over and get both of us. You were a child when we came here and you are still not of age. If you want, I can go and see more senior officers and tell them your true age.'

Tom burst out laughing. 'Is that the best you can do, Iris? You think they care? There's more of us enlisted who are underaged than over. I'm an old timer. There's a kid at the front who's fourteen. *His* sister doesn't tell him to come home for supper. Just leave me alone.' He got up and walked out the door without looking back. It was the last conversation I had with Tom while he was alive. I had many afterwards, when he was dead, but in those I was as silent as I was now.

I wasn't myself in the week that followed. I worried about Tom, what I'd do if he persisted with this plan of his. And I was still tired to my bones. We all were. Miss Ivens had things on her mind too and they were of the kind that made her angry and short with all of us. We'd had a complaint from an orderly who'd returned to England after being let go by Miss Ivens and now Miss Ivens was livid. Orderly Johnston had come to us only three months before. From what I could gather, she had trouble adapting to life at Royaumont. She claimed the conditions were appalling, cited an example of an Arab patient who'd relieved himself on the floor. An orderly was made to clean it up – quite usual when the patients had an accident – but Johnston was incensed. *Anyone who has lived in the East knows well that it is not fitting for a white woman to wait on natives.* She also said the staff accommodations were filthy and flea-ridden – we did suffer terribly with fleas, which came in on the soldiers' uniforms – and that there were unsatisfactory bathing arrangements. This too was a fair point. Most of us got by with a wash every second day and a bath when we went to Paris. As for the accommodations, we shared rooms sometimes with two or three others and during the very busy periods, we even shared beds, one resting while the other worked. Violet and I had done this from time to time and while it was nice to have my own bed – Violet never ever made the bed – it wasn't really much of a hardship as we were rarely off at the same time. Truly Johnston's complaint was a storm in a teacup but it came at a bad time and Miss Ivens had always had a weakness when it came to criticism. She said she would go back to Edinburgh and speak with the committee about the complaint. I told her I thought that unnecessary. 'I just think she's not worth it,' I said.

'She's put it in writing, Iris,' Miss Ivens said.

'You can't just go flying off the handle every time someone isn't happy here.' I was exasperated with Miss Ivens and sounded so. I hadn't meant to speak harshly and the look on her face was one of surprise. I'd never spoken to her that way before.

'Perhaps you're right, Iris,' she said. 'Well, of course you are. We're all under too much strain and people like that just make my blood boil. I'd like to get her back here to tell her what's what at Royaumont.'

'We all would,' I said, more kindly, 'but let me write to the committee, correct her errors and move on to important things.'

'Very wise, Iris,' Miss Ivens said. 'As always, very wise.' She looked at my face carefully but said no more.

A few days later, she sent me off on leave, to Nice this time, in the south of France. She could see something was bothering me and she assumed it was the workload. When I argued against going, she said she wouldn't hear of it and that was that. I went with Marjorie Starr. Just before we left, Miss Ivens told me she was going to recommend me and not Violet for the scholarship. I told her I still hadn't made up my mind what I wanted. She'd told me I needed to have a good think. I didn't know if Violet knew any of this. I felt it had come between us. I couldn't bring myself to talk to her about it.

I worried about Tom, wondered what I should do now. I couldn't just up and leave and take him home, and he wouldn't come anyway. If only there were a way to make him see that what he was doing was worthwhile regardless of what Michaels thought. But perhaps I was being selfish. Many families had watched their loved ones go to war. Perhaps I ought to let Tom do as he wished. And now there was the scholarship, a chance to remain with Miss Ivens, a chance to become a doctor.

On the train from Paris to Nice, I watched an elderly couple who looked like they were returning home from somewhere. The woman tried to make her husband eat – chocolate and flan and sandwiches – some he took, most he left. When he took something, she had some too. He refused the chocolate. She put it back in her bag without eating any, although she took her time, as if hoping he'd change his mind. I realised she could only allow herself to eat if he ate. If he refused, she refrained. If I went home, would that be me and Al in twenty or thirty or forty years time? I wondered. They got off at Antibes. He tried to help her put her coat on. She shook him off, as though she was paying him back for not eating the chocolate.

On the first day in Nice, Marjorie and I climbed a hill to a park where children played pétanque as if there was no war, their mothers sitting on the benches chatting. You would need to look carefully to see that there were also no young men, that many of the women wore black, to know that war was part of these lives too.

Later we walked down to the sea and I was struck suddenly by the futility of it all. The sea was still the sea. Nothing had changed and yet we had been years patching up the bodies of men so they could be torn up all over again. It occurred to me then that the war would go on, it wouldn't matter if a peace was struck, the damage was so great that the war would go on for generations. A little boy I saw on his brave way to school, his mother and sister trailing behind, would have no father, no way to know any more how to be a father. And on and on.

I kept thinking of the Senegalese boy who'd died at Royaumont in our first days as a hospital. He was far from his home, no one to comfort him or even to speak a word he understood in his dying moments. Much has been written about war and its bland cruelty and I have nothing to add that would illuminate matters except to say that every one of those boys from France and England and Senegal and Australia and even Germany was someone's son and many were someone's brother or someone's father. They came from a life with a preference for melted cheese on toast and a missing tooth. We knew them just a little but every one of the millions killed in those four years was a life surrounded by others that would never be the same. So that when you took that one life, you took others and the casualties ran on and on until there was nothing left but grief. It ran like a river through every small town and city of Australia and the world. And for what?

I knew I should do something about Tom; I should leave Royaumont, forget the scholarship, and take Tom home. But he wouldn't come willingly and I wanted the scholarship. I confided in Marjorie, not about the scholarship, but about Tom and what he wanted to do. Her brothers were still home in Canada. Their father wouldn't let them sign up.

'Well, I don't know what I'd do if he were my brother,' Marjorie said. 'He was so young when he started but he's older now. You have to let him go, I think. He's just such a lovely boy, Iris.' Marjorie had worked with Tom to prepare one of the wards in the early days. They always seemed to be laughing.

'I've an idea, Iris,' Marjorie said. We were walking along the promenade on the seafront, listening to the gentle waves as they clattered against the shingle, like distant guns now to my ears. It was our last evening in Nice.

'What is it?' I was miserable with trying to work out what

I should do. Daddy had been consistently clear that I was making the mistake of my life and now perhaps he'd been right all along.

'What if Tom came to Royaumont?'

'How?'

'Miss Ivens already says he's an honorary woman. What if we gave him a job? He can drive. He can fix cars. He can build. He would be wonderful. I bet Miss Ivens will say yes if she knows it's the difference between keeping you and not.'

'What a wonderful idea, Marjorie,' I said. 'And I just know I could convince Tom . . .'

'If you phrase it that we're a bit lost . . .'

'Yes, and what we really need is a man.'

'And one who can build things and fix things.'

'And it has to be a real man.'

'Of course, strong.'

'Courageous.'

'Oh Marjorie, this is so perfect.' I hugged her. 'Miss Ivens will say yes, I know she will.'

Grace

There was a call from Ian Gibson's rooms asking if Grace could drop down on her way out. She'd planned to work late to finish some reports – David was picking up the kids – so she went immediately. The receptionist buzzed Ian, who came out straight away.

'Grace, come in,' he said, not smiling. They went into the office and he waited for her to sit down, taking the seat beside her rather than behind the desk. It was the first time she'd seen him looking not quite in control. She was having trouble catching her breath. 'I have some worrying test results,' he said. 'And I wanted to tell you now rather than wait until you come back with Henry.' He spoke slowly.

Grace could feel the air in the room growing thinner, Ian's voice coming from further away.

'Henry's blood contains high levels of CK,' he said. 'Creatine kinase,' he added when he saw she hadn't understood. Grace still didn't understand. 'I'm pretty sure Henry has muscular dystrophy.' He paused to let the words go in but didn't flinch as he went on. 'We need to do a muscle biopsy to confirm. But given the symptoms, the blood results, I'm very confident that's what we're going to find.'

Grace might not remember CK but she knew what muscular dystrophy was. The muscles failed to develop properly, causing progressive weakness, especially in the legs. 'Are you sure?' she asked.

'Sure enough to tell you. As I say, we'll do a biopsy but that will really just confirm. I think it's Duchenne's.' Duchenne's muscular dystrophy, after Guillaume Duchenne, who first described the symptoms. Funny that she could remember Guillaume Duchenne but not much about the disease he'd named. Duchenne's was the worst one, Grace knew that much. They died as teenagers or young men.

'Don't they think Duchenne's is inherited?' Grace managed to say, her clinical voice failing her. 'That it's an X chromosome thing?'

'Mostly, but not always, and there's no family history.'

Suddenly, Grace wanted to get out of the office. She knew she should be asking questions, finding out more about what it meant, but she just wanted air. It was impolite, it occurred to her, to sit here not speaking but she couldn't make the words come.

'Grace?' Ian Gibson was saying. She was standing up and heading towards the door. 'Grace.'

'Just . . .' She put her hand up in a stop sign. 'I just need a minute.' She walked out of the inner office, through reception and into the cold white corridor. Led Zeppelin's 'Houses of the Holy' was playing on a radio somewhere. Grace found her way to the car park and the safe refuge of her car. She got into the back seat and lay down and made herself as small as she possibly could.

There was a film they'd watched in medical school, a young man in his late teens who could no longer walk, no longer sit up. He had a soft pale face surrounded by wisps of sandy hair. His head was too big for his neck where the muscles were wasting away. He was in a bed, his big eyes darting from one side of a page to the other in order to read, his head unmoving. He could speak but his speech was slow and a bit fuzzy. Grace wasn't sure if the fuzziness was an effect of drugs or disease. The interviewer asked him how he coped. He said he was hopeful that if he ate better and did more of the exercises he was supposed to do he'd be more well. Even at the time, Grace had seen the awful truth, that this poor boy believed if he ate his greens and did his push-ups he'd stem the tide of disease that in reality would eat his muscles over time no matter what he did. He said he had plans for an art exhibition. There was nothing wrong with his brain. That's the tragedy with DMD – there's no muscle in the brain. But the arms, the legs, the back and the lungs and heart – they need muscles to keep going. Near the end of the interview, the boy said that no human being should have to live the way he lived. At first Grace thought he must be feeling sorry for himself – and who could blame him – but then he paused. 'Not so much for me but for everyone who has to put up with me.' Grace had felt moved that he was most worried about the people around him. Now she wanted to find him, to talk to him, to talk to the future for her own son. But he was probably already dead.

She didn't know how long she stayed in the car. She was shivering uncontrollably although she wasn't cold. She knew she was supposed to be in clinic and for a moment she thought she might do that, it might take her mind off what Ian Gibson had said. But when she went to get up, her legs gave way beneath her. She got back into the car, sat in the driver's seat, still not moving.

Henry's had been the easy birth in its way – she'd been asleep for the duration – and that's the thing she can't understand. She would have picked him as the unblemished one, the one unharmed by pregnancy and birth. He was beautiful, perfect. A quiet happy baby. Phil had screamed night after night with colic and when David had broached the subject of a third baby he told her later that he'd thought she'd say no straight away. But she was the opposite. She wanted another baby. She was thirty-six, Phil was out of nappies and had stopped crying. Grace had been happiest when she fell with Henry.

And yet there had been a flawed gene in Henry from conception. The good diet she'd eaten, the exercise classes and, later, the tiny blobs of frozen spinach, the handmade juices, the beef broth, none of it made one whit of difference because Henry had started the first roll of the dice with a faulty gene that would eat away his muscle strength, that would eventually stop him breathing.

Grace knew there was no point thinking this way but she couldn't stop it. She wanted to believe in God so she could scream at him that he was a fucking fucking fuck for doing something like DMD to her son.

It may have been minutes or hours later that she drove home. David had picked up the children as they'd arranged because Grace had been expecting to work late. But Ian Gibson had called him, David said, concerned about Grace. She looked at David and found herself feeling again she couldn't get enough air. She went into the bathroom and closed the door and stayed there until she caught her breath.

She and David couldn't speak freely until the children were asleep. They play-acted normality and Grace was glad for the respite from what she now knew. She lay with Henry until he went to sleep, scooping herself around him in his little bed. He'd insisted on wearing his Superman costume and she didn't object, despite the fact he'd been wearing it all week at day care. As she was getting up, she looked at her small, perfect son and again couldn't believe what Ian Gibson had said to her. She'd never now be able to look at him and not know what she knew.

When she went downstairs, David tried to take her in his arms but she couldn't cope with his touch and said so. She paced the room. He stood at the kitchen bench. 'Ian says he'll need to do another test to confirm,' David said, as if this might give them hope.

'He wouldn't have said anything without being sure. I think that's just to see which one he has. Ian thinks it's Duchenne's. You know what that means, don't you?'

David nodded slowly, folded his arms. 'We'll get through this, Grace,' he said. He looked as if he might cry. 'Where did you go tonight?'

'Nowhere. I just needed a bit of time,' she said.

'You didn't even call,' he said.

'What would you have done?'

'Come and got you.'

'Why?' She kept moving around the room, couldn't stop.

'You were upset.'

377

'And you coming and getting me would stop me from being upset?' She found herself feeling inexplicably angry.

'No, I didn't mean that. But we're together in this.'

'Are we? You made the appointment, you kept worrying at it.'

'Are you saying he wouldn't have DMD if I hadn't wanted to see Ian?'

'No.' Grace sealed her lips. Yes, she wanted to say. Yes, if we hadn't gone to see Ian, Henry wouldn't have DMD, or we wouldn't know. And that would be better. But she knew this was ridiculous.

He walked over to her. 'You want someone to blame. So do I. You wouldn't wish this on your worst enemy. Oh Grace.' He was crying now.

She took a step back. 'I just don't like people round me when I'm upset,' she said.

'I'm not people. I'm your husband.'

'No people,' she said. 'It's not personal.'

'What is it with you? It's all so controlled and ordered. I would have called you first thing. I would have come to you so we could go through it together.'

'We're different, that's all.' Grace knew if she let David hold her she would lose it completely. She didn't want that. She wanted to be strong and vigilant for Henry, who needed his mother now more than ever.

Janis called by at six the next morning. David had phoned her the night before when he hadn't known where Grace was.

'I'm fine,' Grace said.

'You're coming with me,' Janis said. 'Put on your runners. Moving helps.'

378

'No, really,' Grace said, wishing Janis would leave.

'Yes, really,' Janis said, taking Grace's runners from the shoe basket at the door, waving to David as she led Grace out to the stairs.

They ran along Given Terrace to Lang Park. Janis was right. Moving helped. It loosened Grace up enough to start to put words around what she'd been through. 'David thinks I'm an ice maiden,' she said.

'No, he doesn't,' Janis said. 'He was just worried about you.'

'I haven't cried. I can't.'

'You will.'

'I'm not sure I even believe it yet.'

'It will come. We're going to do this every day we're both free while you're getting used to believing.'

'It wasn't even a surprise. It was like I've known all along this is coming. Like there's been something waiting for me, something I knew but didn't know. And now I feel guilty we didn't act sooner.'

They stopped at the war memorial park on Enoggera Terrace. The sun was rising over the city, light falling onto the stone monument at the centre of the park. Grace's eyes found the long list of names. She'd never noticed them before.

'It's not going to make any difference,' Janis said, 'and your guilt won't help. Believe me, I know.'

Grace shook her head. 'When Ryan . . . Did you feel you'd never . . . Did it get better?'

Ryan was Janis's son who'd died at eighteen. He'd overdosed on heroin at the end of a journey away from his family. He was in Sydney at the time. Janis had been informed of his death by the police. She hadn't heard from him in six months. 'Of course. And this is already a grief for you. You'll mourn the loss of an able son, of his future.' Grace had started crying now, softly at first and then sobbing. Janis rubbed her back. 'But it will pass. It really will. The only thing I learnt was this. I couldn't solve the problem of Ryan's death or his use of drugs or his anger at me. All I could do was sit up in bed in the morning and put one foot down on the floor and then the other. Some days that was it. Some days I didn't even manage that.

'I only got into trouble when I widened the lens, when I took it forward into the future or back into the past. The first led me to despair. How can there be a future? The second led me to grief and guilt. How could I have failed my son? But if I just focused on getting air into my lungs right now, getting one leg and then the other out of bed, I was all right. I did that as much as I could and eventually – it took a long time, Grace – it healed.

'I had good friends to help me through, friends like you.' Janis smiled. 'But right now, we're stretching. We've run the sun up into the sky. We're going to stretch and take you home. And this way, you'll get better.'

Grace looked at her friend. 'It will get worse before it gets better.'

'It will,' Janis said, 'but thinking about that won't change it. Come on, let's finish and get you home.'

Ian Gibson said to them, when they saw him to confirm the diagnosis three days later, that research was advancing in leaps and bounds. She'd wanted to slap him. It's what she herself said to families facing disability in a child. She would never say it again, she decided, would look at people straight on and tell them the truth. 'Your child has a congenital illness. There's no cure. Their life expectancy is on average x years.' She would never again lie to a mother, a father. But for David, as distraught as she but differently, not angry, not at all, Ian's words brought comfort and she loved him for it. 'Polio, who'd have thought they'd ever cure polio?' Grace didn't say, But polio's a bug. You can't go back and erase genes. Oh, she wanted to have David's optimism. She'd have given her medical registration for just a day of David's optimism right then. She felt her heart was hard.

Grace was waking at three every morning and spending those black hours staring at the ceiling, thinking about the future, falling into uneasy exhausted sleep just before dawn only to wake forty-five minutes later, the day too near to bother trying to sleep again. She kept seeing the face of the young man she'd seen in that film at medical school. He was the kind of boy you'd be proud to have as a son, so self-effacing, so willing to try in the face of extraordinary difficulties, his giant head compared with his underdeveloped neck and shoulders. Janis turned up most mornings and forced Grace into her running shoes. Even as she protested, Grace was starting to see that Janis had been right. She would only get through this by narrowing her focus, putting one foot in front of the other and going forward.

Henry was oblivious. They'd said nothing yet. Grace wasn't sure what they'd say and David wanted to wait until they'd worked it out. Mia had asked Grace what was wrong but Grace had said work was busy. Grace had no idea how work was. She did her on-call roster. She went in and spoke to patients. She made clinical decisions she hoped were right. Rob Ingram came down to tell her the panel's report had been held up because they wanted to interview more clinicians. It all seemed so unimportant now, she couldn't help but laugh. Rob shook his head and walked away. Grace had told David she didn't want to tell the hospital about Henry, not yet.

The panel. It had seemed so important before Henry's diagnosis. Now Grace couldn't care less.

'Have you told Iris?' David said, late one night after the kids were asleep.

'Not yet,' Grace said. 'I've wanted to feel composed in myself.'

He nodded and rubbed her shoulder. 'I know what you mean. I couldn't tell her.'

'Maybe we don't need to. Except . . .'

'What?'

'Well, Duchenne's. It can be inherited. You don't have it, my father couldn't have had it, so Iris and I might be the carriers. If we want to have more children . . .'

'If we want to have more children, we'll have more children.' David looked at her, his jaw set. 'I mean, he'll just need different things from the girls.'

'David, he'll deteriorate. He won't be walking by the time he's ten. And then, he won't be able to move his legs, his arms. And then he'll die.'

'I just meant, if we want children, it would be all right with me. Henry's a great kid.'

David was right. Henry had saved Grace, had saved both of them in his way. Here he was, still himself, demanding attention, demanding to be loved. He still laughed and called her in the morning to come in and snuggle him. He still worked in the garden with David to pull out weeds, wearing the same broad-brimmed hat, standing hands on hips to survey his work. He was still Superman.

And because he needed her to care for him, because he would need so much more, Grace found herself able to keep going, to get up in the morning and get one foot out of bed and then the other, just as Janis had said.

She dropped the girls at school and Henry at day care, but instead of going to the hospital as she'd planned went back up to Paddington.

Iris was sitting out on the front verandah. 'I saw the mother possum again,' she said as Grace walked up the steps.

'Did you?' Grace said. 'Was she a bit lost?'

'Not at all,' Iris said. 'She still has the other one. I think possums are a lot more resilient than us. I was never so practical, you know. When Rose died, I was . . . I wasn't the best mother to you in those first months.'

Grace didn't want to get distracted. 'I need to tell you something.' She sat down on the chair next to Iris. Grace thought she'd come to terms with Henry. But now, with Iris, her heart felt like a stone in her chest. 'It's about Henry. It seems David was right after all. He's unwell.'

'Really?' Iris said.

'Yes.' She wanted to get it out quickly. 'Henry has muscular dystrophy. It means his muscles aren't growing properly. He . . . It's going to be very hard for him.'

'Oh Grace, I'm so sorry. He'll be all right though?' Iris looked so hopeful, Grace almost told a lie. Yes, he'll be fine.

'Well, we hope so. We don't know what science . . . For now, he's doing well. But he'll get worse, much worse.' And then Grace could no longer hold it together, not with Iris.

A noise came from her. She let out a sob and then another and another. 'He'll die, Iris, he'll die a young man. That's what we do know.'

'Oh dear girl, dear girl,' Iris said, putting her arms out. 'No one should have to bury a child. Oh Gracie, come here.'

Grace sat down on the floor, her head in Iris's lap, and sobbed. Iris sat quietly, stroked her hair, said 'there there' now and then.

Afterwards, Grace felt lighter, as if relieved of a burden. She blew her nose and got back up onto the chair but held on to Iris's hand.

'Tea,' Iris said. 'I'll make some tea.'

Grace let Iris go. She sat looking out to the yard, found it strangely new. Iris brought the cups out and then the pot. Grace didn't even realise she should have been helping.

When Iris sat down again, she said, 'I don't know much, Grace, but I know you'll get through this. You're so strong. You've always been strong. And you'll get through.'

'Well, I have to. There's Henry to be cared for.'

'Exactly. That's your job now. Poor little Henry. That's how I managed about Rose. There was you to be cared for.' She smiled and squeezed Grace's hand.

Grace wiped her eyes on her sleeve. 'There's a chance Henry's condition is hereditary,' she said. 'I'm just wondering if it's in our family. Were there men in your mother's family who died young?'

'I really don't know,' Iris said. 'What about David?'

'If men carry the faulty gene, they have the condition. Only women can be non-symptomatic. It might make a difference to us having more children if we knew. And to the girls, of course. Who might know?'

'My mother had a sister, Veronica. She came to stay with us. But I don't think she had any children. There were no boys in their family. And I really don't know anything about my mother's mother.'

'And your brother Tom?'

Iris looked stricken suddenly. She didn't speak, just stared at Grace. 'Tom,' she said finally. She put her hand to her chest.

'Your brother,' Grace said, as if Iris had forgotten who he was.

'My brother,' Iris said.

Grace waited. 'Of course,' Iris said. 'Oh God, dear God.'

'What?' Grace said.

Iris was shaking her head slightly. She opened her mouth as if to speak and then closed it again, covering it with her hand. 'Tom,' she said finally. She sighed, a long sad sigh. 'Tom was shot in the last days of the war,' she said. 'Oh Grace.'

Iris

I didn't want to talk to anyone but Miss Ivens about my plan. Although some of the women might object to another man working at the hospital, I was sure Miss Ivens would see it differently. But when Marjorie and I returned from Nice, Miss Ivens was away in Paris so I couldn't speak to her straight away.

I saw Violet and told her Marjorie's idea. 'That's ridiculous, Iris,' she said. 'Tom will never go for something as stupid as that.' She was annoyed at me. I didn't understand and wondered if she had heard news about the scholarship and Miss Ivens's decision.

I was hurt. 'Well, of course he will, Violet. He loves helping out here. And Quoyle and the others, they think he's wonderful.'

'I imagine you'll do what you think is best for you, Iris,' Violet said. I felt certain then she must have been told about the scholarship.

'Violet, I didn't ask Miss Ivens to be my sponsor.'

'Sponsor for what?' she said, looking at me.

And then I was confused. If she didn't know about the scholarship, why was Violet so angry with me? 'What's the matter, Violet?' I said.

'Nothing,' she said. 'I must get back to Senlis.'

She left then and I remained confused and unable to settle down to work, worried about Tom and now wondering what on earth I'd done to offend Violet.

And then Quoyle came down to the office to tell me I'd had a note from Tom, delivered by courier the day I'd left to go to Nice. I took the note and went out to the cloister on my own to read.

It seems I'm in a bit of trouble, Iris. I'm sure it will be sorted out but if you get time, come and see me. I'm being held in Chantilly. That was all it said. Held in Chantilly? What on earth has he done now? I thought. Probably some silly prank. I had a feeling Lieutenant Michaels wouldn't be as lenient as Captain Driscoll when it came to boys and pranks.

I went to find Mrs Berry and ask her for leave. 'Go,' she said. 'Whatever could be the matter? He's a postman, isn't he?' I nodded yes but kept thinking of my last conversation with Tom. Had he managed to arrange a transfer and then become worried? I just didn't know.

I went over to the garage. Violet wasn't there – she was in Senlis, I remembered now – but Marjorie Starr was going to Chantilly within an hour to pick up some supplies for Dr Dalyell. We went together. On the way, snow started falling and I remembered the first day I'd arrived at Royaumont, when snow was so new. Marjorie started into a rendition of a song about a bear and I soon caught on and we sang together. I was still in high spirits and had decided I'd tell Tom about our idea, that he could come to Royaumont. I was so sure Miss Ivens would say yes. He could leave Chantilly and come to help us. We needed him so much, I would say.

We arrived at around two. I found Lieutenant Michaels in the canteen. He was sitting at a table with several other officers, soft-looking young men, drinking tea.

He stood up. 'Tom Crane,' he said. He put his hands behind his back. 'I'm sorry to say your brother has died, Miss Crane.'

His words went in but I didn't hear them. 'I'm looking for Tom,' I said. 'He's here.'

Lieutenant Michaels looked at me again. 'Tom Crane is dead.'

'Dead,' I repeated, as if the word might help us understand what he meant.

'I am not at liberty to disclose details,' Michaels said carefully, his colleagues standing now too as if in his defence. 'Your brother was found guilty of cowardice.'

Marjorie was by my side, holding my elbow firmly. I'm sure had she not been there I'd have fainted. 'What are you talking about?' I said.

Michaels could give me no further information, he said.

'But you must,' I said. 'He's my brother. What happened?'

'I am sorry, Miss Crane. You will have to go through the correct channels to request information about your brother.'

'He's in your unit, sir. A postal worker. What's happened?' This was Marjorie.

Michaels was unmoved. 'I have told you what I am at liberty to tell you. You must go through channels. And now, I must ask you to leave.'

Marjorie looked at Michaels. 'We'll see about that,' she said. 'Iris, we'll go back to Royaumont. Miss Ivens will know what to do.' Marjorie herself was shaking and crying but I don't think she believed it either. Somehow, she managed to get me outside. I vomited over the snow, which was falling more heavily now, large soft flakes that fell on our faces and hair. We walked back towards the truck. I wanted to stay there and watch the snow. I felt disembodied, as though I was no longer part of the world, almost as if I was the snow. Marjorie took my arm firmly again and told me we had to go back to Royaumont straight away, that Miss Ivens would be back from Paris and she would fix it. I believed her. I believed Miss Ivens would know what to do, how to find Tom. I remember the noise of the truck as Marjorie started it up. We hadn't picked up the supplies we'd come to get and I remember thinking Miss Ivens would be disappointed in us. The black trunks of trees, the grey sky, the dead dead landscape of murdered France.

Miss Ivens tried to make me drink sweet tea. 'You're in shock, dear,' she was saying as she rubbed my back and held the cup to my mouth. I couldn't hold it myself for the shaking and I couldn't get my lips around the rim, even if I'd wanted to. I knew I'd vomit if anything was put in my stomach. I couldn't stop shaking, I couldn't talk.

Marjorie Starr was on my other side, telling Miss Ivens what details she'd been able to glean. 'It was a firing squad,' she said. 'A British firing squad. They say he was a coward, Miss Ivens, but how can that be?' I saw Miss Ivens put her finger to her lips and shake her head at Marjorie.

'Thank goodness you're here.' Miss Ivens spoke to someone at the door. I turned and saw it was Violet. 'Iris has had some terrible news, dear. Her brother Tom has been killed.'

'Oh oh oh,' Violet said and grabbed the wall to steady herself. Marjorie went to help her.

Miss Ivens stayed by me. 'Oh Iris, dear Iris, this is the last thing you deserve.'

I heard Miss Ivens's words. I would hear words like them many times over the next days and weeks and months. Everyone knew why I'd originally come to France. I'd come to take my brother home. And while I'd done something good instead, I'd served at Royaumont and had made a difference, already the hard nub was forming itself in my brain. I am my brother's keeper. I am my brother's keeper and my brother is dead. And I have killed him just as surely as if I had been one of the riflemen who agreed to be on that firing squad that shot him.

I thought of Daddy then, or saw him, early in the morning, riding out from Risdon. The sun's not even up. He has bread from the baker in town, a flask of bitter coffee that Claire has made; she's arisen especially even though she's been up with the twins in the night. Later it will be a hot day, but for now it's cool and clear. Daddy rides off to the boundary where the fence is down again – cows have made their way through from the neighbours.

Around seven, Garth arrives at the house, finds Claire out the back hanging the washing and then rides off into the morning after Daddy. Claire's face I can't imagine. She wants to go too, to leave the twins in their beds and ride with Garth. She holds back not because of her own boys but because she respects this other family she's fallen into. Still, she wants so much to cushion the blow. She sits silently at the kitchen table staring at the coffee pot she cannot bear to pour a cup from.

Garth finds Daddy easily. To the east, Risdon is flat forever and something the height of a man stands out for miles. Daddy is watching as Garth approaches. He's holding the mallet on one side. His other tools are on the ground around him. Garth gets down from his horse. His eyes are grey, a kind rather than cold grey but he has no kind words. What words are there? he will ask his wife later. He hands Daddy the telegram and says, 'I brought it out here,' because he doesn't know what else to say. Daddy tells him to go but Garth doesn't leave. 'Go,' Daddy says, more forcefully this time. It's enough. He waits while Garth gets back on his horse, waits as Garth rides away, waits until he can't see Garth for the house. Then he rips the telegram open quickly. Iris or Tom? That's all he wants to know. Later he wonders why that mattered, wishes he'd just waited a little while, finished this length of fence he's on, tricky to get around the fig tree, hammered the post, nailed the wire. Tom always did the nailing.

I don't remember the days that followed. Soon after returning to Royaumont, I was taken to bed, undressed. I felt fevers and chills in quick succession, as if my whole body was revolting against the truth. Many of the women looked in on me. I remember Marjorie Starr and Dr Henry but not the others. 'He was such a wonderful boy,' Marjorie said. 'And such a bright spark. I can't believe they'd do that. I just can't.' I asked after Violet but she didn't come.

Miss Ivens called in to see me. She'd been to Chantilly, she said, with senior officers from the Croix-Rouge. They had met with the British officer who had court-martialled and sentenced Tom. 'As I understand it, there was another soldier, not your brother, another one, a British soldier, who had run off from battle and was found guilty of desertion, which, apparently, is punishable by death. Your brother was ordered to be part of the firing squad. He refused and was himself charged with cowardice and found guilty. As far as I

391

can tell, he refused because he thought it was wrong to shoot his own.

'It's unbelievable to me that this has happened, Iris. We cannot stand idle. I have written to the War Office and to the Prime Minister so that these senseless deaths will stop. The committee in Edinburgh is making submissions on our behalf. It makes me ashamed of my country,' she said. 'The one thing we know from this is that your brother was not a coward. In fact, I would be very sure that in this, he was the only one with courage.

'Iris, I don't know if you want to know anything else. I spoke to the doctor who declared the death and to the chaplain who spent his last night with him.' I nodded, wanting to know whatever I could even as I dreaded knowing the truth. 'He didn't suffer. I can assure you his death was quick. And the priest said he died with a clear conscience.'

I was to be relieved of all duties, Miss Ivens said, but I said I would go mad if she did that and she must let me keep working. The next morning, I got up and dressed, smoothed my hair and washed my face and returned to work.

I didn't see Violet for several days. I didn't miss her at the time. But when I did see her, when she sought me out one morning, we both burst into tears. We held on to each other and sobbed and sobbed. I felt I had my friend back, small comfort in the loss I was feeling but comfort it was, at least for a little while.

When we visited the Australian War Memorial in Canberra with Grace as a child, I saw a photograph of one of the hundreds of executions the British Army carried out during the Great War. It wasn't easy to find, although it was listed in the catalogue. I waited at the counter while a librarian found another librarian and another until finally I spoke to an officer who understood why I might want to look at a photograph like that. He'd seen women like me before, mothers and sisters and lovers of those who'd lost someone so wrongly.

It looks as though the soldiers have just fired. The one they have shot is slumped over, held up only because his arms are bound behind him around a stake. He is blindfolded. The background is nondescript trees without leaves, the middle of nowhere and everywhere in France in those years of the war. There are two officers in the frame, the first standing with the firing squad. He has probably given the order to fire. The second, perhaps a medical officer, looks at his watch, recording time of death or simply bored. Of course there is also the photographer, the man who stood by and watched the whole scene, who decided to take a picture right then. There are the men who tried and court-martialled and sentenced the soldier, the men who knew this was happening. There would be hundreds involved in every execution, surely. I cannot understand them, these men, all of whom colluded in the act of killing one of their own.

I contacted the Department of Defence to find out information about the man my brother Tom was killed for not killing. He was a boy too, it turned out. His name was Sidney Martin and he'd signed up when he was fifteen, same as Tom. Just after his seventeenth birthday, he was badly injured when shrapnel lodged in his back. He was hospitalised for a month in Amiens and then sent back to the front. He told his mother, in what was to be his last letter to her, that when the guns started again he felt sick and went to hide in a barn. So he was shot as a deserter. In his earlier letters home, which I also read, Sidney asked his mother to send a picture of herself so he could be reminded of her and home. *I'm so frightened, Mother*, one of the letters said. *So frightened of the noise.*

The British Army included more than a quarter of a million soldiers who were under the legal age of nineteen. The youngest we know of was twelve when he signed up. Their officers must have known. Did they think, eighteen is close to nineteen, seventeen to eighteen, sixteen, fifteen, down to twelve? Did they have sons themselves? Did their sons fight too? And the army executed hundreds of its own found guilty of desertion or cowardice, men who had the good sense to run away from such terrible slaughter. Intentionally, the names of these soldiers are not included among lists of a town's war dead. We accused the Germans of terrible atrocities. I could no longer see us as any different.

For years after Tom's death, I was angry, angry at the great amorphous beast of our institutions, angry at Lieutenant Michaels, who saw in my brother his own broken body unable to fight, angry at Captain Driscoll for leaving Tom. But through all the years I railed against the fact of my brother's death, I would reserve my harshest criticism for myself. I was my brother's keeper and I lost him.

The day I left Royaumont, four months after Tom's death, it was summer, a day hot enough to warm even our poor patients in their cold beds. Jasmine and honeysuckle filled the air, made lazy with the buzz of insects. To me, it wasn't quite real, the dark green of the pines, the iridescence of summer grass, the water chattering away in the stream, and there, the abbey itself, its quiet immutable stone without malice or passion, taking all who seek her, unquestioning.

Although the Armistice had been reached, the hospital would continue to operate until the middle of 1919 caring for those fallen with the influenza and soldiers with a long convalescence. The drivers had all left us. Violet of course, although we knew we'd see each other again. But the others too. We had no need of war ambulances now.

I must have known when I took that well-worn road back to Viarmes that this would be the last time I would see the abbey. But I left without turning back, not once, as if the abbey had been nothing in my life. Perhaps to turn back would have been too painful. I thought of other things, the meeting with Al I was dreading, seeing Violet again. And underneath that, Tom, what I'd failed to do to protect him, how I'd let him die.

Even my farewell to Miss Ivens was what was required and no more. We embraced lightly. I barely grazed her cheek with my kiss. 'Godspeed, Iris,' she said and when I saw the tears in her eyes I told myself I was mistaken. 'I suppose you are quite sure of your course?' I nodded yes, as if I was quite sure, although in truth I was sure of nothing right then. Miss Ivens sniffed and that almost undid me. I told myself these were not tears but Miss Ivens's pesky allergy. Miss Ivens suffered from hayfever in the summer. I told myself this was hayfever and not tears that were for me. I shook my head but couldn't speak.

I had wired Al to come and he came. It was as simple as that and all our lives were decided. He arrived after the baby was born. He'd never suggested we do something else, get rid of the pregnancy – there were women you could go to – and I couldn't have brought myself to do that, not after everything else I'd done. Some of the women at Royaumont had suggested it. Even Miss Ivens had hinted she could help in that way if we thought it best.

The fact Al never suggested it spoke the man he was. We met in London. He looked from me to Rose and said we'd marry.

He'd stare anyone straight in the eye and tell a barefaced lie if needs be, he said. He simply didn't care what people said. I burst into tears. Not that I'd expected less of him. He was the most gentle, generous man I ever knew.

I had told Dugald first, before I told Al, when I was sure of the pregnancy. Later I hated myself for this treachery to Al. I told Dugald and he told me the truth, that he was married, with a family of his own, three children waiting each night for their father to come home. They were in Paris, had been in Paris all those times Dugald and I met there, all the times he'd told me how much he loved me. He'd been planning to tell me the truth, he said, to tell me soon. But he couldn't take on responsibility for a child. Surely I must see that. I didn't feel angry. If he had been dishonest with me, it was only a matter of degrees different from my own dishonesty. I hadn't told him about Al, that I was engaged to be married.

'I did love you, Iris,' he said as I left him.

'I didn't love you,' I said, 'not a bit.'

When Al and I consummated our union, Rose sleeping fitfully in the bassinette beside our bed in a grubby hotel room in London, it was with a minimum of fuss and all the tenderness you'd expect a surgeon and a nurse to create between them. Rose was a difficult baby, colicky with a tiny gullet that needed food every hour or so, just like a baby bird, and all my tenderness was gone by then anyway.

Al wanted more children right away and I didn't know what I wanted so we tried but no children came, not then or ever. There was no science to conception in those days, not even for the medically trained. It was always seen as the woman's problem. We never discussed what was happening. I never mentioned my menstrual cycle or the vague disappointment I felt each month.

We just went on. Somewhere in my mind I thought it was God punishing me. For what I'd done and had failed to do.

Miss Ivens wrote me from France in 1921. She'd driven through Vingré, she said, north-west of Soissons, and seen a monument which had been erected not long before to a group of French soldiers. She'd heard about these soldiers in the early days of the war, she wrote, but she'd thought it was just a story. Following the Battle of the Marne, in November 1914, they'd been in a company that retreated at the order of their lieutenant who had realised the Germans had advanced and were threatening to outflank his men. Subsequently, they were ordered by their company commander to return to their position and this they did.

But the general in charge of the corps was not satisfied that the men had done enough to defend their post and France was troubled at the time by soldiers refusing to fight. So the twenty-four men who retreated were charged with abandoning their posts in the face of the enemy – cowardice – which carried a penalty of death. Following a three-hour court-martial, six were sentenced to death on the grounds that the Germans attacked from the right and those six happened to be on the right so were most guilty of cowardice. At dawn the next day, they were shot by six firing squads. Their entire battalion was paraded past the six dead bodies. They were six of the hundreds of French soldiers '*passés par les armes*', shot at dawn, Miss Ivens said.

Miss Ivens's letter went on to say that in the January just gone, of 1921, the six men had been pardoned and reinstated '*morts pour le France*', died for France. All six were awarded the Médaille Militaire and the Croix de Guerre posthumously.

It reminded me so much of what happened to your brother, Miss Ivens wrote, *that I felt a need to contact you. I have never understood what in human nature could lead to such an act and it's hard to believe that your brother's was not an isolated incident of wrongful death, but that hundreds of both British and French soldiers were executed.*

In France, at least, justice is finally being done. I cannot say the same for my own country. I knew that Miss Ivens and the doctors had pursued their protests about the execution of British soldiers after the war. I also knew their protests had fallen on deaf ears. I couldn't join them in writing to the War Office and pleading Tom's case. I didn't care that he would be remembered as a coward instead of being included among the honourable dead of Great Britain. If I joined in pleading his case I would be consumed by rage. I knew that path would lead to self-destruction.

Iris, I think of you often and wonder how you are, Miss Ivens concluded. *Do write and let me know. Sincerely, Frances Ivens*. I never replied. I never replied to any of them.

I sat on the steps and watched the mother possum and her remaining child on the wire, making the journey from Suzanne's gum to my mango. Poor Henry. I had a picture in my mind then of Tom, ready for school, holding my hand as we walked down the main road towards the convent, chattering away like a little stream, while I worried that we were late. He was so vulnerable even then. All children are.

Grace was helpless, I could see, just as I was helpless. I had wondered when the past would catch me up. I had thought long and hard about truth. It had been Al who'd said we shouldn't tell Rose. And I'd agreed. I was so old now. How could something that happened so long ago reach out still and take more lives?

I would have to tell her now. I would have to tell her the truth. I looked around me, saw the little table on the front verandah, the possum mother with her child, the tree. Just for a moment, I couldn't work out where I was. And then remembered. I was going to talk to Grace.

I went back into the house and dialled the number. She answered almost straight away. 'Is everything all right, Iris?' I looked at the time. It was 12.30 a.m.

'Would you be able to come over tomorrow, dear?'

'I'm on in the morning and have to pick the kids up. I'm off Thursday.'

'Oh well, all right then.'

'How about I finish early tomorrow and come over for lunch?'

'That would be good. And Grace, I love you. I always have.'

'Good, I'll see you tomorrow then,' she said. 'Are you sure you're all right, Iris?'

'Oh yes, I'll see you then.'

Grace

It was 9 a.m. when the phone rang. She'd slept badly, awake through the middle hours after Iris rang, getting up finally at four to finish some reports.

Grace found she was getting used to Henry's condition and she wondered if that was actually worse than railing against it. Iris had helped. Grace had been able to cry and cry and Iris had had the good sense to let her. Grace had felt like a girl again, safe in Iris's arms. And Iris's confidence that Grace would pull through had given Grace confidence.

They'd decided to wait until Henry's symptoms became obvious before they said too much to the children and then give information as each of them asked. To Mia, who knew something was wrong, David simply said that Henry's muscles weren't going to develop in the same way as other kids'. He'd need more help to do things.

David had busied himself researching DMD and setting up therapy. He found a physiotherapist who'd done some work in London with DMD kids. The physio and Henry hit it off immediately. 'We'll keep him moving as best we can,' she said to

Grace and David. She'd come to the house three mornings a week to make things more normal for Henry, she said. Small kindnesses like this – the physio's willingness to come to Henry instead of making him go to a clinic – moved Grace. She bit back tears.

Henry himself had been awake since five that morning and looked like he was starting a cold. Normally Grace would have sent him to day care anyway but today she decided to keep him home. She called the hospital and said to call her if they needed her. David was already at work. The girls were at school.

Grace picked up the phone, sure it would be the hospital and wondering if she could drop Henry with Iris, when the voice at the other end said, 'Grace Hogan? Hi, it's Bernadine McKellar. We spoke once before. I'm Iris's GP. I'm very sorry to say she's gone, Grace. Iris died overnight.'

After she hung up the phone, Grace had that same feeling of there not being enough air to get into her lungs as she'd had in Ian Gibson's office. This time, she called David at the hospital. She couldn't quite say the words. 'Iris,' was all she said. 'Come and get me.' He was there fifteen minutes later. He put his strong arms around her and held her while she sobbed.

Iris's front door was open so Grace went in and through to the kitchen without looking into the bedroom, Henry gripping her hand. David had been scheduled on in theatre and had offered to find someone else to cover so he could stay home with Henry. 'You go,' Grace had said, knowing that finding another consultant would be almost impossible. 'We'll be all right.'

There was a man in an orange safety vest, sitting in the kitchen. 'I told the doctor I'd wait until you came,' he said.

'Who are you?' Grace said, sounding harsher than she'd intended.

'I'm Geoffrey. Iris was . . . Iris was my friend.' There were tears in his eyes and Grace wanted to hit him. What right did he have to cry?

'Who are you?' Grace said again.

'I'm Geoffrey, the postman. Iris was very good to me.'

'Oh,' Grace said. 'I think she mentioned you. Did you find her?'

He smiled weakly. 'She was always back from the shop by the time I got here,' he said. 'Every morning without fail. And if not, she'd leave me a note.' Geoffrey's eyes were red-rimmed, as if he'd spent the morning in Grace's grandmother's house sobbing. 'Every morning, without fail, unless I came early, which I always tried not to do, especially lately when her brother's been giving her such trouble.' He shook his head. 'She always came to the door for the post. It was easier for her than if I left it in the box. And then we'd have a cup of tea . . . She showed me where the spare key was.'

Grace didn't know Iris had shown anyone where the spare key was, let alone a postman. She noticed the bag of undelivered mail at his feet.

Henry spoke. 'Mummy, where's Granna?'

'In her bed, sweetie. We'll go in soon.'

Geoffrey got up then. 'I said I'd wait until you got here. I should be going.'

'Of course,' Grace said. Geoffrey was at the front door when she called him back. 'Thank you for waiting with her. If you write down your number, I'll call when I know what the funeral arrangements will be.'

'Iris always spoke so proudly of you,' Geoffrey said.

After he left, Grace looked at the table, cleared and wiped down, the dishes dry in the rack from the night before, a plate, a saucepan, two cups and saucers, a bowl. On the stove was the little espresso maker Iris used, ready for the morning. Iris had drunk proper coffee for as long as Grace could remember.

She scooped Henry up, opened the fridge, the same food as last time, plus the remains of what looked like a roast pork. It had been Grace's favourite meal when she was young: crumbed, roasted fillet of pork. Grace wanted to cry, seeing the roast there, knowing Iris had probably eaten it alone without Grace, knowing too that she would never eat with Iris again. She wanted to sit down and consume the rest of the meat even as she knew it would make her sick. She wanted to take in whatever was left of Iris, to have this moment go on and on. Henry was pulling on her arm and she wished she'd taken up David's offer to look after him. 'Henry, don't. We'll go in and see Granna in a minute.' She put him down.

In the little living room, on the table next to Iris's chair, there was the book she'd been reading, a new Mary Stewart.

She took Henry's hand to lead him back to the bedroom, not quite sure who was providing comfort to whom. 'Okay,' she said. 'Granna will look different. She won't be breathing and that will look strange. And her skin will be a different colour.'

'What colour?'

'A bit bluey grey, not white.'

Henry nodded solemnly. They stood at the door to the room for a moment before entering. Iris was lying on her back on the bed. She normally slept on her side, Grace knew, so maybe the doctor had moved her. Iris's arms were outside the sheets by her sides. The bed was made around her. It was like Iris and not like her at all. No matter how much preparation Grace had done for her grandmother's death – hearing the advice from Mark Randall, seeing the way Iris had been leaving by slow accretions, her increasingly confused state –

403

nothing would have prepared Grace for this. She let out a gentle sigh. There was nothing she had left to say, none of the unfinished business her friends talked about. 'I just wanted you to stay,' Grace said as she approached the bed. She sat down on the little chair, noticed the shoe horn hanging off the back of it. She pushed a wisp of hair off Iris's face. Her eyes and mouth were closed and rigor was setting in.

'Where's the bullet hole?'

Grace had forgotten about Henry. He was standing beside the bed, peering at Iris.

'What?'

'The bullet hole. Where's the bullet hole?'

'What do you mean, Henry?'

'Where they shot her.'

'No one shot her, Henry. She just died. She was very old.'

He looked more closely at Iris's face as if he didn't really believe Grace. 'I know. So where's the bullet hole?'

'No, Henry, they don't shoot people for being old.'

He nodded. 'She looks the same as asleep. Let's go.'

'A minute,' Grace said. 'You go out to my bag and find the chocolate. I'll be out soon.' He toddled off. 'Iris,' she said. 'You had so much left to live for. It's selfish, I know, but I just wish we'd had you with us a while longer.'

As they were leaving, Grace caught a whiff of the possum and remembered she hadn't done anything about it. She looked in the umbrella box but it wasn't there. Iris had said she was planning to let it go soon. Perhaps she had already. The possum was nowhere in the house when Grace looked so it must be out in the world somewhere. 'Good luck,' Grace said. 'I hope you remember who cared for you.'

* * *

404

When the girls got home from gymnastics David and Grace told them about Iris. Mia cried while David held her. Phil cried for a minute or two and then busied herself interrogating Henry about the body and what it looked like.

In the bath later, Henry told Grace he'd need a new Superman suit soon. The current one was a pile on the floor. 'It's getting tight,' he said. 'Is that because I'm growing?'

'Yeah,' Grace said. 'You're getting bigger all the time.' She smiled at him.

'There's something wrong with me,' he said.

Grace breathed and focused on her hands on the washcloth so she wouldn't cry. It had been such a long day, finding out about Iris, such a long month, knowing about Henry. Grace didn't think she could cope with this. Had he heard them talk? Had he guessed something, noticed the other kids at day care were stronger? It wouldn't help to cry, she told herself, narrowing her eyes and holding her emotions in check. 'There's something wrong with me too,' she said, mock flippant. 'I think I've got a cold.'

'That's not what's wrong with me,' Henry said. Grace didn't respond. She wasn't ready to go here now. 'My penis is wrong.'

'How do you mean?' Grace was racking her brains for DMD effects on penis growth.

'It doesn't have a button at the end. Like the other boys.'

Grace felt relief flood through her. 'Circumcision, Henry. Did I not explain this?'

He looked up at her, his clear green eyes on the verge of tears. He shook his head no.

'Okay,' Grace said. 'They sometimes cut some skin at the end of baby boys' penises. There's a whole lot of reasons people think it's a good idea. But me and Daddy didn't want to do that to you.' David hadn't been circumcised. He'd been in trouble when he first came to the Mater for telling couples it was a barbaric practice, that babies felt pain, that there was no reason you'd do that to a child. Grace had had no strong views either way, but with David as his father, Henry was never going to be circumcised. 'Daddy's the same,' she said now. 'They didn't do it to him. When they do it, boys look like they have a button.'

'I want a button.'

'Yours is better, like Daddy's.'

'No it's not,' Henry said. 'His is all furry.'

Grace smiled. 'That's just because he's a grown-up. You ask him, get him to show you. The other boys, they've had some skin cut off the end. You haven't. That's all.'

Grace leant back and sat down on the floor. She'd nearly rushed in and talked about DMD when Henry first said he wasn't like the other boys. She'd nearly told him. Grace had always been honest with the children, answered their sometimes uncomfortable questions about their bodies with accurate science. The children had a right to good information. It hadn't been her experience as a child. She'd often felt that Iris only told her some things, that important information was always held back. She looked at Henry, so little and thin. Already his muscles were letting him down. Grace wasn't sure she could get through this.

Henry knew he was different. That's what this was about. He was starting to see the differences between him and the other boys. Let him learn slowly, Grace thought, at his own pace. And just answer every question as honestly as you can. She wouldn't lie to him but she wouldn't burden him with the reality of his disease until she had to.

In bed that night, David told Grace that Iris had left

instructions with him about her remains, that her body was to be cremated, that she didn't care what they did with the ashes.

Grace wondered why Iris had talked to David and not Grace herself. 'You didn't want her to go,' David said. 'And I didn't either but I could accept it, I suppose, because she's not my mother.'

'Grandmother,' Grace said.

'Mother,' David said, taking her in his arms. 'She was every bit your mother, and a wonderful grandmother to our children.' There were tears in his eyes. They cried in one another's arms, Grace sobbing, David holding her gently. She leant up and kissed him. He responded, a powerful charge between them. They made love as if it was the first time, in constant contact as they took off their clothes, reaffirming life, after Henry, after Iris, after everything.

The funeral was held in the little stone church of St Patrick's in Fortitude Valley and Grace was surprised at the number of people, over a hundred from across Iris's life, her half-brothers and their families, Dr McKellar and various neighbours and friends from Paddington and the Valley. Grace wrote a eulogy but couldn't bring herself to read it so David read, his English accent strangely suited to the material. It was a hot day promising a hot summer, the sun high in the sky by 10 a.m.

In the eulogy, Grace had focused on Iris as a mother and grandmother, how much she'd given to Grace and David and their children. She'd been surprised at how raw her emotions were as she listened to David read. She'd known Iris would die, she was prepared for the funeral, but her death left a well of loneliness Grace didn't understand. She found herself sobbing, biting her lip hard to stop.

David added some anecdotes that captured something of

Iris, the day she charmed a police officer out of giving her a ticket for speeding through a red light which should have meant she lost her driving licence – how will I get to morning mass if I can't drive, Sergeant? – the day Iris had helped the girl who'd lost her plane ticket, Iris's kindness. The children lasted through the entire service, Henry trying to get high enough to see into the open coffin, probably hoping to discover the bullet hole that had eluded him.

The day after the funeral, Grace went over to the house on her own. She couldn't bring herself to go through Iris's things, not yet. She cleared out the refrigerator and pantry, cleaned the bathroom and swept and dusted. She stripped the bed and covered the furniture. As she was leaving the bedroom she noticed something under the bed she hadn't noticed before, a box that had been hidden by the bedspread. Grace slid it out. She'd never seen the box before. It was a dark wood inlaid with ivory about two feet long and a foot deep. Grace tried to lift the lid but the box was locked. There was no key. Grace pushed the box back under the bed. She'd face all this some other time. She put the umbrella box that had held the possum out on the verandah to air it. She locked the house and left.

Just under two months later, they were on the plane. It was David who said they should go. He and the children would stop in Cambridge and see his family. Grace would go to Paris and attend the ceremony on Iris's behalf. Grace wired the Foundation and they wired straight back that they'd be only too happy to have her attend.

Grace

She arrived at the abbey mid-morning. She'd spent the night in an airport hotel, jetlagged and unable to sleep. She and David and the children had flown together to Heathrow and then he'd rented a car to go to Cambridge and she'd flown on to Paris. That first night, she couldn't get him on the phone and found herself worried suddenly that something had happened. And then he'd phoned, they'd been out for dinner, that was all. She was so relieved.

Grace was surprised at how quickly the compact city of Paris gave way to small fields. She turned off a four-lane highway and drove along a country road to the town of Viarmes. She stopped for directions at the *tabac*, asking, in a little French but mostly English, for Royaumont. The boy behind the counter went to find his mother, who told her in better English than Grace's French which road to take.

She drove slowly through a heavily wooded area. She passed a large house, eighteenth century by the look of it, and pulled over to consult the map the woman at the shop had drawn. She pulled away again, came around a bend and there was Royaumont Abbey.

Grace had seen castles in England and Scotland and David had an interest in Gothic architecture. Royaumont struck her immediately. Whether it was the setting among the trees, the single remaining tower leaning into the abbey, as if nudging it to tell a secret or something else, Grace stopped and got out of the car. It was a sunny day with a lingering fog that gathered around the base of the abbey so that the stonework appeared to float out of nowhere. It glowed, she thought, like something alive.

Grace returned to the car and took the long drive, parking in front of the abbey, her car – a bright red Renault – completely wrong in the medieval setting. This had been a hospital? she thought. Royaumont was a cultural centre now, Grace had read, mainly music and dance. Inside it was beautifully if sparsely furnished, tapestries on walls, dark wood furnishings, modern lighting, a perfect balance of old and new.

Grace found a reception desk, all modern glass and wood. She rang a bell and waited. It was perfectly quiet. She looked up the long staircase. Did they carry patients up those stairs, or have lifts? Iris had told her the hospital was run entirely by women.

A girl of seventeen or so, translucent skin, hair pulled back, rosy cheeks, came out of one of the rooms to the left of the entry hall. 'Can I help you?' she said in French. Grace struggled to explain in French who she was until the receptionist switched to English. 'Ah, you are with the Scottish women,' she said.

'Not really,' Grace said. 'My grandmother was with them.'

'Yes, I know. She is the one called Iris.'

'How do you know?'

410

'Iris Crane. She was the hospital administrator, yes?' Grace nodded dumbly. 'My great-grandmother did the laundry for the hospital,' the girl said. 'Mended uniforms and washed the men's clothes. Emily Fox?' as if Grace might know her. 'She died last year. But she knew Iris Crane well.' The receptionist smiled. 'I am sorry. You did not know your grandmother?'

Grace looked at her. 'I thought I did,' she said. 'Any messages for me?'

'Oh yes, Dr Heron wishes to speak with you. She told me she will be in the cloister. It's a beautiful day.'

Violet Heron, Iris's mysterious friend. As Grace went up the long staircase, she tried to imagine Iris here, a hospital here, but found she couldn't. The layout would be difficult, if not impossible. You couldn't move the stone walls and the long staircases would be hard to negotiate with stretchers. And the abbey would have been so cold within. Would they have had electric light then? It must have been terrible.

Grace's room was small and austere but strangely inviting, a plain spread on a single bed, little table, chair and lamp, with an en suite bathroom. They wouldn't have had the bathrooms in Iris's time, Grace thought. Before she went downstairs, she looked out the window to the cloister. The grass was brown, garden beds bare now in winter. In the centre of the cloister was a little fountain surrounded by stone benches. David had told her that the Gothic had perfected built space. Grace hadn't known what he'd meant but the cloister looked like a place you'd want to linger in the spring when the grass was green and the beds planted with flowers. A group of women gathered around a modern table in one corner. She could hear their laughter but only saw the tops of their brightly hatted heads. There was another woman on one of the benches around the fountain, sitting alone reading. Grace could see wisps of curly white hair under a purple beret and legs too short to reach the ground. Violet Heron.

Grace went downstairs. The women in the group had hair in various shades of blue and grey under their colourful hats and woollen coats, like a bunch of bright flowers in a vase. They looked up at Grace and smiled, trying to place her here. She smiled back but didn't stop to talk. Across from them was Violet Heron, frizzes of curly snow-white hair puffing out from under the beret. She wore large-lensed purple-tinted glasses, the purple beret and a long purple coat, skirt, tights and boots. 'You must be Violet,' Grace said when she went over.

'I must be,' she said. She looked up from her book and closed it. 'And you must be Rose.' She smiled and Grace could see a hint of the younger woman she would have been. She spoke slowly in an upper-class English accent and put effort into enunciation.

'Grace. Rose was my mother.'

'Of course. Grace. Do sit down. I suppose I'm just a little nervous.' Violet was staring at her and Grace wasn't sure if she was quite with it. She patted the seat beside her and smiled again.

Grace sat. 'My grandmother very much wanted to see you again,' she said. 'She was coming because of you, I think.'

'I imagine.'

'She said you were a very good friend.'

'I wasn't. But tell me about you. I believe you're in obstetrics.'

'I am,' Grace said, wondering why Violet would care.

'What do you do about incest?'

'Sorry?'

'What do you do about incest? You must have come across it.' She had a businesslike manner, sharp. She'd annoy people, Grace thought.

'No, I haven't,' Grace said. 'You mean in gynae?'

'Yes, and obstetrics.'

'I haven't had to deal with it that often. We get referrals from psych from time to time. You dealt with many cases, I believe.' Grace hadn't expected to be talking about this subject and wondered again if Violet was quite with it.

Violet lifted her hand as if to dismiss the question. 'Do you remember your mother?'

'No, she died during my birth,' Grace said. 'Did you meet her?' Iris had said something about Violet coming to Australia when Rose was a baby.

'She was a beautiful baby, perfect. I can remember her face like it was yesterday.' If she'd been sharp before, now her features dissolved and tears sprang from those old eyes like tiny diamonds. 'I just want to touch you.' She reached her hand across and caressed Grace's face. Her hand was cold.

Grace pulled back at her touch instinctively, then took Violet's hand in her own and held it. 'I'm sorry. I'm not sure if you realise who I am. I'm Grace Hogan, Iris Crane's granddaughter. You knew Iris.'

'I didn't expect you'd look like me.' Grace looked at her. I don't look like you, she wanted to say. She had the strangest urge to get up and run.

Violet had been holding a small photo album in her lap. 'Well, here goes, as Iris used to say.' She opened the album at a page she'd been holding with her finger. She pointed to a photograph of two women and a young man sitting at a café table. It looked just like Les Deux Magots. Their heads were thrown back slightly as if laughing at something the photographer had said. Grace noticed the young man first, his smile, and then peered more closely at the women. 'Is this you and Iris?' Grace said. Violet nodded. 'She's smoking.'

'That's me,' Violet said.

'Oh, sorry,' Grace said. 'I thought that was Iris. Let me have another look. I do look like you after all.' Grace laughed nervously. She had a strange feeling in the pit of her stomach. Had she eaten this morning? Violet was nodding and looking at Grace very solemnly. 'Is something wrong?' Grace said.

'I just need to touch your face,' Violet said again, moving her hand up to Grace's cheek. The hand was a little warmer now. Grace looked at her and, inexplicably, felt tears fill her eyes. She took Violet's hand again and held it.

'Who's the chap?' Grace said, swallowing emotion, pointing to the young man, dark curly hair, a gorgeous smile. You just wanted to hug him.

'That's Tom, your father.'

Grace said, 'My father? What do you mean?' She let go of Violet's hand. 'I'm Grace, I'm Iris's granddaughter, Violet. I've come to see you after my grandmother died. Iris, you know she died, don't you?' Grace started to feel afraid, for no reason she understood.

'No no no,' Violet said. 'Not your father. Your grandfather. Oh, I'm messing this up. But Iris took the baby. I had a baby. Iris took the baby. This one,' she pointed at Tom. 'He's your grandfather.'

Grace stared at her open-mouthed. She felt as if all the air had been taken out of her lungs.

'I couldn't keep a child. So Iris took the child, your mother. Edinburgh, you . . . she was born in Edinburgh.'

Grace continued staring. 'You need to tell me what this is about,' she said. Her heart was in her mouth. She swallowed hard. What was Violet talking about?

'Iris was angry with me over the scholarship,' Violet said. 'Well of course she was. But how was I to know they were planning to give it to Iris? I wasn't Frances's favourite but Iris was already engaged to that fellow in Australia. She was never going to go off that course. Or at least, I didn't think she was going to. I was sure they'd give it to me, even if they preferred her.

'But Frances said I lacked compassion, a doctor's truest virtue, she called it. Well, maybe she lacked compassion too.' Violet sniffed, sharp again. 'Perhaps I'd have acted differently if I'd known they had Iris in mind. Perhaps not. I'm very selfish.' She smiled weakly and looked at Grace.

'Violet, I'm really sorry but I just don't understand,' Grace said, 'and I need to. You have to help me. What scholarship are you talking about? How are we related?'

'I do think you're being a little slow, dear,' Violet said. 'Never mind.' She patted Grace's hand. 'Iris's brother Tom was my lover. Did you know Tom? Of course you didn't. I'm sorry. He was a beautiful boy. That one.' She pointed at the photograph, her eyes softening.

'But where do I come in?' Grace said, still not understanding.

'I was pregnant. To Tom. I . . . We were lovers. I was pregnant. I didn't know what to do and then he was killed. So I told Frances. She was going to help – get rid of it, I mean. But then I told Iris and she said she'd take the baby. She'd marry her fiancé in Australia and take the baby. And that's what she did. I went back to Scotland and gave birth to the child and then Iris came. She took the child. The others said I only told her to get her out of the way. But I never thought . . .

'I'm sorry I haven't done this better,' Violet said. 'You have to understand it's very hard to talk, even now after all these years.' Her bottom lip began to quiver and she bit it hard. 'I thought about what I should say to you, whether I should tell you any of it. I wondered if Iris had told you already.'

Grace shook her head, taking it in.

'So I'm not Iris's granddaughter?' she said.

'Well, of course you are,' Violet said. 'Blood's not everything. It's not anything really. She's the one who raised you. Of course you are, my dear.' She patted Grace's hand again. 'I gave you up.'

'But Al. I'm not related to Al at all. I'm related to Iris and her brother. And you.' Grace looked at her again and then at the photograph, Violet as a young woman. They did look alike. Grace wished the figures in the photograph could begin to move so she could watch Tom and especially Violet in the world.

Her grandfather. Her grandmother.

Grace had asked Iris once why Iris and Al hadn't had more children. At the time, she'd been old enough to understand how children came about but too young to know that such a question might be difficult. 'It just never happened,' Iris said. Later, when Grace was studying medicine, there had been a suggestion that pre-eclampsia might have a hereditary link. Given that Iris's mother had died of pre-eclampsia, Grace had asked Iris about her own pregnancy. 'I had no problems. Everything was easy.'

'Did you go to term?'

'What does that mean?'

'The full nine months.'

'Yes.'

'How was she born?'

'It was normal.'

'Vaginal, you mean.'

'Grace, please.'

'That's what we call it, Iris.'

'Yes, it was all very normal.'

It had all been a lie.

And even before that. In primary school, Grace had been friends with a girl who'd been adopted. The girl's parents hadn't told her. But kids at the school knew because one of the mothers had told her own daughter and her daughter had told the other girls. Inevitably, someone hurled it as an insult in the playground. 'You're adopted.' The girl had gone home and asked her parents and they'd told her that yes, she was adopted, but to please not ask them anything about it. The girl had confided in Grace. Grace had felt helpless, couldn't understand how the girl could not know where she came from. She asked Iris about it. 'Some things are best not to know,' Iris had said.

'But what if she wants to know?'

'Would you want to know?'

'Of course I would. Who wouldn't?'

'I think children just need to be cared for.'

How had Iris managed to keep this from Grace, and probably from Rose before her, for all those years?

Grace looked over at Violet. It was shocking, completely unexpected. But strangely not unexpected too. It was that feeling of déjà vu, where you remember something from before; Violet speaking to her, the perfect diction, the frizzy white hair, the glasses, telling her this odd, odd truth. Had Grace dreamt this?

'Would you mind if we met again later? I think I need some time to think,' Grace said. She rubbed her forehead.

'Oh yes, dear,' Violet said. 'I did wonder whether to tell you.' She looked so old, so unsure, Grace wanted to embrace her and tell her it was all right but found she couldn't, not yet.

She walked out through the cloister and into the abbey grounds, across what would have been the church – bits of rubble and foundations still embedded in the soil – and into a forest of tall trees. She found a path through the forest, wandered past a little spring.

Her coat wasn't warm enough but she didn't care. The cold was good, real. She sat down under a tree heavily but felt as if she weighed nothing more than the air. She had the experience again of feeling totally surprised and unsurprised at once. Trust, it was a breach of trust. Or was it? She made herself breathe, focus on the trees, their bare branches oddly reassuring. She remembered what Janis had said, one foot after the other, and this way, you go on. But how would she go on after this?

It was as if her life had been predicated on a puzzle, a riddle, and here was the answer. Grace wasn't like Iris. She'd always felt guilty about that, felt she should be more like her grandmother. Iris, the perfect mother, the perfect homemaker. Grace had never been interested in any of that. And when they found out Henry was sick, underneath everything else, she realised now, there was guilt, guilt born of her failings as his mother. If she'd been a better mother, if she hadn't fallen on the ice, hadn't let Henry fall off the verandah. If she'd been home instead of at work all the time, he'd have been all right. If she'd been Iris, she saw now. If she'd been Iris, she'd have saved Henry. She saw the folly of this view, saw too it would lead her into despair. And now, she had learnt, she wasn't the person she'd thought she was anyway.

It struck her suddenly that she'd always felt she had more in common with Al, to whom, it turned out, she had no blood ties. So there you are, she thought. Was she like Violet? she wondered. Hard in her heart? Able to give up her own child? Had she given up all her children in a way, becoming an obstetrician, working in the world that was still the world of men, leaving the children to others to raise, to Iris, who'd do a better job anyway?

Grace leant into the tree under which she sat, the ground cold beneath her, the strong reassuring trunk behind her back. After a little while, she started to cry. Silent tears fell down her cheeks at first and then gave way to hard hacking sobs, one after another, for Henry more than anything, but also for herself now.

She found Violet in the library, sitting with a book open on her lap, staring out the window. Grace paused a moment and took her in. This was her blood grandmother. It was preposterous and yet she had this odd feeling of calm deep within again.

'Is the purple for suffrage?' Grace asked Violet, noticing she'd changed into another purple outfit, crimplene slacks and a blouse and cardigan.

'Purple because I like the colour. How are you, dear?'

Grace pulled up a chair next to her. 'The hospital,' she said, not wanting to talk about her feelings yet. 'You worked here too?'

'Oh yes,' Violet said brightly. 'I was one of the drivers. But Iris ran the place. That's what I always thought. She loved Miss Ivens, the medical superintendent. But Miss Ivens never could have done it without Iris.' Grace let her talk. 'I arrived here yesterday and it was so strange. The track to Royaumont we used to take is a road now of course and the fields are without the flowers we loved so much in the spring. I used to pick those daisies for Iris. He loves you, he loves you not, about her man. What was his name?'

'Al,' Grace said. 'Alastair Hogan.'

'No, the other one. I always wondered what became of him. He was in the Croix-Rouge and afterwards I think he went back to psychiatry. He helped Ruth Berry with some of the mental cases at Royaumont. What was his name?'

'Iris had someone here in France?'

'Oh yes, we all did,' Violet said. 'But the strangest thing was yesterday I came to the abbey and I didn't recognise it. I'd always thought it would come back to me as it does in dreams. After the war, I used to come to France for holidays almost every year. I always stayed away from Royaumont though, from all of what happened in those years. It was the only way.

'But when I saw it yesterday, it held nothing for me. It could have been any old abbey in any old woods for all the effect it had. I think they've turned the entry around, that we came in through the back where the cars were kept, although the stable buildings and garages are long gone. But still, I didn't feel it. All I saw was a long drive, a stream beside it, a fountain, the front door, some church ruins. It was Saturday so there were tourists everywhere, like Brighton Beach.'

'Did you love him very much?' Grace said.

'Who?'

'Tom, Iris's brother, my . . . grandfather I guess.'

'He was so young and sweet and hopeful. God, we were

all young. Oh, the war was horrid. Worse than the next one, worse by far because we all went with such hope and we came home so hopeless.

'He was trying to prove himself. That's what I thought. He'd grown up with Iris as his sister, and she was so much cleverer and better at everything, and she'd mothered him right from when he was small. And she was so bossy with him, always telling him what he should do.'

Grace smiled. She knew that Iris.

'He had a very kind nature but he wanted to fight. He didn't really know what fighting was. None of them did. But he wanted to do his part, felt he wasn't. He was underaged, you see, so they put him in the postal service. Still, he wanted to fight and Iris didn't want him to.' Violet shook her head and swallowed. 'When I first saw Iris fussing over him I thought he was a spoilt brat. I knew her fussing would only make him worse. But I did an even more stupid thing. I treated him like the boy he was. And it made him more determined of course. Iris was so angry at me and I couldn't bear her anger. She was such a dear friend.' Violet put her hand to her face, as if she wasn't sure what to say next.

'The wounded.' She shook her head and paused, lost in thought. 'I felt so helpless. Iris was always much more resilient. I think religion helps. I just got more and more unhappy. And then I got an idea in my head about Tom. I thought if I could do this one thing, save this one boy, it would make a difference. And it would help Iris.

'So I let him love me. I thought it would save him.' She smiled weakly. 'And it nearly did. He'd agreed to stay with the postal service because of me. I didn't tell Iris about our affair. She wouldn't have approved of her younger brother with such an older woman.' Violet laughed, a hard cackling laugh, which changed suddenly into a sob. 'I was twenty-six.

'But I came to love him, you see. He was just so . . . uncomplicated. Oh, I knew there was no future. We all knew that. They were different times. The ambulance on the road at night, shelling nearby, the cloister in the early morning, the patients. At Royaumont, the rest of the world faded away. As I say, I was young,' she said, 'and I've always been quite clever at pretending to be more than I am. That was how I became a doctor after all. Me, who had no compassion.' She let out a sob and her voice cracked. 'That's what Miss Ivens said. I lacked a doctor's most necessary gift. Compassion.'

Grace nodded. This had clearly upset Violet. She'd said it once already.

'Tom was different from the others. He just loved me. And then, the pregnancy. What was I to do? He never knew. I hadn't told him. Perhaps I would have. I was confused. He died not knowing he had a child. I used to think sometimes that if it had been different . . . But that only made it worse, that kind of thinking. I quickly learnt that.

'Iris was angry with me, of course, never forgave me. But I hadn't meant her harm. It just happened.'

Grace watched Violet as she spoke. 'So you had the baby in Edinburgh, you said. Rose.'

'Iris named her. I've never been back to the hospital. Once I was offered a job in Edinburgh, a good job, but I didn't take it because I'd have had to walk back through those doors. I couldn't do it, not then, not ever.' Violet took a breath in and held it, then let it out heavily.

'After the child was born, my mother came and took me home. She came up on the train and took me back with her.

I thought I'd be fine, I'd just get on with life.' She smiled but looked like she might cry again.

'After we'd been home a few weeks, we went to town to a café Mother liked. She ordered scones for herself and for me, although I'd said I wasn't hungry. A young woman came into the café, Amelia Wickham. We'd gone to school together. I recognised her across the café, hoping she'd relieve us, my mother and I, of the need to converse with one another. I smiled. Then I saw she carried a bundle, a small bassinette. But she'd registered my smile and was upon us before I knew. I looked briefly inside the bassinette and saw a new baby, mottled red arms out of a white nightdress, peeling skin. I began to feel cold. It's hard to describe. I didn't really notice the baby. I just began to feel cold.' Violet stopped, swallowed, narrowed her eyes.

'My mother knew Amelia's mother. There had been some tragedy. At the time, I couldn't quite recall the details. Amelia greeted my mother and turned to me. She mentioned that she'd heard I was going to be a doctor. Who'd have thought? she said. My mother ignored this part of the conversation. Medicine wasn't something we discussed. She was against it from the start, felt women shouldn't work.

'So of course my mother fussed over Amelia, who had the far more appropriate life with a husband and baby. Do join us for tea, my mother said. Neither my mother nor I had mentioned the baby. I'm meeting Rob's parents, Amelia said. My mother looked a question. Robert Benton, my late husband. He was in the Somme. Her mouth was set tight. My mother offered condolences, happy now to have got to the nub. She began to ask Amelia about her family, who we knew vaguely.

'I hadn't said a word. I stood so suddenly I felt faint. I excused myself. In the lavatory I vomited and then I sobbed, my heart just a stone inside me.' Violet whimpered. Grace reached out a hand and took Violet's.

Violet withdrew her hand, composed herself. 'The feeling subsided eventually. I returned to the table. Amelia had taken her leave. The child was gone. It's going to be like this for a long time, my mother said. She put her hand on mine and said, You didn't have to do it, you know. I didn't reply.

'What I always remembered about that day wasn't Amelia Wickham who couldn't have known what I'd done. It was my poor mother, trying in her own way to reach out and help me.' Tears were rolling down Violet's cheeks now. Grace felt for her deeply. Violet grinned through her tears. 'And yet I remained helpless.' The smile turned into a grimace. She covered her mouth with her hand, as if her feelings were a surprise to her.

'I used to tell people I wasn't someone who regretted things. And when I did regret what I'd done, I told myself that I had chosen my life. I had made the decision, however badly I felt. No one made it for me. It helped to know I'd made the choice.

'But I've always remembered that day with my mother, her reaching out her hand, trying to help me. We'd never been close, and yet she tried in her way to reach out. I always felt bad that I didn't respond. My mother. You have to understand the kind of life she had, the kind of woman she was. My brother died as a child and she never got over it.'

'What did he die of?' Grace said. In the pit of her stomach she felt a coldness without yet understanding why. But something nagged at the edge of her consciousness.

'Pneumonia,' Violet said. 'There was something wrong with him. He was always sick. No one quite knew what it was.'

Grace looked at her, realisation dawning. 'Muscular dystrophy,' she said. 'Your brother had Duchenne's muscular dystrophy.'

After she left Violet, Grace went up to her room. She couldn't be angry with Violet. Grace had seen the girls come into the hospital who were adopting their babies out. It changed them. You could see that. After Mia was born, Grace wondered how they could do it, walk away from their babies. This was how they did it, she thought now, closing off the past and only looking towards the future. Poor Violet.

She tried to phone David but it rang out. She'd try again later. She didn't want to talk to Violet again for now either. She went out of the room intending to walk again, although it was dark outside and cold. On the stairs, she passed two women, wool suits and hats, one old, one very old. The very old one, holding onto the balustrade, cane hooked on the other arm, put her hand on Grace's arm. 'I knew your grandmother, dear,' she said. She had washed-out blue eyes that lit up when she smiled at Grace.

The woman had said 'grandmother'. She meant Iris, of course, although would Grace ever think of Iris as her grandmother again? She wanted to cry, bit her lip. 'Did you?' Grace said. I didn't know her, she thought angrily.

'You look a bit peaky, dear,' the woman said. 'We were going down for a sherry. Do join us. I'm Marjorie Lanois. I was Marjorie Starr,' as if she expected Grace would know who she was. Her accent was American, Grace thought. 'Iris and I were good friends. And this is Miss May Robertson.'

'Oh yes,' the younger one said. 'Do join us. My auntie Frances thought the world of your grandmother.' Frances Ivens had been director at the hospital, Violet had said. May had spent some time there as a volunteer, she told Grace now.

'We're so sorry for your loss,' Marjorie said.

Grace felt like crying then. She told them she wouldn't join them, she was going for a walk.

'Don't be silly,' Marjorie said. 'Come, join us.'

Grace was about to refuse outright when something changed her mind. She sighed. 'Yes, a drink,' she said, 'and you can tell me about my grandmother.'

She helped Marjorie Starr negotiate the rest of the stairs. 'It's my knees, dear.' She was better on flat land. They went to a little alcove off the dining room, ordered drinks, champagne cocktails for themselves. Grace ordered a neat scotch.

'This was once the monks' bathrooms,' Marjorie said. 'They had a hundred and eighty toilet seats.'

Grace looked at her. They were all a bit odd, she thought.

Marjorie sighed, took a long look at Grace. 'Iris was the one I was looking forward to seeing,' she said. 'So it's lovely you came for her. She'd have liked that. We were all so sad when we heard. She was such a good woman. It wasn't fair, what happened. She blamed herself.'

'What do you mean?'

'Well her brother, dear. She was supposed to take him home. You knew that, didn't you?' Grace nodded. Violet had told her. Iris hadn't. 'That's why she came over originally. And then she got to Royaumont and Miss Ivens wanted her to stay and she and Violet became such good friends. She eventually learnt what Violet was like.'

'And what's that?' Grace said, taking a long pull on the drink. It felt good, calming.

'Violet got the place in medicine, didn't she? That was Iris's place.'

'Iris was going to do medicine?' Grace said, confused. This was something Violet had said too but Grace hadn't understood.

Marjorie nodded. 'Oh yes, Miss Ivens had a scholarship to give out. The Scottish Women's Hospitals were great fundraisers. They had money come in from all over the world, even Canada where I'm from.' Canadian rather than American. 'A lot of those women wouldn't give their money to the war but they'd give it to our hospitals.' Marjorie took a sip of her drink. 'You see, we didn't ever support the war really. We just did what we could for the men. They were lovely, the French soldiers, so kind and considerate.

'The nurses weren't to fraternise with the patients. That was a cardinal rule with Miss Ivens. But goodness me, you put all those young men with all those young women and what do you expect? We used to have concerts and dances. It was a merry place, almost as if the war was all around us but couldn't touch us.'

May Robertson smiled, even blushed. 'It was such a time for all of us,' she said.

Grace smiled too. She couldn't help it. They were such amazing women, crazy but amazing. 'So why didn't Iris get the scholarship in the end?'

'Well, she had the baby, dear. And you know who got the scholarship instead? Violet.' Marjorie pursed her lips.

Grace didn't know if Marjorie knew the truth about Violet and Iris. 'Iris had such a way with people,' Marjorie said. 'And such initiative.' She told Grace the story of the lorry. 'It probably doesn't seem like much now but it was very difficult for us to get anything done. Iris just looked at a problem and solved it. She was a blessing. Miss Ivens would never have succeeded without her.'

May Robertson said Iris was wonderful at cutting through the nonsense to keep them on track. 'She certainly kept my auntie Frances on track and that's saying something.'

'You must be so proud of her,' Marjorie Starr said.

Finally she managed to reach David. The kids were still out with his parents at dinner but he'd come back early to wait for her call. She told him everything she'd found out, that Violet was her blood grandmother, Tom her blood grandfather, that Iris had lied, hadn't done medicine, had felt guilty about her brother, had never talked because of all this, had kept this information from her daughter and granddaughter.

'To be honest, I'm still reeling,' she said. 'The rooms keep moving on me.'

'I knew there was something,' David said. 'If you think about it, for you it's not really any different though,' he said.

'Yes it is. They didn't tell my mother who her parents were. Can you believe that? They didn't tell me. How could they . . .'

'Well, they were a different generation. You didn't tell. You hid things,' David said.

'Yes, but Iris never told me. Iris looked at me and lied.'

'Give it up, Grace,' David said. 'You're starting to sound . . .'

'To sound what?'

'Ungrateful.'

'Ungrateful? My whole life's been a lie. You just have no idea.'

'That's not true. Your whole life hasn't been a lie. Your mother died having you. Your father didn't want you. Your grandmother raised you as her own.'

'But she wasn't my grandmother, much less my mother.'

'Yes, she was. She stepped up and said I'll do this. She was willing. I can't help but think that what she did for your mother, taking her home when she'd been offered a chance to do medicine . . . I can't help but think that took extraordinary courage. And it doesn't change anything.'

'Our son has muscular dystrophy.'

'Would you have done anything differently if you'd known?'

'You mean, aborted a male foetus?'

'Or not had children?'

'No. Maybe. But it's not about that. It's about my right to know.'

Early the next morning, Grace found Violet in the dining room on her own. Grace couldn't face food. She'd spent the night tossing and turning. She remained angry, angry with Iris. And now, she couldn't even confront Iris, couldn't tell her how it felt.

'How are you now, my dear?' Violet said. 'Sit down, won't you?' Violet's face was pleading.

Grace remained standing. 'My mother and I had a right to information,' she said. 'Iris should have told me. She should have . . .' Grace was pointing at the air, her finger trembling.

Violet interrupted her. 'I want you to know that it was me who decided we should keep the secret, not Iris.' She smiled. 'If you want to kick someone, it should be me.' Violet took an envelope from her bag and handed it to Grace. 'I want you to read this. Now sit down.'

Grace did as she was told. She opened the envelope. Inside was a letter, written on soft thin paper in a neat hand.

Dear Violet,
There is news. Our daughter Rose has died. It was a haemorrhage following birth and quick. Al says she wouldn't have suffered at all, which is what you'd hope for. To be honest, Violet, I'm rather in shock, I think, to

have lost what was never mine to begin with. You see, I'd always intended to make amends, to write you like this, to tell Rose the truth. And all I did really was put it off, and then the time was gone. I did show her your photograph and I told her you were once a dear friend of mine who'd become a great surgeon. We'd drifted apart, I said, because our lives were so different.

You know, it may seem queer to you after all your years at it, but I could never imagine you a surgeon. I used to think I was jealous and I was but it was more than that. You seemed too soft for surgery. When I think back to the two of us, I was the tougher one really, although anyone who looked at us, at you, would have been in no doubt that you were, with your boys' pants and your leather gloves and cigarettes. Do you still smoke them? Al says they'll do you no good. It was a brittle strength, yours. Perhaps we were each unsuited to the lives we chose, or had chosen for us. But perhaps after all they've been the better choices.

I'm rambling, Violet, because I don't know what to say. Isn't it strange to think back on your life like this and see it was so different from how you'd always believed it was? I spent many years thinking you had the best of life and I the scraps. I was wrong, although perhaps you don't agree. But I was wrong. I had the best of life, and you couldn't have had better.

We had the funeral here at St Pat's. Everyone came, even the ones who probably shunned us in our troubles. The priest nearly refused to say the mass but Al had a word – I think some money changed hands – and the mass went ahead with a eulogy Al had written that was read by his brother. It was very beautiful and Rose's whole class came, along with faculty and many from the hospitals.

She was so like you, Violet, impulsive and quick to anger and beautiful. Tiny too, not like Al and me. She called us the giants. She'd have been a strong woman in her later years, I think. When she decided on a medical degree, Al was as happy as a man could be. She was at the university in Brisbane and Al and I had agreed privately that when she graduated we'd bring her to you, show you what a marvellous girl she was. You'd have been proud, I hope. We meant to make amends, Violet. We just didn't get to it.

As for the pregnancy, it was me who said Rose wasn't going away, although that's still the done thing. There are homes in all the towns now where girls can go and the Church looks after it all, finds a family. But I didn't have the heart for it and Rose had no idea what to do. I told her to come home to us and we'd manage. I knew people would talk. Let them, I said to Rose. It was no worse than when Al and I came home with her, I thought to myself. They'd move on to someone else eventually, as gossips always do.

So we had her home here and my plan, if you could call it that, was that we'd stand up straight and let the whole world say what it wanted. When Rose had the baby, she'd go back to her study and finish what she started while we – Al and I – looked after the child. I haven't forgotten too much, although I have given away most of the baby things, thinking I wouldn't be needing them again until much later and then I'd probably make new things.

Rose hadn't talked to us about who the father was, although we'd guessed. It wasn't that she couldn't have talked to us, Violet, but on this occasion she kept her own counsel and we respected that. Al was not the type to storm some boy's room and pull him out by the ear and make him marry but I think he'd have liked to know, to sit this boy down and give him a chance to act properly.

He's a nice boy, Violet, from a well-to-do family in Brisbane. He was studying with Rose and they were the best of friends until the pregnancy and then we heard no more of him. I don't know if she told him but he came to the funeral along with her class and he looked so lost. Afterwards, I wrote to thank him and asked if we might have tea. I never heard back so didn't push.

As for the child, she was born eight pounds two ounces with light eyes and fair curly hair. She's the spitting image of you, although she's long and thin so I don't know if she'll be tiny or one of 'the giants'. I can't see so much of Tom in her, except around her eyes.

This has all been quite a circular route to apologising for not contacting you sooner. I wasn't sure what to do. I've never been sure, to be honest. Al has always said we were acting rightly but even Al is faltering now. I want to know, Violet, what you want us to do. We will happily raise the child. Al is still busy at work and though I'm older now than when Rose came home with us, I seem to be stronger, have more verve, rather than less. Al says it's a last great effort before age overtakes me. I hope not.

Anyway, it's hard to find words. We thought, Violet, that you might have some views about the child and if you did, I know we'd be amenable to

something different. I don't know your exact personal
circumstances and you can be sure that I'd be over the
moon to find myself blessed with another child. It's
nothing like that, not from me and not from Al.

I can't make up for what happened to you, not now that
Rose has gone. But I can pay my respects, finally, to you as
this child's – we call her Grace – as Grace's grandmother.

Grace looked up from the letter. Violet met her eyes and spoke slowly. 'I wrote back that it would be ridiculous for me to have a role in the child's life,' Violet said. 'In your life. I told Iris I didn't want you to be told anything. And that was the last of it. Until now.'

'You didn't want to know me?'

'I didn't,' Violet said. 'I had made up my mind and I wasn't going back on it just because the circumstances had changed. That was how I survived. It's all so long ago now but you must understand that I couldn't remain with the loss. It's . . . impossible to convey.' Violet looked sharply at Grace.

'What does she mean, make up for what happened to you?' Grace said.

'When your mother was small, I went to see Iris. We met in Sydney,' Violet said. 'Her man was there, the husband. Al. I didn't much like him, felt Iris could have done better. I always thought he was too interested in keeping her under his thumb.

'I told Iris I wanted the child. I don't know what possessed me. I hadn't planned on saying it but the child was there with us when we met, playing at a fountain in a park. We three sat in a line on a bench and watched her. It was early morning and the sun came in hard lines through the leaves of a large tree.

I don't know why I went. It was like a hunger. You gave her up, Iris said to me. She looked fierce, as if she might pick the child up and run. I was wrong, I said. Well, you can't change now. But she's my child, I said.

'Her man ended it. Listen to yourselves, he said to us, parcelling out a life like so much flour or butter. She's a child and we've created a world for her. It's hers now. It's all she knows. He looked straight at me then. For mercy's sake, if you really care about Rose, you'll leave her settled where she is and never hurt her so.

'As if a signal had been given, the child came bounding up and jumped into his arms and said, Daddy, I saw a lizard, and that sealed her future. She would remain with him and Iris, and I would go back to England and leave them alone. And that's what I did. There were never any papers signed and I suppose Iris was always afraid I might come back. But I accepted what had happened and got on with my life. I closed that door behind me and I wasn't going to open it all those years later when you came along. I'm sorry if that's hard.'

'You said you have no regrets?' Grace didn't believe her.

'No,' Violet said quickly. 'I am not a person who regrets things. And I've used the life I was given well. As did Iris.

'In the end, you have to do what's right. There's a higher good, always, to be found. You have to find it, that's all. And as doctors we have an even greater responsibility because we take part in important moments of so many lives. You can believe in a vengeful God. You can believe in medicine. It will all fall away. Truth runs under the world, a deep black seam of truth and that's in the end what we seek, as doctors and as human beings.'

* * *

After she left Violet, Grace went outside again. She walked back towards Viarmes, taking the road Iris would have taken, a minor highway now. She walked up the hill to the railway station. She thought of Iris coming here all those years ago. She'd been just twenty-one. God, her youth, Grace thought. When Grace was twenty-one, she was fourth-year med and still living at home. And here was Iris, running a hospital, a war hospital, on the smell of an oily rag from what the women had told Grace, and looking after her younger brother.

David had been right. Iris had given up a chance to have a different life in order to raise a child, to raise Grace's mother Rose. Iris's light had shone for those years of the war and then she'd chosen to hide it under a bushel for the rest of her life. No wonder she'd been tough on Grace about school, about study, about medicine. She wouldn't let Grace waste whatever talents she had. She probably felt her own talents had been wasted. Although you'd never have known it if you met Iris. When Grace thought about it, Iris was one of happiest people she'd ever known. Her happiness was hard won, it seemed now.

Surely Iris must have been bitter, Grace thought. Grace had resisted medicine, had thought about doing something else, but had had the choice. That was the point. What if that choice had been taken away from her? Iris never once gave any hint of the sacrifice she'd made. At the time Grace was born, Iris had been about to start studying again, a science degree at the university. Grace had only found out when they'd been clearing out Sunnyside together. She found the application forms and acceptance letter. 'Why didn't you do it?' Grace had asked at the time. She hadn't even noticed that the year was the year of her own birth.

'I decided I was too old,' Iris said. 'And too happy doing other things.'

But some part of her must have watched Grace and wondered what her own life might have been like. How could I have been so unthinking, so selfish? she thought now.

In the town, Grace stopped at the *tabac*, ordered an espresso as Iris might have, bought a croissant from the baker, took a few bites. If Grace had ever thought her generation faced constraints, these women had faced many more. Constraints had shaped their whole lives.

As she came along the drive back to the abbey, Grace saw it with new eyes, Iris's twenty-one-year-old eyes. What hope Iris must have held in her heart. She'd had a chance to become a doctor. And yet she'd given that up, she'd given all that up for Rose and then for Grace. David was right. It had been an enormous sacrifice. And to her shame now, Grace realised, she had always felt slightly superior to Iris. Iris was uneducated. When Grace and Al would discuss a new finding in medicine, Grace wouldn't include Iris in the conversation. The arrogance, she realised now. Iris wasn't inferior. She'd just never been able to take up the opportunities Grace had.

Grace understood now why Iris could never speak of her time at Royaumont, how she'd carried guilt for all those years, had taken her brother's child and then his grandchild and raised them as her own and never once complained about the life she might have lived. It should make her love Iris more not less. Poor Iris, blaming herself for Tom's death. Violet had told Grace what had happened, that Tom had been shot by his own army for cowardice. Iris must have spent her life blaming herself.

When she returned to the abbey, after packing up and

checking out of her room, Grace wandered around alone, the cloister, the chapter room, which had been a ward, the second floor that was now guest rooms but was once wards. And finally, the top floor which had been the laboratory. It really was extraordinary. 'Oh Iris,' Grace said. 'I just wish I'd known.'

Violet spoke well at the reception, managing to mention by name all of those who were present and many who had passed on. There were around a hundred people there, mostly daughters or sons of those who'd served at Royaumont, themselves old now. They'd set up chairs in the monks' refectory, a beautiful space with full-length stained-glass windows.

Violet said it was sad their chief, Miss Ivens, hadn't seen the day they'd come together again, that Cicely Hamilton too had passed on, along with many others, Dr Courthald, Dr Dalyell and Dr Savill.

Violet became teary when she spoke of Iris. 'Of course there was one person who we would agree was the embodiment of all that Royaumont aspired to be. Our dear colleague Iris Crane has passed on.' She paused and composed herself. 'She was not only the best friend anyone could have had. In her quiet way, she ran Royaumont. We all know she ran the chief.' Laughter. 'She was the best of Royaumont, its heart and soul, a perfect expression of its philosophy and essence. She lived her life here with us and subsequently in service. And I'm very honoured that we have with us today her granddaughter, Grace Hogan, who is herself a doctor. Grace?' Grace waved weakly to smiles and applause.

'Iris had been planning to come here to be with us and I'd like you to charge your glasses and toast dear Iris, who made all our lives better.'

437

The women stood and called hear, hear. Grace felt overwhelmed with emotion she couldn't at first put a name to. Pride, she realised. She was so proud to be Iris's granddaughter.

She felt awkward saying goodbye to Violet. 'I need some time to think about all this.'

'There's nothing to think about,' Violet said. 'Iris was your grandmother. You know the truth now, but Iris was still your grandmother. Let's leave it at that.' But when they embraced, Grace sensed Violet holding on. Grace couldn't promise to see Violet again, or bring the children. Grace didn't know what she wanted. But she let Violet hang on to her until she was ready to let go.

'Thank you,' Grace said. 'Thank you for telling me the truth.'

Grace flew from Paris back to Heathrow. As they approached, she asked the flight attendant if she could sit further forward in the plane. There were many empty seats. 'I haven't seen my family for a while,' she said. It was only a few days. It felt like an age. She realised she was crying.

'Of course,' the attendant said, and just before they descended, she came and took Grace to the front of the plane.

As she came through the gate, she saw them. Mia and Phil were holding up a sign, WE LOVE MUMMY!!!!, decorated with red hearts. They were wearing their new red woollen coats and berets, high white socks and black boots. Next to them was David, big jacket undone, cap askew, curls still needing a cut, glasses crooked on his nose. In his arms was Henry, looking at her and waving, a grin on his face. David put him down and he ran to her. She took him in her arms. 'Well, you must be Superman in disguise,' she said, kissing him.

'I'm not in disguise,' he said. He opened his jacket. Under

it was his suit, something resembling scrambled eggs spilt down the front.

'No you're not,' she said. 'And I love you for it.'

They came back to Australia through Melbourne so David could take Henry to see a colleague who'd specialised in paediatric diseases. David had studied under Robin Moreton at Cambridge and almost did paediatrics himself because of the relationship. Grace had met Robin twice before. He was a large, affable man with a grey beard and wisps of greying hair pulled back from his face. His wife smiled and didn't speak much.

DMD wasn't his area, he'd told David on the phone, but he'd be more than happy to talk to them. They went out to his house in the Dandenong Ranges. After lunch, the children went to play while he spoke with Grace and David. His wife went into the kitchen to clear up.

'I know you'll spend time trying to find a way out of this for your son,' Robin said. 'It's certainly what I'd be doing. But working with families, the one thing I've learnt is that you can cause an awful lot of pain for no good.

'I'll be frank with you. We don't know what to do for Henry. We just don't. We don't know what will help him. We don't know what will hurt him. He has Duchenne's muscular dystrophy, to be sure, but today he's playing in the garden there with his sisters. Don't miss that, whether it's Henry walking, Henry in a wheelchair, Henry confined to bed. Because when he dies, and he will die unless something changes in our knowledge, you want to have made the most of every minute with him.' Grace felt completely deflated. She had hoped against hope that Robin Moreton would have an answer for them, or at least hope of an answer, and instead he was telling them to get used to it.

'Do you mean we should stop the therapies?' David said.

'Not necessarily,' Robin said. 'Let me put it this way. I cared for a boy who died last week of leukaemia. He was always going to die but before he did, he had so much treatment that we made him more sick. The family came to me and said they wanted us to keep going. I recommended against it. They didn't take my advice, which is their right. And who knows what I'd do in their place? But afterwards, I couldn't help but feel they missed their son who was alive because they were trying to keep him alive longer. You have to ask yourself, Are we living every minute with Henry, or missing out on that?'

At the hotel that night, after the children had gone to bed, David said, 'I think Robin's got a point. You have to be thankful for what you have rather than try to make it otherwise. He's saying that's all we can do.'

'It's a bit like what Janis said. One foot out of bed and then the other. It seems such a defeatist way to look at it.'

'Or maybe just an accepting way,' David said.

On the plane home, David sat with the girls, reading them *The Hobbit*. Grace sat with Henry. He fell asleep on her lap. She put the seatbelt around the two of them and held him to her. She could smell his sweet nutty hair, feel his breath, his heart beating strongly.

Iris had been Grace's mother. Grace had no doubt about that now. Iris had made such a sacrifice for Grace and for Rose before her and had been a wonderful mother. Violet had made a sacrifice too, although she might not have known it at the time. She might not even know it now, Grace thought.

These last months had been the worst of Grace's life. Henry, her Henry who she held in her arms, was going to be very sick. The person Grace thought she was didn't exist. She was someone else entirely. Her heart had been smashed open, as if God, if he existed at all, was trying to make her see that nothing we think is true is really true at all. Violet had said that a deep seam of truth runs under the world and you could find it. Grace didn't believe that. Nothing she'd thought true had been true. The world wasn't as she'd been led to believe. All she had was the moment she was in, this moment with Henry, as his mother.

She knew there were challenges ahead, some she couldn't yet dream of, a drug trial that looked promising for DMD with unknown risks, in later years blood tests for the girls to see if they carried the gene, Henry's slow but inevitable deterioration. There was Violet and whether she fitted into Grace's life at all, or whether they could ever bridge the gap of all those years. There was work and the report on her performance that was coming. None of it mattered compared with this moment, Henry breathing softly on her breast.

Grace looked out the window of the plane. There in the sky outside her window was a single star. She had the strongest feeling, a familiar feeling, of being mothered.

Creil 1917

It was a warm day; a month ago in Paris she'd worn a coat but now she was in short sleeves. The car seat was hot to her touch.

A tall soldier was walking towards her, British not French. He walked slowly but with purpose. At the last minute he raised his head and she saw under the hat who it was. His face glowed. He was so alive, that was what she'd noticed. He was so alive.

What are you doing here? he said.

I'm waiting for wounded. What are you doing here?

I'm the postie. Want a French letter?

She smiled despite trying not to. A breeze was building from the north. She felt the sun warm on her face. He was staring at her. What are you looking at? she said.

I should ask you that question. You are so beautiful. He moved forward and she thought he might kiss her but he took a curl of her hair and pushed it back behind her ear and smiled. She took him in. He had a cowlick on the left side and his hair kicked up there usually but it was straight and cropped short now.

Tom, she said.

Violet, he said. He stepped back.

Saturday, she said. Chantilly. The picnic spot near the river. We'll walk over. She looked purposefully at him. I'm bringing Iris.

You can bring whoever you like so long as you're there. But Saturday's too long away, he said, and smiled. She shook her head. I'll be there, he said. I'll surely be there.

Writer's Notes

I think it was Grace Paley who said that any story told twice is fiction. I was in the wrong aisle at the University of Queensland Central Library in 1997, having transposed two digits in a call number, when I noticed a title, *The Women of Royaumont: A Scottish Women's Hospital on the Western Front*. Published earlier that year, Dr Eileen Crofton's excellent history recounts the experiences of the doctors who went to France at the start of World War I and established a field hospital in the thirteenth-century Cistercian abbey of Royaumont, north of Paris.

Anyone writing about Royaumont Hospital stands on the shoulders of the women who served there, the doctors and nurses and orderlies and ambulance drivers who gave their time, took enormous risks and were forever changed. I have meant to honour these women, and I have valued fidelity to history as reported. But Grace Paley is right. I am at least three steps removed from the people and events of Royaumont; I cannot know them.

Moreover, my main task has been to imagine a story.

While characters of the novel, including Miss Frances Ivens, share names and backgrounds with women who served at Royaumont and while events match events at Royaumont as reported, my novel is certainly fiction. On occasion, I have even altered history as recorded to suit my story and I have included characters who have no historical doppelgänger. There may have been no British soldiers in some places I've put them, and the Australians probably arrived in Europe later than I have them involved. Most importantly, Iris Crane and her family and Violet Heron and hers are creations entirely of my imagination.

I have wanted most of all to capture in the novel what I believe is the spirit of Royaumont. It's there in Crofton's history and in others written about the women and the hospital, especially Antonio de Navarro's 1917 *The Scottish Women's Hospital at the French Abbey of Royaumont*, which I found most illuminating. It's there in the papers left at Royaumont and the words the women have spoken and written about their experiences. It's in the abbey itself, I believe. And it's summarised almost perfectly in the following unsigned quotation, written in 1915 by a woman who served at Royaumont, which I found in the British Library while researching the novel:

We are a ship's company on a vessel that voyages always in mid-ocean, calling at no ports, speaking to no ships in passing. We are a cosmos complete in ourselves. Our past lives 'before the war' slip from off our memory like reality from the minds of those that dream. Our future – when the war is over – the mind refuses to grasp. There seems no other life. And though we may be quartered in a cloistered abbey, with the ruins of a religious age around us, there is nothing of the institution about us. We are not patterned out to a set of rules and regulations laid down for us. We have grown.

Fondation Royaumont offered me space at Royaumont Abbey to research and imagine, funded by a grant from the Australia Council. The Banff Centre in Canada provided me with a place in the snow to write and edit. I am indebted to these centres for the arts. The Australian Medical Council protects medical education in Australia, and its senior staff and the clinicians and medical educators with whom they work have contributed in no small measure to this novel.

Readers David Mayocchi, Kris Olsson and Kim Wilkins made helpful suggestions, and Cherrell Hirst did her best to correct my medical errors – any lingering morbidity is mine. My agent Fiona Inglis from Curtis Brown Australia, another reader, is all heart, and I love her for it. UK publication was ably assisted by CB's Annabel Blay and by Allen and Unwin's Wenona Byrne, and their passion for Miss Ivens and the Royaumont story has moved me greatly.

Annette Barlow from Australia's Allen & Unwin acquired *In Falling Snow* in faith and editor Catherine Milne helped me reward that faith, with Christa Munns managing a very good process. *In Falling Snow* has now landed at home in England with Allison & Busby, and I thank Lara Crisp and Susie Dunlop for believing in those women of Royaumont.

Thanks to Australian and Canadian friends and family who helped on the journey, especially Antonia Banyard and Clinton Swanson (and Suzanna and Brigita), Debra Bath, Lisa Borin, Karyn Brinkley, Stace Callaghan, Lenore Cooper,

Fumie Craven (and Kyle), Nancy DaDalt (and Robson), Kerry Dance (and Owen), Sharon Doupe and Doug Bell (and Jaden and Mercedes), Dennis Gibson and Catherin Bull, Cherrell Hirst, Nan Hughes and Peter Poole (and John and Irene), Gail Intas and Adrian McGregor, Suzette Jefferies, Tony and Jill Lynch, Jill McAulay, Andrée MacColl, Andrew MacColl, Lachlan MacColl, Ian MacColl and Buffy Lavery (and Cate and Ellen), Christine Maher and Eddie Scuderi (and Benjamin), Wayne McLeod, Laurie MacPhail (and Freddie), Kris Olsson, Ros Petelin, Mary Philip, J. Jill Robinson and Steven Ross Smith (and Emmett), Louise Ryan and Gerard Ryan (and Josh, Ben, Will and Gabe), Cathy Sinclair and Peter Forster, Fiona Stager, Theanne Walters, Alison Watt and Kim Waterman (and Lindsay and Sophie), and Kim Wilkins and Mirko Ruckels (and Luka and Astrid). The team at WildFlour Bakery Café fed my habit while in Canada, and Merlo Paddington provide ongoing supply.

My grandmother Marguerita Lynch (née Crane) never went to war but might have. My cousin Margie Cassidy gave me an idea that grew. My mother Rosemary MacColl led me to believe there were no limits, and she was right.

David Mayocchi and Otis Mayocchi have contributed more to this book and my life than anyone else and I thank them with all my heart.